BANGKOK
W
E
S
Ratchapraprop Rd.
Nikom Makkasan Rd.
Petchburi Rd.
Kamphaeng Phet 7 Rd.
New Petchburi Rd.
Chid Lom Rd.
Witthayu Rd.
Ploenchit Rd.
Soi Sukhumvit 21 (Asok)
SUKHUMVIT
(GREEN ZONE)
Nana
Plaza
Soi 4 (Nana Tai)
Soi Cowboy
Witthayu (Wireless) Rd.
Soi 33
Soi 33/1
Sukhumvit Rd.
Soi 20
Soi 22
Royal Bangkok
Polo Club
Park
Benjasiri
Park
Ratchadaphisek Rd.
Suan Lum
Night Bazaar
Lumpini
Boxing Stadium
Queen Sirikit National
Convention Center
Soi 55 (Thong Lo Rd.)
KLONG TOEY
HORN
0
250m
Rama 4 Rd.
GROOVY MAP
Bangkok
Andaman
Sea
CAMBODIA
Pattaya
Gulf
of
Thailand
Phuket

The Risk of Infidelity Index

THE RISK OF INFIDELITY INDEX

A VINCENT CALVINO CRIME NOVEL

CHRISTOPHER G. MOORE

Atlantic Monthly Press
New York

First published by in Thailand in 2007 by Heaven Lake Press

FIRST AMERICAN EDITION

ISBN-10: 0-87113-974-X
ISBN-13: 978-0-87113- 974-0

Atlantic Monthly Press
an imprint of Grove/Atlantic, Inc.
841 Broadway
New York, NY 10003

Distributed by Publishers Group West

www.groveatlantic.com

08 09 10 11 12 10 9 8 7 6 5 4 3 2 1

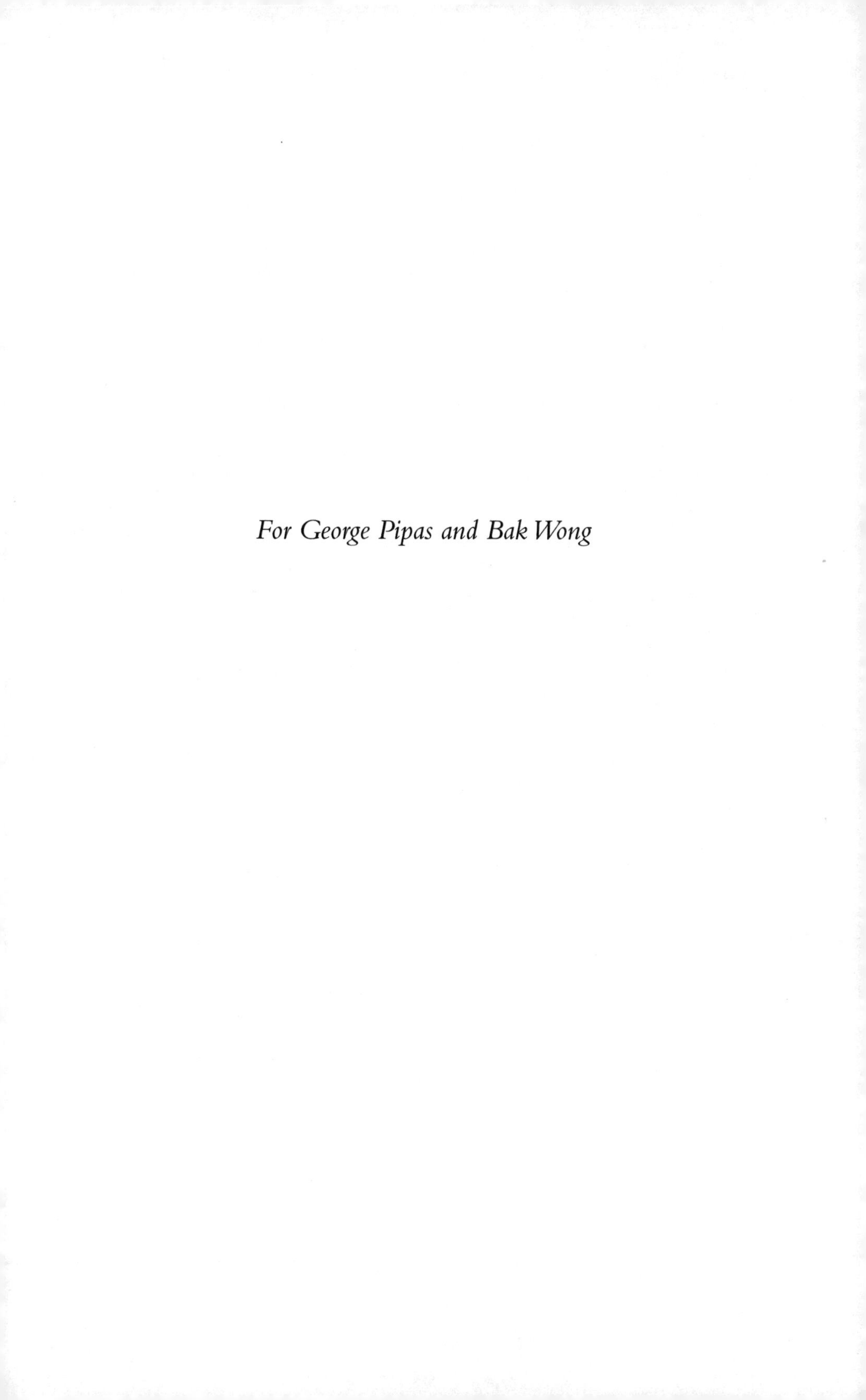

For George Pipas and Bak Wong

ONE

THAIS have a saying about a frog living inside a coconut shell. The frog believes that the world inside the shell is the whole universe. In the private investigation business, Vincent Calvino had clients who were like the frog. What they saw from inside their shell blinded them, made them unable to solve a problem. So they hired Calvino. He knew the drill. Shells offered comfort and security. Leaving could be a dangerous business. Calvino's froglike clients paid him to venture into a larger existence and to find out and report on the wiring of relationships and places and events, how they were linked and fit together in networks.

Drop two alpha spiders into a coconut shell and watch as things become infinitely more interesting. It's still a shell, but the dynamics change from security and comfort to fear and suspicion. No matter that the shell looks the same; it isn't the same place. The landscape is colored with a different set of the emotions. Silky webs mark turf, and spiders patrol their turf. He'd done investigations for spiders, dragging prey back to their shell. Spiders paid well. As far as Calvino would make out, there was no Thai saying about a couple of large, hairy spiders spitting poison at each other in a coconut shell, but when he mentioned it to the Thais, they laughed and said that he knew too much about the country. When a Thai said that, it wasn't a good thing for a *farang*. It wasn't a compliment; it was a warning.

When a potential client walked into his office, Calvino studied the face and body language for some sign: was this person a frog or a spider? Sometimes he knew the answer after the first blink.

Other times, he wasn't so sure. Danielson was a case in point. Calvino collected evidence of a drug piracy operation for this client, an American lawyer who was a partner in a Bangkok law firm. Someone had banged on the side of Danielson's coconut shell and two fearful eyes had popped up at the edge and peered out. Life outside the shell was unstable, dangerous, and darkened by powerful forces. Andrew Danielson was a frog, another borderline ordinary, boring, and predictable frog working in a spider's nest. That's what had confused Calvino. The fee Danielson agreed to pay had been excellent. And there was another reason: the job would help Calvino with an application he had been working on. His mother had sent him an advertisement for a senior investigator job at the World Health Organization. He had never heard of the UN hiring a private investigator, but it made sense. Someone had to investigate where the next pandemic was brewing, who was manufacturing fake drugs—pills filled with chalk and powdered milk—or who was napping at regional headquarters. His mother said Calvino was perfect for the job. He would have a steady income, a steady job, and he would work in New York, closer to her and the family.

His mother had written the letter from inside her retirement home. It was a strong letter, which had cursed the memory of Galileo Chini, the Italian painter, long dead, who had left an everlasting impression on Calvino when he was fourteen years old. He checked out the WHO. It was a legitimate position on offer. With a major bust of an illegal drug piracy operation, how could the WHO not hire him? Vincent Calvino, it seemed, also lived deep in the shell of Bangkok.

On his wall was a framed reproduction of Galileo Chini's *The Last Day of the Chinese Year in Bangkok, 1912*. The original oil painting, which was huge, hung in the Pitti Palace in Florence. Colonel Pratt had given him the reproduction as a birthday gift the previous year. Many years before, in New York City, they had met at a lecture on Galileo Chini and his Siam paintings. Calvino looked up from his mother's letter at the painting. The people, the street, and the dragon glowed in a burnished red hue, shimmering as if caught in the afterglow of flares, tropical hot red as if on fire. The dragon danced, and Chinese in pigtails stood in front of the huge dragon head, as if accepting their fate, waiting to be swallowed. The mind echoed with the sound of gongs and drums and, with each move of the dragon, the tinkling of hundreds of bells.

A new dragon was on the streets of Bangkok. It was a time of great disturbance and conflict. A time of tyrants, a time of visionaries, a time for fools, pretenders, wannabes, and gentle souls, confused and isolated—lives tossing and turning inside their coconut shells. Calvino had pulled out a small victory, one that would please Andrew Danielson but also a feather in his cap that would look good when he sat down with the WHO officials, who would ask what he had done lately for the health of the world. As he entered the narrow dead-end *sub-soi* to his office, he did one of those end zone dances as if he'd scored a touchdown. Looking at his watch, it was just after 5:00 p.m. He thought about the money Danielson would give him. It was more than just another all-cash deal. Sure, he would deliver the videocassette of the piracy operation and get ten grand. But he'd also receive a letter of commendation on Andrew Danielson's letterhead, and a letter from the drug company letting the WHO know this is the guy they need to do their investigations for them.

But in the meantime, Calvino had violated a primary operating principle about fees. Calvino's law: Always get your money first. He had a set speech he gave to clients:

I want up-front money. I'll forget about up-front money if you're willing to have an up-front tattoo. My name tattooed on your right arm with a lot of black magic Chinese symbols for betrayal underneath. I'll look at the tattoo and I'll settle for "hei mo fa" under my name. Do that and I'll let the up-front dough ride.

Danielson never got the tattoo speech. He was a lawyer. Ten grand was nothing for a partner in a Bangkok law firm. And Danielson wanted a performance guarantee. Calvino's mother wanted him to go for the WHO job, so he swallowed hard and didn't make his speech. That was fine. Everything had worked out. He had the evidence.

★

Calvino heard a woman's voice and tried to separate the signal from the noise. *Why was the woman crying?* He stopped and looked around at the buildings on both sides; he couldn't locate where the crying was coming from. The sound of distant wailing suddenly drifted into wet sobs. A woman's voice shuddering, as she recharged her lungs for a new round of even more powerful, mournful notes of sadness. This soulful female moan of despair troubled Calvino. He rubbed the pain in his shoulder. He knew something about pain.

I'm getting old. Too old to be hiking around a strange neighborhood with camera equipment, trying to avoid being noticed. A desk job was just what the doctor prescribed. Ease up, lay back, do the investigative work by computer, hire locals to do the footwork. He had his new job all figured out in his head. Despite the horseshoe kick of pain, Calvino felt in good spirits. High and good, the way a man feels after making a big score, bringing it home, and showing the whole tribe that he might be getting old but can still do the job.

He shifted the weight of the camera bag from one shoulder to the other. On his mother's side of the family, there was a history of arthritis; it was one of those built-in traits, like the mechanics of a ticking time bomb, that waited for the right age, the wrong moment, to spring a surprise. Click, detonate, then a surprise: wave after wave of electricity shooting through the shoulder.

Like the crying woman was a surprise. The sound of her sobbing, half muffled by the traffic from the street, registered on his consciousness. He walked ahead. The sound came closer, coming from the direction of his office. No sound disturbed a man as much as hearing a woman's deep-throated bolts of pure grief. Cursed moans delivered to the world in a universal language of sorrow and loss. It was the soundtrack on the international news every night, but it was never the same as hearing it live. Calvino again shifted the weight of his camera bag from one bum shoulder to the other, the two working like a handicapped relay team looking to cross the finish line and collapse. The video camera, backup batteries, and the other gear felt as if they were pulling him to the ground.

A young *ying* in a polo shirt and loose-fitting pants shot out of the shadows. Her face, a tear-streaked mask twisted by fear, looked terrified. She ambushed Calvino, grabbed him, pulling at his arm, the arm attached to the shoulder with the shooting pain. He cried out but his wail of hurt didn't stop her. Long red fingernails dug into his arm. She tightened her grip, dragging him along until they reached the front of the massage parlor. Then she pushed him through the entrance and into the swamp-green tiled reception room, and walked him down a corridor with orchid wallpaper, under a permanent set of flashing Christmas tree lights, and up a flight of stairs. The décor could have been copied from McPhail's room, exhibiting, like his friend's home, a gangster's flair for year-round Christmas.

Calvino's office was on the fourth floor of the building. The office below his had been vacant for more than a year. The One Hand Clapping massage parlor used the first floor to hook customers before reeling them in to the second floor for a massage. After dark, the red and blue neon sign spelled out the name in cursive script above the door. Some might have called it artistic. A neon image of a woman's hand, the fingers splayed; each finger lit up, red neon for the fingernails, one light at a time until the entire hand was visible, glowing out of the blackness. With slender fingers this sensual hand beckoned to visitors.

When the sign was switched off, the hand didn't move. But even when the neon sign was on, the hand didn't look like it was clapping; it took a leap of imagination to see that. The name and the hand were the first things Calvino's clients saw when they stood at the staircase leading to his fourth-floor office.

A couple of clients had been amused by the presence of One Hand Clapping below the office of a private eye. Others stopped in their tracks, turned, and walked out of the *sub-soi*, phoning later to cancel their appointments, saying they had resolved their problems. A massage parlor on the first floor was hurting his business. Tuesday would be the three-month anniversary of the massage parlor's opening. Business hadn't been good in that period. *Yings* had stood out front, handing out discount coupons to potential customers. His clients sometimes would lay one on his desk and ask if the discount applied to his services. Life was a series of small humiliations.

The area in front of the massage parlor, empty and quiet, normally bustled with *yings* advertising their services. But at the moment it was deserted, except for the *ying* who now had him in an arm lock and was pleading for help, her eyes wild, her hair flying as she pushed against him. She was shivering, her teeth chattering, as if she'd just stepped out of a butcher's freezer.

In the corridor the *mamasan* waited, a lit cigarette held between the fingers of her trembling hand. Her nails had been freshly painted lizard green. The *mamasan* ignored the *ying* who had dragged Calvino down a corridor and stopped before a door. She knocked and yelled but no one inside answered.

"It's locked," she said.

"You don't have a key? Come on. You must have a spare somewhere." He looked around at the blank faces. Business at the massage parlor had been bad, but this was beyond a slump. He noticed there wasn't a single customer on the premises. A deserted massage parlor was an omen, he told himself. Every time he'd ignored one of the universe's signals to beware, he'd regretted it.

The *mamasan* couldn't have been more than thirty-five years old but had the bitter determination of a combat field commander waiting for an attack. "The door's locked from the inside. Help me open the door."

"With what? You need a key to open it." He set down his bag and rubbed his shoulder, still throwing off an electrical storm of pain.

She dropped the cigarette into an ashtray, letting it burn. Then she set the ashtray down on a table stacked with white towels. "No key. No time. I think a big problem inside. We must break it," she said.

The plural "we" meant the singular *farang*. Gimp shoulder or not, he was a man, wasn't he? *Mamasans* had an unrefined way to test a man's valor.

Calvino stared at her, then at the other *yings*. They were all waiting for him to do something. The crying registered a high note. He'd had enough. He turned, set down his camera bag, and slammed a shoulder into the door, breaking it open. Wood splintered. He was the first to go inside. On a chair near the window, a *ying* sat dressed in a red and blue china doll happy coat. The colors of the happy coat matched those of the neon sign. Nicely stitched above the right breast was the name of the massage parlor, along with a picture of a slender hand. This hand didn't look like it was clapping. The *mamasan* shouted at the *ying*, calling her a stupid water buffalo for not unlocking the door. She inspected the damage, shaking her head. She threatened to fire the crying *ying* and to deduct the cost of repairs from her pay. Calvino ignored this sideshow of outrage over the costs of a door. On the single bed was a motionless, naked form with legs and arms sprawled out at odd angles. He knelt beside the bed, careful not to rest his knee in the blood.

Her eyes were wide open, still, and glassy. The veins in her wrists had been cut, and the bed was damp from her blood. Looking at her small body it was hard to believe it could have contained so much blood. She appeared to have done a thorough job opening her veins. Some blood had spurted and clotted on her chin and mouth. Sitting on the edge of a chair a couple of feet away, the other woman rocked back and forth. Deep inside her own world of grief, she ignored the *mamasan*'s tirade.

Calvino estimated from the temperature of the *ying's* body that she had been dead for more than an hour. The air-conditioner hummed softly in the background. The *yings* watched as Calvino examined a heavy necklace, thick as a rope, she wore around her throat. It could have been gold or gold-plated. Other than the necklace, the naked girl was still warm. Calvino circled around the end of the bed. Her clothes were neatly folded on a table beside the bed. He squatted close to the body, watching that he didn't step in the pool of blood. He started with the face and without touching or moving the body, inspected the corpse. He found no bruising. No evidence of a struggle. If she had been fighting for her life, there would have been evidence of a struggle on the body, skin under the fingernails or black and blue impressions. He examined her arms, neck, face, and legs for a sign. He looked for ghost fingerprints on the skin. What he found was that the dead *ying's* skin was smooth, unblemished, without a pimple or mark. Her body appeared to have been, until now, in perfect health; she was a young, fit, beautiful woman, who without the blood all around her might be mistaken for someone lost in deep sleep. Her clothes were neatly folded as if ready for her awakening.

The *mamasan* told him that the dead *ying* had had no customers the entire day. She'd locked herself in the room and refused to come out. The *mamasan* had a spare key, but the *ying* had locked the deadbolt from the inside. Not that it much mattered. The girl was already dead.

As he rose back up, sharp bolts of pain shot volley after volley, as if his shoulder were an artillery range. He grabbed his shoulder, massaged it. A *ying* who had been watching from the doorway silently moved forward—the *mamasan* had signaled to her—and massaged Calvino's shoulder. One of the *ying's* who followed him inside the room offered him a glass of water. He waved it away. He turned to the dead woman on the small bed, lying in a shroud of rumpled sheets. Calvino was more interested in the *ying*, deep lines of grief etched on her face, who sat rocking near the window. The small room had filled with the other massage staff.

"Mamasan, keep the girls out of here. Call the police."

He looked around the room. None of them moved. He shouted for them to all get out of the small room. The VIP room smelled of sour *som tam*, the Isan dish made from hot chili peppers, raw papaya, cherry tomatoes, and fermented fish or crab. An overwhelming stench of garlic made the room suffocating.

"Have you phoned the police?" he asked the *mamasan*. The garlic and cigarette smoke made his eyes water. He wiped tears away with the back of his hand.

"Police no good," she said.

Sometimes a *mamasan* could be so right and so wrong at the same time.

But the police investigation was unavoidable. When someone died in Bangkok, the police and the body snatchers were dispatched to the scene. In a ritual that passed as teamwork, the cops inspected the body, picked up evidence, photographed the scene, and the body snatchers waited for the all-clear before removing the body. If the dead person was someone important, then all kinds of protocols applied, and officials had to coordinate between agencies, committees, and the press. None of that would happen in this case. A dead massage *ying*, a nobody from nowhere, would only result in reams of paperwork.

But the book still required an investigation. An investigation compromised by a dozen idle, crying massage girls walking through the room, picking up things, helping themselves to whatever wasn't nailed down. Food, gold chain, credit card, cash. The thinking was always the same: the victim no longer needed these things. Those who weren't close to the dead *ying* had less resistance to the feelings of bad luck in taking from the dead. From their point of view, the sooner the dead *ying's* worldly possessions found a new home, the better. The fear of ghosts would come later.

He chased out the two girls who had come to stare and went over to the one sitting on the chair, rocking back and forth, as if the window where she sat was the wailing wall and her anguish, now with an audience, had grown more intense. Her chair was positioned to the left of the open window, which was hidden behind white cotton curtains. Calvino asked her why she'd opened the window with the air-con running. She didn't reply. Then he asked her why she hadn't opened the door, and why her friend was dead on the bed. He reached over and touched her hands, held them for a moment, checked the fingernails, and then let her hands fall back into her lap. They were the hands of a *ying* who had recently worked the fields or performed other hard labor. After a couple of months working in a massage parlor, the hands soften. He took her for a newbie.

A shortlist of "why" questions occurred to him. The girl by the window was in no condition to answer any of them, but Calvino asked them anyway. She answered each one the same way: "I don't know."

Didn't know or wasn't telling? He was a *farang* and was getting nowhere. What did it matter? Let the police sort her out. It was their business and not his. They knew how to get answers, and the *ying* knew better than to answer every question with a shrug. The *mamasan* stood in the door, chewing a broken fingernail.

"What's her name?" he asked the *mamasan*.

"Her name's Metta."

Calvino looked over at Metta, who sat with her legs crossed, one of her broad feet with splayed toes, swinging to some soundtrack playing inside her head.

"And the dead girl?"

"Everyone call her Jazz."

The *mamasan* lit another cigarette. What was going through her head? One thought: that suicide in the massage business was never a good thing. Rumors that a ghost, a pale but beautiful young woman ghost, was haunting the building would circulate for months. Suicides spooked the staff and rattled the customers. The *mamasan* was calculating the number of monks she'd have to arrange to purify the premises of a wayward spirit. That was the way of the living. The dead had to be put to rest with burning incense and chanting monks so that the living could get on with their next massage.

For whatever reason, Jazz had lost her will to live. She'd checked out of her misery, leaving a mess for others to clean up. No one had been in a hurry to call the authorities. But when they arrived they brought with them a crowd like the one that showed up at every death scene. Bystanders paralyzed, bewildered, afraid, and confused, but nevertheless drawn to the flame. Calvino noticed two forks resting on the plate of *som tam*. It looked like Jazz and Metta had been sharing food. He had a gut feeling that something was wrong. *Nothing good will come out of this*, he thought. He felt relieved that the police would come and he could get away from the stench of death and the sound of weeping.

The massage parlor staff had involved him in their personal affair. No, that was wrong. He had permitted them to get him involved without fully understanding the situation. It had been, as they say, "up to him." He hadn't known there was a dead *ying* inside. If he had known what was on the other side of the door, he would have immediately called the police. As he leaned against the wall, looking at Jazz's body, it became perfectly clear what would happen next and what he should expect when the police arrived.

The police would question him as to why he had broken down the door. *Under the circumstances, who wouldn't have broken down the door?* he asked himself. But it meant that he wasn't just another bystander but someone—a foreigner with an office above—who had done something physical and violent. How would the police interrogator react? Calvino wondered, if he were the police, what would go through his mind? Would he become a suspect? His thoughts shifted from the police to the pain in his shoulder. He remembered that Ratana had some of his painkillers left in her handbag. He had asked her to keep the bottle for him; otherwise, the temptation was too great to eat them like M&Ms. Four of the blue capsules were still in the bottle. He'd counted them. He remembered them very well and now looked forward to the moment when he could unscrew the lid on the bottle. The thought brought a smile to his face.

The *mamasan* cleared her throat. He looked up to find that all of the *yings* were staring at him. The *yings* watched the pain spread across his face, twisting it, making his mouth angry and desperate. They knew the look from walking on the backs of customers. They had pinned him down. Calvino had been the only *farang* inside One Hand Clapping on the night of the death. He was already regretting that he had put himself in such an awkward position. He should have been on the phone to Andrew Danielson, telling him about the video footage. He should have been at his desk polishing his résumé. Instead he had the sour smell of *som tam* in his nose and the smell of death on his clothes.

TWO

IT wasn't long before four uniformed policemen were inside the massage parlor. The first two cops had parked at the hotel across the street, leaving room in the narrow *sub-soi* for the body snatchers' van. Several men got out of the van and carried a stretcher to the entrance of the massage parlor. Behind the van another police car pulled in, its blue lights flashing across the neon sign, which someone had turned on. The flickering light made the neon hand look as if it were moving, trying to clap.

By 6:30 p.m. the local TV news crews were on the scene. Cameramen squeezed in the doorway, filming the neon sign, the entrance, and the sign on the wall opposite the massage parlor, which read, "Vincent Calvino, Private Eye, 4th Floor." Calvino hadn't thought about covering his sign. If a suspicious death was bad for the massage business, it wasn't good advertising for a private investigator's business either.

Calvino had returned from a long day of stakeout and surveillance. He'd recorded evidence of a major drug piracy operation, and he'd promised to phone Andrew Danielson about it in the late afternoon. He looked at his watch. It was now 6:40 p.m. He stepped into his office and asked Ratana for the bottle of pills. He swallowed two, with a water chaser.

Ratana, her arms folded as if she were hugging herself against a sudden chill, hovered in the way that women do when they are overly tired or angry about something they expect you to know already. "Mr. Danielson has been phoning for the last hour," said

Ratana. She wore a yellow scarf like a bandanna about her forehead and a yellow plastic bracelet on her right arm. She'd told Calvino earlier that it was important for her to leave the office at 5:30, and he'd told her it was more important that she wait until he returned. It was another demonstration in Lumpini Park. For Ratana, going to the rallies and demonstrations had become a new way of life. Recently she had become more determined and vocal. Calvino had assumed her political interest was a passing fashion, a two-week trend that would soon disappear. But he'd underestimated Ratana's commitment to the cause.

He had asked her to stay in the office just in case Danielson called; he needed someone to answer the phone. Having a client phone with no one there to answer wasn't professional, he'd told her. She'd stayed.

"You're late," she said. Worry lines formed around her eyes. A hint of fear mingled with anger.

"There was a problem downstairs."

"I heard a loud noise. It sounded like someone knocked down a wall. I walked outside and I heard a woman crying."

The sound of crying continued to filter up, occupying the silence that fell between them.

"What's going on, Vinny? All those police downstairs."

She'd seen the van. Like the presence of vultures, the arrival of body snatchers meant death was near. Standing on the stairs, she'd wanted to go downstairs and see what had happened but had stopped herself.

"One of the massage girls killed herself."

Ratana closed her eyes, took a deep breath. "That's terrible."

"Cut her wrists," said Calvino. "It happens."

She had gone pale, her hand touching her throat.

"What did you tell Danielson?"

"I told him that you would phone when you got back." She avoided eye contact. More than anything she wanted to be as far away from the office as possible. The dead woman's spirit would be nearby, angry and looking to settle accounts.

"What'd he say?"

"You really want to know?"

Calvino nodded.

"He said, 'Where the fuck is he?'"

"Phone his office. That prick can't talk that way to you." He started to doubt whether Danielson was just another ordinary frog in a coconut shell.

Ratana put through the call. Calvino was told that Andrew Danielson was on his way to the annual Oxford-Cambridge dinner and intentionally hadn't taken a cell phone. The secretary had a great deal of knowledge about Danielson's habits and movements. She took a message. Calvino dictated his message: "I have everything you requested and more. Sorry I was delayed today. I'll phone you first thing in the morning." He asked her to repeat the message until she had it right, and then he hung up.

From his office window, Calvino watched the small crowd of onlookers that had gathered at the foot of the *sub-soi*. He saw Ratana thread her way through the crowd. She hadn't said goodbye before leaving. He studied the people below, waiting for the cops to return for more questioning. In the street, the first customers had stopped on their way to a row of bars named after dead Impressionist painters: Renoir, Degas, Monet. Milling with street vendors, motorcycle taxi drivers, and *yings* on their way to work, all of them gawked at the body snatchers removing a gurney. They'd started the night intending to look for companionship, drink, food, and most of all excitement, to remind them why they were in Bangkok. They were curious. The police gestured for them to move along. Reporters had the cameramen pan the small crowd. That got them to move.

A thin pinkish strip of light behind the clouds was all that was left of the day. The neon sign above the One Hand Clapping Massage Parlor burnt brightly, the fingers lighting up one after another, then flashing applause. One of the body snatchers closed the back of the van. Then he and his companions climbed into the front. The driver looked over his shoulder as he switched on the headlights. His foot worked the brake, the red lights pumping off and on as he reversed out of the narrow lane. One of the police used a bullhorn, shouting at the crowd to make room.

Several police officers remained inside the massage parlor as Colonel Pratt walked up the stairs to Calvino's office. Below in the massage parlor, after an hour of interrogation, the *mamasan* was sick to her stomach and ran to the sink to vomit. Nothing came out. It had to be the rancid *som tom*, thought Calvino. Whatever food had been inside her stomach had been thrown up before the cops had arrived on the scene. *The mamasan played tough, but even the tough ones can get a weak stomach around so much blood.*

"The police officer in charge asked me to take your statement," said Colonel Pratt. Dressed in his police uniform, Pratt looked official, with proper military posture as he sat in a chair across from Calvino. He removed a pen, clicked it to see that it worked, took out a notepad, and closed his briefcase. Then he positioned his briefcase on his lap as a makeshift writing table.

"Are you ready?" asked Calvino.

Pratt nodded, "Okay, Vincent, tell me what happened."

Where to start? He thought about the sound of a *ying* wailing as he entered the *soi*. Calvino closed his eyes as if to rest. Pratt waited, watching, wondering why his friend looked detached, as if he were in another place. Inside that dark quiet place Calvino saw the splash of neon against the long outstretched fingers of the one clapping hand, and then a freshly dead body in a VIP room. A few feet away from the body, neon light spilled through the window, bathing the room in red. A look of absolute terror crossed Metta's face as she sat near the body of her friend.

THREE

JOHN Lovell, his hands under the water, scrubbed his fingers like a surgeon. He was careful to keep his dinner jacket and white dress shirt dry. Jacket and shirtsleeves were pushed up to his elbow. Most viruses and bacteria, he knew well, arrive as self-inflicted wounds. Your hand touches another hand or a staircase railing or another person's drinking glass. The hand, now infected, touches your nose or eye to rub a tiny itch. That tiny itch and the unclean hand are a germ's best friends. If he were a germ, he thought, he'd have an army of itches sent on a long march through the population, day and night. Nearby, a bamboo basket overflowed with freshly stacked white hand towels. None of the awful paper towels or blow dryers which, while not a germ's best friend, certainly were capable of doing its bidding. Or was it pimping?

As he dried his hands, Lovell glanced at himself in the mirror. At thirty-one years old, he could have passed for a man in his mid-twenties. He drew his face closer to the mirror, his blue eyes narrowing as he picked up a small crease in his bow tie. Why hadn't he seen this before? He seriously hoped that no one in the dining room had seen his disgrace of a bow tie. What had been in his head? With his hands now bone dry, he untied the bow. Fifty thousand people die in hospitals in America every year from germs, he reminded himself. And a major breeding place for germs? A doctor's necktie launched a virtual army of lethal bacteria into every hospital ward, killing patients left, right, and center.

A moment later, a young Thai with a light blue Cambridge ribbon pinned to his dinner jacket caught Lovell's eye in the mirror. A wide grin broke across the Thai's face.

"You can actually tie one of those?" he asked.

Lovell worked one end of the tie like a master dresser, expertly threading the ends. He studied his questioner's face in the mirror. "It's not all that difficult."

The Thai removed his bow tie in an instant to expose a hidden clasp. "This is easier. It doesn't take so much time. And time is money."

His attitude was not an uncommon one, Lovell recognized. But it was the enemy of the small gestures and rituals of the past, when time moved more slowly. These were truths that Lovell lived by. He judged others by their desire to learn and master small traditional skills such as tying a bow tie, playing the violin, reciting passages from *Canterbury Tales*. He had an eidetic memory, that rare ability to remember numbers, facts, or pictures to the last insignificant detail. His brain organized, retained, and absorbed information with extraordinary accuracy and speed; it was as if there was no limit to his memory, no boundary line between remembering and forgetting. Such a memory came in handy while Lovell was at law school. During examinations he recalled (as if his head were a Google search engine) entire pages of text. He could flip through his memory of the index, look up the page in his mind, read the passage, and quote it in its entirety.

His mind possessed an image of the perfect bow tie. The bow tie landscape passed from a visual pathway down through his fingertips. While his memory was a rare gift, his bow tie tying skill had been passed down deliberately from one generation to another. A bonding ritual between father and son. The act of tying a bow tie implied civility, self-discipline, and linkage to a gentlemanly heritage. Most people around him believed that the time of that heritage had all but passed, and that the man standing next to him represented those standing on the opposite side of a great divide. Lovell conceded that if no one remembered how to tie a bow tie, the world wouldn't end. Nothing much would change, and few people would notice. But in his opinion the world would have gone that one further notch down the line into coarseness, artificiality, vulgarity, and, yes, a one-size-fits-all pure money drama.

"I'm Apisak," said the Thai.

"Lovell. John Lovell."

"You're Oxford."

The dark blue ribbon pinned to his dinner jacket was hardly a difficult clue. Not the entire city or the whole university, he started to say. But he restrained himself. Lovell nodded in the mirror and put the finishing touch on the bow tie. Checking each crease. It was now, even if he said so himself, a perfect bow tie. Apisak watched the performance smiling, one hand leaning on the marble countertop. He found Lovell amusing, out of place and time.

"I read law at King's College," said Apisak.

Lovell nodded. "I read law at John's."

"First-class degree, no doubt," said Apisak.

Lovell smiled, and this time it wasn't so much a nod as a slight movement of his chin. "Are you working for a law firm?"

"Jackson and Gleason."

It was one of the best in Bangkok and counted major banks, auto assembly companies, and real estate and property development moguls as clients. It was also a competitor of Lovell's firm.

"And you? Where are you working?" Apisak had a slight English accent.

"Peron and James."

Apisak offered his business card with both hands. Lovell accepted the card and, opening a silver case, produced his own. Like two Japanese businessmen they studied each other's cards, taking in the quality of the paper, the embossing, the size of the font, any hint of title or status.

"How long have you been in Bangkok?"

"Five months," Lovell said. "Almost six months."

"And you have Thailand all figured out by now?"

"Keep away from street demonstrations. Don't pat anyone on the head or point your foot at them."

"That's pretty much everything you need to know," said Apisak.

"I forgot. Most Thais aren't very good at irony."

"Sorry, I'm a little nervous. I have to speak tonight." Apisak cleared his throat. "I'm making the toast to Oxford. I'm not certain what to say."

"You haven't prepared a speech?" Lovell would have written a speech weeks ago and practiced it for days on end.

"I'll wing it." Apisak produced a bottle of prescription medicine and set it on the marble countertop. "These help." He unscrewed the lid and tapped the side. A red capsule fell into his palm. With a flick of his wrist, it shot into his mouth. "That should do the trick."

A photograph snapped in Lovell's brain: the bottle, the lid, the red capsule, and his hand moving to his mouth. He could play the sequence backward and forward, speed the image up, slow it down, or stop the action at any point.

Andrew Danielson, hair silver-gray, wearing a dark blue ribbon on the lapel of his dinner jacket, walked in as Apisak swallowed the capsule. He looked distinguished as he washed his hands, but Lovell could see there was something wrong with him. Danielson's face, ashen and sallow, looked as if someone had kicked him in the guts. He staggered, caught himself.

Lovell thought Danielson might fall down or throw up, or possibly both. Taking deep breaths, he steadied himself against the counter, eyes closed, sweat rolling down his face and falling into the sink. He was a physical mess. Lovell had never seen his boss in such a condition.

"Are you okay, Andrew?" asked Lovell.

Danielson hyperventilated, bubbles of snot dripping down his nose. It was strange to watch him pretend that none of this was happening to him. A case of pure denial as the body entered an emergency state.

"Tomorrow, Khun Weerawat will come to the office," Danielson paused as if to catch his second wind. "I want you at the meeting." Danielson's voice, thin, frightened, seemed in freefall. His normal confidence and energy drained.

"Yes, sir," said Lovell. "Is there something wrong, Andrew?"

Danielson sighed, dipped his hands into the water running from the faucet and splashed his face. "I received some disturbing news." Danielson's voice trembled and he continued to brace himself against the counter with both hands. He saw Apisak's slender brown bottle of prescription pills and read the name Zoloft on the label.

"I sometimes get panic attacks. These pills help take off the edge," said Apisak.

"Do you mind?" Danielson's eyes never left the small bottle on the counter.

Apisak shook two pills out of the plastic bottle over Danielson's outstretched hand. The red capsules were serrated down the middle. Danielson tilted his head back and swallowed the two pills in a gulp. Almost immediately something eased in Danielson's disposition. There was a lot of literature on the placebo effect of medication. The speed of Danielson's recovery could have been a textbook example of such an effect. Lovell had worked with Andrew Danielson for six months, in demanding situations with considerable pressure. They had even pulled several all-night sessions for a couple of cases, but there had been no indication that his boss suffered from a neurological condition that would have caused the anxiety attack.

"Great bow tie, John," Danielson said. He dried his hands before going into one of the stalls and bolting the door. Lovell took another glimpse of himself in the mirror. The bow tie was indeed great. The comment had been Danielson's feeble attempt to appear his normal self.

Apisak held out the bottle. "Do you need one? You seem to be very anxious about that bow tie."

Lovell shook his head. "The tie's fine. I'll pass, thanks."

For a moment, Lovell thought that he should wait for his boss. What had been so disturbing as to cause a panic attack? The closest Danielson had ever come to making a personal comment was one late night after a thirteen-hour negotiation. After everyone packed up, Lovell had followed his boss back to his office where, for the first time, Danielson opened up. Shuffling his papers, he had looked up from his desk and said "you know exactly when you get old. Your dreams are filled with people who are dead. Your parents, school friends, and people you knew professionally. They find you in a departure lounge, but it isn't in an airport. In my dream, on the other side of the doors was a vast Ferris wheel a thousand miles high, and every gondola filled with people I recognized from before. Not one of them was alive." The next day he regretted having mentioned the dream or his feelings of getting old, and he told Lovell to forget what he had said. That was the surest way to make certain someone never forgot.

Apisak had already left for the main dining room. Lovell caught a final glimpse in the mirror and then knelt down and looked under the door to the stall. He saw Danielson's trousers around his ankles. He rose back to his feet. "See you inside," he said.

Danielson didn't reply. Lovell returned to his place at the table.

After the waiters cleared the tables and poured more wine, Apisak rose to give the traditional toast to Oxford. "When I was in the toilet the idea came to me that Oxford is stuck in the past. Oxonians not only love the past, they live in the past. I watched as an Oxford graduate tied his bow tie in the mirror. This was what an Oxford education had given him: a skill. But as skills go it has a very limited market, and I doubt anyone is challenging Bill Gates because he can't make a perfect bow tie. You see, this is the problem with Oxford: they teach their graduates horse riding, building model steamships, leather work like saddles and stirrups, and Morse code in case a Mayday message must be sent to rescue their sailing ship. All very important talents. But may I suggest, rather on the nineteenth-century side of the equation. When I think of Oxford, I think pre-computer, pre-cell phone, pre-automobile, earnest and relatively harmless bow tie aficionados. In Cambridge we do things a little differently. A clip-on bow tie frees our hands to make a phone call and check our e-mail. We prefer to multitask, listening to our iPods and surfing the Internet for fun-loving companions and times-aving gadgets. While our brethren at Oxford have both hands tied up doing what? Tying a bow tie. A no doubt noble act, like the archer of the Middle Ages who also had the ability to tie a bow tie in between stringing the odd arrow to fell an invading enemy. So I would ask all Cambridge graduates to rise and offer a toast to Oxford, the last bastion of hand-tied bow ties and garden parties with thinly sliced cucumber sandwiches."

Lovell's face burnt red as Apisak raised his glass and looked directly at him. He regretted that he hadn't taken the Zoloft. It sounded like the name of a Russian satellite rather than a drug prescribed for anxiety and panic attacks. He felt a jolt of anxiety surge through him as Apisak gestured with his glass in his direction, and the eyes of the other diners caught him, laughing at him. Apisak had gone out of his way to publicly humiliate him. An article of faith was that Thais were non-confrontational and would go to great lengths to avoid causing another person to lose face. Lovell looked down at the table, his face burning, wondering if it was about to come loose from his head.

FOUR

WITH the last of the speeches delivered, a hardcore group of old boys removed their dinner jackets and loosened their ties, staying behind to smoke cigars and drink brandy. Lovell felt the presence of someone standing beside him. The conversations had stopped. He turned around in his chair. A uniformed police officer politely asked him if he would mind answering some questions. He got up from the table and followed the cop to a deserted table in the back. The officer gestured for him to sit down. He explained that Danielson had been found dead in a toilet stall. It appeared he'd been dead for some hours. His black dress trousers were around his ankles.

The hotel had phoned a private emergency service team that had discreetly arrived and, without drawing attention to themselves, waited for the police before they removed Danielson's body from the restroom. After the police had finished, the emergency service team had left through a staff-only exit. The guests had no idea what had happened, though now the word spread like wildfire among the few members who were scattered among the nearly empty tables.

Later the autopsy revealed that Danielson hadn't eaten dinner. He had alcohol in his blood from three or four glasses of wine. They expected further analysis to show chemical traces as well.

A police detective wondered aloud if Lovell might have been the last person to see Danielson alive. It was an old technique, one that sometimes yielded a confession. A waiter had told the police that he had seen Danielson go into the restroom. He had seen Apisak emerge, and then a couple of minutes later Lovell had walked out.

"Did Danielson look ill?"

Lovell said that there had been something wrong. Danielson had been sweating and shaky on his feet. "He said he'd had a disturbing phone call."

"Disturbing?"

"That's the word he used."

"Who phoned Danielson?"

"I don't know. He didn't say."

"You didn't ask him?"

"It wasn't my business. He's my boss. I don't ask him personal questions."

"What did you talk about?"

"An appointment tomorrow with a client."

"Great bow tie." Had those been his boss's last words? But he withheld those words from the police officer. What good would come of repeating those words?

"Did you see anyone else in the restroom?"

"Khun Apisak. He gave Andrew two red pills."

The officer looked up from his notepad. "Do you know what kind of pill?"

"Zoloft. Danielson took two of them."

The investigating officer lay down his pen. He had already taken Apisak's statement and knew about the drug. Lovell had simply confirmed what he already knew. "You saw Danielson take the pills?"

Lovell nodded. "Danielson asked for the pills."

"What does that mean, 'asked for the pills'?"

Lovell saw the officer scribble something on the notepad. But it was in Thai and he had no idea, reading the script upside down (or right side up for that matter), what the police officer had noted. "Danielson walked in just as Apisak had taken out the pills. He saw them. He knew what they were. In my opinion he was having some kind of anxiety attack."

"Are you a doctor?"

"I am a lawyer," said Lovell. "A doctor of law."

As if that made any difference. The police officer looked down at the notepad as he wrote down what Lovell had said.

"A doctor of law knows Zoloft?"

"I only know what I saw and what Khun Apisak told me."

He left out the part that his blink reaction to the pills was they looked like a prototype for a Russian spacecraft. "The autopsy report will confirm that," he added. "I presume there will be an autopsy."

The detective let Lovell's question about an autopsy pass without comment. He busied himself making a note of the name of the drug. Lovell knew that the officer had already interviewed Apisak. He was simply doing his job, unraveling the story of two young lawyers huddled in front of a restroom mirror as Danielson walked in. Pills being passed around like candy. A middle-aged *farang* minutes away from a massive heart attack, swallowing a couple of reds before locking the door of a stall and dying. The detective put the end of his pen against his upper lip. He wondered whether Danielson had walked in on something that he wasn't supposed to see.

"Is there anything to suggest that it wasn't a heart attack?" asked Lovell. "He was old, wasn't he?"

"Fifty-three," said the cop.

"That's not exactly young."

When you are thirty-one, fifty-three is a faraway world, another galaxy, and one that may never be reached. Lovell wondered if he should mention what Danielson said about the Ferris wheel a thousand miles high, each gondola crammed with dead people. In law school he'd learned to never volunteer information to an investigating officer. And when they go fishing for information, don't go for the bait.

"Khun Apisak and you have been friends for how long?"

Lovell glanced at his watch. "Under three hours."

"You came to the party with Danielson?"

Lovell shook his head. "We live in different parts of the city. We came separately."

"You work together but you didn't sit at the same table tonight. Did you have some kind of conflict?"

Lovell digested the detective's last couple of questions, and he didn't like the direction that he was taking. As if he were somehow a suspect. Did he think that somehow he had something to do with Danielson's death? Was this cop crazy? What else could explain this line of questioning? It had been a heart attack, right?

"No, we didn't sit at the same table. We didn't come together. We had no plans to leave together. Danielson is my boss. Or was my boss. But he wasn't my master. There is an important distinction. I don't know how he died or why he died. I am very sorry he's dead. But I don't see how I can tell you anything more than what I've already said."

As he walked away from the table, Lovell felt that this would not be the end of it. The cop tapped the pen against his lip, watching Lovell as he glanced back. He now had a new job in his law firm: appointed talking head to explain the details of Danielson's last moments. It didn't seem fair. The banality of mentioning an appointment and the superb quality of his bow tie were not enough to satisfy anyone. The police had wanted more out of him. The police detective gave the impression that he thought Lovell was holding back something. And how do you explain that nothing else was said?

FIVE

RATANA prayed in front of a spirit house, her head bowed, eyes closed, lips moving. The spirit house, like a dollhouse but larger, with tiny windows and entrance door, was perched on a thick white marble pedestal. The structure was substantial, solid; the durability gave it an ageless quality. Someone had spent a serious amount of money on it. The back of the spirit house nestled against a fence at the dead end of the *sub-soi*. The owner of a secluded, three-story building behind the fence had installed the spirit house several years ago. A motorcyclist who had consumed half a bottle of Mekong while celebrating a World Cup victory ran his motorcycle into the old spirit house, knocking it over. The impact, which had hurled shrapnel twenty meters, had destroyed the old spirit house, sending the roof to the second-floor balcony of the building behind the fence. If the roof had been a football, it would have been a perfect field goal.

The force of the collision had shattered the old spirit house into rubble, scattering pieces of debris over the lane. The motorcyclist, who had been knocked out, had broken a leg. Motorcycle drivers from the injured man's queue had loaded him into a *tuk-tuk* and taken him to a hospital. Many people after the accident who lived on the *sub-soi* believed that bad luck followed such an accident. Any spirit living in that house, would, in their view, take revenge. A homeless spirit could become angry and vengeful.

The old woman who lived in the three-story building had

received most of the old spirit house in the accident. She knew the neighbors had gossiped about the meaning of this. She heard the rumors, or perhaps she was one of those who started them—the evidence wasn't clear on that score. She felt the chill of insecurity among her neighbors and was afraid herself. In any event, she paid for a new, better, and sturdier spirit house. Gossip in the neighborhood was that she paid a great deal of money. Some said the new spirit house used the roof from the old destroyed one, and the spirit house contractor had given her a personal warranty. No one said what the warranty covered. The main benefit had been to restore a sense of harmony in the *sub-soi*. Everyone was grateful to the old woman, knowing that in reality when people become old and live behind a fence, putting things right with the world of spirits was a small price to pay for collective peace of mind.

Flowers, incense sticks, and plates of fruit were pushed against the front of the temple. Tiny plastic figures, standing and sitting, some knocked over like stiff drunks, populated the background of the shrine. Most of the time, the modern, new Thais in the *sub-soi* went about their business without thinking too much about the spirit house. And Ratana was a modern woman. Only rarely had she gone to the spirit house to make an offering. Once when her mother was ill, and another time when a client refused to pay a bill.

On the morning after the suicide in the massage parlor, she had gone to the spirit house alone. Other people working in the *sub-soi* had already left their offerings. Flies hungrily buzzed over the glasses of fruit juice, bananas, oranges, and mangos. No one mentioned that the death of the massage girl had suddenly caused everyone in the *sub-soi* to want to appease the spirit of the place, to help Jazz's ghost rest in another, faraway place where the tenor sax was mellow.

Using a plastic lighter, Ratana moved the flame under the end of three incense sticks until they caught fire. She blew out the flames, watched the smoke curl upward, and then stuck the incense sticks one by one into the sand covering the bottom of a small aluminum bowl. She prayed for him to take Jazz's ghost away from the *soi*—or the spirit could have been a her. Whatever god or spirit, he or she would take notice. Then she lit a single fat yellow candle, the wick burning bright. Ratana leaned over and placed it in a bowl beside the burning incense sticks. Her back was turned to the office. Unaware that her boss had been watching from a distance, her body was perfectly still. Only her lips moved, fingers touching in a *wai*. Like smoke signals from an Indian tribe on the eve of war, Ratana's presence signaled a message to the spirits to lift her sense of dread and blunt her anger. Calvino continued walking. He stopped at the foot of the stairs, where a half dozen massage *yings* in their One Hand Clapping uniforms lounged and smoked cigarettes. Squatting on stools or leaning against the staircase, they chattered to each other and stretched like cats. Their eyes were red from crying. For most of them, it had been the first dead *ying* their own age they'd ever seen. It had unnerved the toughest of them.

Calvino waited for Ratana to end her meditation. Upstairs he heard the faint sound of the office phone ringing. He ignored it and walked down the *sub-soi*, stopping not far from the spirit house. She pretended not to notice him. He was, after all, invading her space, her private moment of bargaining with the spirits. There was no easy starting point for the conversation. Her silence made it more difficult. A thin white line of smoke from the burning incense and wax broke apart above the spirit house. He tried to say something several times but couldn't find the words. He started over, stopped again.

"I don't want to bother you," he said, "but is there something I can do?"

She turned her head, studied him for a long moment.

"I'm sorry about what happened yesterday," he continued. "It's been terrible for everyone."

"I'm not here because of what happened," Ratana said.

Both of them avoided referring directly to Jazz or the fact that she had apparently killed herself. Calvino had stood in the room of the dead *ying*. Death encircled him. Once he had disturbed the spider web of death occupying the VIP room, something had been altered. Calvino had witnessed a great deal of violent death. But no violent death had ever happened this close to his office. Ratana took this as a kind of omen.

He wasn't certain what he expected from Ratana. The heavily garlanded spirit house showed off the offerings from the early morning visitors. A lot of money had been spent on flowers, fruit, candles, and incense. The death of a young *ying* had caused a chain reaction. Appeasement of her spirit had been on the Thais' minds all morning. His secretary had come to pay her respects for other reasons.

"I'm confused," said Calvino.

"You've not seen the newspaper," she said. It wasn't a question; apparently his lack of knowledge was a fact.

"More street demonstrations?" he asked. "I get tired of reading the papers."

"Danielson's dead."

Calvino looked as if he hadn't understood her.

"Your client. The one you missed phoning yesterday because you stopped to knock down the door of the dead girl. That Danielson. There is a story on page four and his photograph. This offering is for him."

"Dead?"

"Heart stopped."

"That's cut-and-paste newspaper talk. Of course his heart stopped. But why did it stop?" asked Calvino. He sucked in a deep breath, and, as he exhaled, the pain in his shoulder nearly made him cry out.

"He was your great hope." What she meant was "our great hope." Danielson had become a kind of savior in the intolerable situation of a massage parlor below the place where she worked. They had calculated that Danielson's fee would more than cover the cost of buying the massage parlor lease. Business was terrible and they had been ready to sell out.

She was unaware that Danielson's death had cut another blow; there would be no letter of recommendation for the WHO job. He'd kept his plan a secret, thinking that his chances of getting the job were too remote. And if by some miracle he got the job, he'd need a secretary. She'd go with him. It had all seemed so simple.

"Are you praying for Danielson or for another client to replace him?" asked Calvino. He felt numb as the full impact of Danielson's death slowly registered.

"Both."

Calvino lit incense and candles.

"You don't believe in this," Ratana said.

"It can't hurt," said Calvino.

Head bent in a bow, she closed her eyes, her lips mouthing a Pali chant. When he opened his eyes, Ratana had disappeared. He turned and saw her hurry past One Hand Clapping and climb the staircase to the office. Calvino had never seen her emotionally close down, as if her own system, their entire history of working together, and each and every window and door of her mind had slammed shut. It wasn't a good sign. There were dark days, and then there were days so black that darkness seemed to cast a shadow of hope.

Calvino told himself he would find a way out. He always had.

SIX

A Bangkok headhunter was complaining that she'd been phoning Ratana for an hour. She was calling with a job offer. Ratana listened to the soft sell and then the hard sell. "It's a great opportunity to advance your career." Then a pause. "You aren't getting any younger, and lots of others will want this job."

She remembered how Vincent Calvino had looked defeated and helpless and very alone as he awkwardly stood in front of the spirit house, not knowing what to say, starting and stopping himself before he got it right. He was always careful to take her feelings into account. But that wasn't anything she could tell a headhunter.

From the first day the massage parlor had opened downstairs, she'd felt a downward spiral starting. The business, the political situation, her personal life—the whole bundle of laundry in the bag of life—had been thrown onto the back of a garbage truck and she was trying to pull it off. Each time she walked past One Hand Clapping she was painfully aware of the stares and whispers. The presence of the massage parlor felt like a deep insult to her. She'd hurry by it, ignoring the *yings* outside on the stools, but it never worked. Her stomach knotted, a threatening storm mixed with resentment and sorrow and anger.

What if her mother stopped in the office to visit her and had to elbow her way through a group of massage girls loitering outside? Her mother would have a heart attack to think that her daughter worked above the One Hand Clapping Massage Parlor. What would she tell other members of the family? Or say to her friends or neighbors? It was too appalling to contemplate. She would have to lie to them. Her father's reaction would be more predictable and practical. He would go into a rage and lock Ratana in the family house and throw away the key. And she couldn't blame either her mother or father. She would have done the same thing in their place. The only ways out were for the massage parlor to go or for her to find another job.

The headhunter was frustrated by her long silences. "Hello, are you still there? Were you listening to what I just said? I think this job at Science Park with a foreign joint venture company is perfect. I can get you double your current salary. You will be working in a highly professional and international environment. You will have a chance for promotion and overseas training. Why are you thinking twice about it?"

The question rang like a bell across a valley. But she had been thinking twice, three times, and more before making a decision. Working for Vincent Calvino wasn't just another job. But even at the best of times it wasn't a highly professional environment. Promotion? What chance was there for that, working for a one-man operation? Now with Danielson dead, the future of working for Calvino had never appeared so fragile and alarming. How could she explain to the headhunter that her current situation was more than just work; it was a relationship that had been built up over many years. Leaving the work was always easy, but walking away from a relationship was an entirely different matter.

By the time she finished the call, Calvino was at his desk on the other side of the partition. She made no effort to lower her voice on the telephone in talking to the headhunter. It was the Thai way of getting a double message across. After the call ended, Calvino reread the article about Danielson's death in the newspaper. Ratana had used a yellow magic marker to circle the article and photo. In the classified ads, there were two jobs advertised for experienced administrative assistants, and they were also circled. His secretary was actively job-hunting, and leaving messages of her intentions in the newspaper. *She might leave.* He let the smooth marble of that idea bounce around the sides of his mind.

From the other side of the office partition, he heard Ratana shifting through papers. She was reading his surveillance report, in which he had detailed the stakeout. The report included the time of the stakeout, registration plate numbers of vehicles, descriptions of people coming and going. Danielson would have been pleased with the completeness of his work. But in the world of the living, the "would have been pleased" counted for nothing. Ratana's chair scraped against the floor. She appeared in his office, holding the Danielson file.

"You're leaving me?"

"I've had an offer," she said. "A very good offer."

"More money." In a war for employees, this amounted to a declaration of surrender. Calvino couldn't hope to match a salary offered by a big company with a steady revenue stream. In his stream the water level was only occasionally deep enough for two fish to swim.

Ratana shook her head. "It's not the money."

"It's about the massage parlor door?" He felt that if his timing had been right, then Danielson would have taken his phone call and relaxed in the knowledge that Calvino had a solid piracy case. It might, just might, have made a difference. Danielson might not have died of a heart attack. Calvino knew that he was reaching for explanations.

"It's not about the door."

She hadn't liked that he had got himself involved in the suicide downstairs. She had not said that what he'd done was stupid, but he said it to himself. Now when he thought about breaking down the door, the image of him slamming his good shoulder into it made him flinch. How had it happened? At that moment, he had felt he had *no choice* but to open the door. At the time, it seemed there was no other way. Actually, there had been another way: Metta, the girl at the window, could have unlocked the door. But he hadn't known that at the time.

Ratana sat patiently in the chair, holding the file. She had gone silent.

Women expected men to know what was on their minds. The two looked at each other. If she knew so clearly, then it had to follow that he obviously knew as well. Calvino understood that line of reasoning. He had tried to guess, then, why she was planning to leave, but she wasn't giving him even a hint. Had she found out about his plan to apply for the WHO position, and was this her way of dealing with it? That would have made it too easy. *It's up to me to guess from a long list why she is considering the offer.* She finally placed the Danielson file on his desk. She leaned back in the chair, legs crossed, arms hugging her knees, waiting for him to say that he fully understood what was inside her mind.

"Let's go over it again. It's not about the money. It's not about the door. It's not about . . . Can you help me a little bit here?"

She looked at him the way a mother looks at a child who has left his room a mess but literally can't see the clothes, socks, books, plates, and papers scattered across the floor and furniture. She rarely sat in that chair, which was the hot seat for clients. It was a time for unusual events. Ratana had also rarely made offerings to the spirit house in the *soi*. It had been twenty-four hours of rare events and incidents and sightings. Which made him think about the video footage of workers churning out fake drugs. He was supposed to deliver it to Danielson. But dead men don't pay.

"Someone else will take over from Danielson," said Calvino. "I'll get paid."

Ratana shrugged. "I hope so." There was little conviction in her reply.

Whatever her reasons for leaving, she kept them to herself. It wasn't anything he had guessed, so it must have been something he had done to offend her. "Is it mid-life crisis?"

"You walk past it every day. But you don't see it."

Calvino looked around his office. "Something on my desk?"

"No, not on your desk. It is something downstairs."

"The massage parlor." His face brightened.

"I don't think it is funny," she said.

His smile disappeared. "I know it's not funny. I never thought it would make me laugh. I smiled because now I know why you are circling job ads in the newspaper. You don't like the massage parlor as a neighbor."

Her smile masked an unsettled feeling that had been building for weeks. "It makes me feel . . ." She paused, choosing her words carefully. "Not good about myself. Every day I see something that makes me feel bad. Can you understand that?"

She turned and returned to her desk. He followed a couple of minutes later. "I'll buy their lease."

She sighed, still smiling. "That would be good. But I think it is quite expensive."

"I'll borrow the money."

They both knew this was unlikely. It was easier to coordinate a bomb attack than to borrow money in Bangkok.

"I think it is hard for a *farang* to get a loan, Vinny."

He saw her effort to be understanding but her true feelings hovered close to the surface. If only he weren't a *farang*. Then he'd understand. Then he could borrow the money. It made her suffer in a way that Calvino regretted.

To say that Thais go out of their way to avoid conflict was true, but to say that they aren't filled with conflict would be a lie. The conflict inside Ratana kindled a roomful of oily rags and old papers of regret until they exploded into flames. She was raging inside, burning up, running, screaming, though on the outside, a wall of calm fenced off her internal mayhem. What made matters worse was Calvino's trying to find a large sum of money. His desperation was the kind of personal humiliation that she hated herself for fueling. If only the spirit of the place would answer her prayers. If only there were forces beyond who would respond to incense sticks, candles, flowers, and prayers—and lend funds to a *farang* private eye with a balance sheet written in red ink.

Did the gods have time to rescue such a business? She promised herself to make another offering tomorrow and the next day, building merit.

"Even if I can't get the money, there may be another way," he said, brushing the back of his hand against his cheek. "What would you think about moving our operation inside the UN?"

She blinked as if she might be dreaming. "Are you okay, Vinny?"

"I am serious. The WHO is looking for a senior investigator. I'm thinking about applying. Of course, you would go with me."

"Where?"

"New York."

She broke out laughing.

"And leave my family and friends? Leave Thailand?"

Calvino stood his ground. "I said it was an option. I didn't say I would take it." A moment later he had logged onto the WHO website and was reading the job description again, looking for some detail he might have overlooked.

SEVEN

LOVELL had been in his office a few minutes, checking his e-mail, when Cameron, the senior partner of the firm, sent his secretary to escort him to the conference room. This was not unexpected. A department head had died the night before. The office was in turmoil. His computer screen was papered with stick-on messages of missed phone calls. He peeled off a couple but hadn't finished his e-mail when the big boss summoned him. It was understood that he would immediately drop everything.

Siri, his girlfriend, came into his office. Lovell slumped forward from his chair, hands holding his face. "John, are you all right?" she asked.

Lovell lifted his head. "Cameron wants to see me, now," he said.

She smiled as if it were just another day. Her hair was pulled back from her shoulders, with not a single strand out of place. Her makeup looked as though it could have been applied with the finest brush of a portrait painter, leaving not the slightest blemish showing. She might have been a model or a movie star. Siri asked him if she could do something to help out. He slowly shook his head. What could she do? What could anyone do? She meant well and that was the important thing. Cameron's secretary came back into his office and made it clear that she intended to wait until he left for the appointment.

Siri, seeing that he was trapped by Cameron's secretary, sighed.

"Call me when you finish," she said.

"I'll do that."

"You look upset. I would be, too. But it will be all right," she said.

"Sure thing," he said, pulling on his suit jacket.

He felt things were pulling. But he still had his balance, and he'd always found a way to turn things around in the past. The quality had made him a good lawyer. As he was about to leave, one message caught his attention: a call-back message from the police detective who had interviewed him after Danielson's death. He had phoned twenty minutes earlier, saying it was urgent for him to return the call. Lovell had resigned himself to the fact that everyone would now have an urgent need to talk to him. Looking at the mountain of messages, three from the police, he expected that his law work would have to give way to days of answering questions, giving interviews, and making statements. And because of the way his memory absorbed the smallest of details like a camera lens, he felt confident that he could recite every last frame of what he had seen in the restroom the previous night.

In police work, a rule of thumb in every detective's training manual was that the last man to see a dead person alive was at the very least a material witness. He may have seen crucial events that, taken one by one, would prove to be the pieces of the puzzle of how it happened. In the case of murder, the last man to see the dead person before he or she died was also, by default, the prime suspect. In the case of a heart attack, the last man could describe the victim's condition and confirm that a medical event had happened. The man sweated, clutched his chest, and was short of breath. Heart attack, panic attack: like twins, they shared similar footprints.

Another message on his computer was from a private detective named Vincent Calvino. Behind it was a second, a third, and a fourth note from the same private detective. Four clients and two other lawyers in the firm had also phoned. None of this mattered so long as Cameron waited. His future in the law firm wasn't a question for the police but was in the hands of the firm's senior partner.

When Lovell entered the conference room, Cameron's back was turned to the door. His long thick mane of bushy white hair made his head look enormous. He paced in front of a bank of floor-to-ceiling windows. Thirty-seven floors below, the traffic had ground to a standstill. A pencil couldn't be shoved between the bumpers. Motorcyclists had taken to using the sidewalks, until they, too, were stopped by the surge of people. Hundreds of demonstrators with placards marched along the road, spilling over onto the pavement. *It was the best of times; it was the worst of times,* thought Cameron. Charles Dickens would have been at home.

Lovell entered the conference room so quietly that he was forced to clear his throat before Cameron turned around. The man with the big hair and even bigger ego owned the law firm and everyone in it. Dressed in a tailored, double-breasted gray suit, Cameron could have been fifty or seventy years old. No one was ever sure of his age. He was also uncommonly tall: six feet and five inches at least. Too distinguished to be confused with an aging 60's rock band drummer, he looked more like a Nobel-winning scientist who had discovered a secret door to the quantum world. Clients trusted Cameron in the way that people trust gurus–with complete faith–and he used this power to humble anyone who doubted or questioned his authority.

"Someone in the police forensic department says Danielson may have been murdered," he said. His voice was never much above a whisper. He had cultivated a low-register tone of voice because it had forced people to bend into it so as not to lose a word. Controlled, constant, with unwavering certainty and conviction, his voice sounded as if it were delivering the Ten Commandments even when it was ordering a coffee.

"Last night the medics said it was a heart attack," said Lovell.

He sat down hard at the conference table.

"In Thailand, there are no medics. There are volunteers who collect bodies."

"Then the police."

"You're not sure?" Cameron glanced down at the ant-like creatures moving along the streets with their banners and handmade signs.

It was one of his most gifted techniques, making others doubt themselves and then offering up the solution to resolve that doubt.

"No one said anything about Andrew dying from anything other than a heart attack."

"That was last night. Today they are questioning whether it was acute myocardial infarction." Cameron's voice dropped to just above a whisper.

"What killed him?"

"They found traces of several drugs in his blood."

Lovell smiled. "He took two Zoloft pills for anxiety. I saw him swallow them."

Cameron arched an eyebrow. "He swallowed pills in a ballroom filled with people?"

"He was in the restroom at the time. He didn't feel well. There was another lawyer at the sink. His name is Apisak."

"He's with Jackson and Gleason?" asked Cameron.

Was there anything Cameron didn't know? thought Lovell. "As a matter of fact, yes." He stared at Cameron. Maybe he was God after all.

"Go on."

Lovell took a deep breath. "Apisak already had the pills out. Andrew was trembling. He'd had some bad news that rattled him. He asked for the pills."

"What if I told you that Andrew didn't die from Zoloft," asked Cameron, "but from something else?"

"What are you saying?" Lovell sat down at the conference table, hands clasped in front like a schoolboy on judgment day.

Cameron turned away from the window, walked around the conference table, and leaned forward, his fingers splayed out to balance himself. "What better place to kill someone? With two hundred of the top movers and shakers of Thai society nearby. If you wanted to kill someone, wouldn't that be a perfect place? Where would the police start? Questioning people from influential families, people with titles, people who work at the highest levels of government, banking, and commerce? Where would you start?"

"With the last person who saw him alive."

Cameron smiled, his eyes not blinking as he stared at Lovell. "We are paid by our clients to extricate them from difficult circumstances. Circumstances which make them uneasy, which can be messy, costly, or embarrassing. You are a lawyer in this firm, and you are in a difficult situation. The law firm functions for its clients. You have made it difficult for me. I must make a judgment." At that moment, Lovell looked across the table at Cameron. Moses-like, he said, "It is for me to decide whether you can continue to function as a lawyer in this office."

"I didn't do anything."

"How is that relevant?" asked Cameron, his voice like thunder. "Do our clients care whether you did anything? No, they only care that their law firm has lawyers who do not spend their billable hours trying to pry themselves free of accusations." His voice diminished again in the way an unhappy god's voice might trail off into silent disappointment.

Lovell said nothing but waited for the full weight of Cameron's whisper to lift him from his seat and carry him to the window of the thirty-seventh floor, where unlike a leaf he wouldn't float but fall. A faint smile crossed Cameron's face as if he had recalled a private joke. He shook his head and smiled again. "Danielson will be missed. But we have a practice to run. Clients expect us to look after *their* interests. Your interests don't concern them. The question is whether you can deliver work to our clients despite your own substantial personal problems."

"I can, sir. And I will."

"Let's take it one day at a time." He sat down in the chair opposite Lovell. "I want a complete list of all the cases Danielson worked on for the past two months. We will need to reassign the files to other lawyers. And I want a list of your cases, too. No client can suffer or be left uncertain or confused, is that understood? We must repair any damage caused to this firm by his death. And we must repair it fast."

"You said a drug was found in Danielson. What was it?"

"Zoloft and traces of other substances."

"What other substances?"

Cameron ignored his question and returned to looking out the window. "The people marching in the streets want to believe in justice. That is their hope and desire. But justice, like a suit, comes in many different sizes and styles. It is never one size fits all. No client list from Danielson's office will be disclosed to the police unless I personally authorize it. Is that fully understood?"

The giant of a man left the room without waiting for an answer.

EIGHT

ALONE in the conference room, Lovell collapsed, resting his head on the polished table. He focused his mind on recalling all of Cameron's half-whispered words. The fresh memory of Cameron's voice—trailing off here and there, threatening, baiting, comforting, remote, and intimate—haunted him. Danielson had been a buffer between Cameron and Lovell. They had rarely spoken to each other. Lovell found Cameron unsettling and overbearing. Andrew had said the law firm was Cameron's private bus, that Cameron was the driver and owner, and that those who did well kept their heads down. Like anonymous scribes, they focused on the case at hand. Danielson had been the only lawyer who never showed any fear of Cameron, even standing up to him in meetings and conferences. Cameron had tolerated Danielson for a couple of reasons: he never made Cameron look bad in front of a client, and Danielson's reputation attracted business clients.

When Lovell returned to his office, even more messages littered his computer screen. He felt sick looking at them. Cameron had made his priorities clear, and Lovell did what he was told: he organized Danielson's case list. Most of the cases were already in his memory. He double-checked the computer files, verifying clients, status, and outstanding bills. Lovell was too inexperienced to have acquired his own clients in his short time with the firm. Cameron knew this. It was his business to know who brought money into the firm and who took it out.

Soon after he had finished with the first draft of the report, the bamboo telegraph had sent the message that Lovell had returned and locked himself into his office. Siri had phoned him several times. His secretary had intercepted each call. When he finally returned Siri's call, she was frustrated, upset. There was a coldness, a distance, in her voice. He invited her to his office so that he could explain what had happened with Cameron in the conference room.

Her anger turned to sympathy as she came into his office. "Are you okay? You look terrible," she said.

"Cameron wants a list of Danielson's clients."

"Get his secretary to do it. That's not your responsibility."

Lovell fought back the urge to scream. "He asked me to do it." *In that whisper of his*, he thought. With the Thais, every assignment had to fit into the hierarchy. Like in a beehive, where every bee had a duty to perform certain tasks. Asking the wrong bee to do something made the entire hive buzz with discontent.

"There's a database of all our clients," he said. "Why doesn't he check that?"

"What if he suspects that Danielson had clients who aren't on the database?"

"Yeah, like Danielson was running a black bag operation for Bill Gates." He mimicked Cameron's whisper.

"It's not funny. And don't try to sound like Cameron." She circled around his desk and looked out the window. Half-turning, she looked back at him. "Just be yourself, John."

"I don't want to fight, and I have a lot of work to do. We can talk over dinner," he said.

"He didn't blame you?"

"Blame me for what?"

She studied the perplexed expression on his face, smiled, and reached for his hand. "He's worried about the fallout with our clients."

"Old people die all the time. The clients will understand."

"I hope so."

She toyed with a gold bracelet on her wrist, turning it around as if it were some kind of tuner, and whatever frequency she was plugged into made her colder and more remote. The newspaper with Danielson's photograph was on Lovell's desk. She reached over and picked it up. "He wasn't that old, John."

"He was fifty-three. My dad's fifty-two."

The phone rang and he picked it up. Siri left his office, closing the door behind her.

"Vincent Calvino?" Lovell repeated the name into the phone.

"Danielson hired me to investigate a drug piracy case. I'd like to meet with you about evidence. I've got a video of the operation."

Lovell had accidentally stumbled on the case and Danielson had told him it was a personal matter. Gould was the managing director of Avenant Pharma, a local distributor for several of the major drug companies. Sales of some high-profit drugs for high blood pressure and diabetes had been sliding down, just when all the medical statistics showed a significant increase in the number of Thais suffering from these diseases. Doctors had been prescribing the new wonder drugs in response, and a check of hospitals showed that prescriptions had been up by thirty-two percent. But sales of the imported, brand-name drugs were down fourteen percent.

Danielson had asked him to say nothing about the case. Lovell's hunch was that his boss's need for discretion had something to do with his hiring Calvino. He hadn't been in the loop when Danielson had engaged a private detective.

"As you might understand, I've lost a friend and boss. I simply don't have the time to meet you this week."

"What I have will make your client happy," said Calvino. "I have a video of the operation. The drugs are trucked in. I checked registration plates and found the trucks are out of Chiang Rai. It's like what Danielson thought was happening. The goods came down from China by the boatload. I've got them uploading tons of product. It's exactly what Danielson wanted."

"I'll keep that in mind. Right now I'm putting out fires. Danielson's death has made many clients less than happy." He found himself reading from Cameron's script.

There was a pause at the other end. "Phone me when you're free. We need to move on this quickly."

"Sure thing," said Lovell, knowing that he was telling Calvino what he wanted to hear, and that it would buy him some time.

After he ended the call, Lovell asked his secretary to bring in the Avenant Pharma file. Looking it over, he saw that billings to date had run to ten thousand dollars, and Stiles had billed most of the time. But there was nothing about Andrew Danielson handling a piracy case. Nor did the name of Vincent Calvino appear in the file. That was no surprise. Gould, as Danielson's personal client, wasn't in the law firm computer system; there was no way to know about their financial arrangements. Lovell stretched back in his chair, looked up from his computer screen, and swirled around, looking at the family photographs of his parents on the shelf. His father looked good in the photo. Strong, full set of teeth, dark hair, and slender. But the photograph had been taken a few years earlier. His mother had lines around her mouth and, especially because she was looking into the sun, creases around both eyes, making them look more like bullet holes.

Thumbing through Danielson's case file, he found a copy of a letter written on personal stationery, asking Gould to give him additional funds. No explanation was given as to what the funds were for. There was also a printout of an e-mail from Gould, confirming the importance of keeping the case confidential to just the two of them. The request for money and Gould's e-mail had been exchanged one week ago. Danielson obviously had continued working on the case even though the firm's policy was that all work stopped on any case where the client was in arrears of payment.

That was a minor issue. Taking a case and keeping it off the books was an entirely different matter. Danielson had violated more than one rule. The phone rang again. It was Lovell's secretary, a middle-aged, unmarried woman with wide hips and flashy jewelry. She was reminding him that he had a meeting with a client. She endlessly snacked at her desk, leaving a trail of crumbs that once a month jammed her keyboard. Her nickname was Wan, or Sweet. Lovell had speculated that when she'd been assigned to him, her main job had been to watch him and report to Danielson. Now he wondered if he'd gotten that chain of command wrong. He'd told Siri he felt Wan's Thai nickname must have come from her addiction to sugary food rather than her personality, which was dark and brooding. Siri had bristled, saying that Wan had worked for the firm since Cameron had started it twenty-two years ago. She had joined straight out of university.

As he walked past Wan's desk, she informed him that Cameron

would be attending the meeting. There was a hint of menace in her voice, a subtle message that he was being carefully watched. Others in the office had gone strangely silent, too. Or was it just his imagination? In between the states of silence and menace, Lovell searched for a mental place where he could consider what the unexplained correspondence in the file meant.

NINE

CAMERON sat at the head of the long conference room table of polished teak, looking like God—who, if he had decided against better judgment to manifest himself as a lawyer, could have done no better than manifesting himself through Cameron's body. At the table next to him was a Thai-Chinese man in an expensive Italian suit, a Liberty tie, and a three-carat ruby ring. His moussed hair rose in rows of glistening spikes. But the haircut couldn't fully mask that the head belonged to someone in his early forties. Weerawat threaded the fingers of his ruby decorated hand around a china cup of coffee and clicked the ring against the cup. He used his other hand to touch his upper lip as he looked at his reflection in the highly polished surface of the table. Beside Weerawat's coffee cup and saucer lay two sleek, black-bodied cell phones, the kind with a little flashing red light like a beacon in a rural one-runway airport, facing off like two budget air carriers with cowboy pilots at the controls. Above the cell phones, stationed like a centurion guard, a pair of high-tech sunglasses—silver, ultra thin, with tinted glass the color of a mysterious and moonless night—looked like an ultra-light ready to launch.

Each time one of his cell phones rang, Weerawat glanced at the number, smiled, and then pushed the busy signal. He received a lot of calls, thought Lovell. The teak had been polished to the point where it reflected images that looked like distorted faces in an amusement park mirror. Chatting at the table their images half merged on the highly polished surface, creating the weird optical illusion of a third person embedded and moving inside the glass. Cameron tossed back his head, sending his white mane flying, and his mouth opened wide, and what came out was a deep laugh echoing across the room. The laughter ebbed away as Lovell crossed the conference room and took a seat at the table. He recognized Weerawat. His face often appeared in the business section of the *Bangkok Post* or *The Nation* and his boyish good looks filled the society pages and peered out from magazine covers. Weerawat was a local celebrity known for his close connection with the government. Danielson had talked about him many times as a sensitive and connected client. "He is a revenue stream with the power of the Amazon," Danielson had once said. "The river as well as the dot-com." *It's funny,* thought Lovell. *He's only just dead and already I'm thinking of him as a resident of the past.*

Danielson had thought of Weerawat's interconnected networks of families, friends, and colleagues as a vast coral reef—honeycombed chambers, passageways, and towers hidden beneath the surface. With each generation the family coral reef expanded across the ocean floor of Thailand multiplying, building new layers, making everyone richer, stronger, more secure, and more committed to protecting each other. At the center of the reef was Weerawat, and with him his Uncle Suvit, a former cabinet minister who was also an honorary member of the law firm.

Danielson had said, "Draw charts of the families. Diagram them the way you diagrammed sentences as a kid learning English. And for the same reason. That's how you understand the structure of grammar, and it's also how you comprehend the structure of a culture. In this culture, there's just one commandment: nurture the important coral reefs. They are a living entity. If they're damaged, then they will die. The Thais know this. Khun Suvit knows this, as does Cameron."

Still, it was unusual for Weerawat to pay a personal call. Even stranger was Suvit's absence from the meeting. He should have been at the conference table at the side of his famous nephew, though there had been rumors that the old man had been in ill health lately. No one had seen him in the office for weeks. Weerawat's empire of companies brought in a great deal of business to the law firm. Even God laughed at the jokes of a rainmaker, thought Lovell has he folded his hands on the teak table.

"Khun Weerawat has volunteered to help us," said Cameron.

Weerawat grinned and nodded as if Lovell were a potential swing voter in a district that he needed to carry.

The statement was pure Cameron: hopelessly vague, opaque, and hinting of danger. Volunteers were required for tough, dangerous missions. In the movies the loyal and brave walked through snake-infested swamps, with coiled serpents ready to drop from low branches, while along the banks unseen enemies prepared to spring an ambush. Lovell's father, who had been in the army, had taught him from an early age that "volunteer" was the only dirty nine-letter word in the English language and that he should avoid it at all peril. The two men looked at him, as if sizing him up. Lovell wasn't certain what he was supposed to say. "That's great. We need all the help we can get."

Cameron's eyebrows knitted into the shape of a pair of open handcuffs. He opened a folder, removed a document, and slid it across the table to Lovell. "It's a confidential report. For our eyes only. It seems that someone working in the forensic lab made a mistake. They found Zoloft. But they also found something strange. Several drugs used to treat HIV and the presence of a deadly dose of wasp venom."

Glancing away from the report, Lovell looked confused. "He took two Zoloft pills. I saw him."

Cameron nervously cleared his throat, twisted his neck—that was one of his signature gestures, signaling his unhappiness. "The report has been corrected to state that traces of Zoloft were found in Danielson's blood. Your statement was of course of great importance. Tomorrow the final verdict will be made. Andrew died of a heart attack. He was far too young. It makes you think. A heart attack can hit just about anyone. Though it wasn't a great surprise. He had been taking statin drugs for his blood pressure. It was the statins that confused them. One of the doctors misinterpreted the results. Khun Suvit phoned Khun Weerawat and asked his opinion. Let's just say, he has successfully straightened out the problem."

"That's good," said Lovell. He looked at Weerawat and then at Cameron, wondering if he had said the right thing.

"He's a team player, just like I told you," Cameron said, turning and addressing Weerawat, who was picking up one of the ringing cell phones. The ring tone wasn't a normal ring but the sound of a flock of geese in flight. He had gone to the trouble to assign different signature rings to everyone in his address book. He held up a finger as a gesture for Cameron to pause. Weerawat turned, cupped his hand over his mouth and phone and spoke in rapid Thai. He rang off looking addled, as if he had found a loaf of bread with a large dead rat stuffed inside.

"Khun Weerawat also needs us to help him."

Lovell noticed that Weerawat had lost his smile. Weerawat looked like someone born to captain a yacht on which his family and friends enjoyed champagne under a bright orange sun. He was the mellow, charming storyteller with hundreds of best friends. It was hard to imagine Weerawat screaming.

"What can we do to help Khun Weerawat?"

"My very good friend—I have known him since school—has a problem. I want to help him. There's an American making some trouble for him. It's not a big problem. It's quite simple. You stop handling one of Danielson's cases. It's a small case but it gives my friend a big headache." His smile flashed back as if it had been set on an egg timer, and then morphed as he screwed up his face as if to express the pain felt by his friend. He still hadn't directly answered Lovell's question, circling around it without actually pinning himself down. Weerawat, ten years older than Lovell, scrutinized the young lawyer's reaction using the traditional Chinese art of face reading. Weerawat, who had half a tank of Chinese blood running through his veins, fell back on the true and tried principle of his ancestors that a man's face, eyes, and nose revealed everything important about his true nature. Properly read, a face could not hide the truth.

"The Gould case," whispered Cameron. "I am not quite certain how we came to take on the case. I've explained it was never an official case of the law firm. Perhaps you can support me on this point, Mr. Lovell."

"Mr. Danielson..."

"There is no point in assigning blame to anyone for taking the case. But I understand it was a personal client of Andrew's. Mr. Gould, in fact, asked Andrew to keep the case, for whatever reason, off the books. Is that true?"

Lovell nodded, knowing that this would seal the client's fate.

"Write a letter to Mr. Gould informing him the firm will not be continuing Andrew's private arrangements with respect to this case. I want a copy of that letter on my desk before the end of the day.

And arrange to have a copy of the letter to be delivered to Khun Weerawat's office."

Cameron had opened the lid of a magic music box, and Weerawat liked the sound of the music. He smiled, stood up from his chair, *waied* Cameron, and then turned and performed a degenerated version of a *wai*—the begrudging *wai* returned to *waiing* servants, junior janitors, and shoeshine boys—to Lovell.

Outside the conference room, Lovell leaned against the wall and drew in a long breath. His heart thumped. He wondered if he might be suffering from a heart attack at age thirty-one. *Christ almighty, Andrew was taking HIV medication,* he thought. *I had no idea.* The main thing, he told himself, was that Cameron had given him what felt like a last-minute reprieve from a certain execution date. No police would be coming to his office to ask further questions. He could get on with his career and settle down to a good life with Siri. It was as if he were being reborn as he stood in the corridor, clerks and other lawyers passing him. And the best part was the low price he had to pay: cutting loose Gould was hardly a difficult call to make. He had stopped being an official client of the law firm. When he had shifted status and become Danielson's personal client, then Gould had become just another outsider.

Lovell sensed some people in the firm were worried about him, though. Gould was an ex-client who landed on a watch list. And then there was the private eye, Vincent Calvino, who had phoned about the case, but he obviously didn't know Gould's name. He turned over in his mind how he would handle Calvino. He was another complication he'd rather not deal with.

He couln't prove it but Cameron's decision to backlist Gould had Weerawat's fingerprints all over it. Weerawat had gently put the squeeze on Cameron. The hand that made the graceful *wai* was also the hand that grabbed and held onto Cameron's balls, he told himself. What was new about that? It was the nature of the ecology built by the people who lived in the world of business and law.

It was like making orange juice, which is all about applying the necessary pressure to get the juice out of the fruit without splattering it all over the table and floor. You don't want to destroy the orange; you just want to harvest the juice.

The law firm would survive; he would survive. He took off his jacket and draped it over the back of his chair, sat down, and checked his e-mail. Delete, delete, read, and reply.

Lovell was working at his desk when Graham Stiles, the lawyer two offices down, walked in without knocking and flopped down in a chair. Stiles, a five-year veteran in the corporate department, put his feet up on Lovell's desk, his shoes pointing at Lovell.

"You aren't supposed to point your feet at people in Thailand," said Lovell. "It's in all the cross-cultural books."

"Read the fine print. It only applies to Thais."

Having made his point, Stiles swung his legs around, his feet dropping to the floor. Stiles' male-pattern balding made him look older than he actually was. His athletic build advertised a ghostly presence of youthfulness. His stylish, hip suit and bald head sent a mixed message. Women thought he was too old; clients thought he was too young. Stiles had a combative nature. He had been kicked out of litigation after three months for alienating the Thai lawyers, several judges, and three clients. Cameron, though, tolerated him for reasons that God and Cameron kept to themselves. Each day Stiles' mission was to pick a fight.

"You were at the hotel when Danielson checked out."

Lovell tried to ignore the comment. But Stiles wouldn't let it go. He laughed at his own sick joke. "Check out? Hotel? Don't you get it?"

"He was in the restroom," said Lovell.

"Taking a dump and his heart stopped pumping," said Stiles.

"I've got a lot of work to do, Graham."

"Think about it. Your last words are, 'Grunt, grunt.'"

"I don't think that's at all funny."

Stiles had the kind of sense of humor fueled by reference to violence, muggings, assaults, extortion, and remote controlled explosive devices. The more gruesome the image, the more he laughed and expected others to find this funny.

"You still don't get it, do you? To work here, you better learn some jokes or you won't last. Cameron says he can tell originality is present when someone makes him laugh. That's because he's heard just about everything before."

"How's your billing this month?" asked Lovell in the same jokey tone of voice. It was like asking how your golf handicap was or how much you bench-pressed. Competition required reporting and comparing the results.

"I had a good month," said Lovell. "And your billings?"

"Out of the ballpark."

About once a week Cameron, as the senior partner, advised that all lawyers should keep up their billings, but they had to find a balance. Why would Andrew Danielson keep the fees from Gould off the books? He wasn't a crook or greedy; it wasn't in his nature to cook up a scheme to cheat the firm. Lovell circled around the issue and kept returning to the same conclusion. *Gould had paid cash to Andrew.* It had to be done discreetly and in a way that guaranteed Cameron would never discover the payment.

Once after a meeting, he had asked Stiles about the relationship between Cameron and Suvit. He already knew that Suvit was the silent, steady hand behind a family empire fronted by Weerawat. But he also knew there was much more about the family empire that no one openly talked about in the firm.

Stiles had told him that Suvit had taught Cameron everything he knows. The need to stay fit and in the game by keeping the client thinking that some progress is being made. You must be practical. There are ways to help both sides. If you're going to bust the chops of the other side, you use all available resources. Strike hard, strike fast. Do whatever you have to do, but don't fail. Keep the client happy, keep the police happy, and then people in power and in business are happy. You'll always have clients. You'll never go without success. "Isn't that a worthy goal in life?" he had asked.

"With what I'm bringing in as a bonus this month, why don't I take you out for drinks after work tonight?" said Stiles.

"I've got plans for dinner."

"Then after dinner. You need to unwind after what you've been through."

Lovell thought about the logistics of dinner, then explaining to Siri that he had an appointment to meet Stiles for drinks. He had all but signed a covenant in his own blood not to go to bars.

"Who in the bamboo telegraph reported that I saw Cameron?"

"Was it a secret?"

The oldest lawyer trick in the world, replying to a question by shooting back another question.

Word of the deal he had just made with Cameron had already leaked to Stiles. Secrets were difficult to keep in the firm. A couple of times a week, Lovell caught Stiles outside his office handing a bag of cookies or custard cakes to his secretary. She obviously liked him, and Lovell suspected that she whispered information to him. The old bird hadn't liked Lovell from his first day at the office.

Lovell comforted himself by recalling that it was not important how Stiles had found out about the meeting with Cameron and Weerawat. In a small office—or a large one for that matter—if a celebrity appears and is escorted into the conference room with the big boss, there is no way to keep that confidential. There was another possibility. A rumor circled that Stiles acted as Cameron's guide into Bangkok nightlife, where every fetish could be satisfied. Rumor had it that Stiles combined his inside information on Cameron's sexual preferences with his ability to drive his boss discreetly to some back door for an afternoon session. These skills had been his ticket to access, and access was power.

Stiles got up as Lovell's phone rang. "We'll hook up at eleven. I'll phone you and let you know where to meet."

"One more thing," said Lovell. "Are you still handling the Avenant Pharma account?"

Stiles stared at him. "That's an interesting question."

"That's an interesting answer."

"See you later, Lovell." Stiles disappeared before Lovell could reply, leaving the door open. Wan, standing in the doorway, did something Lovell thought she was incapable of doing: her lips spread into a motherly smile.

★

When Lovell picked up the phone, he heard Vincent Calvino's voice: "We talked earlier. I don't think I made it clear. I have the evidence that proves the piracy of your client's goods."

"The case is no longer active."

"What does that mean?"

"The person in question is no longer a client of the firm. He had some special arrangement with Andrew. I have no idea what they were doing. I don't want to know. It's our firm's policy—a lawyer can't have private clients. I'm certain I don't have to spell out the reasons why that isn't allowed."

"What about my outstanding bill? Danielson said he would clear it."

"I'm sorry, Mr. Calvino. But that is between Danielson and you."

Calvino paused, thinking of his next move. Suddenly his necktie started to strangle him. He used his free hand to loosen his collar. Looking at the computer screen, he looked at the amount outstanding. It was a large sum of money.

"Give me the name of Danielson's client. I'll contact him directly."

"I can't do that. I'm sorry, but I really can't help you."

Talking to Lovell was as useless as holding up a mirror in front of a blind man and asking him to describe his features. Calvino had smashed into a dead end. He blinked at the four hundred thousand baht figure on the screen, his stomach twisting into knots, sweat breaking out on his forehead. "You're joking, right?"

"Why would I joke with you, Mr. Calvino?"

"Danielson phoned me from your law firm."

"What Andrew did was wrong."

"I want what is owed to me," said Calvino.

"I thought that I made it clear. Let me repeat it. What Andrew did in that situation was way outside the rules of the law firm."

"Maybe you didn't hear me. I want my money."

"You want the firm to pay you off?"

"No, I want to be paid for what Danielson hired me to do. I did that. I've got the video. I did my job. Pay me."

What rang in Calvino's ears long after he had put the phone down were Lovell's words, "I really can't help you." Cold, definitive, blunt words ringing like a gunshot in the middle of the night.

With Andrew Danielson dead, his associate had made it clear that the piracy case, as far as Danielson's law firm was concerned, never existed. No file had been opened, no file needed to be closed. No money, no joy, no nothing. He thought about phoning Lovell back and telling him that he had ways of tracking down Danielson's client. The reality was different. Danielson could have been acting for someone who had no authority. If it had been a straight-up transaction, there would have been no need to keep the relationship off the books. *Who do you call? What do you say? I'm the schmuck who didn't know who he was representing? Who's your mama?*

When he was a child, Calvino overheard his mother calling his father a *schlemiel* for not getting money up front. Her voice had been raised when she said, "That's why your family are gangsters. They have to chase after money they should have already had in the bank. What are you thinking? Get the money up front. When you don't get the money up front, you can't sleep at night. When you can't sleep, I can't sleep."

As far as Calvino could determine, he saw no clean path to the ten grand Danielson had promised him. And the letter Danielson had promised to write to support his WHO application? Another promise dissolved by Danielson's death. Calvino was angry. He wouldn't stop until he found a path, clean or not, to his money. When someone owed you money, the rule was you collected it. Shrugging off the loss wasn't an alternative. Find the money. Money had a purpose. Just in case the WHO job didn't come through, Calvino planned to use the money to buy the lease from the *mamasan* of One Hand Clapping. Her business had never taken off; the *yings* were restless, moody, killing themselves. The price for the lease had dropped. The *mamasan* had even approached him and asked if he was serious about the lease. He'd told her that he had the money. It would be an all-cash deal. She'd looked happy, like someone who had just emerged from the molten core of the planet with just a bad rash, knowing that she would survive. Now he had to go back to her and explain that he didn't have the money. He would get the money but he would need some time. He'd ask her for an extension. She wasn't going anywhere soon, not with her business like a coma patient laid out for the long sleep. Calvino pulled his .38 police service revolver out of his shoulder holster and checked the safety. It was on. Feeling the hard, cold steel in his hand made him think of a serious intention to cause bodily harm. The lack of funds meant some major disappointment for Ratana. He shoved the .38 back into his holster, got up from his desk, put his jacket on, and, covering the holster, went to lunch.

TEN

AS usual, Old George perched at the end of a booth beneath an enormous stuffed water buffalo head, nursing a bottle of Singha beer. He sipped, made a face, and then smacked his lips. "I don't know what you're doing back there, but whatever it is, don't stop."

Oy, a waitress at the Lonesome Hawk, balanced herself on her knees behind George, combing and tying his long black hair into a ponytail. At eighty-four years of age, to have enough hair to tie into a ponytail was a miracle, but to have a bar filled with personal attendants proved there was a God.

As she brushed Old George's hair, he said, "The first house I ever owned was in Berlin. I bought it in 1945. I bought it for two hundred cartons of cigarettes. I still own it. Goddammit, would someone change the music? I want country western. Break that CD. I don't ever want to hear that crap again." George hated Elton John's music. The *mamasan* of the Lonesome Hawk liked Elton John, and their music wars were a daily affair. The DJ was like a straggler caught in their crossfire.

In the back of the bar was the toilet. McPhail was inside pissing in a urinal filled with large chunks of ice. He refused to stop even when nothing more would come out. Like an artist examining his own creation, McPhail decided the ice sculpture looked like a tiny saddle on a miniature horse. This urinal ice sculpture gave him a sense of accomplishment. He walked back into the bar and found Calvino sitting two booths down from George.

"George, where do you get ice that size?"

"Antarctica," said Old George. "Hauled it in just for you to piss on."

"Yeah, yeah."

Calvino told a waitress that he wasn't hungry. She scowled and took away his plastic placemat. Instead he ordered a cold beer. Rubbing his shoulder, he wondered if the beer might help kill the pain. At the bar, several regulars sat with a stranger, a drunken Englishman, who was bragging about how he never used a condom in his life. He joked with Jack, one of the regulars. They seemed like friends. From the look of them, it was a good guess that they'd been drinking most of the morning. Unless the slur in their voices had been caused by sudden strokes. The Englishman, who was in his late thirties, stared at Calvino. He whispered something to Jack, who whispered something back, and then he raised his beer bottle and clicked the neck of Jack's bottle. The Englishman was the kind of drunk who couldn't sit still. He was on the stool, off the stool, pounding the countertop, screaming, "The taxman, the taxman! Fuck the taxman!" It made no sense what he was shouting. Then he pushed off the stool again and walked over and leaned on Calvino's table.

"Calvino, are you the only private dick in the world with an office above a massage parlor? One Hand Clapping and one eye spying." Calvino ignored him. Drunks and barking dogs were best left alone. He turned and walked back to the stool, picked up his beer again, and drank. Turning back, he stared at Calvino. He walked back to the booth.

"Someone said you were a fuck-up as a private eye."

Calvino looked up, finding the Englishman fixing his eyes on him.

"They said you couldn't find pig shit in a pig farm."

It was the wrong day to push the needle the wrong way over the record.

Calvino leaned forward, swinging his legs out of the booth. The Englishman snorted as he laughed at his own joke. He looked back at the bar as if he expected some applause, but Jack had turned his back on the Englishman and was drinking straight from the beer bottle. The Englishman had finished and half-turned toward the bar, still making his snorting noise. Calvino shoved a fist into the Englishman's shoulder blade, and waited until he craned his neck around. Then

Calvino head-butted him with enough force to splatter blood over the back of Jack's shirt and sluice blood across the bar top. The Englishman opened his mouth but made no sound for three seconds and counting. The customers at the bar waited for the deathly quiet to end. No more snorting or laughing. The Englishman's eyes rolled to the top of his head and he slumped forward, his head hitting the top of the bar, bleeding. Jack grabbed him before he fell onto the floor.

"Goddammit, Calvino, you can't beat up people in my bar," said old George.

"I didn't beat up people. I hit an Englishman. Not the same thing."

Bar owners made their profit off drunks like the Englishman and Jack. Morning drinkers were a blessing for the bottom line. It hurt to see a face smashed up to the point where it was hard to see how a bottle of beer would fit into its mouth.

"I've decided I want the special after all," said Calvino.

Old George sighed, shook his head. "Get him a special and get a bag of ice for that guy, whatever his name is."

The waitresses, displaying a mixture of excitement, horror, and sympathy, gathered around the Englishman, holding him up. He looked smaller now, more fragile, like a bantamweight boxer who hadn't seen the right cross land with speed and force on his own head.

Jack kept saying, "Eric, can you hear me?" He was shouting this in the Englishman's ear. The scene of mayhem attracted a crowd, and Jack assumed the role of official spokesman. The cook came out of the kitchen, wiping her hands on her apron. Old George gestured at her. "I said get some ice, goddammit! I want ice out here."

His request created a slight problem. All of the ice had been dumped in the men's urinal. McPhail watched as the cook went into the men's room with a bucket. He thought about saying something but then thought, *What the fuck.* The cook carried the bucket of ice and set it on the bar. She wrapped a hunk in a towel and applied it to the Englishman's face.

"I told you that Englishman was a pisshead," said McPhail.

The cook shot him a frown.

"I ain't giving you mouth to mouth, Eric," Jack said.

The Englishman moaned, leaking blood on the bar. The bartender, on the opposite side, tried to slide a towel under his head but he only groaned louder.

"You shouldn't have done that, Calvino," Jack said. "You've hurt him."

Calvino didn't say anything. He turned around and went into his booth. A plate of spaghetti had appeared during his absence. He pushed it away and ordered another beer. He slipped a waitress twenty baht to ring the bell. That made Old George happy enough to forgive Calvino. The two bartenders served a drink to all eight people in the bar, stuffing the tab for the drinks into Calvino's chit cup.

McPhail scooted across Calvino's booth, dangling his feet over the side, facing the bar. He ignored the Englishman's moaning, which had now upgraded to the low-pitched howl of a kicked dog. Shaking his head, McPhail watched the ice melting on the Englishman's face.

"You hit him pretty hard," said McPhail. "I think you broke his nose."

"A warbler like Eric has got to learn when to fly away," said a regular from across the bar.

After the waitresses fanned out and delivered free beers, including one for Old George, he shouted, "Next time don't be so goddam touchy, Calvino. You won't get any new clients fucking up my customers."

"I'll remember that, George," said Calvino.

"You do that."

Jack helped the Englishman over to the other side of the bar, where he sprawled out on his back, taking up the entire bench in one of the empty booths. He pressed a towel of pissed-on ice over his nose.

One booth away, Howard, another lunch time fixture, was hunched over his laptop. His thick, drooping moustache covered his upper lip. He pulled the cigarette out of his mouth and it looked like a magic act, the cigarette appearing out of the scrub of his moustache. Smoke curled out of his nose as he looked over the screen at the Englishman. Howard took a long sip from his whiskey and soda and wrinkled his large, red nose. "I'd bet you got a broken nose. I'm going to take a picture of that and put it on my website."

Jack sat back and drank the beer that Calvino had bought. The Englishman held the towel wrapped around the ice over his nose. He no longer moaned. McPhail wondered if the Englishman could smell his piss leaking through the towel. Probably not, he decided.

Howard snapped two shots with his digital camera. He showed them to a waitress who gave Howard the thumbs-up.

"You should get that nose looked after," said Howard, taking another shot as the Englishman moved the towel, exposing his face, wrinkled around the eyes, the skin a pale blue. The nose was flattened to one side. "I once had a friend who broke his nose. Tried to set it himself and it just ruined the look of his face. Every time you looked at him, you thought that he was signaling for a right-hand turn."

McPhail's Jameson with ice arrived with two ice cubes floating in the amber. He pushed the ice cubes with his finger, licked his fingertip. The blood had been wiped off the bar, the stool, and the floor. The *mamasan* nudged the DJ aside and put on Johnny Cash's "A Boy Named Sue." That song seemed to calm the patrons. McPhail gestured for a waitress to bring Calvino another beer. He sipped the Jameson. Calvino didn't look like he was in any mood for conversation. McPhail lit a cigarette and stretched out in the booth, listening to Johnny Cash singing in "Folsom Prison."

Calvino stared straight ahead, trancelike, eyes unblinking, saying nothing as the waitress set a fresh beer, lines of cold sweat rolling down the sides, on the table. He wasn't paying attention. Instead, in his head, Ratana's voice was playing on an endless loop. *Danielson was your great hope. He was our great hope. Now he's dead. What is there to hope for?* Ratana had been right. That was before he'd told her about the WHO position. She had shaken her head. *I mean, what real hope is left?*

He'd got the goods on the drug piracy operation. Just as he thought, the row of shop houses was just a transit point for knock-offs produced in China. They were making their own fakes. Never, in all of his years working as a private eye in Thailand, had he captured an illegal operation with such precision. Like a bank security camera tracking a robber standing at the teller, wearing no mask, no hat—no nothing—just showing his face to the camera.

He knew that what he had done was valuable and explosive. The ten grand was nothing to what the big drug companies were losing in sales. He'd made a transcript of the wiretap that recorded a Thai rapping with his plant manufacturer, who needed cash to buy ingredients. These guys had been in business in a big way. Voice tape and transcript and videotape—the package couldn't have been better. Leverage was one thing, but having a case on video and audio, that was a lever that would let you lift the moon and stars.

With Johnny Cash driving the prison population crazy with "A Boy Named Sue," Calvino couldn't stop asking himself questions like, why hadn't Danielson said he was acting outside normal channels? He should have told Calvino that he was getting into a backdoor operation. At least then he could have mentally prepared for something going sideways. He thought about the lawyer he'd phoned, going over and over what he'd said. Each time, something in his gut told him that there was more involved than what he was being told. Why was Lovell holding back the name of Danielson's client? Calvino knew the main players in the pharma business. He just couldn't figure out how to track down the right one. Cold-calling a dozen people wasn't the way to get paid, but it might be a good way to tip his hand and get himself killed.

It was a time of secrets and half-truths, of intrigue and fear, of deception and anger. The legal business, like every other business in the country, had dried up. Everyone was in a holding pattern until the lingering political storm blew over. Fear was hot in the air, fear of not knowing what was going to happen next.

What was left of the Englishman's nose twitched against the towel. "Smells terrible," he moaned. The cook, looking guilty smelling the pissed-on ice water in the towel, blushed, turned away, and fled into the kitchen. None of the waitresses squealed on her. They figured that kind of information ought to have value, and blurting it out for free was a waste.

McPhail clinked the rim of his glass of Jameson against the neck of Calvino's beer. "Vinny, your beer's getting warm."

Calvino looked at him and smiled. He drank straight from the bottle.

"Good head butt on that asshole," said McPhail. "The waitresses are already telling him where he can get a new nose for five thousand baht. Why does it always come down to money with them?"

"I need two hundred fifty thousand baht to buy the lease downstairs," said Calvino.

"I thought your new client paid you more than that?"

"He's dead."

"Oh."

"Heart attack last night."

"Fuck, man."

Calvino drank again from the bottle.

A waitress ran her arched fingernails over McPhail's happy Buddha belly, spilling from his unbuttoned Hawaiian shirt. She looked at her damp hands—each of her fingernails was painted a deep ivory green—and wiped them on a towel. "You too hot," she said. "Sweat too much."

"And you, dingo-worm, talk too much."

George, walking slowly past the booth, patted Calvino on the shoulder. "What you're talking about, Calvino, is a lot of money."

"Tell me about it," said Calvino.

"Unless you break it down into four parts," said McPhail.

Not exactly two hundred fifty thousand baht but close enough to keep his interest. Calvino looked up from his beer. He rubbed the side of his head, feeling an egg-like bump in the hairline above his forehead. The head butt had left what felt like a growing horn. "What's that supposed to mean?"

"I'm taking a cooking class." McPhail leaned forward over the table.

"Cooking?"

McPhail nodded. "And there are four *mem-farangs* in my class."

"And they are going to give me two thousand dollars each?" His head throbbed and his shoulder ached in a two-part harmony of pain.

McPhail, balanced on his elbows, rocked back and forth. "They have rich husbands. I'm telling you, Vinny, these women have money to burn. Charge them a couple of grand American and they won't blink. It's chump change if you know how to handle them."

"And you do?" Calvino drank from his beer bottle and thought about taking two painkillers.

"Vinny, I am trying to help you, goddammit. I'm learning to cook pasta and they yap away about the usual women things. The usual bullshit worries about getting older, and they gab about spas, beauty products, traffic jams, maid problems, but the conversation always comes back to the same thing. They're afraid that their husbands are fucking around with a young Thai girl. If this fear could be bottled, it would be enough renewable energy to turn oil overnight into some sticky black shit you leave in the desert."

A Calvino law said, "Better a clean defeat than a dirty victory," but he lived in a world where this law had been amended. The new version was, "If you can win a dirty victory, take it; never surrender for a clean defeat."

ELEVEN

CALVINO hovered inside the door. McPhail, humming the Bee Gees' "Stayin' Alive," walked ahead into the kitchen. Taking an apron from a hook, he wrapped it around his waist without breaking his stride. He passed a row of sinks and ovens. Looking back over his shoulder, he pointed at Calvino, then leaned over and whispered something to the chef, a large-boned man, with a shaved head under his chef's hat and a square jaw stubbled with one-day's growth of beard. He stared at Calvino, sizing him up, nodding as he listened to McPhail. After McPhail finished whatever lies he had to tell, the chef winked and gestured for Calvino to come out of the doorway. Calvino pushed away from the doorway and crossed the kitchen. The smell of tomato, garlic, and black pepper mingled with more faint smells of perfume and body odor.

McPhail introduced chef Elmo Valerio.

"I am very happy to meet you," said Elmo, shaking his hand. "Your famous grandfather must have taught you many things."

Calvino's hand froze, he pulled it back. He shot McPhail a hard look.

"My grandfather taught me many things. Telling the truth being one of them."

McPhail had told the chef how Calvino's great-grandfather had been a famous painter in Florence and had designed the set for Puccini's opera *Turandot.* And how in New York, Vincent's grandfather had been a famous chef. The city had put up a bronze plaque in Union Square with Calvino's name on it. Why the city would make such a tribute (or where in the square) to honor an Italian chef had been left vague. The chef had taken McPhail's explanation at face value.

Elmo had been born in Detroit. His acquired Italian accent, like the chef's hat and starched white uniform, was a finishing touch on his image. He was perfectly cast in the role of a chef, matching an upscale diner's vision with his dress, how he held himself, and how he spoke.

Also in the room were three women, two blondes and a redhead in their late thirties to forties—but that was a wild guess. They had reached an age where the years collapsed into the universal middle-age range, depending on Botox. They could have been sisters—same mother but different fathers. Open, friendly, and attractive, in any other city they would have been highly sought after. Men would have elbowed each other to get close to them, lavished money, gifts, and time on them, and made promises and commitments. But they weren't in any other city; they were in Bangkok.

They had been accustomed to exercising real power over sex. Turn it on; turn it off. Place, time, conditions were theirs to plan. The husbands went along to get along. Call their leverage a monopoly, and one was getting to the truth. It was a woman's weapon, her tool kit for enforcement—crowbar, monkey wrench, or jackhammer. After a couple of weeks in Bangkok they awoke to find that nothing in the old toolbox worked. The monopoly was busted; weapons rendered dysfunctional. Here all bets were off. That left them a few avenues, such as learning how to cook Italian.

McPhail sucked in a long, deep breath, holding in the toxic fumes of Jameson, and said with some forced flair, "Here's the Fab Four."

"That was the Beatles," said Janet. "We aren't that old." She liked teasing McPhail. The women had often used FabFour as a shortcut to talk about themselves. Of the three, Janet was the most attractive and had the kind of honest, natural face that attracted men.

"Okay, then the new Fab Four."

"Fab Four works," said Debra. "I don't have a problem." Pudding-faced, quick to smile, she had blonde hair that showed no brown roots; it was the real thing. She played along with Janet's fake ignorance.

McPhail quickly introduced the women, like a schoolteacher reading out names at assembly: Janet, Debra, and Ruth. He looked around, "Where's Millie?"

Ruth blinked away a couple of tears and then used her hand to brush away a few more following the first two down her cheek. "Her husband died. She won't be coming to class for a while." She had an angular face, thin lips, a long neck, and small blue eyes now flooding with tears. Her broad-brimmed pink hat was pulled down on her forehead. The hat and the white apron gave her a motherly, stay-at-home look.

The others nodded. "She might not return. We're not sure. She has so many arrangements for Andrew's funeral," said Ruth. Something about her eyes made you believe everything she said.

Calvino cleared his throat, "Andrew Danielson?"

Ruth sniffled and nodded. There was no hint of fake histrionics; she had been genuinely affected by Danielson's death. Debra squeezed her hand. Playing mother was what Ruth needed.

"You knew Andrew?" asked Janet.

"He was a client."

Then Janet offered her hand to Calvino. "It's sad to lose a husband."

Calvino shook her hand, though the way she'd held it out had suggested an invitation to kiss it. *Almost as sad as losing a client who owes you a lot of money*, he thought as he held her hand. She had the kind of smile that used every muscle to pull back her lips far enough to expose the back molars. Janet's face had not even a hint of a line or crease. It was unnaturally smooth. Her fingers were needle thin, and her nails glistened with a clear polish. They could easily transform into claws to leave streaks down a naked back. If there were a search for the all-American sweetheart next door, she would be a finalist.

McPhail slipped in next to Calvino and whispered, "You knew Millie's husband? Why didn't you tell me, man?"

"Why didn't you tell me you knew Millie?"

"Why would I do that?"

"That's what I was thinking, McPhail."

"You're right. Sorry bud, you know me with names. I can never remember."

Chef Elmo clapped his hands, "You are in my kitchen to learn how to cook Italian. Back to work," he said. The women circulated among the cutting boards, racks of pots and pans, stainless steel washbasins, imported ovens, and countertop gas cooktops. It was like watching flight attendants scatter after the captain's voice came over the intercom, ordering them to prepare for landing.

Chef Elmo adjusted his chef's hat as he strutted down the line. A walk he'd learned on the lot of a second-hand car dealership. His white top and trousers were freshly pressed and spotless. He walked the line between his students, closely supervising their activities with military precision. Meaning, he stood close to them, touching their hands, showing them the proper motions for chopping, slicing, and dicing. Onions, carrots, spears of white asparagus, and celery. Each woman had been assigned a task, a knife, a battle station, and an apron. The light flashed from the knife blade. Janet nibbled pine nuts from a bowl. The setup seemed to give the women a sense of purpose and happiness.

Chef Elmo worked three saucepans like a carnival juggler. Lines of sweat rolled in jagged rivulets down his neck. A wet stain appeared around the collar and under his armpits. He had mastered the stage movements and look of a professional. Chef Elmo knew how to command and entertain. He had left Detroit in the dust. McPhail knew of Chef Elmo's secret reinvention and his history of second-hand car sales in Detroit.

Calvino noticed that the women had developed a collective personality. Janet, the backbone of the group, watched as Chef Elmo—he was everywhere at once—stirred the chicken broth with one hand and guided Debra's carrot slicing with the other.

"You are lucky," said Chef Elmo. "Today we make osso buco. You like osso buco?"

"*Vorrei un piatoo con il manzo*," said Calvino.

Chef Elmo lost his smile. "I didn't catch that."

Debra clutched her throat, "You speak Italian. That is so, so romantic."

"I said a good osso buco depends on the quality of the broth," said Calvino. What Calvino had said in Italian was that he wanted a dish containing beef. Elmo hadn't understood. Now that was out of the way, Calvino could concentrate on what other lies were being told. Instead of focusing on Chef Elmo's deception about his Italian heritage, his mind raced around the fact that Andrew Danielson's widow was part of this group of expat women. They knew her, and, if he played his cards just right, they might lead him to his only chance to settle the bill owed by her late husband.

"*Posso avere una bottiglia di il succo?*" Calvino asked the chef for a bottle of juice. But got a blank stare in return.

The point was not the chef but the women, who swooned.

The chef squealed. "That is so right. You learnt this from your grandfather."

Calvino didn't acknowledged him, but figured it was better not to show up the chef. He didn't want to kill any chance of a return visit. In the world of expat cooking schools, keeping everyone happy was the goal —especially the women. You scratch my back, and I'll see the pasta sauce is served up, and you can have the women after class. Calvino got the message.

Chef Elmo moved over to Debra's workstation. She brushed back her ponytail as she sweated over the onions. Tears welled in her baby blue eyes. She used the back of her hand to wipe them away but it was useless and ran down both cheeks. "Debra, slice and dice the onions. Like this." He took one of the onions and his hand became a blur. The onion disappeared into a million little pieces.

Debra took out a tissue from a box on the counter and blew her nose. "You are so talented," she said.

Chef Elmo shrugged. "It is practice. You can learn to do it."

"I'll try," she sobbed, lower lip quivering.

They'd all been crying over the news about Millie's husband.

The restaurant kitchen had become their private sanctuary, an oasis away from the stark strangeness and cheap threats Bangkok represented. Their children attended international school, their husbands spent hours away at the office, and their maids rattled around pretending to clean their company-provided houses. This translated into a life with substantial dead time, starting in the early morning and ending in the evening with the children's return from school and the husband's phone call to say he had a meeting and was running late.

Or in Millie's case (exceptional but not unheard of), a call saying her husband was dead.

The wives were cast in minor roles in highly scripted daily lives, while their husbands received star billing. The women had few lines. A camera might capture a quick walk early in the morning and again late at night. Blink and what they did could be lost. In return, the Fab Four lived a life of comfortable isolation surrounded by luxury and convenience. But rather than happiness and contentment, their days and nights were filled with gnawing doubts about their husbands' fidelity.

In Chef Elmo's kitchen, they were back home. They mixed, chopped, stirred, tasted, and checked the temperature of the oven and found a place where they could easily mix, avoid the traffic and the crushing crowds, and shelter together. In Chef Elmo's kitchen they were productive. They occupied a space where they counted. What they did in the kitchen could be stretched into an activity with purpose and meaning.

Calvino had worked for women exactly like them. The assignment was to catch their husbands in full regression to their sixteenth year, giggling and nudging the *yings*, who made them feel like high school football stars. But the similarity was mostly on the surface. Underneath, each case had its own set of misery, conflict, threats, and abuse. No one, from the cops to private eyes, had much use for domestic cases.

After the cooking class finished, the women sat at the table together. The chef had disappeared, apparently afraid that Calvino would strike up another conversation in Italian. The osso buco, salad, bread, and wine had done the job. They relaxed, talking as if McPhail and Calvino weren't present. "His secretary was phoning at night," said Janet. "And what was she talking about? Her personal life and how lonely she was. I said fire her. He said, 'she's a good secretary.' And I said, 'a good secretary doesn't phone her boss at ten at night to talk about her sex life.'" *This is a good thing*, thought Calvino.

Maybe McPhail read the group psyche correctly, thought Calvino. The key, he told himself, was to get Janet signed on to the husband surveillance program. Then the other two women would follow like ducklings following mother duck across the road.

"This is my friend, Vincent," said McPhail. "He specializes in domestic surveillance. He can help you."

Janet Herron swirled the wine around the rim of her glass.

"Does he really?"

"I've handled a few domestic cases." But he had tried to avoid taking them. The code of *omertà* operated among members of the expat community with regard to sexual matters. A man could get killed if he violated it.

"He's the best private eye in Bangkok."

Calvino flinched every time McPhail made this puffed-up claim.

The best private eye was invisible, honorable, walked through the mud without complaint, and didn't track it through your living room. Tracking foreign husbands to short-time hotels was pure mud, right up to the hips. He wasn't happy with himself.

"I've heard that before," said Debra. "But everyone always says they're the best of the best. Am I right, Mr. Calvino?"

"Would you prefer someone who had no confidence, Debra?" Clients in domestic cases were mostly conflicted, emotional, and irrational. They had invested too much of themselves, and however such cases turned out, the line between right and wrong was blurred.

"But you're so busy that you have time on your hands to attend our cooking class," said Debra, touching up her makeup. She didn't bother to look up from her compact mirror.

"He's interviewing us?" asked Janet.

"I asked him to come, ladies. He canceled his afternoon to come here. All I am trying to do is help. Every time I come to class, you are talking about some young bar *ying* or secretary or whatever throwing herself at your husband. It was Debra who said that the worst part is not knowing," said McPhail. "She's right. I'd want to know. Don't you?"

Janet took a sip from her wine glass. "Ed is right."

"Jack would never cheat on me," said Ruth. Her gray eyes gave her a distant, sad look, and what looked like a D-cup gave her a certain built-in advantage over the locals.

Debra rolled her eyes. They were still bloodshot from cutting up the onions.

"How much do you charge?" Debra asked.

Calvino did some mental math. Since Millie Danielson was no longer a potential client, he'd have to recalibrate his fees if he had any hope of buying the massage parlor lease. "Three thousand," he said. "That's U.S. dollars." It was enough money that he was convinced they would turn him down and he could get on with finding the money a dead lawyer owed him.

"What do I get for that?" She fingered her necklace.

"For three grand? You get a professional. I send you photo graphs, video, and a full report of my stakeout. Normally it takes two or three weeks. Sometimes a case can run on for a few months. But I am thorough. If he's cheating, I'll find out where, when, and the names of the women."

Ruth sprayed wine out of her nose. "You mean more than one woman?"

It was time to spin them a war story. "One guy I followed was sleeping with five women. Not all at once. He did have two or three at the same time. But he never had five at once. At least I never caught him with all five. It was an exhausting case."

The kitchen was silent except for a running dishwasher. None of them knew how to react, or what to say.

"What a lot of energy that must have taken," said Ruth. She was the quiet one in the pink hat.

"He was in good shape," Calvino allowed. He wondered if she ever made love wearing that hat. A voice inside told him to walk out the door. Did he really want money from the dirty part of the business? Want didn't figure into it. He wouldn't walk out—couldn't walk out. His back was against the wall.

"No, I meant, following him, getting all of those prostitutes on video. It must have been exhausting," said Ruth.

"He already said it was exhausting, Ruth," said Debra.

"I'd rather not dwell on numbers," said Janet.

The women went silent. Were they thinking about the size of his feet or the number of women in the story? It wasn't clear.

McPhail glanced at Calvino and nodded. Like dolphins, women had a way of communicating when they were only thinking and not talking. Whatever sonar system they used, they had reached some tentative understanding in those few moments of silence.

"Who wants to go first?" asked Debra.

Ruth pushed away her wine glass. "I think we should draw straws."

"That's fair," said Debra.

"Can't we get some kind of group discount?" asked Ruth.

Her husband was on his second tour. She was a veteran, so bargaining like a local had become second nature.

McPhail smirked, pulled a funny face, "He's already giving you a discount," he said.

"There are other private investigators. Some work for less," said Calvino. "I will give you some names." For a moment, it appeared that they would take him up on the offer. He started to relax, found himself smiling. He would go back to the office and figure out how to track down the client who had gone to Danielson for evidence about the drug piracy operation. Yeah, as his mother had said, "Get your money in your hand. Then go out the door." He always had faith that things would turn out for the best.

Janet gestured at the wine bottle. "That won't be necessary, Mr. Calvino. We know all about the other private investigators in Bangkok. And we've not been impressed."

The other two women nodded in agreement. "We should open a new bottle of wine."

"Another bottle of wine, Janet? Are you sure?" asked Debra.

"We finally have a new project. So why don't we celebrate?"

Calvino's law: When a man takes a woman to a short-time hotel, what happens inside the hotel room stays in that room. He believed that what passed between a man and woman was their business. Profiting out of another man's bedroom activities was no different from pimping. It was no way to make a business. But there were more private eyes in the city now, and the old ways were breaking down. *Omertà* no longer kept the secrets between men. He told himself that the expat community had changed, morphed into factions, and splintered loyalties. The packaged *farangs* only played at being expats. They were never really in the game. They were bystanders, amateurs, or careerists out for themselves. Calvino asked himself what he owed them. Birds of passage with comfortable, all-expenses-paid nests learned the deeper law, that they had their expense accounts and salaries, but they were outsiders. He ran through the arguments. Something inside his skull told him it still wasn't right.

As far as the women were concerned, three thousand dollars was a small price to pay to prevent them from becoming invisible, no more than after-images in their husbands' lives. What price could anyone put on the dawning of a new day, a fresh start, inking in the possibility of hope they would survive Bangkok? Arms around each other's waists, with Ruth in the middle, her pink hat framing the picture, they smiled at Calvino, "Okay, three thousand dollars is fine. We'll pay it," they said in a synchronized voice.

He'd trapped himself. "I have some cases to clear first."

It was a lot of money. Calvino saw the sign for One Hand Clapping being lowered.

"You'll need these." Janet quickly lay down four photographs as if dealing a deck of cards. They looked like passport photos. Each man dressed in a suit and necktie with faces staring back with that "don't fuck with me" look, drilling holes straight into the camera lens. Andrew Danielson's face peered out from one photo.

"There's something else," he said, looking down at the pictures of the four middle-aged *farangs*. It would have been difficult to distinguish one of them from another in a police lineup, or on barstools in a dark bar. Calvino touched the edge of Danielson's photo, dragged it with his finger out of the group. "Isn't that Andrew Danielson?"

McPhail looked over his shoulder. "That's Danielson?"

Calvino nodded. Janet's face flushed, "Yes, that's Andrew. I forgot to take out his photo."

"He looks like Alec Baldwin," said McPhail. "How can someone who looks that young die of a heart attack?"

"He was fifty-three," said Ruth.

"Man, I wish I looked that good at fifty-three," said McPhail.

"You didn't look that good at thirty-three," said Calvino. He couldn't take his eyes off Danielson's picture. "Did Danielson hang out with your husbands?"

The three women exchanged glances, looked down at the gray tiled floor as if they were searching for a way to escape down the metal drains in the corner. Janet reached out for the photo of Andrew Danielson.

"My mistake. I mixed Andrew's photo up with the others," Janet said. As if this explained why she had all of the photographs to begin with.

"We socialize as couples," said Ruth.

"Then your husband knew him?" asked Calvino.

"Of course. Why do you ask?"

Calvino smiled. These ladies' husbands just might lead him to finding his money. "It's my job to ask questions. For example, why you ladies would carry around photos of each other's husbands? Was it in case you ran into a private eye, so you could brief him fast? Follow this one, and that one. Oh, this one is dead. No need to follow him."

"Please don't be cruel," said Janet.

The Fab Four looked defeated, embarrassed. "Don't get upset. It shouldn't have happened. But it did. Get over it," said Debra. She grabbed the photo before Janet could get it. Debra slipped Danielson's photograph in her handbag and closed the clasp. Calvino wasn't upset. Calvino smiled, feeling that a way may have opened for him to follow the money Danielson owed him. One of these husbands whose photographs he was staring at might know the name of the client Danielson had been working for outside the normal channels. This wasn't something Calvino could rush; he'd have to play out which husband had the ammunition he needed before he could celebrate.

"I said Andrew's photo got mixed up," said Janet, as if that explained why the women were fighting over the photograph of a dead man.

"Any other photos you hand out like pizza?" asked Calvino.

"No." They were on the defensive.

"Can you give me Millie Danielson's phone number? I can return her husband's photograph." He had them cornered.

"I think we should ask her first," said Janet. The feeble defense collapsed into the emotional fall-back posturing. "She's gone through so much."

"Why do you want her number?" asked Ruth.

He'd proved his credentials by spotting Andrew Danielson's photo. "I knew Andrew. I wanted to tell her how sorry I am for her loss." *And he owes me money.*

Debra tilted her head the way a mother does when a child says exactly the right thing. "I'll give you Millie's number." She reached inside her handbag and pulled out a well-thumbed booklet. Calvino caught the word "Index" as she turned it over and wrote the phone number on the back. She handed it to him.

★

On his way back to the office he looked at the thin hardcover book, half an inch thick. The yellow cover was printed with the words "The Risk of Infidelity Index." He flipped through it, finding pages of charts and tables listing cities, countries, and geographical regions. It had fallen open to the page about massage parlor culture. One hundred and twenty-three well thumbed pages documenting the history, culture, and rituals in Thailand. Even at a glance, large sparks from ax grinding flew off the page. He folded the heavily creased booklet and slipped it inside his jacket. His hand nudged against his

.38 police service revolver.

More than one millionaire owed his fortune to what the Thais called *ruang tai sadue*: stories, tales, rumors, jokes and gossip about what happens south of the belly button. Part self-help, part how-to, part almanac, and part recipe book, the *Index* coached women how to use food to control sex-addicted husbands: "You must catch him emotionally—in the guts. Forget about all those lectures you heard about morality or appeals to reason, logic, or commitment. These cold blooded, sterile speeches mean nothing when he's being pulled by dozens of young, available women. When he comes home, have dinner waiting. Give him something special to look forward to—yellow tuna is good. Why not try wasabi guacamole? The sensuality of slow-roasted tomatoes, Zuppi di Pesce, amd blackened roast pumpkin is guaranteed. Keep a bottle of Dom Pérignon on ice. Constantly refine yourself through your cooking skills and the other talents will be magnified."

Calvino figured that *The Risk of Infidelity Index* was the latest story below the belly-button or *tai sadue* money-making machine. Another of Calvino's laws had come into play: The person who raises the suspicion of activities occurring south of the belly button makes a fortune, while the private eye hired to do the footwork of looking for the evidence is asked for a discount. Like all markets, it was best to buy on rumor and sell on fact.

TWELVE

SIRI traced an invisible line along the edge of a wine rack. She looked bored, withdrawn. Every time she glanced at Lovell, emotions welled up and she looked away. It was the way a woman looked at a man she found repulsive. Lovell hadn't noticed in the dim light of the cellar. The four walls of the wine cellar had wraparound floor to ceiling racks. Vintage wines from France, Australia, Italy, Spain, and California. Lovell slid a bottle of Château de Vialle out of the rack. He carefully studied the label. She had been witness to Lovell's wine choosing ritual before; only then, she'd thought it was charming, suggesting a high degree of learning and wisdom. Now his habit annoyed her.

She watched him reading the label, as if looking for hidden meaning in an indemnity clause. Lovell puffed up his cheeks, sighed, and pursed his lips before he turned the bottle over and read the back label. With his memory, she knew that every detail of every label had been lodged in his brain. Why did he read information over again when he already knew what it was? Was he trying to impress her? She resisted the sudden urge to strike him. His smug self-importance made her want to attack, to draw blood. She hated herself for this feeling.

Lovell, head down, reached inside his jacket for a crib sheet of Robert Parker's ratings. This was another one of Lovell's rituals that was no longer endearing. Parker said this wine was "leathery" and, not being just complex, it had dried figs on the nose. In the low light, Lovell checked the list again and rechecked the label before putting the bottle back in the rack. It was beyond his budget. He planned, in the not too distant future, to order Château de Vialle for a special celebration. The book was closed on that option for the evening. He moved on to the Italian section of wines and selected a bottle of Merlot. A Merlot that would never have been sniffed by Robert Parker.

Siri had commented that it smelled like burnt toast and olives. It was the same wine they had drunk the month before. He had enjoyed the previous bottle.

Turning to find Siri watching him, he smiled and held out the bottle of Merlot. "This should be good."

"I don't want that one. It smells and tastes like a hospital," she said. She balanced herself against the table in the center of the room. The chef had allowed them to be alone in the wine cellar.

Lovell blinked as if he didn't believe what she had said. "A hospital?" Parker had never compared a wine to hospital smells. And exactly what does a hospital taste like? But before he asked the question, Siri had taken the bottle from him and put it back.

"Can't we try something different? Why do you always choose the same wine every time we come to this restaurant? You look at that list, but you never choose a bottle from the list. Why do you do this? Can't you see this isn't normal?"

"You're upset," he said.

"I am not upset."

"You're angry."

She stood with her arms folded. "Please choose a wine. I'm cold."

"I thought I had."

"I don't want that wine. It's . . . it's not pleasant for me."

"Siri, this isn't about wine, is it?"

Siri glanced down with a long sigh.

"What is it?"

"Skip the wine. I'd rather have water. Besides, after dinner you're going barhopping with Stiles."

He slipped another wine bottle out of the rack, walked over, and reached for her hand, but she pulled it away. He hadn't bothered to read the label. "We're not going to a bar."

"You're going out with Stiles. That's where he will want to

go."

"I told him that I wouldn't go to a bar."

She clicked her tongue. "What else did you tell him?"

"That you don't want me to go."

"It's up to you," she said, hands on her hips. She squared off, staring straight at him. "You blamed me?"

He wilted, clutching the bottle to his chest. "I didn't blame you."

"Why couldn't you just say, 'It's not my style. I don't like going to bars'? You could have said that. But, no, you avoid any responsibility."

"I want to find out about his work on the Avenant Pharma file. To do that, I need to go out with him. Talk to him when he's relaxed. I need to let him feel it was his idea to go out. Or he'll think that I want something."

"Which you do. So why not just ask him at the office? If it's business, I don't understand why you have to discuss confidential client matters in a bar."

Lovell bit his lower lip and shook his head. "We shouldn't argue about it. This is something I need to do. Besides, it won't take any longer than a drink. It's not useful to argue."

Siri's eyes widened. "Not useful. Who taught you to say that? Are you making fun of me?"

"Not useful" was one of her stock expressions when she wanted to close a line of conversation, avoid a topic, or gloss over a mistake she had made. Being angry had exhausted her, and whatever depleted emotional resources she could draw on were rapidly running to empty. She had reached that point of no return, when something snapped and the animal brain reset the vocabulary to full-throttle attack mode. Lovell wondered what was driving her to distraction, making her irrational.

"*Mai wai jai.*" A hiss in her voice strung out the word "whoremonger" as if it were an oral banner half a mile long.

"What I don't understand—"

"Is . . . I don't trust what you say."

"If it's not about the wine, why don't you tell me the truth?"

The picture of him in her head had altered. She simply saw him in a way that made her question herself. "Why do you want me to have doubts about you?"

"I don't want that."

He couldn't stand the sight of her distorted smile.

"Your actions don't say the same as your words."

"Are you saying that I'm lying?"

He was getting angry despite his best efforts.

"Sometimes people lie to themselves."

"I don't do that."

"Because you have a perfect memory, right?"

Danielson was dead, and the truth of the matter was that Lovell had avoided going to the *wat* to pay his respects. Funerals and dead people made Lovell feel uneasy. He didn't want to think about the possibility of dying. And after all the police questioning, and then the meeting with Cameron and Weerawat, he felt detached, alone, as if he could see himself through the telescopic lens of others. He didn't like what he saw. More than anything, he wanted to shut out death, investigations, and the law firm. With a bottle of wine and his girlfriend, the truth was, he wanted to halt time, make it stop, walk outside of it—if only for a few hours. Then he wanted to ask Stiles some questions.

"Well, are we going to stay in the wine cellar all night?" she asked.

Lovell looked up at her, reaching out for her hand. She walked ahead, climbing the stairs and then stopping to look back. "I'm coming," he said. "Give me a minute."

"I can give you all the time you want." She vanished up the stairs.

It was as if he had seen Siri for the first time, not as a woman he'd made love to or someone he was seriously involved with, but as a stranger. It was a stranger who swept out of the half shadows and disappeared from the low light of the wine cellar. He had his work and he had Siri—the two poles of his existence, the axis on which his twenty-four-hour day rotated. He closed his eyes, smelled her perfume, and then leaned back against one of the wine racks. Nothing was working out the way it was supposed to. It was as if he had turned a corner and everything had suddenly changed. It was incomprehensible how fast it had all occurred. With his full workload at the law firm, he had been ignoring her. He told himself it was his fault. They had been going out for more than four months and this had been their first serious fight. The experience left him feeling unsure of his feelings. Seeing another side of Siri had raised a small voice of doubt. It was impossible to ever know a person completely, but he realized how little he really knew about her, and how little she knew about him. They shared a surface knowledge fed mostly by casual and safe encounters.

He replaced the bottle he was holding, pulled out the Merlot she had said smelled like a hospital and had a burnt taste, and climbed the stairs to the restaurant. He could have hurried after her. But he decided it was a matter of principle. *Hold your ground,* he thought. *Think it through.* It's what Danielson would have done: advised, written a memo, emailed, and then followed up with a hard copy. See how it plays through. The truth? Sure, it was important. But truths competed like racehorses. Which truth would cross the finish line first, that was the question. The truth lodged in your dreams? Your accounts? Your résumé? The memory of your friends and family? Many truths. He would explain all of this to Siri over dinner. They would make up, go back to his place, and make love. That was the truth he clung to as he reached the top of the stairs.

She was gone. The waiter came over and said, "Your friend, she leave."

He sat down at the table as the waiter picked up Siri's place setting. After a moment, there was no trace that she had ever been at the restaurant, at the table, or in his life. The waiter inserted the corkscrew, opened the bottle, and offered him the cork. He smelled it. No hint of ash and smoke, he told himself. He tasted the wine, and then the waiter filled his glass. He drank it down, and before the waiter returned, he poured himself another glass. He sat alone, drinking. "Here's to the truth. Here's to Andrew Danielson."

THIRTEEN

LOVELL still felt a twinge of apprehension about meeting Graham Stiles. When Stiles called, he considered making up an excuse to cancel the evening. Stiles, rather than discussing the matter, gave him an address and told him to come when he'd finished dinner. Lovell drank the rest of the wine and paid the bill. A taxi waited outside. He climbed into the back and gave directions to one of the private members' clubs located in the heart of the Sukhumvit Road green zone.

Stiles was a card-carrying member of the club. Technically the club wasn't the same as a go-go bar. No one swung from chrome poles, and no *farangs* wearing shorts, T-shirts, and sandals were allowed inside. The dress code was smart casual, preferably shirt and tie. The hostesses dressed in evening gowns and silver high heels. Pulling to the entrance, a doorman opened the taxi door and waited until Lovell paid the driver. As he got out, Lovell realized that he only wished that he had done this before. The club was an elegant world cut off from the traffic, beggars, broken pavement, and heat.

He could use some elegance. His thoughts drifted back to Siri glaring at him in disgust. She had kept her distance from him in the wine cellar. *What do you know about the truth?* she had said. That had opened his mind. Hadn't he tried to please her, to keep the relationship at the level they both had agreed was comfortable? She couldn't leave what was already perfect alone. As far as he was concerned, her storming off was a childlike way to punish him for meeting Stiles. She had reminded him of the bargain he'd made with her, but meeting Stiles for a drink in a nightclub wasn't a bar, so technically it wasn't a violation. She'd drawn no comfort from his narrow lawyer's argument. It wasn't about logic. She wanted, needed, something he wasn't giving her. This had been a revelation.

Stiles, hands loose at his sides, walked over to him. He had a strong, certain movement in his stride. He stopped close to Lovell, stretching out his hand. "I wasn't sure you'd make it, you know," said Stiles. They shook hands. It seemed an odd thing to do, shaking hands with Stiles, who had no problem sticking his shoes on Lovell's desk.

"No bars. That is the only limit," said Lovell.

"Ethics must serve some purpose, Lovell," said Stiles. "Explain to me how not going to a bar is ethical? Only a fucking moron uses women and ethics in the same sentence."

"I promised her that I wouldn't go to the bars. And I keep my promises. I guess that makes me a fucking moron." He left out Siri's name.

"A moron with a memory card like the one in your head can be rescued."

It wasn't necessary but Lovell reached over and straightened Stiles' tie. "Cameron said you were strange."

"Is Cameron your model of normality?"

Stiles felt that he was getting somewhere. His eyebrows knitted when he looked serious about something. He had a strong, masculine jaw line, and his brown hair was combed neatly back. Women in the office found Stiles handsome. He flirted with them. And in the case of Lovell's secretary, Wan, he knew how to corrupt them with a bag of cookies.

"But you aren't living *in* Bangkok."

Lovell fell silent. Stiles' eyebrows folded into a single line over his eyes. That meant he was being serious. But it seemed like a trick question.

"Right, then where am I living?" asked Lovell after a long pause.

"In the office, which is located in Bangkok. But you aren't living in Bangkok. That's my point."

"I stay focused, if that's what you mean."

Stiles pulled one of the hostesses onto his lap. Half-startled, she giggled and squirmed as he wrapped his arms around her waist. She made no real effort to get away. Customers had privileges that came with membership. All the *yings* knew the rules, and if any were unhappy, then market forces would take their course, and they'd be replaced by other *yings* with smiling faces. The alternative was a massage parlor like One Hand Clapping, and life in such a place was worse.

"I should have been born a troubadour two hundred years ago. Isn't that right, darling?"

"You funny man," she said, pinching Stiles' cheek.

"Bouncing *yings* on my knee, singing them songs, reciting epic poems, teaching them how to sing and dance."

"What's your name?" she asked.

"Khun Phaen," Stiles said. "The most famous Thai lover of all times. I've been reborn and you are my Nong Phim." He squeezed her cheeks, kissed her. His hand explored her face and neck, and then worked down the front of her gown, where he found her breasts.

"I don't think she's enjoying that," said Lovell.

Stiles broke out laughing. "Enjoying it?" He made a fist of his hand inside her gown, punching his knuckle out like an erect nipple. "It makes her happy. Right, darling?"

"Nong Phim," she said, laughing. "My Khun Phaen." She leaned over and kissed Stiles on the forehead. He gave her the gesture to leave, and she pushed off Stiles' lap in a long, graceful movement. She *waied* him and left.

Lovell sat forward in his seat, enraged, boiling over with anger.

"In the epic poem," Stiles said, "Nang Phim was shared by two men. Khun Phaen, the one she loved, and Khun Chang, the ugly, fat fart. But he had money. He took care of her, gave her gold and silver. Do you get the message? It is subliminal with the *yings*. He's a good man, he takes care of me. That's what has been taught for two hundred years. Khun Phaen slips into Nang Phim's room, fucks her, then goes into her stepsister's bed and fucks her, too. They don't say 'fuck.' It's all this funny, flowery language about ships being lashed by the winds and the sea, but everyone knows they're fucking. And everybody accepts the situation as perfectly normal. Troubadours for hundreds of years went around the country telling the story of Khun Chang and Khun Phaen. The tradition never dies; it just changes into TV and movies and books. Or they the men wear Khun Phaen amulets. Kids still learn the poem in school. Siri would have learned it. Ask her sometime about Khun Chang and Khun Phaen. It's *her* culture. Infidelity is not only taught, it is celebrated. You gotta love that. Remind her that what she's asking of you not only has no poetry, it is against the most famous of all Thai poems. And to think, when I was a kid, I hated poetry. But we never had poems like this in New Jersey."

Lovell wasn't certain whether to believe Stiles. "Bullshit," he said.

"Ask Siri about Khun Chang, Khun Phaen. Nang Phim bounced between them like a ping-pong ball, with one, then the other, and back and forth. You know what happened to Nang Phim?"

Lovell shook his head. "No idea."

"She was drawn and quartered. That means pulled apart by horses."

"I know what it means."

"Do you really? It means the *yings* have always been dispensable. If they can't make up their minds, you get rid of them and start over. So ask yourself what else you don't know about where you are living. Lovell, you need to wake up. Smell the orchids. That is what Danielson would have told you."

"He would have said 'roses.'" He looked around the room. "I can't imagine Danielson in this place."

Stiles lit a cigarette and exhaled. Lovell batted away the smoke. "Then you need a new imagination. Did I tell you that Danielson was a member of this club?" he asked, sucking on the cigarette.

Lovell stared at his drink, moved his hand over the top like a magician over a top hat. "I should have gone to the *wat* tonight. But I couldn't face it."

"I went," said Stiles. "Most of the firm was there. Your absence was noted."

They sat at a table and a waitress brought a hot towel and wiped Stiles' face. Another waitress started to wipe Lovell's face but he blocked her arm.

"I didn't think that Danielson and you got along," Lovell said.

"That was at the office. After hours, we got along just fine. We shared the same desire for a daily dopamine hit," said Stiles. He shivered as he said the words. "The need to explore."

Lovell wasn't listening. He could only think of Cameron looking over his glasses at the *wat*, searching but not finding him among the mourners.

"What do you mean, my absence was noted?"

Stiles smiled and pulled one of the waitresses onto his lap. He was gearing up for the second act of an epic poem.

"Cameron asked where you were. Andrew was your boss. I guess he expected you to come to the *wat*. Show your face. Pay respects. Lead the mourners in song."

"What did he say?"

He was too quick off the ropes and Stiles was waiting for him.

"Only that he was surprised he hadn't seen you."

"You know what troubles me, Stiles?" The wine had made him light-headed.

"You're going to tell me. So tell me."

"Why Noah Gould wouldn't have gone to you with his piracy problem. You handled his corporate account. Instead he went to Andrew. That's seems strange."

"Noah did come to me with the problem," said Stiles. "We were working on it. Clients get a fire in their pants."

"But you were getting nowhere."

"Who told you that?"

Lovell shrugged and twisted his neck to one side, and then to the other. "If you were getting results, Gould wouldn't have gone to Andrew for help."

"I'd say you'd have to ask Andrew about that." A smile crossed his face. "But that is a little difficult. Or you could ask Noah. But I'm not certain you really want to go there. You're in enough trouble already. Not showing your face at Danielson's funeral tonight is a black mark, John. He was your fucking boss."

Lovell had worked until eight and Cameron had stuck his head into his office and given him the thumbs-up. "Always the last one to leave," said Cameron. "You have a future in this firm." But he hadn't mentioned about going to the *wat*.

And now Stiles, the smug bastard, massaging the waitress's breasts, implied that he was in serious trouble. His absence had been noted.

"You dropped the ball, Lovell." He smiled and refilled his glass. "Dropping the ball isn't fatal. You pick it up and run with it. Just don't walk off the field shuffling your feet like a sore loser."

This is what passed for moral support at the law firm. Stiles hadn't exactly gloated, but he hadn't shown a great deal of compassion, either.

A nightclub was about passion; compassion was never part of the deal. Membership clubs avoided anything that would remotely make a customer uncomfortable. Just the opposite: Lovell's discomfort gave Stiles a degree of comfort, if not outright pleasure.

"I'll go to the *wat* tomorrow." Lovell sipped from a glass of whiskey and soda.

"Tonight was the big event, the water-pouring ceremony. Everyone queued up and poured water over Danielson's hand. His right hand was the dull color of a polluted klong. You can't keep bodies very well in this climate. They start to go off right away."

He paused, raised his glass. "I'd seen where Danielson had put that hand. And it wasn't just in his pocket. It makes you think. This could be my last grope on earth. The last breasts I'll ever touch. Lights out, and a queue of people I never liked are pouring lustral water over that same hand."

Bitter bile rose in Lovell's throat, as if the wine had begun the long return journey from his stomach up to his throat and mouth. He leaned forward and spit into the now cool towel that a waitress had sought to use to wipe his face. She sat on the sofa next to him, her hands folded, smiling and trying to look happy. Lovell saw that like Siri, the hostess was upset with him; she didn't want to be on the sofa, and he could see through her half-hearted attempt to mask her revulsion.

"Taking you out tonight was Cameron's idea," said Stiles.

Stiles had walked up to Danielson's body and poured water over his hand. Everyone in the office had poured water. I was getting drunk and fighting with Siri, thought Lovell.

"Hello, are you listening to me?" Stiles noticed how Lovell's eyes had glazed over as if he had gone into a trance. He smiled, thinking it was the waitress on the sofa who was distracting him.

"Cameron noticed that I missed the bathing ceremony at the *wat*."

Stiles sighed. *The guy was basically hopeless*, he thought. "It was his idea that I take you out. Introduce you to the place where you work."

"What else did he say?"

Stiles cleared his throat, and then in a Cameron-like whisper said, "Lovell's a good man. But he does nothing but work. I worry about the boy. It isn't human to work that hard and never go out. We don't want machines in this firm. We want lawyers who understand how Thais think and act. That is the value we give to our clients."

"Cameron said that?" Though he realized that if he'd closed his eyes, it could have been Cameron talking.

Stiles nuzzled his face between the ample breasts of the hostess, who had escaped and come back, suggesting she had never wanted to escape in the first place. He was making a child's blubbery noise of twisted helicopter blades. She giggled and pushed his head back and dropped another cashew into his mouth as if she were rewarding a seal for performing a trick.

"Get that boy on the street," he said in Cameron's whisper. The waitress put a finger over his lips and he kissed it. "You have the meter running all day. She has it running all night. That's why she gets along so well with lawyers." He kissed her on the cheek, pulled her tight and ran his tongue into her mouth. Lovell looked away. He wanted to vomit. "'Show him a good time,' is what Cameron said. And he gave me a wink and a nudge."

That part about a wink and nudge had put a dent in Stiles' credibility. He couldn't imagine Cameron ever doing something like that. It was vintage Stiles, and not something in Cameron's character.

"You don't believe me?" asked Stiles.

Lovell broke off eye contact. Stiles had stonewalled about Avenant Pharma and Noah's decision to take the piracy case away from him. It was hard to believe anything that he said. He thought in silence about Danielson coming to this club, seated where he was sitting, the same women at the table, and Stiles with his tie unknotted, kicking back, rubbing his face between the breasts of a young waitress.

"And you know what I told Cameron?"

Lovell waited for him to tell him.

"I said, 'I am certain Lovell is for making good relations between the sexes.' And Cameron cuffed me on the shoulder and said, 'Show him the ropes. Explain the poetry of the place to him. He's a bright boy, he'll get it.' We had an unspoken understanding. And now I'm here. And you're sitting there."

"Showing me the ropes. Explaining poetry." Sliding your rough tongue down the throat of a hostess, he thought.

Stiles pulled his tongue out of the *ying's* mouth, threw back his head, and laughed as if this were something funny.

"You know why I'm laughing?"

It was a mystery, the entire evening. Why Stiles was telling him all of this, and now laughing at him. Cameron, if he had said anything, would have wanted it kept in confidence. Danielson had said that Cameron placed value in loyalty, silence, and fear. That he flirted with invisible forces: determination and ambition. His oversized life was too large to sit comfortably on any mantel.

"What's so funny?"

"I told this one that you are Khun Chang. She knows I am Khun Phaen. And I told her she had to choose. And you know what she said?" He tickled her under the armpit. "Tell him, darling."

"Cannot decide."

"That's the essence of the whole twenty-two thousand lines of an epic poem in two words."

"Is this why Cameron chose you?" asked Lovell. "Because you have read Thai poetry?"

"He chose me because I live the poetry." The hostess continued smiling as she leaned forward and gracefully slipped ice cubes into Lovell's glass. Stiles had unfastened himself from the waitress, leaned back expansively, smiled, and patted a passing waitress on the ass. She emitted a high-pitched yelp and playfully slapped his hand.

"Just calling for the bill," Stiles said. He pulled out a wad of notes and called for the bill.

"How much is my share?" Lovell reached for his wallet.

Stiles raised his hand like a traffic cop. Being in Stiles' debt bothered Lovell. He was the sort of person you didn't want to owe anything to. "I can afford it," said Lovell, grabbing the bill as the waitress brought it on a silver tray. "It goes on a client account."

"Avenant Pharma?" asked Lovell.

"Why not? We did talk business." Stiles shrugged, leaned back, pulling the hostess with him. Lovell looked at the bill, his eyes focusing in the twilight of the room. He checked his wallet for more cash, swallowing hard. The bill was New York prices. He caught Stiles smiling at him from across the table.

Stiles slipped five thousand baht onto the tray. "Let's go," he said.

Lovell blushed, his cheeks glowing a bright red. Not having enough cash ranked with the humiliation of accidentally tripping a fire alarm. It felt vaguely like an insult, one that rattled him, making him grateful in a way that wouldn't have happened if he'd just let Stiles pick up the bill as he had offered.

"Piece of advice. Always carry fifteen thousand baht when you go out. Walking-around money. Think of it as Khun Chang money. If you come up short of cash, the girls can get the wrong idea. The lack of cash confuses them. Makes them afraid."

"I'll remember that."

"Poetry."

"I'll remember that, too."

"One more thing, Lovell. Don't get involved with the Avenant Pharma file. Just a friendly piece of advice."

"That almost sounds like a threat."

Stiles slapped him on the back. "Loosen up. Try not to think about the office."

Lovell felt a sense of relief that the evening was ending. The bill was paid and they were hardly out the door when Stiles flagged a taxi, opened the door, pushed Lovell in, and slid in behind him.

"One more stop before we call it a night."

"No bars."

"Has Siri put you through some kind of aversion therapy? You're like a parrot, 'No bars, no bars. Polly wants a cracker! No bars.' You're out of the cage. Try spreading your wings. You can fly. I promise no crash landing."

The taxi driver started laughing at Stiles' parrot voice. Stiles had a knack for imitations. Being good with impressions made him popular in the law firm, inside taxis, and with the *yings*. His social skills had secured him a place in Cameron's inner circle. That wasn't a bad place to be. For the first time in the evening, Lovell envied Stiles' position in the law firm. Lovell had witnessed the way Stiles handled himself, always at ease, funny, and in control. Stiles had batted away the questions about Noah Gould and Avenant Pharma as he would swat away a fly.

One more stop couldn't be a bad thing, Lovell thought.

Stiles turned, lost in thought, and looked out the window. His fingers drummed a beat on the edge of the door. He kept the beat of a song running inside his head. It was as if he were running a soundtrack through his mind. What ran through Lovell's mind was a question: why had Danielson's death made such a shallow impact on Stiles?

FOURTEEN

ACROSS the *soi* from Nana Plaza, Vincent Calvino occupied a hotel coffee shop booth. From his seat, he had a clear view of the door and of the other booths, which ran along the east wall and, beyond them, of the tables with chrome legs in the center of the narrow room. The coffee shop staff waited for the rush that came once the bars closed. More than half of the tables and booths were empty, so for the moment they had it easy. They stood in groups, talking. Then more customers started to arrive. One waiter checked his watch. The evening rush had started. The bars had turned out the lights. The first bar *yings* had undergone their metamorphosis, shedding their bikinis for street clothes to transform from one kind of butterfly to another, and moving from one part of the jungle to the next.

The men who walked through the door were from all walks of life—ancient grandfathers, office workers, teachers, travelers, and locals with no visible means of support. At one end of the bell curve were the faces twisted as if their shoes were too tight, or their underwear. At the other end were men with their faces slack, drooping as if they'd forgotten to put on their underwear before checking out of a short-time hotel. In the vast curve of the bell were the faces awash with expectation and desire, burning for a hookup.

Calvino recognized one or two of the faces but couldn't quite place them. When he saw people out of context, it took him a long time to figure out who they were. Sizing up people on a stakeout required a lot of concentration. He sat still, looking over every feature and detail of each person coming through the door, trying to remember if he had seen him before, filing away the face in his memory. He had the three photographs from the Fab Four memorized. On the table next to a cup of coffee was *The Risk of Infidelity Index*. He had begun to read it while looking around the room, only to find himself rereading the same passages.

The book made many claims. For instance, it asserted that people can't distinguish between causation and correlation. Like farm hens who believed that the crowing of the rooster made the sunrise. Or the peasants who believed that rich men were innately good, and cared for and looked after their women. There were sections in the booklet about how men liked the hunt part of sex better than sex itself. How men sought out the new woman because she was new, not because she might be any prettier or younger or better in bed than his wife. His interest was focused on what he hadn't fucked. A new woman gave a man a surge of endorphins, which was a drug, and that caused some men to become women junkies.

Calvino put down the booklet, sipped his coffee. It had gone cold. He resisted the urge to pick up where he had left off in the booklet. Looking around the room, the middle-aged endorphin junkies piled in, eyes constantly moving around the room.

Bangkok crawled with these ghost-like predators stalking prey, the coffee shop and parking lot their watering hole. Sooner or later the prey would have to creep down for a drink. Calvino had come to the water's edge in search of Howard Herron, Janet's husband. He was a big man, slightly overweight at two hundred pounds. Howard was fifty-two but looked in his mid-thirties. They'd met at college. Janet had been working in her father's pawnshop in Seattle. He had come in to pawn a gold chain. They had gone out for coffee and had never been apart since. Now Calvino was waiting for Howard to make another coffee run with someone other than his wife.

Colonel Pratt came through the door and spotted Calvino sitting alone in the back, leafing through the booklet, with a half-empty cup of coffee on the table. He sat down next to his friend and a waiter handed him a menu. Since he was dressed in civilian clothes, apparently no one knew he was a cop. Without opening the menu, the colonel ordered tea and a fresh coffee for Calvino.

"Aren't you gonna get something to eat?" said Calvino.

Pratt put down the menu. "I already ate."

"The Chinese noodles are good."

Pratt nodded. "Have you eaten?"

Calvino looked at a plate of cold French fries. "I'm not hungry. I can't eat when I'm working. I don't have an appetite."

"I hear you have a new case?"

"Three new cases. It's a package deal."

Colonel Pratt smiled. With his back to the door, he followed Calvino's eyes as they scanned the faces behind him. "Then you're doing well."

"Life couldn't be better."

"I'm glad to hear that. You had a tough time lately. Who are the clients?"

Calvino explained how his three clients were expat housewives who had nowhere to go and little to do around the house once the kids were off to school, so they signed up for expensive cooking courses. Before Chef Elmo, they had studied with many other local chefs—Japanese, French, Thai, Korean, Swedish—all of them charging through the nose for turning them into forced labor and making them feel good, as if they were actually learning something useful.

"Teaching housewives the art of cooking is a racket," said Calvino.

"Is that what your clients said?"

"Victims to the slaughter never complain until it's too late." The classes had become the centerpiece of otherwise pointless lives. He imagined the Fab Four had enough certificates to wallpaper a small room.

"One of the women gave me this," said Calvino. He slid the booklet across the table. Colonel Pratt opened it and read the title page.

"*The Risk of Infidelity Index.* Interesting," he said. "What's it mean?"

"It falls between a horse racing form and a hedge fund report on commodity futures. The target market is expat wives. They buy the book because it has a statistical chart that predicts the chances of their husband cheating on them. There are sixty-three cities ranked according to risk of a husband's infidelity. Bangkok's number one."

"Only the top one percent of fools would buy this.

"Worldwide, that's a big market," said Calvino.

"Your clients believe their husbands are cheating on them?"

Calvino shrugged, scanning the faces of people in the restaurant. The colonel was right about believing in numbers that were shuffled out to prove a point. No one wanted to go to a party and get ditched. Figuring the odds of that happening had good business potential. The pitch went straight to the heart of the matter—assessment of the risk a woman faced, with a promise to show her exactly where the landmines were clustered.

"Infidelity has gone international. No one ever tells them that, while globalization makes places and markets easier to get to, the people in those places are different. Some of these guys have money, white shirts, and neckties. The women smile at them like they mean it. The next thing is the guys take it personally. These women get under the men's skin in a way that hasn't happened in years. The men's wives pick up on the change in their husbands' attitudes. The wives want to know what they should do next."

"This book promises them answers?" asked Pratt.

"It's a marketer's dream. Ten steps to save your marriage when you move abroad," said Calvino. "It gets women thinking too much about the wrong things."

"Or gives them a substitute for thinking. But it can be good for the private investigation business," said Pratt.

"I'm not complaining."

"That's life. No matter what, there's always an upside for someone."

"And a downside for someone like Andrew Danielson. I told you that Danielson's wife is a member of the group, right?"

"I wouldn't be here if you hadn't. Now explain to me how you connected them to Danielson?"

"His photograph was one of the four they showed me of their husbands."

"Strange."

"Weird. But there it was. I figured one of the husbands might lead to the man Danielson was fronting for."

"One of the husbands is going to name Danielson's client?"

"It's a possibility." Calvino clenched his jaw. "Pratt, I am going to get my money."

Colonel Pratt sat forward, arms resting on the tabletop. This information about the Danielson connection with the expat wives' cooking group had caught Pratt by surprise. Pratt flicked through the booklet, not so much reading as considering the possibility that one of the expat wives could be useful in tying up some of the loose ends surrounding Danielson's death.

Calvino saw Colonel Pratt staring at a page of the booklet.

"Bangkok's number one," he said.

"A hub of marriage destruction?" asked Colonel Pratt.

"The guys who wrote this are performing a valuable public service."

The *Index* expertly twisted every stereotype, pumping up emotions with random numbers, feeding anger and fear as if the number-one designation had special significance. No doubt this sort of booklet had been good for the private investigation business. Private eyes should be flooding the publisher with letters, asking if they could do quarterly updates rather than annual ones.

"You should thank them. But no one writes a letter anymore," said Colonel Pratt. "It's all email."

"I'll email them with your suggestion. Anything else I should say?"

A waiter in a white long-sleeved shirt with an open collar and black cotton trousers arrived with a pot of tea and poured it into a cup for the colonel. The colonel added milk and half a teaspoon of sugar, and stirred the mixture until it bleached white.

Raising his teacup, Pratt said, "'The gods are just, and of our pleasant vices make instruments to plague us.'"

"That's Shakespeare."

"*King Lear,*" said Colonel Pratt.

Calvino thought about an elderly *farang* raging and pulling out his hair over the women who had betrayed him. Calvino let the thought linger as he glanced at the colonel, who was turning another page in the booklet.

Colonel Pratt paused from his reading and looked up to catch an intent expression on Calvino's face, with his eyes fixed on the *farangs* filtering into the coffee shop.

"You said that one of the women had a photo of Andrew Danielson."

It had been a sufficient reason for Colonel Pratt to leave the comfort of his home and join Calvino at his stakeout position. "Yeah, and I don't believe it was an accident. They wanted me to see it." Like dealing a pack of cards, he snapped each of the three photos of the suspect husbands on the open page of *The Risk of Infidelity Index*. "One of the women did something like what I'm doing. Danielson's photo was with these three."

Colonel Pratt examined each face. "Where's Danielson's photo?"

"Debra, one of the wives, grabbed it. Said it was a mistake to have included it."

"Any idea why she thought that?"

Calvino rotated his shoulders, checking for a blade of pain. There was none and he relaxed. "They were giving themselves an out. 'Oh, how did that photo get here?' I didn't buy it. I don't think they know how we've all been through the honest mistake excuse."

"Don't you find it strange that one woman had a photo of all four husbands?"

"You've read enough of the *Index* to know they must have been on high alert."

Colonel Pratt shook his head. "How did she look when she took back Danielson's photo?"

"Embarrassed."

Calvino pointed at Howard Herron's photo. "That's the guy I'm looking for tonight. Apparently hangs out in the coffee shop."

Colonel Pratt picked up the photograph, examined the face. Pouring himself more tea, he stirred in sugar and then sipped it black. This time he looked at the face in the photograph more closely, wondering how well this *farang* (and the others) had known Andrew Danielson. He wrote down Howard's full name, and the names of the other husbands, too. The names of the husbands had been written on the back of the photos, along with other details—height, weight, date, and place of birth. The *Index* had a page of instructions about briefing investigators. Putting down personal details on the back of photos was one of the recommendations. He took down this information as well and closed his notebook.

"There's a good chance that Danielson's toxicity report was altered," said Colonel Pratt.

"What's behind that?"

"One possibility is someone didn't want a report that conflicted with the verdict of heart attack."

"Someone in the department?"

Colonel Pratt never committed himself on such matters. "I don't know."

"You're saying Danielson was murdered?"

"I don't know. There isn't enough evidence to draw that conclusion. Just because it was altered doesn't necessarily mean anything. There might have been a mistake made in the first report and they corrected it."

The Colonel had gone into defensive mode. The policeman's code was to defend and protect fellow officers, especially from outsiders. And Calvino was not only not a cop; he was a *farang*. That made him a double outsider. Pratt had gone as far as he was comfortable in going.

"Just assume Andrew Danielson was whacked and someone wants to cover it up. What's the motive? Let me guess—it was either personal or business." The standard official explanation for a murder case divided the world of murderers into those two categories. The newspapers quoted this dual theory in most murder cases. It was a boilerplate phrase used by the police, and no matter what happened or why, the journalist sooner or later was vindicated as having identified the motive at the outset.

"Danielson owed you a lot of money," said Colonel Pratt, smiling.

"Come on, Pratt, you can do better than that. The other three husbands could end up like Danielson."

Colonel Pratt's face had a faraway expression. "Anything is possible."

"The Fab Four are knocking off their husbands one by one, and I stumble into their plot and feed them with the information. That would make me an accessory," said Calvino, rolling his eyes.

When Pratt looked into the empty teacup, he tried to read the leaves inside. "Maybe the wives want to be sure before they take the next step," he said.

Calvino rubbed the knuckles of one hand, stretching out his fingers. "They're like me. They want their money. I respect that. It makes me understand them."

"Money is only one kind of revenge."

That was one of Colonel Pratt's stock phrases, a kind of policeman's default view of a world that was never stable or predictable, where anything could float away. A world where all options remained open, and agendas never closed.

"A friend who works in forensics told me about the toxicity report," said Colonel Pratt. He was trying to give Calvino something.

"Tampered with? I hope they find whoever did it," said Calvino. "But I need to get back to work."

"Is it possible that Danielson's death had something to do with the piracy case you were working on?"

Now he had Calvino's full attention. He thought for a moment whether to tell Colonel Pratt how Danielson had kept the case off the law firm's books. For a partner in his position to break the rules, Andrew Danielson must have a good reason.

"What if it was Danielson's private case?" he said.

The Colonel called over a waiter and asked him for more hot water in the teapot. Then he turned back to Calvino. "Private? I don't understand. What does that mean?"

"The law firm has no record of the case. That means Danielson for some reason wanted to keep it off the books."

"Why would he do that?"

"A conflict of interest? Or he got the fee up front and didn't want to split it with his partners," said Calvino.

"Any idea who Danielson was working for?"

Calvino sighed, sucked in his teeth. "That's what I'm trying to find out. I've got the drug manufacturer. But I can't phone and ask, 'Hey, guys, did someone in your department go to a now dead lawyer named Danielson and cut a side deal to bust a piracy operation? Could you put me through to someone in your office who knows about this?' Who do they put me through to? Pratt, I need more information. I've got three leads. The three husbands married to girlfriends who hung out with Danielson's widow. That's better than nothing."

"But you have no idea if they can help."

Calvino scratched his head where the head butt had left a lump.

"I agree, but it's a start. What I don't get is why someone would kill him. He's a lawyer. Take him out and whoever hired Danielson finds another lawyer. You gotta go upstream and take out the prime threat. The guy who ordered his lawyer to hire me."

Pratt sniffed at the tea and put his cup carefully down onto the saucer. *Vincent has no idea who hired Danielson*, he thought. Piracy was a cat-and-mouse business. Local gangsters were often caught running back-*soi* operations. They paid a fine, moved shop, and started up business again the next day. Getting closed down was just a cost of doing business; it was hardly a reason to murder someone.

"We've already questioned an American lawyer named Lovell," said Colonel Pratt. "He worked as Danielson's associate. He was the last person to see Danielson alive. He might give you background information about your case."

"I already tried that. He told me to fuck off."

"He's under a lot of pressure, don't you think?"

"He needs a reason to talk."

Everyone in business hid something; what they hid was slightly different from what scam artists and conman drug manufacturers were hiding. Law firms were paid to hide things under the cloak of confidentiality and privileged communications. Calvino had practiced law in New York and understood that a lawyer provided a reinforced bunker in which to house sensitive information. A professional confidence rule was as good as a bulletproof vest. But the case had never appeared on the books of the law firm. There was no confidence to keep. It was a subtle distinction, one that Lovell had been bothered by.

Colonel Pratt sipped the hot tea.

"I didn't say I'd given up on Lovell," said Calvino, and he was about to say something else. He stopped mid-sentence and looked down at the plate of cold french fries. He picked one out and chewed on it. He checked his cell phone. He had missed three calls from Janet Herron. Calvino glanced at Pratt, who waited for more information about Lovell.

"You gave him a reason to talk to you?"

Calvino nodded. "I got a video of the piracy operation. It's beautiful, Pratt. I caught them making the shit, putting it in boxes and crates. It's a video of Piracy 101."

"And Lovell still wasn't interested?"

"It was like the case was radioactive. There has to be a good reason to distance himself. I'm telling him I want my money, and he's telling me to go somewhere else to find it. He tells me that this client had nothing to do with the law firm. He said it was against firm policy. What Danielson had done was wrong. *Not a bad policy*, Calvino had thought. After talking to Lovell, he thought he'd decided to write off the case. He had three new American clients who would pay for him to shadow their husbands. But a deadbeat, dead client was something he told himself he would never get over.

"Perhaps I should ask Lovell about Danielson's client," said Colonel Pratt.

Calvino brightened at the thought Colonel Pratt could get his money for him. But he tried not to show his excitement. "He wouldn't tell me. Maybe he'll tell you."

"I'll let you know."

"I should have got the money up front. But I didn't. End of story."

"Beginning of story."

Calvino rocked back and forth like a prizefighter resting on a stool between hard-fought rounds. "Some stories don't have a beginning or an end."

"That's why I love Shakespeare. He knows where to begin, and how to end. That's art."

"I don't know from yesterday about art. But I know I've got a job. Now. Tonight. To nail Howard Herron so that his wife can say, 'You're busted.' I get paid, Howard loses everything he owns and loves."

"That's a beginning and one possible ending. Another ending is Howard tells you the name of Danielson's secret client."

"I never guess an ending."

Calvino spotted his target, Howard Herron, the moment he walked into the coffee shop. He arrived alone. He stopped a couple of feet inside the door, scanning the faces of women scattered around the tables. He looked younger in the photo, and in much better shape. Howard squinted, fiddled with his glasses, taking them off, putting them back on—a nervous tic that gave the impression he was trying to decide if it made any difference as to what he saw. In the photo his hair had been dark; in person it was short and graying. His white dress shirt had sweat stains under the armpits and his green striped tie was loosened, but his tailored dark trousers hadn't lost their crease. The expensive shoes looked as if they had just been shined. His no-nonsense look marked him as someone who hadn't come to relax on a holiday.

He looked tired, agitated, and stressed, as if his company's quarterly report hadn't racked up the projected numbers and he was personally responsible for the shortfall. *Caffeine could make a man jumpy, even though he's bone tired,* thought Calvino. *Or other, more powerful drugs. Or else Howard's personality is wired toward high anxiety.*

Howard, a line of sweat on his upper lip, walked into the coffee shop as if he were expecting to meet someone. His gaze bounced around the room, jumping from face to face. Nothing. He moved on a few steps, wiped the sweat off his lip. After he finished his pass-through, a look of disappointment registered on his face. He had failed in his mission, and something about Howard suggested he didn't take failure well. He turned around and opened the door, disappearing into the night.

Calvino slid out of the booth. "That's my man," he said.

Pratt watched him go out the door.

"Vincent," Pratt called after him. Calvino turned. "I'd like to see the video you made for Danielson's mystery client. And let me know how it ends."

"No problem. Tomorrow."

He watched Calvino disappear into the night. Colonel Pratt hadn't raised the matter of the WHO application. He sat in the booth enjoying the last of his tea. There were many possible endings. He had trouble thinking of a UN job as one of those ends for Calvino.

FIFTEEN

THE thin trickle of people passing through the hotel parking lot at 2:30 in the morning had turned into a full-blown tsunami of humanity sweeping in, wave after wave, from the bars. Each surge brought more people, bodies pushed together in the heat of a moonless night. The parking lot was gorged with people, standing shoulder to shoulder, laughing, chasing around, smoking. Some of the men in shorts and sandals, their eyes bloodshot, walked around with bottles of beer. The party atmosphere spread to the street, where people spilled out and blocked the traffic. The after-hours meat market had officially opened. Prime rib circulated, displaying itself as available for those with a late-night appetite.

"Look at the size of the crowd," said Lovell. "The embassy warned against getting involved in street demonstrations."

"It's not a demonstration," said Stiles. "This isn't political. It's social."

The taxi with Lovell and Stiles in the back stopped across from the police kiosk on Soi Nana. Uniformed officers sat inside the kiosk, looking bored. They got out of the taxi. Stiles edged through the street vendor carts and crowd before stepping off the pavement and into the street. Swarms of *yings* and men on the hunt crossed the street to the parking lot. High on speed pills, some of the *yings* buzzed like fireflies around a campfire. One of them, in sunglasses with white plastic frames, homed in on Lovell, grabbing his arm. Ahead a rat scurried past Lovell's feet, darted over the curb, and ran along the gutter before disappearing down a hole. A few hours before Lovell had drunk a bottle of wine, but the effect had now worn off.

"You handsome man. I go with you. You give me money, okay?"

Lovell stared at the tattoo on her shoulder, a heart. Underneath the heart was the name "Rick" in blue Gothic lettering. One of her friends with an ulcerated herpes sore on her lip butted in, "I go with you, too."

He felt hands grabbing his arm and increased his stride, but he couldn't shake off the *yings.* They had a genius for holding on, like a pride of lions bringing down a slow moving water buffalo. Stiles whispered in the ear of the *ying* with the tattoo that Lovell was gay. By this time, he had grabbed Lovell's hand and nodded in his direction. Not a gesture that went unnoticed by the *yings.* Rick's tattoo *ying* jerked away as if Lovell had a dangerous infection. She told the other two *yings*, and they broke off formation and flew off on a new mission.

"How'd you do that?" asked Lovell.

He let go of Lovell's hand. "I told them that you were gay."

"And they believed you?"

"It's an imperfect world, Lovell. They want business. They don't stick around if they think you don't want a woman."

"We need to talk about a few things."

It was difficult talking over the noise. Stiles hadn't caught what Lovell had said, or if he had, then he'd pretended not to hear it. "Follow me," said Stiles, half-shouting.

"I've seen it. I want to go somewhere quiet where we can talk." Hundreds of people were swarming, touching, and recoiling.

Stiles waited until Lovell had caught up. "If any ninety-pound *ying* threatens you, just let me know. Think of me as your human shield. Cameron will have my full report tomorrow. I wouldn't want to say John Lovell couldn't hack it."

Stiles elbowed slowly through the crowd, blowing the occasional kiss. Lovell followed him, fingers of sweat rolling down his neck. He unbuttoned the top button of his shirt. The humid air felt suffocating. Food vendors sold pork and chicken on a stick, and carts loaded with fried grasshopper and water bugs were also doing a good business. As the crowd closed in, Lovell felt blackmailed, hot, disoriented, off-balance, and afraid. The scene repelled him. But at the same time, the more he walked along, the more fascinated he became with the experience.

Stiles had been basically right: his world had been no more than the law office and his condo. His world expanded only far enough to include Siri. The Nana Hotel parking lot after two in the morning pulsated with possibilities, personalities, and promises made and broken. The women, mostly young, stood in groups, faces freshly painted. Just emerged from a ten-hour shift of groping, dancing, hustling, being hustled, rejection, and cat fights, they wandered into the parking lot, hoping to find a man.

"You don't have to go to the bar. The bar can come to you," said Stiles.

They stopped in the middle of the parking lot. A couple of feet away, a *farang* and a *ying* were standing in the street sucking each other's spit. Wrapped in her arms, he had one hand inside her jeans. As far as the eye could see were *yings*, expectant, making eye contact, smiling, and flirting. Cigarette smoke curled out of the nose of the *ying* closest to Stiles. She offered him a cigarette and he accepted the offer. Lighting it for him, she gracefully placed it between his lips. "You like, Dew?"

"I like Dew," joked Stiles.

She playfully punched him on the shoulder. "You forget me?"

Stiles dropped the cigarette and ground it under his heel. "I never forget you."

"Why are you talking baby talk to her?"

Stiles ignored him. "Cannot tonight." He folded two hundred baht into her hand and squeezed it.

"You gave her two hundred baht for a cigarette?" asked Lovell.

"Kill fee. She phoned me earlier. I said I'd be here. But I'm not taking her."

"You gave her money not to take her?"

"I am bored with her. I don't want her to lose face. So I gave her money to go away. That buys me the right to ignore her. She got something, and so did I."

Cameron was right, thought Stiles. Behind his back, Lovell's nickname was Bubble Boy.

Lovell turned around in a full circle.

The parking lot churned with frantic bar *yings* in short skirts and high heels, others in jeans and T-shirts, supercharged by the knowledge that this was their last chance to score. Fashions accented the pelvis and hips. Kittenish and sensual, there were *yings* for every taste—geared up for food, drinking, drugs, and sex. The subliminal message ran in the humid air: take me out of the parade and let's go to the game. Small hands reached out, fingers touching Lovell's hair, tie, and shirt. Tall and young, they were drawn toward him as if he were a rock star. In comparison with the other *farangs* watching the parade, Lovell was different: young, handsome, fresh meat. Stiles had seen it before. Their built-in radar allowed bar *yings* the ability to track a customer who, innocent and new, held the possibility of a large score.

Locked inside this increasingly tense circle just inches from them, all lipstick and white teeth, Lovell and Stiles were among the last to know what had caused the shouting from the street. A couple of minutes passed before Stiles glimpsed the first uniforms moving through the crowd. Nobody had any idea what was happening, but the pent-up desire for sex washed away almost immediately.

They were in the midst of a police raid. A Toyota pickup edged into the *soi* and parked in front of the parking lot. Behind the pickup, a half-dozen officers on motorcycles stopped and climbed off their bikes. The doors of the pickup opened and an officer climbed out, walkie-talkie in hand, shouting orders to the other police, who moved into the crowd. Like hens in a henhouse reacting to an intruding fox, the *yings* shivered, cried, and ran, bouncing off each other, falling, scraping knees, and losing shoes. Reporters and TV camera crews had hitched rides to witness and record the raid. They'd been tipped off in advance.

The TV crews filmed the cops grabbing the first *yings*, who cursed and yelped and struggled. The cops shoved them in the back of the pickup. As with the bombing of Pearl Harbor, the element of surprise had worked in favor of the police. The cameras captured surrealistic images of cops picking up *yings* like fifty-kilo bags of rice and hauling them away.

"Now what?" Lovell's legs trembled. He wanted to run but didn't know where he would be safe.

"Relax, it's not political. It's not about crime."

"What is it about?"

"Looking good, making out that they're doing something useful," said Stiles. "Nothing to piss your pants over. Just watch the show. Next time you're back for a high-school reunion you'll have something to talk about."

The circle of *yings* that had surrounded them had broken up and scattered. Some had shown enough running ability to make the Thai Olympic sprint team."

A dozen uniformed cops fanned out, blocking the driveway out of the parking lot. Others ran down Soi 4. The *yings* in the parking lot looked for a way through the police line, running in all directions. The cops gave chase. Each cop, even the overweight ones, returned with two or three girls. They loaded their catch sardine-style into the back of the pickup.

Also caught in the dragnet were a few odd fish: *katoeys*—women trapped inside male bodies; some having had undergone the final cut and the full Monty of hormone treatment, while others were saving up and dreaming for the day of their surgery. Wobbling on high heels, one big-boned *katoey* was as tall as Lovell, her feet a size larger, her voice half a tone deeper. She screamed in her baritone voice at the cop who was having trouble keeping hold of her arm. Her beef was that because of her size she should be allowed to sit up front in the pickup. Her fight for special treatment wasn't ever going to work. Two cops pushed her into the back of the van, where she broke the heel on one of her shoes. Tears streamed down her cheeks, wrecking her makeup, making her look more and more like a man as she screamed "*hia*" and "motherfucker" at the cops, who laughed in response. Then one of the cops slammed her across the face and that shut her up. When the pickup was overfilled with human cargo, it departed. For the excess *yings* who had been arrested, the cops flagged down taxis and pushed their catch into the back. A procession of taxis left the *soi* with a half-dozen prostitutes in the back of each and a cop riding shotgun in front. The taxi drivers laughed and joked. All of those hot *yings* bundled in the back of the taxi made for good eye candy in the rearview mirror. For most of the crowd the scene was *sanuk*, just good fun, except for the *yings* who were going to the police station to pay a thousand baht fine. The newspaper photographers and TV crews followed the police, filming the chase, the collars, the resistance, and some long shots of *yings* too fast for the out-of-shape cops to catch. Those shots would be edited out later. The drama of near escape played better on video. And it was much safer to play success than failure.

Later the newspapers would report that the cops had arrested thirty-two girls, two of whom were *katoeys*. Most of the *yings* who were arrested wore miniskirts and high heels. Even a fat cop could catch a *ying* in a tight miniskirt and high heels. It was an unfair handicap. The ones who escaped had worn flip-flops and jeans. The street was littered with discarded flip-flops. High heels were more expensive, and the instinct to keep them had sealed the fate of those wearing them.

During the confusion, one of the *yings* who stayed in the parking lot had the idea that to avoid arrest, she had better grab Lovell's arm. She was a *katoey* with a six thousand baht nose job and too much lipstick. When the cop came for her, she hissed, "I'm with my husband. How dare you?"

Lovell started to protest, as a reporter snapped several pictures.

"That's right, officer, they've been together for years," said Stiles.

The light of a TV camera hit Lovell as he reached forward and removed a loose thread from the officer's shoulder, balled it up between his finger and thumb. The cop looked at his shoulder, then at Lovell's tiny ball of thread.

"It's a habit," said Stiles. "He can't stand clutter."

The cop smiled, glanced at his other shoulder. After all he was on TV. Then he told Stiles in Thai that he should tell the *farang* that in the middle of a crackdown, raid, bust, whatever, it isn't a good idea to indulge in grooming the police. They might misunderstand. Meaning the *katoey's* story suddenly had credibility.

"I'll never forgive you," said Lovell, his voice emitting a growl expressing an animal-like low-grade rage.

The cop looked at Lovell, then at the *katoey*, "Then you and your wife shouldn't be here."

"We were just going for something to eat. We had no idea," said the *katoey*. "Darling, you know how hungry I am. Let's go."

Lovell could feel her nails bite into the flesh of his upper arm. She was incredibly strong and her message couldn't have been more direct and clear: fuck me over with this cop and your arm will never be the same. The bluff had worked well on the cop. A moment later he gave chase to another *ying*. The raid was mostly over. Stiles walked on the other side of the *katoey*. She led them to the coffee shop.

The night had gone so horribly wrong for Lovell. He played back the tape of the evening's events. The heated exchange with Siri in the wine cellar. Skipping the first night of Danielson's funeral. Cameron had looked around the *sala* at the *wat* and noticed Lovell's absence. Instead of pouring water on Danielson's hands, he was at a nightclub. Hostesses clung to Stiles who explained about the place of Khun Chang and Khun Phaen in ever-shifting Thai sexual relations. Then Lovell felt that he had no choice but to follow Stiles to the largest open-area *ying* collection in the known universe.

Inside the coffee shop, the *katoey* let go of Lovell's arm and without a word walked to a booth where Howard Herron sat, brooding, folding and unfolding his hands, his shirt sleeves rolled up and exposing his hairy forearms.

"Where were you?" she asked Herron.

Calvino, who had followed his mark outside, followed him back inside as the raid started. This was the "other woman" that Janet Herron had paid him to find. He took out his digital camera and snapped several shots of the couple in the booth.

SIXTEEN

PRATT found Calvino behind his desk, working on the crossword puzzle in the *Bangkok Post*. He tapped the end of the pen against his chin, his lips pursed, eyebrows knitted together. Without looking up, he asked, "What's a four-letter word for 'literary fury'?"

"Lear." Pratt sat down.

Calvino wrote in the word. He seemed satisfied with himself.

"Yes, Lear. You were quoting from that play last night."

Colonel Pratt filtered violence, sex, betrayal, loyalty, and trust through the prism of Shakespeare, and this ability set him apart from most Thais.

Pratt opened a copy of *Thai Rath*, a mass circulation Thai-language daily newspaper, thumbed through a couple of pages, stopped, found what he was searching for, folded the newspaper in half and laid it on Calvino's desk. "It's not a crossword puzzle. But it is a mystery. Have a look at the photograph."

Calvino looked at the photograph. Lovell had a surprised, wide-eyed look and the *katoey* on his arm was staring dreamily at him. "Lovell."

"With a friend. Do you think that Danielson knew about him?"

"Knew what?"

Pratt smiled, sitting back in the chair, arms folded. "His secret life. Going on gigs with *katoeys*, sneaking out to late-night pickup spots on Sukhumvit. Lovell was the last person to see Danielson alive. And he's refused to help you. He's hiding something."

"After you left, I hung around until late and then went back to the coffee shop. Bingo. There was Howard. And there was Lovell, with the *katoey* holding on to him," said Calvino, grinning.

"Like a happy couple," said Colonel Pratt, tapping the photograph in the newspaper. Had there been an ending to the story?

Calvino shook his head. The veins in his neck popped out as he sat back in his chair. "Not exactly. She went over and sat with Howard Herron. They obviously had something going on."

"What's her connection to Lovell?"

Calvino thought about this. Lovell, the secret nerdish pimp, who supplied Howard with his fix? He shrugged. "I have no idea."

Calvino reminded Pratt that Howard was the focus of his current professional interest, not Lovell. The last thing that he had expected was that Lovell would deliver the evidence.

"What did Lovell do after she sat beside Howard Herron?"

"He left with another guy. A *farang*. Someone I've never seen before."

"A friend? A colleague? Someone he just met in the parking lot?

"He could have been anyone. I didn't talk to him. And, no, I never saw him before tonight."

"Lovell's boss has just died. He turns up in the middle of a police raid with a *katoey*. I'm getting the picture of someone who doesn't seem to be in mourning," said Pratt.

Ratana came into the office with a glass of water for Colonel Pratt and set it on the table. She also put down the videocassette that Calvino had shot at the factory. Close-up shots of the loading bay. A half-dozen men unloading bootlegged drugs from a ten-wheel truck with Clint Eastwood mud flaps.

"I heard something. But I don't know if it's useful," she said.

Calvino sat back in his chair and lifted his arms, palms up.

"What did you hear?"

"It's about Danielson."

"Who were you talking to?" asked Calvino.

"The *mamasan* downstairs."

That took Calvino by surprise. Ratana had avoided the massage parlor as if she might catch a contagious disease there. She looked at Colonel Pratt, watching out of the corner of her eye the astonished expression on her boss's face.

"You actually talked to her?"

"I thought it might help. She'd be more likely to talk to me than you or Colonel Pratt."

Colonel Pratt sipped from the glass of water. "Please tell us what she said. "Calvino and Colonel Pratt exchanged a glance. Calvino shifted in his chair and gave up on the crossword puzzle.

"She told me about Jazz," she said. Ratana was unable to bring herself to use the name of the massage parlor, One Hand Clapping, or to admit that such an establishment existed. "She said that Jazz may have cut her wrists but she really died of a broken heart. Danielson was a regular customer. He visited her a couple of times a week.

"How long was this going on?" asked Colonel Pratt.

Ratana thought about this. "A few months. Ever since *that* business opened. Two days before she killed herself, Danielson gave her a bronze necklace. He said that it had belonged to his mother, and that when she died, he had inherited it. He wanted her to have it. Not his wife. He wanted it for Jazz. That's what I was told."

"I don't get it. Danielson gives her something from his mother and she kills herself," said Calvino.

Ratana stared at the photograph of Lovell and the *katoey* in the newspaper spread out on Calvino's desk. "The *mamasan* said that Khun Andrew took the necklace from a large bag of junk jewelry. Inside were many bracelets, necklaces, and earrings. His line was that the necklace was something very special. But it really wasn't worth more than a few baht. It was junk. I am not certain it was really from his mother." She shrugged her shoulders. "He made a habit of getting involved with a massage girl or bar girl, and he sealed the relationship by giving them something from his mother. He was a *farang*, and maybe he didn't know that when a man gives a Thai woman something from his mother, something personal, that means he wants her as part of his family. It isn't just money. It means that he thinks about her like a wife. Jazz must have thought that she was very special to him. She wore that necklace to bed at night. She treated it like an amulet. Jazz wouldn't go with other customers; she sat and waited for him day after day to come around. Then she found out he had lied to her."

Ratana paused, waiting for a reaction from Calvino or Pratt. Neither man said anything. The silence grew until it was nearly unbearable. Danielson had been coming into the *soi* for months. But he'd never mentioned his involvement with Jazz.

"He never said anything about having a girlfriend downstairs," said Calvino.

Had Danielson been using Calvino as his beard to cover his frequent trips to the massage parlor? If he was being followed, he'd had a solid alibi—that he had a meeting with Vincent Calvino on a piracy case. Sometimes that story was true. Mostly, though, he hadn't any intention of going to Calvino's office; his mission was downstairs at the massage parlor, unloading his mother's phony jewelry.

Calvino's law about guys like Danielson, addicted to working *yings*, held up. His wife could threaten him, scream at him, and he'd promise to stop. But the promise never held for long. The law was simple: That dog never will stop chasing cars.

"How did the *mamasan* find the jewelry?" asked Colonel Pratt.

"Jazz's girlfriend told her. Metta's her name. The two of them got into a fight. It all came out. Metta found out about the bag of fake jewelry. She told Jazz after hearing her brag about how this *farang* loved only her, how she was special and he was different from the others. That did it. Metta told Jazz that he had given his mother's jewelry to lots of girls. Jazz wasn't anyone special. She was one in a long line of throw-down girls.

"Jazz refused to believe what she heard. Then she did some checking. When she discovered the truth, she lost face. And she killed herself. She couldn't bear to live and know this truth about a man who she thought had really loved her."

"Why didn't Metta tell the police about this? It wasn't in the report," said Colonel Pratt.

"Metta could be lying, or the *mamasan* could be trying to blame the *farang*," said Calvino.

Pratt and Ratana both looked at Calvino, waiting for him to explain what had happened the night of Jazz's death. "All I'm saying is all of this is third-hand gossip. When is the last time you heard of a *ying* killing herself because some old fart customer scammed her with some fake jewelry?"

"She may have had real feelings for him," said Ratana. "Just because Jazz worked in a massage parlor doesn't mean she wasn't human."

Why is that girl crying? Calvino had asked himself walking into the *soi* the day before. Her friend was dead. Could it have been that she was crying because she understood why the girl had killed herself?

"I'd like to talk with Metta," said Pratt. He wrote down the name in his notebook and noted: "Dead *farang* rejected by mother? Possibly mentally unbalanced with women. Check out his wife's alibi and knowledge of poison."

"Metta," from Pali, means compassion, Pratt recalled. Buddhism rests on the idea of compassion; it's the shock absorber on the bumpy path to enlightenment. But compassion isn't always what it's cracked up to be. There are costs, expenses, fees, tributes to be paid along the road of taking into account the feelings of others.

"Did Metta see her friend cut her wrists?" asked Colonel Pratt.

Ratana wasn't certain how to answer that question. The *mamasan* hadn't said anything about the timing of Jazz's death and Metta's showing up in the room.

Colonel Pratt continued, "She was interviewed by the police. And she told the police Jazz was dead when she came into the room. Maybe she said something to the *mamasan* that was different from what she told the police."

Ratana squirmed, clasping her hands together, then rubbing the tips of her fingers together. She regretted having talked to the *mamasan.* Getting involved in a police investigation wasn't what she had intended. Sometimes she could forget that Pratt wasn't just her friend Manee's husband and Calvino's best friend; he was also a cop.

"She said Jazz was already dead when she came into the room."

"Why did she lock the door?"

"I asked her. But all she could say was that she was frightened."

"Did she say why she felt afraid?"

"She blamed herself and thought she might get in trouble."

Colonel Pratt scribbled down her words in his notepad. No one was sure what time it had been when Metta had entered the room. The fact was she remained a suspect; he needed to know more about her. Was she cunning enough to spin a story that Jazz was already dead when she entered the room? Had she told the truth to *mamasan*? And had the *mamasan* told Ratana the truth?

"If you think of anything else she said, let me know. It might be important," said Colonel Pratt.

"Would you like more water, Colonel Pratt?" asked Ratana.

"No," he said. His wife, Manee, had been talking about Ratana over the past couple of weeks. They'd been attending demonstrations together and had, so he gathered, become quite close. They wore the same yellow bracelet on their right wrists, and around Ratana's neck was a yellow silk scarf, elegantly tied. Her friendship with Manee made him feel closer to Ratana. The things she told him, making certain Calvino was present to listen, were her way of showing respect not only to him but to Manee.

He swallowed the last of his water and put down the glass, slowly shifting in his chair. Ratana had left the two of them to pick up the conversation.

"Do you still want to see the videocassette?" asked Calvino. "I'll burn you a DVD."

"I want the original, Vincent."

Calvino frowned. "Let me make a backup."

"Later. Show me what you've got." He glanced at his watch.

Colonel Pratt had come specifically to see the videotape. But what Ratana had told him was a major distraction. He needed to filter through his mind what it meant for his investigation. Andrew Danielson and his girlfriend died only hours apart. Inside the department someone with significant influence had put in motion a cover-up designed to keep Danielson's official cause of death a heart attack. Calvino had kicked down a door and found Metta crying and Jazz dead on the bed. The dead girl had deep slash wounds on her wrists. In a suicide, even the most depressed person has a natural aversion to slashing the wrist. Most of the time wrist slashing is a glancing cut, just enough over the threshold of superficial to draw blood. Men cut themselves more deeply. It was hard for women to work up the degree of self-violence that matched self-hatred. The depth of the wounds on Jazz's wrists troubled him. It wasn't consistent with what he had seen many times over.

What did he have? A woman named Metta who might have acted out of revenge. A dead massage girl named after American music. Danielson's bag of junk jewelry inherited from his mother. The photograph of Danielson's young associate in the arms of a *katoey* had run in one of the leading local newspapers. Lovell had been caught in the middle of a raid where the police nabbed more than two football teams' worth of prostitutes.

"I got the angles right. It wasn't that easy in the dark. The lighting was low. It doesn't matter. You can see the faces. I've got close-ups of the boxes. They put the names of the drugs on the labels. They were going directly into drugstores and hospitals. You can bet on it."

"Let's have a look at what you've got."

Calvino hooked his digital video camera to his computer, slid the cassette into the camera, and waited for it to load. He turned around his monitor for Colonel Pratt's benefit. Then he walked around to Pratt's side of the desk, pulled up a chair, and sat next to the colonel. Calvino alternated between looking at the screen and watching the colonel for reactions. The colonel watched as several workers loaded a pickup with packages. One fell from the trolley and broke open. Hollywood blockbuster films, with stars on the packaging, spilled into the street. There was no narration. It was like an old silent movie, maybe with the Keystone Cops. The view from the street cut abruptly to an interior shot. A warehouse with pallets stacked along one wall. Another cut and several women in jeans and T-shirts worked alongside one another at a long table.

Overhead neon lights shone down over the main floor area. Computer monitors flickered from three desks pushed together against the far wall. On one screen a movie was playing, another displayed a waterfall screen saver, and on the third a woman worked on an Excel file. The women looked bored. In the middle of the floor an assembly line with conveyor belts fed packets of pills to women who stuffed them into small boxes and then stacked them inside larger boxes.

He counted eighteen women and seven men inside the warehouse, each with a job. Outside, three men patrolled the grounds, watching the street. Large barrels of ingredients were stacked on pallets in the area inside the loading bay. A forklift worked in the small turn-around space, shifting the barrels to the mixing area. One of the women operated a machine that stamped logos on sheets of plastic pill wrap, and several other machines dropped the pills into place and sealed them in tiny see-through compartments. The packets then passed along a conveyor belt to women who stuffed ten into a box with the drug company logo printed on the front. Another woman wrapped cellophane around ten of the finished boxes and handed each package to the last girl down the line, who stacked it in a large shipping box. No question, from the layout and staffing, that it was a highly professional operation. Colonel Pratt watched the scene, one that he had witnessed before, without any expression.

"How did you get inside the warehouse?" Colonel Pratt asked. Impressed by the videotape, he asked Calvino to play it again.

"Behind the warehouse is a row of shop houses. One was empty. I drilled through the common wall."

"They didn't hear the drill?"

"There was a lot of noise inside and out. It's a factory. They go deaf after a few months working in a place like that."

They watched the video again. The brand of diabetes pills, clearly visible, jogged Calvino's memory. He picked up his pen and wrote in a word—diabetes—completing the crossword puzzle. It gave him no satisfaction to have finished it. Colonel Pratt wrote in his notebook as he watched the video for the second time. Both of them were thinking about Jazz. Calvino's thoughts wandered to the room where he'd found her. The initial verdict was that she'd killed herself. Despondent over a love affair, she had opened her wrists and bled to death. Fake jewelry had been around her neck and a razor she had bought herself at a 7/11, sticky with blood, lay beside her on the bed.

After the second playing of the video, Ratana re-entered. "You should take this call," she said to Calvino.

Lovell was on the line.

"I'd like an appointment," he said.

"The last time we talked, you said there was nothing else to say."

"Things haven't changed," Calvino continued. "I still want my money. Do you understand what I'm saying?"

Colonel Pratt wasn't looking at the computer screen.

"It's a personal matter," said Lovell.

"How personal?"

"I've got a problem with my law firm."

"What kind of problem?"

There was a brief silence. "I've been fired."

Calvino traced a line over Lovell's photograph in the newspaper. He wasn't all that surprised. "I saw your photo in the newspaper. I recognized the *katoey* you came into the coffee shop with."

"The senior partner in my law firm recognized me."

Colonel Pratt heard Calvino's side of the conversation, making notes. Ratana came back with a plate of mango and set it in front of the colonel.

"She dropped you pretty fast the other night."

"That was the only good thing that happened. But of course no one took a photograph of that." The panic in his voice raised it an octave. He sounded like a frightened schoolboy. The confident state he had occupied when he had brushed Calvino off had dissolved into a mist of fear.

"Who was your friend you came into the coffee shop with?"

There was a long pause. "His name is Stiles. He's another lawyer at the firm."

"He managed to stay out of the photograph."

"A fact that hasn't gone unnoticed by me."

Another period of silence followed. He could almost feel Lovell's sense of desperation. Near tears, he was as close as a man can come to pleading.

His voice was firm. "I am not going to roll over for them. You want your money. I want my career. Let's find a way to make a deal."

"I'm looking at my diary, and I see that I do have time to meet with you."

SEVENTEEN

MCPHAIL greedily gulped down the last swallow of Jameson, rattled the ice inside the glass, and raised it to signal the bar that he wanted another. Grasping the glass, he raised his hand above his head just as Calvino walked into the Lonesome Hawk Bar. Old George guarded his territory from his station below the stuffed water buffalo head. From his vantage point no one came or went without passing him. He knew his regulars and greeted them, and he eyed strangers, who had no idea as they came in off the street who the old guy under the water buffalo was, and that he was a walking history of the twentieth century.

"Calvino, I like your trade, but if you beat up another customer I'm gonna personally eighty-six you. Got it?"

"George, screen your drunks."

"Are you telling me how to run my bar?"

"I am suggesting there's a line. The Englishman crossed it."

"I know he did. That's why I am not saying much. But next time, take them outside to do your business."

"I'll try and remember that, George."

"You're gonna give me my first gray hair if you're not careful, young man."

He loved Old George. The Lonesome Hawk was one of the few places on earth where the owner greeted him as a young man. Calvino got Old George's message, all right. If you live that long, then you have a right to call a few shots.

"Now tell me, how's your mother doing?"

That was an Old George thing. He'd threaten to eighty-six

Calvino from the bar and a couple of seconds later he'd turn around and ask about his mother.

"The same. No change at her age."

"How old is she?"

"Eighty-two."

His eyebrows arched, his double chin spreading out to reveal two more chins. "Shit, she's just a kid."

"Calvino, you've got a problem," said McPhail. He nervously played with the cellophane on his cigarette pack, tearing off a piece at a time, blinking each time he peeled off another thumbnail of it. He was like a cat dissecting a small animal, except his action was mindless.

Calvino slipped into his usual booth. A waitress, who was a grandmother but could still pass in low light for a late thirties *ying*, staggered half-drunk down the bar. She reached Calvino's booth and set down a Mekong and Coke.

"Let me drink this first," said Calvino. "And you, don't go anywhere."

McPhail watched as the Mekong and Coke disappeared down Calvino's throat. He handed the waitress the empty glass.

"One more?" she asked.

He nodded. "And one for yourself."

The last thing she needed was another drink from a customer.

"Oy's drunk," said McPhail. "I already bought her three Mekongs. For a grandmother she can pack 'em away." He sneezed, and the pile of shredded cellophane blew all over the table.

The waitress giggled, handing a tissue to McPhail as if he were a prematurely aged child. He blew his nose. "I gotta tell you about the Fab Four. It ain't good."

"I don't come here to hear about problems. I come here to get away from problems. Got that, McPhail?"

McPhail's glass of Jameson arrived and he slapped the grandmother on the ass, reached around and pulled her back for a hug and tickle. Some quick movement had triggered the impulse to pounce on a prey. She quickly squirmed away, and he made no real effort to hold on to her. After she left, he lit a cigarette. "You want to hear about this problem or pretend that there's nothing wrong with your expat ladies?"

"I nailed Janet Herron's husband. He was holding hands with a retrofit. I caught him in a public place. He's cornered. He's got no way out. They should love me," said Calvino.

"I know, I know. But it don't work that way."

"What way are you talking about?"

McPhail sighed, "You're looking at it from your point of view. Not from their point of view."

Calvino shrugged, "Okay, I've got it. They don't want to admit what happened with Janet's husband might be happening in their lives. That their husbands are cheating on them. That's natural. Human nature."

McPhail blew out a lungful of smoke, shaking his head. "It's more complicated. Man, they'd be as happy as a one-legged ballroom dancer at a wheelchair convention if Janet's husband had been caught with a young lovely girl. Let me say that again. Girl. You caught him with a *katoey*."

There are stories that everyone knows are stories. You hear them, laugh, and then move on. Then there are stories that suck you inside, make you *feel* that you are in the center of what is happening. You experience turning around three hundred and sixty degrees, finding that in every direction you are inside it. It isn't some story. You are there. That is what had happened to the women in the Fab Four Cooking School Club. Howard Herron's story buzzed around inside their consciousness like a blue bottle fly inside an empty milk bottle, bouncing off the edges, panicky, angry, and desperate.

Calvino had, in his mind, already pocketed the full fee from the three women and he had handed the money over to the *mamasan* to buy out the One Hand Clapping lease. It was a done deal, wasn't it? Done only in his mind. Another Mekong arrived silently and replaced his empty glass.

"What are they saying?" asked Calvino.

"You need to talk to them again."

"They want to cancel the deal?"

McPhail raised one eyebrow and shrugged. "Women want to know and don't want to know at the same time. It's fucked up. But that's how they're wired."

Nothing in business was ever straightforward or easy. After Danielson died, or was killed, Calvino had been orphaned. He'd done his job but hadn't got his money. The expat women were the first glimmer of hope suggesting a way to rescue the situation. One hand washed the other; only it wasn't working out that way.

As a private investigator, Calvino had done what he'd been hired to do. He'd got the dirt on the piracy operation. He had photos of Howard with his paws all over the *katoey*. The point being that truth and evidence were only a small part of the equation when it came to getting paid.

It hadn't occurred to him that Janet would make a big deal over the original gender of the retrofit captured in the picture. Maybe she hadn't. The other women might have worried about the consequences of finding out that their husbands had some kinky dark secret extending way beyond the ordinary boundary of infidelity.

"When do they want to meet?" asked Calvino.

"Three tomorrow afternoon. I fixed it with Chef Elmo. It's no problem for us to meet in his kitchen. Oh, one thing. He asked if you'd go easy on the Italian. He says he's rusty and it makes him look bad in front of the women."

"He's an Italian prince," said Calvino. "Tell him I said so. In English of course."

"He's doing you a favor, buddy. Come to think of it, I'm doing you a favor."

"Janet won't answer her phone. She owes me information about Danielson."

"She don't want to talk about anything to nobody. She's all fucked up, buddy."

"What about my money, McPhail? I help her and she's too distraught to talk to me?"

"Tomorrow, ask her for the money," said McPhail, sucking on a cigarette, dragging in the smoke slowly.

"She'd better be there," said Calvino, his hands tightening into fists.

"What do you want me to do? Slap her around? 'Hey, bitch, pay my friend or that's the last pasta you're ever gonna eat with that set of teeth.'"

"Get her on the phone. She'll answer your call. And then give me the phone."

McPhail choked out a cloud of smoke, his face turning a bright red. "Man, she'll hate me."

"Consider that a positive outcome, McPhail."

Paranoia was the best friend for professionals—private eyes, doctors, lawyers, and accountants. A seed of fear or doubt, once planted, flourished. The clients watched in enveloping horror and amazement as the tiny seed grew and grew. Matters quickly got out of control. Too much excitement made people edgy, irrational, ready to bolt. Too much paranoia made them run for guns, drugs, or a hired gunman. It was a delicate balance: taking charge of a frightened, emotional person's life, making them a plan to uproot the evil plant before it could grow into a forest blanketing every part of their lives. Calvino realized that he might be too late.

McPhail placed a cell phone to his ear and, rising from his seat, whispered as he handed the phone to Calvino.

"Janet, before tomorrow, you ask your husband one question for me. Can you do that for me?"

There was a long pause. "What kind of question?"

"You ask him to give you the names of Andrew Danielson's buddies who have any connection with the drug business," said Calvino.

"Whatever you might think, Mr. Calvino, my husband doesn't know anything about drugs."

"I am talking legit drugs, not opium. Like penicillin or aspirin. All the big companies sell their stuff here. Danielson was helping someone on the side. It had to be a friend. Find out if he knows anyone who fits the bill. You can help me on this, Janet. I walked the extra mile for you. That means you owe me."

"Don't tell me what I owe you, you scumbag."

"If I were a scumbag, I would have gone up to Howard and said, give me a list of Danielson's friends and I delete the photos of you and your friend. And I tell your wife you're a good boy."

He handed the phone back to McPhail, who shook his head, got up from the booth and walked out the front door. Calvino glanced at his watch. He had another hour before his appointment with Lovell.

Calvino put his head back and closed his eyes. When he opened them, Old George sat across from him in McPhail's spot. "You sound like a Jewish mother. With all of this 'you owe me' business."

Calvino's eyes popped open wide and he stared hard at Old George. "You got nothing better to do than listen to private telephone conversations?"

"Listening? Huh. You were fucking shouting. I'd had to cover my ears not to hear."

"So I sound like my mother. What's your point?"

"How is she up here?" Old George asked, tapping the side of his head with his forefinger. He'd been thinking about Calvino's mother.

"Are you trying to say something about my mother?" The heat was rising.

Old George waved his hand. "Don't take everything the wrong way. I was asking you if her mind is still okay? A week ago you said she was having some problems. Something about a UN job she was on you to apply for. Excuse me for asking."

Last time Calvino had visited his mother in a rest home, she'd sat in a dressing gown on the edge of her chair, rocking back and forth. She leaned forward, stopped, looked around the room before whispering, "Do you see that man over there?" Calvino saw an old grizzled man with a fringe of white hair and watery eyes in the far corner.

"His name is Glenn. He's responsible for the place falling apart."

Calvino couldn't imagine the harmless old man was responsible for anything more difficult than remembering his toilet training.

"He's eating the place, bit by bit. He thinks no one notices what he's doing. But I have caught him. He's sly. He thinks he's so smart. But I see him eating things."

"Eating what?"

"The furniture."

A couple of months later, he'd had an email from one of his mother's doctors, who confirmed that the man in the striped pajamas, a spidery web of wild hair growing inside his ears and nose, had been discovered to have been secretly removing the screws from the furniture. An orderly had caught him swallowing them whole. When the doctors had operated on Glenn, they'd discovered more than ten pounds of screw sludge sloshing around inside his gut. He would never have made it through an airport metal detector. And in the sunroom where residents (they never called them patients) played cards, watched TV, or read, the furniture had been falling apart. One fat lady of seventy-eight had crashed through a screwless chair and broken her hip. Several other patients had less serious accidents involving sitting on or leaning against the deceptively solid chairs and tables. The table holding the TV had suddenly collapsed and the TV had crashed onto the floor. The exterminators had gone through the rest home and found no species of insect capable of eating the furniture. No one except his mother knew the cause that had defied gravity.

After Calvino had exchanged a few more emails with the doctor, he had renewed respect for his mother. He'd thought, for a moment, that she had lost her mind. Just the opposite, she had been the first person to discover the reason the furniture in the rest home had become a minefield for elderly patients. No one on the staff had believed her. They'd written her off as a dotty old broad with a screw loose. But his mother didn't have any loose screws rattling around inside her head. If she'd had any, Glenn would have eaten them.

Old George smacked his lips with approval. "She's one smart cookie."

Calvino smiled. That was a good definition of his mother.

"I had a friend in Guam; his mother was in a rest home. One day he went to visit her and she froze, turned pale, and became very still. He thought she might be having a stroke. She pointed at a house lizard on the wall. 'You see that?' He looked at where she was pointing. It had sharp, black eyes and a tongue licking the air. And you know what his mother said? She said, 'Alligators. They're everywhere. I can't sleep. I see them crawling on the walls. Can't you find a way to get rid of the alligators?' And he said he'd try his best. That's what I mean about having all of your marbles. If you start seeing things and confusing reality with imaginary worlds, then it's over."

Calvino stuffed a five hundred baht note into the chit cup.

"My mother was a saint," said Old George.

"That's a good thing," said Calvino.

"Only if you're religious."

EIGHTEEN

LOVELL wore his best lawyer's suit for the appointment at Calvino's office. A couple of the girls in front of One Hand Clapping were impressed enough to get off their stools and rush at him, trying to drag him inside. He stood his ground like a mule. The Nana Hotel parking lot had served as his basic training. He was a veteran. One of the *yings* gave him a fifteen-percent discount coupon in case he had time after his appointment with Calvino. He stuffed it in the outside pocket of his suit without reading it and mounted the stairs. They shouted after him, "Don't forget us! We wait you."

Reaching the top of the staircase, Lovell adjusted his tie, refastened the button on his suit jacket, and walked inside the reception area. Ratana looked up from her keyboard. It was rare that any of Calvino's clients were worth a second look. She broke into a girlish smile, one of those involuntary grins that last a few seconds too long. "Can I help you?"

He handed Ratana his business card. "I have an appointment."

She wanted to say that she had been expecting him. But she hadn't been expecting him to look this young, this smart, or this handsome. His photograph in *Thai Rath* hadn't done him justice; in person, he was much better looking. The photograph captured an unflattering look of astonishment. Those large deer eyes caught in the high beams. In the clutches of a *katoey,* the confident man who stood in front of her desk had appeared wounded. Blunted around the edges, toned down, vulnerable, and geeky. She got up from her chair and walked around the partition to announce that the client had arrived. *He even smells good*, she thought, as she walked past him.

Calvino clicked on to Google Earth, typed in the coordinates, and from a satellite way above the planet's surface, he homed in on the short-time hotel where Howard Herron had taken the *katoey*. He switched coordinates to his office, to his mother's rest home, and back to the warehouse loaded with knock-off prescription pills. His earth was scattered with the locations of work, confinement, and illegal operations.

He downloaded the image to a folder named Howard_H. He had sent the folder to Howard's wife. And Janet Herron had already downloaded the digital images of her husband and the *katoey*. She was the only person (other than Ratana) who had access to the folder. When Howard had woken up that day and gone into his study to check his email, he found that Janet had used a montage of the photos as screen savers on his computer. She heard his agonized whine all the way in the kitchen. Calvino savored the moment and barely registered that Lovell had stepped into his office.

"You can help me," said Lovell.

He sat down and opened his briefcase, removing a half-dozen files. Lovell looked like a graduate student on his first job interview. His hand in a briefcase, fishing around for the big trout, the trophy fish to show off.

Calvino looked away from the computer screen, watching Lovell scramble around for a hidden object that somehow eluded him. But he didn't say anything for over a minute, letting the college boy sort out his presentation.

Lovell had lost his train of thought. He started a conversation then disappeared from it as if he had better things to do. If this were a personality trait, it would take some getting used to. Calvino waited through the blanket of silence until he felt Lovell had gone mute for too long.

"You said I could help you." Calvino waited until Lovell's face turned up from the briefcase. Once he'd established eye contact, he continued. "I recall telling you the same thing, and what did you tell me?" asked Calvino.

Lovell remembered exactly what he had said on the telephone. "I said I couldn't help you. And that was true when I said it. But now we can help each other. And I can help you to get your fee paid."

The kid had a point, thought Calvino. Truth never stayed true for long; it was always zigzagging across the floor, up the wall, along the ceiling, circulating around to the point where it wasn't clear where it started.

"What about your law firm?"

Lovell shook his head. "Like I said on the phone, I've been fired."

"You lost your job. And now you want revenge. Blow them out of the water." Law firms avoided hiring circus performers (especially jugglers and trapeze artists), bohemians, free-thinkers, poets, and anyone else who might embarrass them, making them look stupid, weak, like asses. No one had confidence in a law firm run by freaks, except other freaks, and those kind of people never had any money.

Calvino found the *Thai Rath* newspaper under a mountain of debris on his desk and tossed it to Lovell. "That's not good for business."

"That's what my boss said. But it wasn't my fault."

Rolling his eyes, Calvino sat back in his chair. "Exactly whose fault was it?"

"If we're going to work together, I don't think you should be so hostile."

Calvino saw the young lawyer's eyes study him. "What are you staring at?"

"Your tie. The knot is wrong."

Before Calvino could respond, Lovell reached over the desk, undid the necktie, and quickly made a perfect Windsor knot. "That's better, detective."

Calvino wondered if Lovell has some kind of mental condition. Normally a stranger wouldn't reach over the desk of another man and retie his necktie. No one had called him "detective" since he'd opened shop.

"Don't call me detective."

"Sorry, Mr. Calvino."

"You can call me Vinny."

Lovell squirmed, rotated his shoulders, processing the name request. "I'm more comfortable with Mr. Calvino."

Calvino nodded. "Okay, call me detective. What's your problem, other than unemployment?"

"Where to start?"

"Why not with the case Danielson hired me to work on?"

Lovell swallowed hard. "Okay. Andrew was helping out a friend."

Calvino sighed, a wide smile crossing his face. He hadn't felt this good in a long time. "Tell me about the friend, John."

It turned out Danielson's friend was an American client, Noah Gould. Gould managed an independent distribution company called Avenant Pharma, which had deals to distribute big-name brands: Pfizer, Upjohn, Roche. Noah had lived in Bangkok for a number of years and was a friend of Andrew Danielson. They were roughly the same age and had met at a chamber of commerce meeting and struck up a friendship. Their wives were also extremely close. Ruth Gould, the one who had worn the broad-brimmed pink hat, and Millie Danielson, the expat wife that Calvino hadn't met at Chef Elmo's cooking class.

"My guess is that Noah asked Andrew for a favor," said Lovell.

"I don't see why it would be a favor. It was business. He's getting ripped off. Your law firm does intellectual property work. What's this about doing a favor?"

Danielson hadn't struck him as someone who did outside work as a favor. He was businesslike, direct, and setting up realistic expectations.

"Gould was getting stonewalled by the corporate department. They had promised to close down the piracy operation. But nothing happened. So he went to Danielson and told him the problem he was having."

It was starting to make sense, Calvino thought. There was some internal political problem and Danielson was going outside the usual chain of command. "Who was stonewalling him?"

"Stiles for a start."

"The lawyer you were with last night?"

Lovell made a face. "Yeah. Not so cool, I know. And then there's the senior partner, Cameron. Stiles is close to the big man."

"Why wouldn't Danielson go to Cameron and tell him an important client wasn't getting the attention he deserved?"

"You practiced law?" asked Lovell.

"In New York, last life."

The revelation came as a jolt. A one-man private investigator in

Bangkok who had once practiced law in New York made Lovell suspicious. Calvino saw Lovell withdraw into himself. "Why didn't Danielson raise hell with Cameron?"

Lovell shook his head, his eyes narrowing, shoulders slightly hunched as if he were about to spring. "You don't know Cameron. I'd seen it happen before. There would be strong cases that Cameron killed."

"Okay, but what specifically was it about Gould's case that made Danielson bring me into the picture?" asked Calvino.

The young lawyer groaned. "I don't know."

"What do you think happened?"

"He knew that Cameron wanted Stiles to stonewall Noah on the case. Andrew made a private deal. It's something you would do to help a friend. Noah's business was going down. He was in big trouble with his company. The drug companies were threatening to cancel his distribution deal. That would be my guess."

"You haven't answered my question. Why would Cameron want to stop Danielson?"

"Because a piracy case might hurt Khun Weerawat's reputation and business. He's an important businessman. The firm represents him. His uncle is honorary chairman of the firm."

Calvino made a note of the name. "How would it hurt Weerawat to help Noah nail the people destroying his business?"

Lovell had researched Weerawat's background as a businessman with investments in restaurants, private schools, franchise fast food, and real estate. These companies paid large retainers and even larger fees to the firm. He also suspected that not all of Weerawat's businesses operated inside the law. From his first week at the law firm, he'd heard rumors but nothing solid about the dark side of Weerawat's empire. His businesses had grown up fast, and Weerawat had become rich and influential. This was coded language for someone who was untouchable, beyond the reach of the law. If that were the case, it made sense to go outside the firm.

"Did anyone know that Danielson had gone cowboy on this case?"

Lovell felt a chill as he thought of himself ending up in a small office above a massage parlor, an ex-lawyer scraping by with two-bit investigations.

"Who knew about Danielson taking on Noah Gould's case? His secretary, maybe a law clerk, a research assistant, someone in the library."

"He was pretty careful. I was close to him. I didn't know about it."

"But you're not Thai."

"I came across a company registered on New Road. I thought you might find that interesting."

He had caught Calvino off-guard. He'd gone to one of the *sois* on New Road for his stake-out. The videotape of the drug piracy operation hadn't been more than two hundred meters from the wharf along the Chao Phraya River. Lovell laid out some documents on Calvino's desk. One was a detailed map of the *soi* with the warehouse circled. "Is that the place where you shot the video?"

Calvino nodded, and looked up from the map. This part of Bangkok wasn't on the tourist map. There were no hotels, shops, or restaurants in the area; it was bleak and dismal rows of shop houses snaking down to the waterfront. "How did you make the connection?"

"Danielson asked me to do a database search on a company name. I got all the shareholders' and directors' lists from the ministry of commerce. I searched the registered address of each company. It's here on that map," said Lovell, putting his finger on the spot. Much of what Lovell had pieced together came from public information, but he needed to know where to look and how to decipher the Thai language documents. "I used the law firm's computer system to check and compare the list of directors and shareholders of that company with every registered company we knew was controlled by Weerawat. I compiled a chart showing the overlapping nominees or proxies. Weerawat's nominees repeatedly showed up on many different companies. Some of Weerawat's shareholders and directors were also used for the company registered at the warehouse. The nominees were maids, drivers, gardeners, and handy-men who were on the payroll."

"What did he tell you about this company?"

"He said check it out. We didn't discuss the background. Or why he wanted me to do the search. He was like that. It was okay with me. I liked the work. I asked him about it. I needed to know how to bill the time. He billed the time to one of Weerawat's companies."

"Didn't you think that was strange?" asked Calvino.

"Danielson said it was for a reorganization of companies and we had to do due diligence on a number of Weerawat's companies. Some of them had big contracts with government agencies. Land deals, housing and road construction, and a big project at the new airport. It wasn't my job to cross-examine my boss." His voice turned edgy; he squirmed in his seat.

"What did he say when you showed him all of this?" Calvino gestured at the stack of documents.

"His face turned white. Like the blood had drained from it."

"A partner who didn't know his client's business structure?"

Lovell shrugged. "I'm telling you how he reacted. You can read it any way you want."

Lovell, without any notes, took Calvino through the complex interlocking shareholders and directorships. He knew every name, address, occupation, and age of the shareholders and directors; how long they had served in their capacity for the company. He even had at his fingertips family connections based on the last name of the nominees.

Calvino's jaw dropped. "How do you do that?"

"That's how my memory works."

"You've got one of those genius memories?"

"I never forget," Lovell said, thinking that Calvino's jaw was about to unhinge.

"I file things in my head, compare them, analyze and dissect them like in science class, when you have to cut open a rat and draw and label all of the organs and muscles. I never had any problem doing that. I could do it in my sleep."

He started to sketch a rat. "That's the superficial fascia."

"Just as I always remembered it," said Calvino. "Don't draw me a rat. Draw me something like a picture of what your law firm does for Weerawat." It was more than a little intimidating to sit across from a genius. If that was how Lovell's talent could be described.

Lovell opened a folder and pulled out a spreadsheet, handing it to Calvino. "It's a list of the active cases involving Weerawat's intellectual property and corporate work. We also represent him in a couple of infringement cases against Chinese companies."

He'd momentarily forgotten that he was no longer part of the "we."

Lovell had begun to trust Calvino. He looked up from the spreadsheet. "I sometimes wondered where someone like Weerawat would hang. It's a location game."

"What kind of game are you talking about?" asked Calvino.

"The Lair. It's a piece of software that lets me guess Weerawat's location within five-percent, plus or minus."

"Did Danielson know about this? Or Cameron?"

Lovell smiled, gestured like a student. "It was my private game."

Calvino was silent, wondering what kind of wheels within wheels and knobs and bolts and circuits Lovell's mind embraced. The Lair had a ring to it; Calvino had his own, everyone needed their lair in which to hide away from the world, to lick the wounds, to rest for another day.

NINETEEN

SUVIT said of his nephew that, after he returned from earning his Ph.D. in America, he seemed to have unlimited energy. What he didn't say was that the sole purpose of that energy was to increase and preserve the fortune of the family. Weerawat was their educated, modern, and media-friendly face. The old man beamed with pride when his nephew's name came up. Inside the firm, Suvit's office was filled with framed photos of his nephew with leading businessmen, politicians, movie stars, and television talk-show hosts. A framed reproduction of Galileo Chini's *The Last Day of the Chinese Year in Bangkok* had been placed above a small Chinese shrine. Danielson's diagnosis of Weerawat had been that he was the classic overachiever. Most cultures produced the driven man who rarely listened to anyone. No one ever started out in life planning a career of shady deals and deception. But some ended up at that end of the road, not feeling even a small amount of shame.

Weerawat had the sheltered childhood—private schools, tutors, summers spent in Canada or America, invitations to the right social events. Each time he came to the law firm, it was as a sort of visiting dignitary. No one dropped rose petals along his path, but more than one secretary and clerk handed him a note with her cell phone number.

Weerawat managed to never look crumpled or tired. He floated on an air cushion of social and political connections. He was someone on the inside hub of business circles, a man who pulled the levers of power with ease and delicacy, in a polished, subtle, understated way.

His great grandfather had arrived from China in 1911. Weerawat was the pinnacle of their shaping and developing the family business into a new age. In his early forties, he had built his own private, secure compound surrounded by a band of loyalists. There had been talk of a cabinet position for him in the next shuffle. He was a man, they said, who didn't need to cut corners because there had been none in his life. In their place were smooth curves that he navigated easily.

⋆

"What kind of work did he give your firm?"

"Mainly real estate and joint ventures."

"Legal work with a foreigner attached to the deal?"

Lovell nodded. "Most of the time."

Cameron made the foreigners feel secure. He sat at the head of the conference table, making certain the foreign partners felt Cameron's job was to protect them.

"When your intellectual property department represented a foreign client, did Weerawat or his uncle ever interfere?"

"They didn't need to. There was an understanding about what outside cases the firm took on."

No wrecking ball punching big holes into other people's business. It was more like a crowbar quietly dismantling a structure. Calvino thought of his mother and the guy named Glenn who ate screws. Cameron had a system to flag cases that were sent to Suvit, who met with his nephew, and Weerawat decided if the case went nowhere. A stealth system, where the lawyers continued to bill the client, make reports, promises, and action lists.

"When was the last time you met Weerawat?"

Lovell sighed. "Recently. At a meeting with Cameron."

"Then I called you."

"And I told you that I couldn't help. That was a mistake."

Lovell recalled how Cameron had told him that Danielson's private case didn't exist as far as the firm was concerned. That he should keep up his billings and never bring up the Gould matter to anyone inside or outside the firm. He should know who his friends were and the meaning of loyalty. And at the end of the lecture, as Cameron wound down from his godlike commands, he'd winked at

Lovell and said, "You need to find a better balance in life."

Calvino listened as Lovell opened up about his relationship with Cameron. According to Lovell, Cameron had advised him to stay fit and stay in the practice of law game. His job, according to Cameron, was to keep the client believing that progress was being made. He recalled conversation months earlier, when Cameron had said he had cautioned him to be practical. There was something for both sides. Look for the middle path. You set up the bust first. Your job was to set up a small-time operation staffed with some cutouts. Have the police arrive and your people with the video cameras to record it. You show the video to the client. The client is happy, the police are happy, the people in power and doing business are happy. Isn't that a worthy goal in life? The problem was Stiles hadn't given Noah Gould anything for coverage, nothing to reduce the heat, and out of frustration he'd asked Danielson for help.

The goal was to make certain that the right people were happy and not in conflict, Cameron had said. Noah had been unhappy. Danielson had also been unhappy for his own reasons. Lovell had been staring in silence at the painting on Calvino's wall.

"Weerawat's uncle, the one in our office, has the same painting in his office," said Lovell. "Only his hangs over some kind of shrine."

Calvino wasn't convinced. "There are lots of paintings with this theme.

"Is this Galileo Chini's *The Last Day of the Chinese Year in Bangkok*?"

The young lawyer read the answer on Calvino's face. "I thought so," said Lovell. "Painted in 1912." Lovell walked over to the painting and pointed at the youthful Chinese man walking in full stride past the dragon as if on an urgent mission. "Suvit said that was his father."

★

As they left the office together, Calvino saw that Ratana had taken more than her usual interest in a client. Lovell was oblivious as she devoured him. Ratana looked dreamy-eyed as she returned to the computer screen. Lovell followed Calvino downstairs to One Hand Clapping. At first he looked confused. Then Lovell pulled the discount coupon out of his jacket pocket and handed it to one of the *yings*.

"It's not your first time," said Calvino watching the coupon pass between them.

"I got it less than an hour ago. From her." Lovell pointed at one of the *yings* who had rushed him.

The *yings* who clustered around Lovell pushed through the entrance of the massage parlor. It was as if they had woken from a deep sleep, smiling. Enthusiasm spread from *ying* to *ying* as they waited to be embraced by Lovell.

"I don't want a massage," said Lovell, holding his hands above his head as if he were surrendering to an overwhelming enemy force.

"Later, later. We're here about Jazz," said Calvino. The mention of the dead *ying's* name was sufficient to free Lovell from his captors. "I want to show you something."

They walked down the corridor, stopping at a shattered door to the VIP room. The *mamasan* arrived on the scene with a cigarette hanging out of the corner of her mouth. She seemed unfazed that Calvino wanted to see the room where Jazz had been found. She chewed on the filter of the cigarette and gestured with her hand for them to go inside. The room had been cleaned up. Sheets had been stripped off the bed. The bloodstains looked like the shadows of sleeping cats.

"Danielson's girlfriend died here," Calvino said. "Her wrists were cut."

Lovell turned pale and looked like he might be sick. He stared at the bed. Shaking his head, he lowered his briefcase to the floor. Behind him the mamasan had put out her cigarette.

One of the *yings* had given her a plastic cup with cola and ice; she crushed ice between her yellowish teeth, swallowing.

"We cleaned up the blood as best as we could. No one will use the room. They're scared of ghosts," said the *mamasan*. She scratched her arm as if to ward off the feeling of the razor haunting the room.

Calvino wanted to see Lovell's reaction to Danielson's mistress. They had died within hours of each other. "Danielson had a girlfriend who worked here. She died the same night he died."

Lovell, his legs wobbly, sat in the chair by the window. Metta's chair, the chair of the crying girl. "I don't believe it. I know his wife, Millie."

Calvino put a hand on Lovell's shoulder. "Yeah, he was married.

But he had Jazz on the side. When I found her dead, Jazz was almost naked. She had no clothes. But she wore a necklace Danielson gave her. I guess that still makes her naked. Danielson gave her some sentimental bullshit line about the necklace being a gift from his mother. Danielson had a habit of using that line on women."

The news visibly shook Lovell as he played with the watch on his wrist. Danielson had given it to him, saying it was an heirloom from his father.

"Are you sure about that?"

"There are some things you can never be sure about. It says something about Danielson. The evening Danielson died I found her. See the door? I had to break it down." Calvino circled around the end of the bed. It seemed small, bare; an empty room like a tomb robbed of its body. He hadn't known her; he couldn't remember her in front with a fistful of discount coupons. At nineteen years old, how much was there to know about someone? She hadn't lived long enough to accumulate enough friends and enemies who knew the details of her life. Like her name, Jazz was like a song that sounded good at the time but was soon forgotten.

"What time did you find her?"

"Around five," said Calvino. "What's on your mind?"

"When Andrew came into the restroom he was very upset. He said that he'd received some bad news."

"Someone might have phoned him about his girlfriend."

Lovell looked out the window. Several taxicab drivers were playing cards at a makeshift table. He could just make out the hand of one player. But he wasn't certain what game they were playing, or the stakes. Having a mainframe memory didn't make it any easier to assemble the pieces and process the infinite possibilities. "I'm not certain what I know anymore."

"A genius admitting he doesn't know." Calvino shook his head, leaned back, a smile crossing his face. "Maybe you are smarter than I thought. Maybe not. It doesn't mean you will be able to fill in the blanks. What you're looking for is information from the street. People who get their information from books are mostly illiterate when it comes to reading the street. It's a different vocabulary."

⋆

Lovell turned away from the window. "More than fake drugs is involved. They have companies ripping off watches, airbags, auto brakes. You name anything with a large profit margin; they're making it. I have the files. The letters, memos, and opinions. It's all here. Take it." Lovell had dug the last of the folders from his handbag. Calvino looked at him across the single bed in the small room. "They are from memory. I copied them out."

This was a different Lovell from the one who had sat in his office. He'd been waiting, deciding whether to give the full or edited version of the law firm's business to Calvino. A walk through Jazz's death scene had made the decision for him. Through the open door, a jazz riff drifted into the room, the tenor sax and piano of Michael Lington's "Two of a Kind."

The *mamasan* had disappeared with her ice and cigarettes and changed the Thai music to jazz. She thought it might make the *farangs* want to stay longer; maybe both of them would take one of the *yings* to another room.

Calvino looked at the stack of files resting on the bed. Leaning against the wall, he watched Lovell's hands moving like a concert pianist, flipping through folders and taking out documents, charts, and graphs. The *mamasan* hadn't switched on the air-conditioning. The temperature inside rose until sweat dripped off the end of Lovell's nose. Calvino continued to watch as Lovell worked to some drumbeat of memory. The kid had been holding back, playing with him, doling out information in small amounts. "Why are you doing this?"

This wasn't the response John Lovell expected. He sat back in the hard chair like a rejected schoolboy. He glanced at the wristwatch, biting his lower lip. Lovell felt that he understood exactly how Jazz had felt. The watch had been from Danielson's father, but maybe that was a lie, too.

"Revenge against your law firm?" Calvino continued.

"Stiles and Cameron wanted to scare me. I've memorized all of the procurement contracts they wrote for Weerawat's companies. But they don't know exactly what I know. Still I let Stiles bully me. I'm not very proud about that," said Lovell, a hitch in his voice, a soft, guttural catch a moment before the first tears rolled down his cheek. "I'm not going to roll over for them."

Calvino arched an eyebrow. "There's a reason that I can understand."

"I thought it was all about money for you."

"Don't forget the purpose of money."

As they walked down the corridor of the massage parlor, the tape had changed to Gerald Albright's "The Night We Fell in Love." On the way out, Calvino told the *mamasan* that she should put that song on a continuous loop. *Farangs* liked the sentiment of the song, what it promised, and repeat customers were mainly romantics who believed in finding love in a place like One Hand Clapping. She grabbed his arm and jerked him to the side. "You help me with the cost of the door." It wasn't as much a request as a command.

Lovell stopped a foot away, turned, thinking Calvino had some business.

"I'll leave you to it," he said.

"Stay where you are," said Calvino.

"You give me two thousand baht," said the *mamasan*.

Her eyes were hard, menacing, determined. "Put a report into Khun Ratana. She handles that side of the business."

The *mamasan* let go of his arm. "Better you pay now."

"Get the money from Khun Ratana." They both knew the *mamasan* wouldn't have the guts to go up the flight of stairs and ask Ratana for the money.

"You break the door. Why you don't pay?"

"Good question. Ratana has the answer. Just ask her."

She had the last word. She called Calvino an *ai hai*, a kind of large, ugly monitor lizard. Thais had been known to kill someone who hurled that insult at them. There was no English equivalent that packed as much hate into one word, nothing that came close to the emotional heat of the insult. Calvino laughed, walked back to Lovell, "Let's get out of here."

"What's she calling you?"

"A term of affection."

"It didn't sound like she was being affectionate."

"That's as affectionate as a mamasan gets when she's squeezing you for money that you won't pay."

TWENTY

CHEF Elmo's cooking school in the afternoon echoed with the sound of Verdi. Speakers positioned on shelves against a wall in the kitchen enveloped the kitchen with opera. Chef Elmo in a bass voice sang the libretto from Verdi's *Otello*, hitting some notes, missing others. His passion almost compensated for his lack of musical talent. No one would have hired him to give singing lessons. But Elmo enjoyed himself, dancing around the kitchen in his chef's gear, swinging his knives, checking his pots, adjusting the flame on the gas stoves. He was like a dictator with a singing disability. The funny thing was, his voice soothed the members of the cooking class. The three women moved their hips to the tempo of the opera. The smell of freshly ground chili peppers overwhelmed the more delicate mint scent. The oven, fired up, glowing red inside, waited as he lifted a casserole and slid it inside. Closing the oven door, Chef Elmo glanced inside the inferno and wiped the sweat off his brow.

"Opera means 'work' in Italian," said Chef Elmo. He'd brushed up on his Italian overnight seeking to reclaim some of the lost ground. The women hadn't said anything but it was clear they now suspected his purported Italian origins.

"I didn't know that," said Ruth. She was letting him off the hook.

"As in work of art?" asked Janet.

"As in real work."

Chef Elmo broke into song. He had scored another point with one of the ladies. "No, you slice like this," he said, taking her knife and demonstrating how to slice a carrot. "And why did you throw that away?"

Ruth stared at the top of the carrot. "Because I always throw that part away."

"In a restaurant we don't throw away food."

"What will you do with this?" She held up the green carrot top, challenging him.

"It goes into the soup over there."

"Of course," said Ruth. "Silly me." There was a hint of something dark and unsettling in her voice.

"Democracy never works in the bedroom or kitchen," said McPhail.

Janet stared at him, raising a large spoon she'd been using to stir one of the pots, looking as if she might throw it at him. McPhail raised his arm to shield his face. "I was joking."

"No one is laughing," said Ruth.

He slowly looked around the room. It wasn't true; Chef Elmo was laughing. That was something. But he also understood what Ruth had meant; none of the women were laughing. They were the ones who counted. If they weren't laughing, then it wasn't funny.

The Fab Four (they still counted Millie Danielson, whom they considered to be on sabbatical leave) worked like slaves over the cutting board and stove, listening to Elmo's singing above the *Otello* tape as the out-of-tune chef strutted down the line, cracking the whip. Ruth smoothed her apron, lifted her hands, giving the chef a little wave, then she measured out two cups of flour for the eggplant gnocchi. She looked relaxed, carefree.

"With men, it's understanding the moving parts," Janet said. "Assuming the parts aren't too tired or old to move."The others laughed.

"That doesn't look right," Debra said, pointing out a limp eggplant in the acceptable pile.

"It's borderline." Janet picked it up and examined it again.

"It looks okay to me," said McPhail.

"Check it again, Janet. That eggplant should have a pair of large breasts. I think Mr. McPhail is a breast man. Am I right?" said Debra, using a large spoon to shove them into a breast-like formation.

The other women snickered. Creases webbed out from their eyes. Real, genuine laughter works those muscles around the eyes, like focusing a pair of binoculars, making the image of delight written in lines.

"I think that Italian is so much more sexy than Thai," said Janet.

The good thing about Chef Elmo was he not only taught them how to make a decent eggplant gnocchi, he left them to tune in to whatever emotional frequency they collectively agreed was the right one to set the mood for their mincing, chopping, washing, and cutting. Preparing food was physical. The women worked with their hands, the white skin rubbed raw, the red spreading out from their fingers to their palms. They inhaled the cooking smells. They felt the weight of the knife.

The group had evolved, over the many cooking classes, a shorthand language of women in close proximity, slang, and green zone ghetto lingo, expat talk. McPhail caught only fragments: men and whores and *katoey*.

It wasn't much, but it was enough to get an idea of the destination of the conversation. Janet laughed, dropping an egg on the floor. Ruth, snorting with laughter, blew flour over the table onto Debra. The laugher increased. Whatever secret they shared suggested that it had been at someone else's expense. It was the kind of laughter that bonds people against a common enemy.

Shafts of light extinguished one after another until there was total darkness. It was a power outage. The darkness dulled the laughter until it died out altogether.

"The power will be on in a minute," said Chef Elmo, illuminated by the glow of the oven behind him. The Verdi opera ended. The kitchen was not only dark but silent. The glow of the oven cast a reddish spell.

In the darkness of the kitchen anything was possible.

McPhail felt up a thigh. There was no resistance. He somehow felt that might be the case, even though he had no idea who the thigh belonged to.

When the power came on, Vincent Calvino was standing in the middle of the kitchen. It was as if he had materialized out of thin air. McPhail's face flushed red, an instant before the lights went back on, he had taken his hand from the thigh.

Debra gasped, involuntarily clutching at her throat. "My God, it's that private detective."

"You frightened me, too," said Janet. "You didn't make any

noise." Her hands clutched at her throat.

"He's not supposed to make noise," said Ruth. "That's what they are taught in private detection school. Otherwise how would he follow someone without him being noticed?"

"Or her," said McPhail. "He does have women he follows." Somehow it came out the wrong way.

"I bet the women you follow know how to work in the dark. Isn't that right, Mr. Calvino?" said Ruth.

Debra wiped her hands on her apron. It had been her thigh that McPhail had felt during the temporary blackout. "The really bad things always happen at night. Or in the dark. If you can't stomach blackouts, well, I think it would be very hard to do your job. We had one private detective who was just so hopeless."

"Debra, don't you think we should cut more onions," said Janet, giving her a gentle nudge. Both Ruth and Janet were rolling their eyes, wondering why Debra would say something that shouldn't have been said.

"You've hired other investigators. They didn't do the job. Now you've hired me," said Calvino. "Ask Janet if I did the job."

Janet's face flushed red. She was speechless. Picking up a knife, she cut onions until tears filled her eyes. Calvino let his observation hang like a pop-up fly ball to right field.

"The others disappointed us," said Debra. Her knife slipped and fell to the floor. She leaned down to pick it up.

"How many others?"

"Two," said Ruth. Calvino had been concentrating on Ruth. Noah, her husband, Danielson, and himself had a connection. He wondered how much she knew about her husband's side deal with Andrew Danielson.

"Three," said Debra as she washed the blade under the water tap.

"Can't get the numbers straight."

"Technically it was three because there was that guy who asked me to go to bed with him," said Ruth. *Some men are turned on by women in big hats*, thought Calvino."What you're saying is that you have a considerable history of hiring private detectives."

"You make it sound like we did something wrong. We didn't," said Janet. She turned to Debra, "Enough onions, already. I'm starting to cry. I don't want to cry."

Calvino said to Debra in Italian that she shouldn't cry. He had to explain it to her. Chef Elmo listened a few feet away, shooting dark, deadly looks at Calvino and then at McPhail. When the opera ended, Chef Elmo, seeing his control of the kitchen had once again been lost, stormed out, throwing up his hands and talking to himself.

★

Infidelity cases were big income earners in the investigation business. Emotions raw and festering, money was never an object. That was a good thing in any business. As with anything that good, others came to the party, expecting a place at the table, and gorged on the feast. "Private eye" was just a two-word statement. No degree, no standard, no oversight; the perfect condition for grifters who hung around bars, talking to *farangs* who had fallen in love with a bar *ying* and proposed marriage, or with some *ying* they'd met long-distance through an Internet chat room or dating service. Maybe a mule kicked some of them in the head, so that at the last moment, common sense made them decide it might be a good idea to check her story.

Small minor points in the narrative needed clarification, such as whether she was already married with a bamboo house full of snot-nosed kids playing barefoot in the dirt. Turning up the paranoia dial on the relationship was what private eyes did best.

Calvino had mostly steered clear of cases from *farangs* who hired him to check out whether their Thai girlfriend was faithful. These clients were middle-aged men insecure about the loyalty of bar *yings*, forgetting the basic rule: the object of their affection worked in a business where sexual loyalty was an occupational disability.

When they got his report, some broke down and cried. They couldn't believe that the promises, the guarantees of fidelity, hadn't just fallen apart; fidelity had never existed. And the best he could do was to deliver the report and photographs. It was like an X-ray revealing a hairline fracture that ran through every bone in the body. The messenger of a person's worst fears was never a hero. Knocking the ground out from under their reality made them angry, sad, embarrassed, or ashamed. No one liked to discover that the shark fin in their bowl of soup was swimming at them.

When an expat woman hired him to track a husband, the dynamics changed.

"You didn't get what you wanted," said Calvino. "You should have told me."

Ruth groaned. "It wasn't a secret."

"Now you're having second thoughts."

"And third and fourth thoughts," said Debra with a sigh.

"Ladies, you never told me about the other private eyes," said McPhail. He looked at the three women. Debra smiled, Ruth looked at her makeup in a compact mirror, and Janet had a faraway, distracted look. "You should have told me. Vincent's my friend."

"Friend?" asked Debra. "Is that why you spied on us, Ed? Told him about our *private* conversations? You overheard us talking. How could you do that?"

"Why wouldn't I tell him?" asked McPhail.

The hook had been baited. She waited for Calvino's jaws to snap down.

"I'll come back another time," said Calvino, spitting out the hook.

Ruth, who had snapped the compact closed, reached over and grabbed Calvino's arm. "Please stay. Debra isn't really upset with you, are you, Debra?"

Debra blinked her eyes, swallowed a laugh before it could escape from her lips. The flour from her hands smeared on her face, giving her a ghost-like appearance.

Calvino sat down in a chair and opened his briefcase. "Let's talk this through," he said. "Because I'm confused with what you want. And I'm confused that Debra gave me the wrong phone number for Millie Danielson. So as you can see, ladies, I have some issues to clear up."

"I may have written down the wrong number," said Debra.

"Can we try again?"

Calvino handed her a pen and piece of paper. She tapped the pen against her lip. "And Ruth, Noah and Andrew were good friends. Am I right?"

"What does that have to do with *my* concerns?"

"When I do an investigation, a man's friends are a woman's concerns. They tell me where he socializes and the kind of people I am dealing with. Does that answer your question? Now if someone would give me Millie Danielson's phone number I can get on with my investigation."

He paused long enough for his words to sink in, waiting for Debra to write down the correct phone number. Ruth and Janet stood beside her, whispering. Chef Elmo suddenly appeared out of the back.

"Secrets, secrets, I can't stand secrets," said Chef Elmo. He popped the pan of eggplant gnocchi into the oven and left the kitchen in a huff. He had disappeared as quickly as he had arrived.

"Tell him about the book," said Debra.

Janet sighed. "Millie read the book first."

"It changed our lives," said Ruth. "The way we think about men."

They exchanged knowing smiles between themselves.

TWENTY-ONE

SAMUEL Thomas had been someone who hadn't shown the slightest amount of confusion about what women wanted or what they feared the most about their marriage. He marketed *The Risk of Infidelity Index* in such a way that it had been irresistible. Thomas had started up the *Index* as a hobby business in Paris, Texas. A billionaire born-again Christian, Thomas had endowed a fidelity foundation with several million dollars, using the donation as a tax deduction. Samuel's main insight was that the holy mission of the bible was designed to promote monogamy. He might have halfway believed in the venture. But his stroke of genius was to exploit women's anxieties about men. Samuel Thomas understood that such insecurities were as old as human history. What he invented was a product designed specifically to help married women who were going abroad with their husbands, a small but highly lucrative market. His *Index* confirmed women's hardwired feeling that men were nothing short of walking sexual catastrophes, and their repulsion by and attraction to that sexuality at the same time. The Dow-Jones-sounding name added an element of science and rationality, the whiff of a system or method that had a factual, objective basis.

If you are going to a foreign country with your husband, went the pitch, then you must buy *The Risk of Infidelity Index*. It also was filled with homespun advice. Take hot yoga classes, the *Index* advised; a wife who calms her mind and keeps her body slim will have her husband rushing home from the office.Don't accept inferior private investigators. Fire them unless they are professional.

★

"Why are you staring at me like that?" asked Janet.

"McPhail says you want to fire me. Now that makes sense. You fired two or three others. I'm next in line for the ax, is the way I figure it."

The three women turned their attention to McPhail as if a Judas among them had made the ultimate betrayal. He had been privy to their private thoughts. Debra had even let him feel up her thigh. What an outrage! They'd forgotten, McPhail was no different from any other man. The fact that he was in their cooking class had lulled them into the false belief that he was on their side, one of them. Instead he carried back their private doubts to Calvino.

"I thought we could trust you," said Janet under her breath but loud enough that everyone could hear.

"But that's what you said." McPhail defended himself before the first verbal attacks were launched. Appealing to the truth cut no ice with them. It was beside the point.

"No one ever said that Mr. Calvino should be fired," said Janet.

"Man, you were all upset after you found out that Howard hooked up with a *katoey*. You said that you didn't want to know this. It was too much."

They had said these things. But that had been then, not now. The problem with men was their failure to understand the difference between those two temporal states of thinking and being.

"But Debra and I have decided. We want you to continue your investigation," said Ruth.

The others nodded. "Please, Mr. Calvino. We insist."

Calvino's law: Never be surprised in an infidelity case to be fired and rehired in the same week.

Something must have happened to explain the turnaround.

"But that's not what you said yesterday," said McPhail.

"That was yesterday," said Ruth.

Debra still hadn't written down Millie Danielson's phone number. She looked up from the paper, nodding in support of Ruth.

They left it to Ruth to explain the change of heart.

They had been initially upset when they had heard about Janet's husband caught cuddling a retrofit in a hotel coffee shop. But the fact that Howard's wife, a factory original, had been replaced by a *katoey* translated into a perverse kind of good news: Janet had suddenly lost her most basic fear that another woman might replace her. She had reclaimed her lost power and, having the advantage, she wasn't about to let off the pressure. She had told friends how Howard had made her swear that she wouldn't show the pictures that Calvino had taken to anyone he knew at work or to his friends. He was desperate that no one close to him should know about his specially friend.

She had received from Calvino her husband's secret life, and he now lived with the fear she might expose him. What had he been thinking?

And what did Janet want from Howard in return for her silence? She demanded what every wife dreams of: she made Howard promise to do whatever she wanted. *Anything* she wanted. Whenever she wanted it. She had mastered Chef Elmo's cooking class main lesson: make the others in your kitchen your slave, throw away nothing, brook no dissent, command and punish at will. He'd been an excellent mentor.

Ruth and Debra were excited by Janet's revelation. Janet scored with a knock out one minute into the first round. Her husband hadn't seen the right cross that landed him sprawling and helpless. They couldn't wait to get the right kind of dirt on their husbands. For the others it was clear that short of death, the only way to bring a husband into light was an extreme measure.

"We want the same results as Janet," said Debra.

"What you did was beautiful," said Ruth.

"Mr. Calvino, I am personally grateful," said Janet.

The other women smiled, nodding their heads.

"Man, I could use some fresh air," said McPhail.

Calvino pointed at him. "Stay put. You aren't going anywhere."

"I like a forceful man," said Debra.

They wanted dirt on their men. Real, honest to God mud. Calvino listened to them competing for his attention.

"When McPhail told me that you'd changed your minds, I took on other business."

There was a gasp from Ruth. "You're saying that we've been fired by you?"

He touched Ruth's hand. "I want information about emails between your husband and Andrew Danielson over the last couple of months."

She pulled away her hand. "I thought you were working for me? Now you want me to spy on my own husband?"

McPhail rolled his eyes, slammed a lid down on a pot.

"That's exactly what I want you to do. Download the emails on a thumb drive and give it to me."

Ruth turned away and left the kitchen without saying another word.

"You've made her very upset, Mr. Calvino," said Janet. "We don't trust our husbands. But we do love them. So don't ask us to do anything funny."

Chef Elmo walked back into the kitchen and opened the oven door. The room filled with the scent of eggplant. "Ten more minutes. Then we can eat," he said.

Calvino's stomach groaned. He was hungry. He explained that after McPhail had told him how unhappy they were with him, another client had offered him a significant job. That was Lovell. It was a job. But they hadn't gotten around to payment.

"Is that your stomach growling?" Janet asked.

Calvino felt that his guts had suddenly taken on a life of their own, gurgling like a drowning man. His shoulder started to ache as if it were the bass section of a dysfunctional band.

"You must be very hungry," said Debra. She cut a piece of eggplant, slid it on a plate and put it before Calvino.

"We need to find a way to help each other. You know what I want. And I can deliver what you want," he said. He showed no reaction to the eggplant.

They watched him carefully. It was one of those Bangkok eggplant standoffs with no one giving ground.

Calvino reached over, picked up a fork, speared the eggplant and swallowed it straight down.

Ruth quietly returned and stood slightly apart, holding a plate given to her by Chef Elmo.

"You will help us?" asked Debra.

He stuffed his mouth again, juice spilling down the corners.

"He'll do it," said McPhail.

"Does he speak for you?" asked Ruth.

Debra had refilled Calvino's plate. She had cut him two large pieces of mushroom pizza. He bit into a slice, holding it in his hands.

"Show me Noah's emails to and from Danielson."

"Why don't I help you contact Millie Danielson? She would have Andrew's emails to Noah. He's dead. It's no problem, I think, for her to do this," said Ruth.

Calvino knew this was as good as he was going to get. He grabbed it. Like the eggplant, when a man was hungry, it didn't much matter that there was better grub down the street. He had something on his plate. Going with what he had made him feel like he was finally on the road leading to the place where he wanted to end up.

TWENTY-TWO

AROUND mid-afternoon a hundred and fifty people assembled at Wat Thong for Andrew Danielson's cremation. They were mostly *farangs* with a few Thais scattered among them. Danielson's secretary, driver, and maid formed their own group in the corner. Plastic chairs had been set in rows facing the cremation oven. Half of the chairs were occupied. A cat scampered across the open area. Dogs slept under some of the unoccupied chairs. They took no notice of the cat. The organizers had expected a larger crowd. Mourners milled around the open concrete grounds around the crematorium, looking for shade outside the *salas* that lined the sides of the main courtyard. Small rooms decorated with funeral urns, chairs, and flowers. Floor fans circulating the air.

Groups of mourners from the law office clustered together, whispering, waiting. The heat of the midday sun, bright and unrelenting, gave a sense that they were all being slowly cremated. Millie Danielson, in a neat tailored black dress, stood closest to the elevated platform with Danielson's coffin in the center. She received people who stood in line, the queue snaking down the stairs and around the corner. Each mourner, having reached the top of the stairs, said a few words, shook her hand, kissed her on the cheek, wiped away their tears and, after paying their respects, departed, placing a small piece of sandalwood shaped into a flower on the coffin. The Thais called it *dok jan*; it was their way of saying goodbye. Millie was in her early fifties, but with her blonde hair, smooth skin, and long, unblemished neck, she looked ten years younger.

Ruth, Janet, and Debra approached her together. They all hugged each other, smearing their eye makeup and lipstick. Ruth Gould's hat was knocked crooked. Millie reached out and straightened it. They laughed, and then cried again. Janet told her how much they had been missing her and that they hoped she would come back to class soon. Debra was going to say something about Vincent Calvino but Ruth stopped her, saying it wasn't the time or the place. The Fab Four had their brief reunion and then separated again. Noah Gould followed next, holding Millie's hands, shaking his head, tears in his eyes.

After the women and Noah had left, Lovell was next in line. His instinct was to follow after Noah. But it was too late; Millie had already caught his eyes and nodded for him to step forward. Lovell wore a dark suit and black necktie. Millie offered her hand.

"Andrew felt so proud of you. It was as if you were his son," Mrs. Danielson said.

He was at a loss for words. Finally he said, "I miss him." He embraced her.

"We all do," she said.

"If there is anything that I can do . . ."

He didn't know what else to say, and no doubt she had heard the same phrase a hundred times since her husband died. Was this the best he could do? "What I mean is you are going through a lot. There may be things on the legal side that you don't understand. Just give me a call."

"Andrew was right about you. You are such a nice boy. And I know he wouldn't have liked the way Cameron has treated you. He didn't have the decency to wait until the services for Andrew were finished before he fired you. It's terrible."

There she was comforting him as an attendant lit the cremation oven for her husband. The first time he had met her was at dinner in an expensive French restaurant. Danielson had flown him to Bangkok for interviews.

Millie had been kind to him, offering to help him with the logistics of an international move. At that first dinner, flashes of sadness showed, but she quickly brought them under firm control. At her husband's cremation, she was using that skill, he thought. Others in the queue behind were becoming restless, grumbling about Lovell taking too much time.

"We'll talk later," he said. Lovell had already worked out how he would ask her about the wristwatch supposedly inherited from Andrew's father.

"That would be a very good idea, John. Thank you for coming. I know how difficult it must be for you with everyone from the firm here today."

As he climbed down the stairs, he looked around for Noah Gould. He saw him in the distance and quickly crossed the pavement under the hot sun.

"Noah, I'd like to talk to you," said Lovell. "I worked with Andrew."

"I can't believe he's gone," said Noah.

"The investigator he hired has got the evidence Danielson asked him to get for you." He blurted it out and was immediately sorry. No context had been laid out, no winding slowly down the road before gathering speed.

Noah Gould looked terrified. "I don't know what you're talking about."

Gould turned to walk away but Lovell pulled his arm.

"What are you doing?" he asked Lovell.

"I know what happened," Lovell said.

"Please keep your voice down."

"I checked Andrew's personal client records with the law firm's database. Your name didn't appear. He risked his career to help you. Because he knew Avenant Pharma was getting nowhere with Stiles."

"I really don't know what you're talking about." He pulled his arm out of Lovell's grasp. As he left, Apisak came out of nowhere and blocked Lovell's path. He saw Noah and his wife quickly leave through the far exit.

"Did you finally get your bow tie on straight?" asked Apisak.

"You turn up at some quite interesting times," said Lovell. Lovell turned around and saw another group of lawyers watching them. "I was trying to have a conversation with a client and here you are in my face."

"I heard you got the boot."

News of failure traveled at the speed of light; news of success never broke the sound barrier. "Bad news travels fast."

"The bamboo telegraph is even faster."

Apisak grinned as if something Lovell had said was funny. Lovell reminded himself that Thais often grinned not only when they were happy but when they were feeling pain, loss of face, shy, or embarrassed. The smile was the default setting for the whole range of human emotions. That made their faces difficult to read. Like first-class poker players, no one could easily guess the hand they were holding.

He associated Apisak with Danielson's last moments. The last time he had met him had been in the restroom of the hotel where Andrew Danielson had taken two Zoloft pills from Apisak, swallowed them, gone into a stall, pulled down his trousers, and died.

"You're glad that I was fired," said Lovell.

"Don't say that, John. These things happen. A year from now, you'll be back in Los Angeles where you'll be working at some big firm, and what you'll remember is a strange land where things didn't quite work out. No big deal. You have options. And that is everything. So don't take it so hard. Move on to bigger and better things. Getting fired was the best career move you could make."

Lovell wasn't buying it. He couldn't help looking at Apisak's eyeglass frames. The frames were out of balance, sloping slightly to the right. The crooked frames threw off the entire angle of his face. He looked slightly dopey.

"Why did you come here? To keep an eye on Noah Gould?" asked Lovell. Reaching into his pocket, he took out a small tool kit with a tiny screwdriver. The steel glimmered in the sunlight.

"I came because Khun Andrew was a colleague. It is our custom to pay respects when a colleague dies."

"A colleague?" Nothing in Lovell's memory suggested that Danielson had ever thought of Apisak as a colleague. He couldn't ever remember his name coming up. Not ever. "I am certain his widow will appreciate your gesture," said Lovell, slipping the tiny screwdriver into his pocket. He started to walk away but Apisak walked alongside him.

"As a goodwill gesture, let me give you a suggestion."

"You mean recommendation."

"I mean something to think about seriously. Don't go doing anything crazy."

"Like what?"

"Making a problem."

"For you? How would I be making a problem for you?"

"I think you know."

"No, I don't know. Tell me what kind of problem you mean?"

Apisak grabbed Lovell's arm. The man who had charmed the Oxford and Cambridge dinner crowd had some hard edges. He could be all fangs and fins and scaly sides. "I am trying to be your friend. Stay away from Noah Gould."

He didn't sound remotely friendly.

Why shouldn't I talk to him?"

A coldness in Apisak's eyes struck Lovell as he felt a sharp pain. Apisak was twisting his arm. The pain shot straight through his body. The unexpected warning, followed by a physical confrontation, sent the message that this wasn't the polite, witty man who had delivered the speech at the dinner. "Khun Weerawat isn't someone you want as an enemy." He let go of Lovell's arm, brushed the lapels on Lovell's suit, the smile reappearing.

Cameron came around the corner and brushed against Lovell, knocking him into Apisak. It took Cameron a second to recover and use his favorite ploy of turning a defense into an offense.

"You two are hiding out in a corner, and look to be up to no good. This is a funeral. No one would know it looking at you." He was carefully reading Lovell's face. Surprise, shock, anger, and a pinch of fear played across Lovell's face.

"He offered me a job," said Lovell. This set Cameron back on his heels.

"A job?" Cameron's lips narrowed, his voice a hoarse whisper. He could see from Lovell's face that this was a lie.

Apisak hunched his shoulder, glanced at his watch, then at Lovell. "I'll catch up with you later. Got to go." He walked a couple of steps, turned, and looked at Cameron. "Make certain he is on the plane to Los Angeles."

Cameron set his jaw and stared at his shoes. It was the first time that Lovell had ever seen anyone intimidate his boss, make him back down.

Apisak walked away. Cameron watched him disappear.

"Looks like I failed your test," said Lovell.

"I made a mistake, John." He strained to hear Cameron's whisper above the voices of the mourners. Cameron's voice trailed off into a vapor of regret. "Forget about Andrew. Forget about us."

"I thought I'd been hired because of my memory."

Cameron's face looked drawn, tired. "I like you, John. Don't make things more difficult than they need be."

"Apisak said that I was going to Los Angeles," said Lovell.

Cameron reached into his jacket and removed an airline ticket. "I have a business-class ticket. I'll arrange for someone to drive you to the airport. It's all for the best."

Lovell stood staring at the ticket and when he looked up, Cameron had vanished into the crowd. Apisak reappeared, a false smile on his face, and nodded at the ticket. "You got it. That's good, John. Very good."

He glared at Apisak. "Is that the same deal you gave Noah?"

★

Months earlier, Lovell's future with the firm had been ironclad; he was guaranteed to make partner. He *was* the firm's future. All these reassuring words had come from Danielson, who had invited him to a private dinner party. That evening his boss had been in an expansive mood. Afterwards, Millie had left the two of them alone in the living room, the windows overlooking the nightscape of Bangkok. It was a dramatic view of the skyscrapers running along Sukhumvit Road and the lake beside the Queen Sirikit Conference Center. Danielson had opened a bottle of brandy, poured two glasses, and handed one to Lovell. Andrew stood at the window looking out.

"To your future in the firm." He raised his glass and touched the rim of Lovell's brandy glass.

Lovell raised his glass and stood beside Danielson, looking out at the night.

"Did you ever wonder how Cameron came to *be* Cameron?"

He hadn't been certain at first what Andrew had meant. Had Cameron once been someone other than Cameron? It was a story that Danielson's brandy had inspired that evening.

"Cameron started off at a powerhouse bold-name law firm in New York. But after a number of years, it didn't look like he was going to make partner. He'd had word from a senior lawyer that the committee was passing him over for a partnership. But the firm still wanted to keep him. He had certain skills they valued. Cameron had gone to university in San Francisco, where he had stumbled upon a psychologist who had done pioneering research on reading faces. It was half medical mumbo jumbo about the number of muscles. What struck Cameron was that once you understood how to read expressions, you were in the driver's seat. It was very difficult for people to lie to you without your seeing it on their face.

"He mastered a couple of thousand expressions. The ones that were the most important were the involuntary ones. The expressions no one can really control. Not long after he learned that this parlor trick wasn't going to get him a partnership, he met Khun Suvit, who was in New York. The family was buying a building in Brooklyn and the law firm was handling the transaction. They got onto the subject of reading expressions. Khun Suvit is from the old Chinese school that says you never do business with anyone unless you have a master who can read the face of the stranger. Was his a wooden face? Or fire? Or was the face one of earth, metal, or water?

"Suvit carried around with him a lot of family photographs, and he explained how a Chinese master would read them. Cameron was quiet and waited until Suvit finished, and then he studied the expressions. One after another, he was able to describe the emotion of each person with deadly accuracy. He had caught Suvit off guard. The next day, Suvit insisted that Cameron go to Brooklyn and meet with his company's owners, the manager, and someone who wanted to invest in the project. Again Cameron cut to the heart of each person, making a personality profile that Suvit received as something that came from the gods.

"Suvit introduced him to Weerawat, who brought along an album of pictures. It was filled with employees, gardeners, maids, bodyguards, partners, school friends, and girlfriends. They spent six hours straight going through the album. Firings, demotions, dismissals, and disappearances followed. This was fifteen years ago. It was a test. Cameron went through every picture, studying the expressions and making conclusions about the emotions on the people's faces. Several people in the album disappeared after that meeting. A week later, Suvit offered Cameron a deal. Two million dollars deposited in an offshore account and his own law firm in Bangkok. He could build up the law firm in any way he saw fit, but his main duty was to help the family business. To pinpoint faces to avoid, faces to send packing, faces to be trusted. He got another three hundred grand a year offshore. The funny thing was how little of the Thai language Cameron ever learned. Suvit discouraged him from learning more than the usual left, right Thai."

Lovell sniffed his brandy.

"Left, right Thai?" he asked.

Danielson grinned. "Thailand is full of *farangs* who know enough Thai to tell a taxi driver to turn left or turn right, but their language ability drops off after that. They try the left, right Thai in an office or shop and no one can understand them. In the bedroom with a hooker, they pretend they're fluent. But they're not. That's left, right Thai, and that pretty much explains Cameron's Thai speaking ability. But that doesn't matter, he reads the Thais better than anyone who can speak the language like a native."

"Why are you telling me this?"

"I want you to remember that whenever you talk with Cameron, don't think you can bullshit him. Or that you can cover up what you are really thinking. It won't happen. Your face will give you away."

Lovell had felt from the first day he had been interviewed that Cameron had wanted his memory skill in the same way that Suvit had wanted Cameron's skill in reading faces. "He didn't ask me anything about law. He was only interested in my memory. What's the deal?"

Danielson refilled his brandy glass and then Lovell's glass. He paced in front of the window, looking out at the view as if something in the night had been drawing him. "You're right. Cameron is intrigued by your memory. He's been looking to hire a lawyer with an eidetic memory. Then you came along and fit the bill. I don't have to tell you there are hundreds of thousands of lawyers looking for work."

"They didn't get a law degree because they had no memory."

"They can memorize. Yes. But do they have a perfect memory?" Danielson's shook head. "Why should you be surprised or upset, John? Your memory has always been your greatest asset."

"There's more to law than just memory," said Lovell. "Take the ability to work with clients. Make them feel comfortable and secure."

"Cameron assumes you can handle clients."

"I don't know why he would assume that. He doesn't know me."

Danielson sipped his brandy, wondering if Lovell would come around. "Cameron has great plans for you, and sees your potential for the law firm's clients. That's the bottom line. He's in love with your mind. That's not a bad thing, John."

"Did Cameron say what love making plans he had for my mind?" His hand shook and he put down the glass. Danielson's laugh echoed off the walls. He couldn't ever recall him laughing. Suddenly Lovell felt uncomfortable, and he needed air. It might have been the brandy, he told himself. But he knew that wasn't true. No matter what else he had to offer, it always came down to one thing: his eidetic memory. It wasn't who he was, he thought. But it didn't matter what he thought; it was the opinion of others, like Cameron. "Just explain to me what I will do in the firm?"

Danielson shifted the brandy around his glass, sniffed it, and then drank. "For instance, you could memorize a highly complex structure of interlocked companies. There would be no other record except in your brain. No backup documents, no computer files. The storage would be in your gray matter. But first he needs to trust you totally."

"Cameron plans on testing me?"

A smile crossed Danielson's face. It was clear from the way he glanced at his watch and turned that he wasn't going to answer Lovell's question. He had already fished his keys from his trousers.

"You look a little pale. Why don't we walk down to the street together?"

On the street, a taxi pulled up. They shook hands and Danielson slammed the taxi door after Lovell got inside. Standing on the curb, Danielson waved as Lovell's taxi departed. Lovell turned in his seat and saw his boss climb into another taxi.

The light changed and Lovell's taxi turned right, and Danielson's taxi disappeared in the traffic. He thought that it was odd to walk him to the street, wave him off, and then get into another taxi. Sitting in the back of his taxi, Lovell wondered what kind of test Cameron had in mind. And when he would be informed that he had passed.

★

At Danielson's funeral service, Lovell still wondered about that night after the dinner party when his boss had climbed in the taxi and disappeared. Not that it mattered. What did matter was Danielson had protected him. That shield was gone. He was fair game and the only question in Lovell's mind was who would blink first.

Lovell had crossed halfway through the parking lot when he heard his name called. He knew her voice, and he remembered that tone of high indignation when she was angry. He stopped and waited for Siri to catch up. She needed a moment to catch her breath once she had caught up with Lovell. He had caught a glimpse of her earlier at the funeral. She had been standing near Stiles, who looked like a bat hanging from an old church belfry. She had slipped away when Stiles came out from the shadows and told him to forget the road to success.

"Don't you know that you are a freak? Always touching other people. Untying and tying their ties. Messing with their glasses. Looking at their shoelaces. And now you're running away from your boss's funeral. How can you be so lame?"

She had done the Thai thing: waited until she could be alone with him. A one-on-one chance discussion in a neutral place would limit her potential loss of face. Confronting him in the parking lot of the *wat* was the perfect place. She could accuse him of his brain fart tics and condemn him without any direct witness.

"Hi, Siri. I've been trying to call you. I called you dozens of times. But you won't return my calls."

"Do you have any idea what you've put me and my family through?"

The photograph taken with the *katoey* pawing him in the parking lot of the hotel would have made for an interesting dinner conversation at her household.

"I thought that when two people really loved each other they stuck by them through the difficult times," he said. "If you ever loved me."

She clenched her fists. He thought she might hit him. "You have no idea how much you've made me suffer. When my mother saw that picture, she cried. And my father had to face the people he works with. You made my mother and father miserable. If you had killed someone it would have been better. I never want you to phone me or try to see me again."

It was a genuinely impressive performance, thought Lovell.

She had cut him loose in front of a two-year-old BMW in the parking lot of a *wat*, the black smoke from the cremation chimney curling skyward. Another member of the law firm walked past. He nodded and Lovell nodded in return. They waited until he had disappeared.

"You want to break up? You don't need my permission."

"How can I possibly see you after what has happened?"

"You can do whatever you want to do. It's okay."

She swung at him; it was a windmill punch and easily missed as Lovell stepped to the side. "Don't ever talk that way to me."

"Cameron said my new duty was to forget. Why don't I start with us?"

Her anger propelled one more failed attempt. This time he caught her fist in his hand, held it for a moment, leaned forward and kissed her forehead. "Have a good life," he said.

Tears welled in her eyes. "Good," she said. "I'm sick of babysitting you." She turned away but he grabbed her arm.

"What do you mean, babysitting me?"

She tried to break away from his hold but he was too strong. "Nothing. Let me go."

"The firm paid you to look after me. That's it, isn't it? To keep me in line. Who did you report to? Was it Cameron? Or did you report to Cameron, Danielson, and Stiles? Your little illiterate essays must have made interesting reading for them."

"They made a mistake hiring you," she said.

He let go of her arm and watched her hurry back to the main pavilion. As she disappeared through the main gate of the *wat*, he thought, *I have no job, or legal career, and no future in Thailand.* She had used the same phrase that Cameron had used. He'd been a mistake. Soon she disappeared, and he had never felt so thoroughly rejected. Short of jumping in the cremation fire with Danielson, he knew he had to step back and do something. Lawyers were supposed to examine all of the options to solving a problem. Apisak's advice was to fly back to Los Angeles. Cameron had given him a business-class ticket and requested a memory wipe of everything he had learned about the law firm. He pulled the ticket envelope out of his pocket, flipped through it. It was a one-way ticket. He smiled, put the ticket back into the envelope. The departure date was forty-eight hours away. What would Danielson have done?

He wouldn't have run. That wasn't in Danielson's nature. He was a fighter. Lovell turned and looked back at the *wat*. Smoke curling skyward from the crematorium. That was all that was left of Danielson: smoke and ashes. Should it end here in the cremation fire? Should he forget everything? Danielson had stood beside him, guided him, and given him a chance to prove himself. Or had he been just like Siri, another set of eyes for Cameron? He wasn't sure of anything or anyone.

Lovell walked through the grounds of the *wat* and out onto Sukhumvit; he climbed the stairs to the Skytrain. When the train came, he found an empty seat and looked down at the wristwatch Danielson had given him. All around him in the car were ordinary-looking people, going about their ordinary business. He recalled the image of his ticket from his memory and focused on the departure time as if his memory might also locate a message inside that information, waiting for him to discover it.

The train stopped, and new passengers pushed and shoved their way into the car. Two *yings* looked at him, whispering and smiling. He returned their smile. "There are lots of other women," he told himself. "Siri who?" Perhaps forgetting wasn't such a bad idea after all. They smiled again, and one of the *yings* brushed back her hair, her eyes sparkling and happy.

It seemed, for a moment, that the Skytrain car was filled with available smiling women.

One of the *yings* stood in front of him. "Hi," she said.

"I've been dumped," Lovell whispered to himself.

He wasn't focusing on the attention of the woman.

"What did you say?"

"I just broke up with my girlfriend," he said, thinking of Apisak's face as he looked at the business ticket in Lovell's hand.

The *ying* standing above him in the Skytrain smiled. She sighed, "Broken heart?" she asked.

He looked up at her. "Can I buy you a coffee?"

TWENTY-THREE

CALVINO leaned forward on both elbows, as he stared at himself in a small compact mirror perched on top of two books beside his computer keyboard. A towel, tied around his neck, showed the curled debris of hair trimmings, a mixture of brown and gray. He coaxed a strand of hair between his fingers, then slipped the scissors inside along the edge of the strand and cut. Hair fell down onto the towel and bounced over the keyboard.

On the computer screen, flickering with UN blue, was the WHO website page listing the senior investigator's position. He glanced from the mirror to the WHO logo, featuring a snake coiled around a spike. The job description said the senior investigator would direct investigation. He must be able to recommend corrective action and prepare fraud risk assessments. Bingo, thought Calvino. I can do all of that. As he looked at his hair in the mirror, he worked the blades of the scissors as if warming them.

Calvino had started cutting back on expenses two months ago. Self-barbering was his brainchild. Cutting his hair at his office desk saved on expenses. On the street or at a bar, he'd meet someone he had known for a long time and find them staring, jaw open, at his hair. Or was he imagining things? He was self-conscious the first time he had tied a towel around his neck and pulled the scissors from his drawer. He had waited until Ratana had left the office. Switching on all of the lights, he experimented with the position of the mirror until he had found the right spot on his desk. Trimming a little bit here and there until he had greater confidence that he could cut his own hair. The bitch about self-barbering was the difficulty cutting the hair on the back of the head; it was like shooting a rifle over your shoulder at a moving object you had to squint to see. It would have helped if he had been a contortionist.

A month into the experiment, he gained enough confidence to cut his hair before Ratana had left, and the first time she had walked into his office while he was in the middle of a self-administered haircut, to his great surprise, she took his latest cost-saving enterprise with a matter-of-fact nod. Nothing he did ever surprised her. She accepted his haircutting as if he had always cut his hair himself. There was comfort in a woman who took a man's strange behavior in stride, as if his actions were perfectly normal and expected.

She asked him to turn around and she examined the back.

"You've missed a couple of spots around you neck," she said.

He strained to find the spots. "I know. I'm still not very good at the back. It's a haircutting blind spot. It's like that old nursery rhyme 'Three Blind Mice.' Though they've probably changed it to 'Three Vision Challenged Rodents.'"

A small smile crossed her lips.

"Give me the scissors." She walked around his desk and stood behind his chair. Three, four snips of the scissors later, he had a clean hairline at the neck. Handing him the scissors, she picked up a file from his desk and went back to her side of the partition.

He sat in front of the mirror, holding the scissors, looking at himself, and wondering if it had actually happened or if he had dreamt it. He liked the sound of the blades, like a guillotine, like a pair of smooth thighs in nylons gliding across a room.

Lovell showed up at the office without an appointment, bending his head around the corner of the reception area. Ratana looked up, saw his grinning face, and she was as starstruck as ever.

"Hi," she said. "You don't look so well."

"I just left a funeral," he said. The smell of the cremation clung to his nose.

"That would have been Mr. Danielson's funeral." Calvino had told her that it had been scheduled for today. He had decided against attending. If anything, his presence would advertise that Danielson hadn't always played by the rules of the firm. The place would be crawling with lawyers.

Lovell nodded, thinking this was one clever secretary. "I talked to his wife, Millie."

"It must be a very sad time for her." She wondered how much

Millie Danielson knew about the dead massage girl in One Hand Clapping and her husband. The degree of sadness no doubt was inversely related to the extent of her knowledge of the nineteen-year-old named Jazz.

Lovell dropped his chin the way a schoolboy does when he looks down, that humbling look at his own shifting feet, the awkward, honest gesture that no woman can resist.

"And you want to tell me something else?"

Lovell's nose twitched, and he nodded. "I got dumped."

Ratana wasn't exactly certain what that meant. "Dumped where?"

"It happened at the *wat*. My girlfriend stopped me in the parking lot. Her name's Siri. We were planning to get married. But it's over. She dumped me at Danielson's funeral. His smoke was in the sky. It rolled right over us. She didn't care. She said that we were finished."

"That's terrible," she said, thinking this was the best possible news in a long time.

He grinned. "Not really. You see, I have a plan," Lovell said. "I know I don't have an appointment, but I really need to talk to Mr. Calvino."

That wiped the smile from her face. She cleared her throat and sighed. "When would you like to see him?"

That's how it was. He was a star but he wasn't ever going to be within her reach. Her mood had gone from the top of a mountain to a crash and burn in the deepest valley. Lovell's girlfriend had ended the relationship. She had a chance. He had a plan to win her back. Crash and burn, baby.

"Could I just go in? Like now?"

Ratana thought about letting him have his own way. What tipped the scale was Calvino's haircutting. She liked the idea that Lovell would catch Calvino cutting his own hair. It served both of them right. And only a woman could understand why that was the way it was.

Lovell marched straight into Calvino's office. He found the private eye hunched over his desk, clipping his sideburns, pulling his face to one side, staring in the mirror. "Mr. Calvino," he said. "I hope I'm not disturbing you."

Calvino glanced up and sighed. "Of course you're disturbing

me." He worked the scissors as if he had Lovell's necktie in mind. He went back to his trimming exercise.

"I can come back."

"Sit the fuck down and shut up for two minutes."

He tried to decide whether he liked Lovell. The kid was clueless to the bigger picture. On the documentation he likely ran circles around everyone else. But in the land where the written word had as much weight as a paperclip in zero gravity, what he did and what he thought it meant were the difference in distance between earth and Mars.

"I cut my own hair now," said Calvino. "That's an important event. Do you know why it is important?"

"I am not sure," said Lovell. It sounded like a trick question, the kind law professors asked about a point in a legal judgment. "Because you have more control and freedom?"

What a freshly minted, American fallback answer, thought Calvino.

"It has nothing to do with control or freedom. Cutting your own hair is the first sign that you don't give a shit. It's something you communicate to the world and yourself. You are saying, 'I've reached a point in my life where nothing can touch me. No one or no thing can make me sad, depressed, or hopeful."

Lovell was staring at the sideburns. "They're not even."

Calvino examined his face in the mirror. "What's not even?"

"The left sideburn is slightly lower."

He's that kind of lawyer, thought Calvino. Lovell was one of those guys who spotted every typo, every missing comma, and knew the difference between using brackets and parentheses."

He had the classic personality type, which in large doses would drive most people nuts. You paid a pile of money to leash his obsessions and put them in the service of your case and then held on for the ride.

"Lovell, I always leave the left one slightly lower." Calvino leaned forward across the desk, holding the scissors with both hands. "It's a signal. Call it a code."

Lovell swallowed hard. "What kind of signal?"

"Symmetry don't matter. Lies and truth rarely balance. What you try to do is explore the gap without getting sucked into the cosmic deficit." He leaned back in his chair, opened the drawer of his desk and put the scissors and mirror inside. He untied the towel, folding it so as not to lose the trimmings, and set it on the floor. "That's done. Now what is it that you want?"

"I didn't see you at Andrew's funeral today," said Lovell.

"Do you think he missed me?"

"I thought you would have gone."

Calvino shrugged, the guilt trip bounced, dropped, rolled to a stop. It hadn't touched him. "You were a Rhodes scholar," said Calvino.

Lovell nodded that he had been one.

"Out of law school you landed a position at a major Los Angeles firm."

Again Lovell nodded. "Until Danielson recruited me." He left out the part that Cameron had a fixed agenda about the qualifications of the new associate.

It had been decent of Danielson to shoot straight on what Cameron had planned for him.

"Your ex-girlfriend has it right."

Lovell's eyes narrowed. "You were listening to my conversation with your secretary."

"I am paid to listen. To watch, to report. But that's not my point."

"I was paid for my memory. So what's your point?"

"You've failed. Fucked up. It is probably the first time in your life you lost. The thing to remember is the first time is the hardest. But having never failed, you don't have a clue how it feels. You don't get it. Reality hasn't touched your brain. You are like Humpty Dumpty and all the king's men and all the king's soldiers can't glue you back together again. Are you listening?"

Lovell looked as if he'd drifted off into his own fog of thoughts. "I'm still listening."

"You come to the office of a man who can't afford a barber. How am I gonna put your life back together when my own life is in more pieces than I can count?"

"I don't like what's happened. I don't like the way it's happened."

"Go on." He could see Lovell boiling over but holding back.

"They fucked with me. I don't like it."

Before Lovell could add the usual conclusion, that he was on his way back to the big leagues, Calvino said, "Who does? Failure isn't something that gets better over time any more than crashing a motorcycle gets less painful over time. But you learn from your mistakes."

"I haven't made a mistake." Lovell's reaction was a half-a-beat too fast.

"Yeah? Then why are you here?"

"I know the entire structure of something I shouldn't know. Cameron thinks crucial parts of information were left out. I'm glad he thinks that."

"The entire structure of what?"

"Weerawat's business empire." He had in his head more than a structure; he had put to memory the vast coral reef hidden in deep waters. Lovell knew every entrance and exit point, the organic living, breathing whole, where monsters lurked, and where whispers and echoes of past crimes reverberated.

Calvino looked up at him. "What do you want to do with that information?"

"Use it to find out why Noah Gould is running. Why Danielson is dead. And why they had a Thai lawyer babysitting me, pretending to be my girlfriend. Isn't that enough?"

"More than enough," said Calvino. "At thirty-one years old, you had a good job, money, and lots of women."

"One woman."

Calvino raised his hand as if to stop him. "Let me finish. When you get older, things slow down but time speeds up. It's one of those contradictions. You stumble, and you fall down on your face. You taste the dirt and grit between your teeth. You get up and fight or stay on your knees in the dirt."

"I'm ready to fight," said Lovell.

Calvino leaned his head back against the headrest of his chair and rocked, using the heel of his shoe to make an even, steady motion.

"It's never that easy or clean. Sometimes it's better to stay in the dirt and live."

"I don't believe you believe that. Why don't we find a way to help each other to our feet, Mr. Calvino?"

"Detective. Remember we decided you'd call me detective."

"Okay, detective."

"How you comin' along on The Lair Game? Got all of Weerawat's locations on a map?"

Unfastening the top button of his shirt, Lovell fished out the thumb drive, which he had hung there on a necklace, and put it on Calvino's desk.

"It's up and running. The program. It's not a map. Anyway, what I have on the drive are all of the files for the eight other intellectual property cases that Danielson handled. The ones I mentioned last time."

"Did you memorize all of this?"

"All of it," said Lovell, his face beaming. He was proud of his capacity to memorize and retrieve the data.

"Why are you giving me this?"

"I want you to see something. Each case has one thing in common. Different companies but one owner, and each case was about theft of identity or intellectual property. Sometimes they stole the brand. The pattern was always the same. The idea was to investigate and create two files: the actual report for Weerawat, and the cleaned-up report that went to the client."

Calvino plugged the thumb drive into his computer and downloaded the files. After he finished, he removed the small drive and handed it back to Lovell.

"Did I tell you my grandfather could tie a bow tie?"

Lovell looked confused. "I'm talking about assessing major fraud and you bring up your grandfather's bow tie?"

"You need to learn patience. It's not all one straight line to connect the dots. My grandfather Vito immigrated to America from Florence. He arrived during the Great Depression. He left Italy after Livia, his mother, drowned in the Arno River. It was suicide. She had ceramic tiles from Galileo Chini's factory in her coat pockets as she slipped over the side of the Ponte Vecchio. Under the glassy, translucent surface of the tiles were Chini's Siamese nudes, young women forever smiling. The tiles pulled Livia to the bottom of the river.

"A month after the funeral, Galileo Chini enrolled Vito in art school. But he lasted three weeks, got a refund on the tuition, and used the money to go to New York and start up a plumbing business. After a few years the business grew. He had seventeen employees working for him. He also killed a man. It was late at night. He was on his way home after work. There were three men who pushed him against a wall. One of them called him a 'bastard wop.' If they had simply said, 'Gimme your money,' or maybe called him just a 'wop,' Vito probably would have turned his pockets inside out. But they didn't just want to rob him; they wanted to humiliate him, put him in the dirt, saying he had no father. That was a touchy point with Vito. The man Vito killed had his hands around my grandfather's throat. He only let go when Vito broke his neck. The others ran away. My grandfather got sent to prison for seven years. When he got out he started a plumbing business."

"Seventeen employees."

"He killed the man over a matter of honor. When you live here for a long time you understand how that kind of thing happens. And the thing that makes men kill is what they call face in Thailand. But we call it honor. Later, he was forced out of business because he needed a license to be a plumber in New York. He couldn't get one because he was an ex-con. He accepted it as the price for his honor. Vito didn't sulk or get drunk; he went to work for one of his employees. I grew up with this story. It was one of the reasons I wanted to become a lawyer. Justice was something worth fighting for—or when you're young that idea gets into your head."

"So does that mean you'll help me?"

Calvino closed down the WHO website and opened the downloaded files. Page after page filled with photographs of fake products scrolled down the screen: Prada bags, baby milk powder, braking systems, pills and more pills, and a list of movie and music DVD titles. "It means I choose my fights, and I don't let those who want to fight choose me. That's what my grandfather taught me. You can't break the neck of every jerk. If you do that, by the end of the week, you won't be able to count all of the bodies."

"He tied his own bow ties?"

"Perfect knots every time." Calvino looked away from the computer screen that looked like an online shopping mall. "Let me know one thing. What do you want?"

"I want to know if someone killed my boss."

"Why do you care?"

"Because he believed in me." He uttered the words with such complete sincerity that Vincent Calvino thought there was a good chance John Lovell had finally found a reason for doing the right thing.

"What about getting back your girl?"

"I decided to forget her."

"She may not forget you."

Lovell wrinkled his nose. "You can use this information?"

Calvino smiled, leaned back in his chair and let out a long breath, "Tell you what, kid, I'll have a look at it and get back to you."

That wasn't what Lovell had wanted to hear. But it had been a day of disappointments. He closed his briefcase, rose, and walked to the other side of the position. Ratana looked up and smiled. "He's thinking about it," whispered Lovell.

"That's usually a positive sign," she said.

TWENTY-FOUR

WEERAWAT'S driver parked the silver-gray Lexus outside Calvino's office building. Getting out of his car, he stretched his arms and then he reached back to pull out a leather briefcase. He took two steps before stopping at the entrance of One Hand Clapping. Sitting on plastic stools, the *yings* outside dressed in their black Toby coats with the name of the massage parlor printed over their left breast, stared at him, trying to size him up. A customer alert flashed across their faces. But something about Weerawat's appearance made them hold off the usual hustle. He looked familiar, not in the sense that they had seen him on the *soi* before, but in the way a celebrity is familiar. One of those faces memorized from TV that ran on a continuous loop somewhere just outside of consciousness. It was the small things—his carefully manicured fingers and stylish haircut, and his cultivated-from-the-camera grin, a practiced expression with a history of capturing hearts.

Weerawat rested the leather briefcase on one of the empty stools. He was the kind of man who liked to keep his hands free. He wore a light brown Armani suit and Italian shoes, smiled as if he remembered something that had amused him. Confident, determined, and still boyish even though they could see he was on the wrong side of forty. He didn't look like any customer they'd ever seen. Still trying to place where they'd seen his face, they watched his every step. Without any need to communicate their thoughts, collectively the *yings* concluded this fish was too large for their net. He walked up to them, trying to read their frozen smiles.

"I am looking for Vincent Calvino," he said. "He's a *farang*." He spoke Thai with a slight Chinese accent.

As if they wouldn't know Calvino was a *farang* name.

Three *yings* in unison lifted their hands and pointed up the staircase on the left. Weerawat nodded, smiled, picked up his briefcase and walked to the bottom of the stairs. On the wall was a small sign that read "Vincent Calvino, Private Eye." He had the idea that was the extent of their contact with the *farang* investigator. They knew him, but didn't know him. A light flashed behind one *ying's* eyes. "You're Khun Weerawat," she said.

His smile widened. He thanked them for their help, and they *waied* him. He replied with a *wai*. The exchange had been brief, precise, and civilized, and everyone understood exactly what their position was in the scheme of things. Like Khun Phaen's on-and-off wife, Nang Pim, their fate was written on their faces and the nature of the *wais*. Weerawat climbed the stairs to Calvino's office.

Ratana recognized Weerawat in the blink of a cat's eye.

Weerawat hovered over her desk, waiting for her to acknowledge his presence. His face had a caring, supportive, easy going look, the sort that set off a woman's hormones, priming an avian-like instinct to collect pieces of strings and leaves to build a nest. She tried to look busy at her computer screen and pretended he didn't exist. Finally, she turned, smiled, and rose from her chair. He took his time looking around the reception area as an appraiser valuing the artwork, plants, chair, and the office equipment.

"Nice office," he said, smiling at her in a friendly way that she remembered from seeing him on TV.

"Khun Weerawat?"

He was used to being recognized. He broke into a smile. The kind that says, "What's a good looking woman like you doing behind that desk?"

"If Mr. Calvino is free, I'd like to speak with him."

Her initial reaction hadn't been much different from the *yings* sitting on the plastic stools in front of the massage parlor. Ratana's instinctive reaction combined a mixture of confusion and awe. Her hands froze over the keyboard. It was one thing to see celebrities on TV or in newspapers and magazines; it was another to have them standing at one's desk and passing compliments about the office.

She didn't ask if he had an appointment. Men like Weerawat

didn't need appointments. They simply showed up and expected to be seen. Immediately. Ratana knew that Calvino was on the phone, arranging a stakeout for one of the Fab Four. And also that he had spent the morning studying the files that Lovell had given him. Weerawat had no problem placing her in an awkward position. He was used to exercising his power. It never required much. An arch of an eyebrow, a smile, or the hint of unhappiness would be enough to ensure he got his way.

Suggesting that Calvino didn't have time to see him would have been an insult. He was accustomed to his status ensuring that he'd be quickly ushered through the no-waiting zone. Especially if the person to be seen was a *farang*, a private eye *farang*, in a small office in a building featuring a massage parlor on the ground floor. She felt insignificant and suddenly found the office small, cluttered, and in need of paint.

She kept smiling, eye on the phone to see when the red light for Calvino's phone went out. When she saw Calvino was no longer on the phone, she dialed his number. "Vinny, Khun Weerawat is waiting. He wants to see you."

"Tell him I am busy."

She swallowed hard, looking up to smile at Weerawat. "It is important."

"People without appointments always think they are important."

"Trust me."

He sighed, knowing this wasn't a battle he would win.

She put down the receiver, stood up from her desk. Weerawat was taller than she expected. She showed him into Calvino's office. She placed Weerawat's name card on Calvino's desk and disappeared to the other side. Calvino stared at the name card. It had no details other than his name and a cell phone number. No address. No business, no company, no title. Calvino turned the card over as if to discover a message written on the other side. It was pure white.

"What do you do?"

Weerawat looked around Calvino's office. It was small, the desk a mess of stacks of paper and folders, and the curtains hadn't been cleaned for years. *It was a one-horse operation, with a rather old horse in the stable*, thought Weerawat. The oil reproduction of the Galileo

Chini Bangkok painting stopped him cold. His face contorted, the mouth rigid, unyielding, and his hands clenched. His face became a ghastly mask, like the face of someone who had witnessed a train crash.

"You like Italian paintings?" said Calvino.

"I didn't come to discuss art," said Weerawat. His face flushed as he looked away from the painting with the look of someone caught in an ambush.

"Almost no one ever does."

Weerawat recovered quickly. Once over the hump of whatever had disturbed him, he got straight down to business. There was no point in generalities with a *farang*.

"Americans don't like foreplay so much," he said. "So I'll come straight to the point."

Calvino figured Weerawat's clothing would have paid his rent for three months—no, make that six months, he corrected himself, as he glanced down at the shoes. Ratana had said into the phone, "Trust me." And this was what she meant. She had sent someone who wasn't only rich, but someone who looked like a million dollars into his office. He trusted her all right. This was a very Big Cheese on the buffet table of the business community. Calvino knew the name from John Lovell. Weerawat was an important client for the law firm.

"What is your point?" asked Calvino.

"I want to put you on a monthly retainer of seventy-five thousand a month."

The names of Weerawat's various companies whirled inside Calvino's head. He leaned back in his chair and glanced at his computer screen. The company names were a couple of keystrokes away. They were in one of the computer files he'd downloaded from Lovell. Calvino clicked the mouse and opened the Word file.

"You want me to work for you? Which company? And what kind of work would that be, Mr. Weerawat?" He looked up from the screen.

Weerawat smiled. "You would come to work as chief of security."

The words "Senior Investigator" flashed through Calvino's mind. That had been the title of the UN position. "You want me to be your bodyguard?" Calvino scratched his head, looking at the name card. *A nervous frog wants to pull you inside his coconut shell*, thought Calvino.

This made the powerful man laugh. "No. I've not put it very well. Let me start again. I have a number of businesses. Security is always a problem. I need a professional security person to monitor my operation, report to me, keep the security tight."

Calvino nodded. He knew about the businesses, and Weerawat was smart enough to have understood that Calvino had a relatively good picture of the family empire. "I am the wrong guy for that kind of job. Go to a headhunter. They'll find someone who is a professional for your kind of business."

Weerawat sat in the chair looking across the desk at Calvino. "I am not that smart. But I know how to find the right people. I know what to look for in people." He studied Calvino's face. Thick, dark eyebrows, the eyes a little too far apart, long, narrow face, strong jawline.

Weerawat paused, expecting Calvino to ask him what exactly it was that he did look for in the people he hired. Only Calvino didn't follow the script. He let the pause grow into a period of silence that only Weerawat could break.

"There are two qualities I look for. The person I hire must be clever and talented. The two don't always go together."

"When would I start?"

"Today." Weerawat pulled out a stack of thousand-baht notes and set it on Calvino's desk. It had a bank wrapper holding the notes together, one of those wrappers with a printed statement that one hundred notes had been machine counted.

"Just like that," said Calvino, snapping his fingers. "Today. I'm on the payroll. This is the interview. Seventy-five thousand baht a month."

Weerawat shrugged. "Today or tomorrow. That's for the first month plus expenses."

"I need to think about it. As you can see, I have a business. It's not easy closing up shop."

What Weerawat saw wasn't a business, but the hope for business.

"I thought you were a man who wanted money," said Weerawat.

"Only the money that's owed to me." Calvino made no move

toward the money.

A bargaining ploy was how Weerawat read Calvino's response. "I expected you would be too busy. The best people always are. Return any retainers you're holding from clients, and I'll fully reimburse you. Tell them you have made a change of careers."

"Yeah, I guess I could do that. Tell you what, why don't I get back to you on your offer."

Weerawat rose from his chair with his briefcase. "You have my phone number."

Calvino fingered the name card, remaining in his chair. "Yeah, I have it."

Weerawat stopped at the door, turned back. He positioned himself so as to avoid looking at the oil painting on the wall. "I know the owner of this building. He's an old friend. He once offered it to me for a good price. I wouldn't be surprised if that offer was still open. Between the massage parlor and your office is an empty floor. You might consider expanding your massage parlor business up another floor."

It would have been easy to straighten out the facts of his relationship to the massage parlor. But Calvino let it slide. Let Weerawat run with the idea that One Hand Clapping was his operation and the private investigation business a sideline. It was the perfect welcome-to-reality flash after hearing the bullshit speech about how Weerawat only hired talented professionals.

Once Weerawat was out the door, Calvino sat back and thought about the offer. And he wondered what had upset Weerawat about the Galileo Chini painting, why he avoided looking at it, and why a copy of the same painting was in his uncle's law office above an altar? Mostly, he wondered if Weerawat had been serious. The monthly retainer was enough cash to look after his mother and secretary. He searched through his files, remembering a memo in Lovell's Word files about Weerawat and his connection with a string of local companies, businesses spanning real estate, media, shipping, and mining. Lovell had called it the "structure," the vast assembly of interconnected details he had memorized and could recall at will.

Calvino was standing in the center of a runway and Weerawat had decided he was going to set down his private airplane whether Calvino moved or not. He'd pretended to give Calvino a choice. They both knew that it was no choice. The deal he'd been offered was clear. Calvino wasn't being hired for security; he was being hired to look the other way. This didn't make Weerawat a liar. From a wider perspective, it made him dead honest about his intentions. He wouldn't stop there; Weerawat would be asking advice on how to increase the security blanket for his operations. His Uncle Suvit had recruited *farangs* for their unique abilities. In Cameron's case, he had an uncanny ability to read expressions, spotting those flashes, tiny involuntary micro-expressions that exposed true feelings.

What was Calvino's special talent? No eidetic memory like Lovell; no face-reading ability like Cameron; and not even the technical skill to tune up his Lexus every six thousand kilometers.

The track record was that no one was hired without that kind of extraordinary skill. Calvino didn't have one and that worried him.

Weerawat may have figured out that Calvino had information that made Weerawat, if not fearful, at least uneasy. The way to settle the unease was to hire Calvino, bring him into the operation, another layer to protect his family against men like Danielson. Ten minutes after Weerawat left his office, Calvino wished that he'd asked Weerawat one question: had he ever made a similar offer to Danielson? If he accepted the offer (he refused to think of it as a "job" offer), then like Lovell's old law firm, Calvino's business would close, and he would be like Cameron, another *farang* on the payroll, keeping the lids on pots, making certain they didn't boil over. Or he could blow off Weerawat (it was a possibility, he told himself) and continue working for expat wives who were paying for dirt on their husbands and tracking down Noah Gould, making him talk about who had scared him.

Debra was flaky but had a good heart. Janet was suspicious and jaded. Ruth, Noah's wife, appeared on the verge of a nervous breakdown. And there was the elusive Millie Danielson. He'd phoned her but it was never convenient to talk; she was sure that he understood. What he understood was that this morass of damaged people who wanted to use him had become his life. An alternative was for him to work with Lovell and follow where the information led. But the kid's motive made him nervous. Like Jazz, Lovell was enraged to find out that the family heirlooms were fraudulent. Going up against someone like Weerawat meant stirring up people, watching their hands drop the soupspoon in their rice bowl as they reached for their guns. Calvino's law: only walk on point when you know that your back is covered.

He stood at the window in his office and looked down at the street. Weerawat had reached the bottom of the stairs. Calvino watched as all the *yings* from One Hand Clapping in their skimpy coats – a fashion statement combining a kick boxer warm up jacket and sexy lingerie – waited in a line beside Weerawat's Lexus. As Weerawat approached his car, he juggled his briefcase until one of the *yings* offered to hold it while he took out a pen. He signed his name. Each of them had a small notepad or piece of paper.

The first *ying* in line was the *mamasan*, coy and schoolgirl-like, and all smiles. He hadn't seen that smile when she had hit him up for two thousand baht for the busted door, he thought. He watched her bow; thumbs and fingers pressed tightly together, she *waied* him. Then the next *ying* stepped up and handed Weerawat a piece of paper. It had the name of a five-star hotel on the letterhead. Smiling, he signed it. All the One Hand Clapping *yings* wanted his autograph. What would they have done in return for seventy-five thousand baht a month? He knew the answer: anything and everything. That was how the system was wired, and guys like Weerawat knew where every last wire went.

★

Ratana ate lunch alone at her desk, working on Calvino's stakeout schedule for the rest of the week. She had location names, *soi* names, names of *mamasans*, and sometimes of the *ying* who was the suspect target of the stakeout. There were two schedules for the remaining two wives. On her screen were JPEGs of the four husbands, lined up in a row like on a police computer. Typed underneath Danielson's photo: Deceased. And under Janet Herron's husband photo was a second photo of the *katoey* he'd been photographed with.

"Some guys have it all," she said, after Calvino crossed to her side of the office. She could always tell when Calvino wanted to talk. His body language was different, the way his arms moved, the tilt of his head.

"Some guys who have it all think like they are dirt poor. They always want more. No matter how much they have, they're insecure." To Calvino, Weerawat was like a woman with anorexia, who looked in the mirror and saw a circus-freak when everyone else saw the wreck of a skeleton racked by famine. In Weerawat's case, the self-image problem wasn't about food, but about money.

"He's very charming and famous." She ate sticky rice and grilled chicken slices with her fingers.

"You like Weerawat?"

She licked the tips of her fingers, smiling. She said nothing, tearing a piece of meat from the slice of chicken, and with her fingers rolling it together with a small ball of rice.

"He asked me to work for him. What would do you think?" So far he hadn't told Ratana about Weerawat's connection to Danielson's law firm, or that Lovell had a long list of related companies under Weerawat's control. The man might live in a coconut shell, but it was a luxury shell and one Weerawat had every intention of keeping.

"I'd say, take it." The pause between his question and her answer was less than half a beat. She knew the answer before she'd been asked.

"And then do what? Close the office?"

"Why close it? He offered to buy you the whole building."

Ratana stared at the hundred thousand baht in Calvino's hands.

"You listened to our conversation."

"You got your money," she said.

"It's money. But I am not certain it is *my* money."

"Whose money is it?"

"The money for the Danielson investigation. That's the money I want."

This was stay-still money, keep-quiet money, buying-a-man's-loyalty money. Each time Calvino considered the possibilities, he came back to the beginning: Weerawat wanted him off the street, off the case, and where he could see him. Holding the money in his hands, watching Ratana looking at it, he felt that what he held was unclean. For most frogs deep in the coconut shell, there is no such thing as dirty money. There is just money, and if it's in your hands, then it has to be good. Weerawat had dealt him into the game. Was he going to play? And if he didn't play, when would the hammer fall? Questions Vincent Calvino pondered as he returned to his office, slapped the money into his desk drawer and locked it, put on his holster, and checked his .38 police service revolver.

TWENTY-FIVE

READING by the ambient light from the street, Calvino checked his schedule. He read a printout containing personal details about Ruth's husband. He studied Noah Gould's features from the photograph. He was looking at a man who at some stage in his life had been attracted to women in large hats. His tastes seemed to have changed. Noah fit the bill of a man who owed him money. There was no way to be sure of Noah's role short of channeling Danielson in the hereafter or getting Noah Gould to come clean. Thinking through the two possibilities, Calvino decided the channeling approach might be easier. Noah was a cornered rat, scared. Calvino hadn't decided how he was going to play it with Noah.

He watched people moving along the pavement.

Calvino sat in his car on the "Dead Artists" Soi. He'd parked no more than a hundred meters from his office. So close, but yet another world of high-end expat bars, clubs, massage parlors, and restaurants.

The Dead Artists bars were named after Renoir, Picasso, Manet, Dali, and Monet. According to his wife, Gould was a regular at Renoir. From where Calvino parked, he could see anyone going into or coming out of the club. McPhail knocked on the window of his car. Calvino looked up, saw McPhail's lopsided grin, and rolled down the window.

"Man, I thought that was you. Everyone knows this car. What are you doing?"

"I'm working."

"You can almost see this place with a pair of binoculars from your office window."

"McPhail you got something for me? Other than advice on how to run a stakeout?"

McPhail walked around to the passenger side of the car and climbed in, slamming the door a little too hard. "Sorry, sorry, I know that I look wrecked." A maniacal laugh burst from his lips. He recovered, shaking his head and grinning. "Nothing major. I'm dancing on the other side of happiness. I tend to lose muscle coordination when I go to that side."

He opened a yellow plastic bag and took out a Styrofoam container. Placing the container on the plastic bag on his lap, he opened it. The whiff of garlic, olive oil, pepper, and cheese expanded to fill the car. He took out a piece of grilled bread with a thick wedge of thinly sliced tomatoes and handed it to Calvino.

"We learned how to make bruschetta."

Calvino sniffed the air. His stomach growled. Taking one bite, then pushing the rest of the toasted bread into his mouth, he chewed. "Not bad," he said. He held out his hand for another one and McPhail obliged. The thing with Calvino was Italian food calmed him down. McPhail could talk to him now; nothing like two slices of bruschetta to make a man human.

"Next week is the last class."

"Do you have a final examination?"

"We prepare a six-course meal. You're invited."

"Chef Elmo isn't still pissed off at me?"

"He talks about your grandfather."

McPhail turned halfway around in his seat, spilling some of the sliced tomato on the car seat. "Hey, you're making a mess," said Calvino.

McPhail gestured at a *ying* walking past on the sidewalk in white pants, high heels, and lips with a perfect pout. "That's an RTS. Number twelve for today."

They both watched the *ying*. Calvino looked away first, remembering he was on a stakeout. "And what is an RTS?"

McPhail chewed the bruschetta. "Man, you don't know RTS?"

"If I knew, would I be asking?"

"It means Reason to Stay. A reason to stay in Thailand. We live in a definitely weird place. It's life inside a comic book. Unless you have a lot of good reasons to stay, then you should leave, or it can make you insane. Every day you gotta add up the RTSs and subtract the RTLs and check the balance. Got it?"

"Like a bank account? You're in the red or the black?"

"I'm walking down the sidewalk after the cooking class, minding my own business, and a motorcycle nearly knocks me down. That's an RTL, a reason to leave. Or a couple of days ago an asshole in a red BMW barrels straight at me. I'm in the middle of the crosswalk. There are white lines protecting me, right? Wrong. Those lines mean nothing. He kept driving straight at me. I jumped out of the way at the last minute. I stood in the road and gave him the finger. He stopped his car. I gave him the airport ground crew signal for him to back up his car. I wanted to kick his ass. But he thought twice and drove off. That's an RTL. That *ying*; the one who just passed by. Did you see her? Look, man. That one. That's a reason to stay. She blanks out all the assholes on motorcycles and driving BMWs. You want the last bruschetta?"

Calvino looked over at the container. He shook his head. "You go ahead and add it to your RTS."

McPhail looked at the last piece of bruschetta and, deciding against eating it, closed the container. He wiped his hands on his jeans and took a half-smoked joint out of his shirt pocket. He lit it and inhaled deeply. He offered it to Calvino, who shook his head, opening his window preparing for when McPhail exhaled.

"I got something to tell you," said McPhail, after holding the smoke in his lungs for a long time, then exhaling.

McPhail paused as another Reason to Stay slowly walked past Calvino's car. Under a short skirt, her thin, smooth, long legs streaked with flashes of red and green from the reflected neon lights, gliding with a grace and perfection that made McPhail sigh. Calvino waited but McPhail had lost his train of thought.

"You were going to tell me something," said Calvino.

McPhail drew in another long hit from the joint before stubbing it out against the heel of his shoe. "I know, I know. I'll clean it up."

"That's what you came to tell me?"

McPhail's laughter was more like a bark, the happy bark of a dog happy to be fed. "It's about the women in my class. Ruth and Debra can't make up their minds."

"Tell me about it."

"They aren't sure they want you to get the dirt on their husbands. Ruth sprung the news that her husband was being transferred to Denver. She danced around the kitchen. Man, was she one happy lady. Singing and jumping around like a high-school cheerleader after her team won the homecoming game. She even threw that big hat of hers in the air."

"So she's dropping out?"

"She said, what's the point of an investigation? Going back to Denver was all she ever wanted. Now she's got that. She doesn't want to know about Noah shagging *yings*. She says it would only cause trouble. What she wants is to forget that Thailand exists."

"And?" said Calvino, gripping the steering wheel with two hands, white knuckles showing.

"Ruth and Debra ain't paying you. Oh, yeah, Janet's short of money."

Calvino closed his eyes, his head touching the steering wheel. He raised his head and looked over at McPhail, who was taking another toke.

"I thought we'd been through that."

McPhail shrugged. "Women change their minds. That's what they do. All I can tell is that's the situation. Tomorrow, who knows? Maybe Noah's transfer will be cancelled and Ruthie will be begging you on her knees to catch her ratbag husband in a trap. But I fought for you, man. I told them what they were doing wasn't right. They had to pay you. And they said they'd think about something. I figure a forty percent haircut ain't ugly."

Noah Gould emerged from the Renoir with a *ying* on each arm. With two Reasons To Stay, Denver must have seemed a million light years away. They walked to the street. He radiated adolescent happiness, the kind that normally is killed and buried by age thirty. He gave no indication that he was on his way back to the States.

Noah was the man who owed him ten thousand dollars. The man who had arranged with Andrew Danielson to close down the bootleg drug factory because it was destroying the bottom line of his business.

"That's Ruth's husband," said Calvino, glancing at the printout photograph. He reached over and picked up the Styrofoam container and opened his car door. A motorcyclist swerved at the last moment to avoid hitting the door.

"Hey, where are you going?" asked McPhail, as Calvino got out of the car with the container.

He slammed the door and bent down. Head in the window, he mouthed the words, "Watch me."

Calvino crossed the street and followed behind Noah Gould and his two beautiful companions. They hadn't had much of a head start. Calvino caught up with them just as Noah flagged a taxi. "Mr. Gould," Calvino called out.

Noah Gould turned around, looking for the person who called his name. He didn't recognize Calvino. "Noah, isn't it?"

Gould nodded, "Do I know you?"

"We have people in common. Such as Andrew Danielson. And your wife, Ruth. In fact I know her quite well. I'm really going to miss her bruschetta after you two go back to Denver. It's difficult losing people you're close to. Oh, yeah, here's the bruschetta we made today at cooking school." He handed him the container. "You really gotta keep an eye on her once you get back. The Thais call a woman like Ruth *kai kae mae pla chawn*." The two *yings* on Noah's arm laughed. "It means a veteran hen. Someone who knows the ropes, has learned a thing or two about how to please a man."

Noah looked like he was going to cry until a wave of anger took hold.

"You bastard." His fists balled up.

Calvino moved in close and personal. "That's why she hired me. The same reason Andrew Danielson hired me to get the dirt on the people selling counterfeit drugs under your nose."

The garlic on Calvino's breath made Noah turn his head to the side.

"Get away from me." His teeth showed like an animal.

Calvino didn't back away. He stood in close and whispered, "Enjoy the bruschetta."

"Is this a shakedown?"

"You owe me ten grand. I want my money."

"For what?"

Danielson hired me to investigate the fake drugs for you. And I did that. I found where they're making them. You don't believe me? I'll fucking take you there right now. You wanna go now?"

"I'm not going anywhere with you."

"Knock off drugs, Noah. Fakes. Do you understand what I'm saying? I found the factory producing shit and putting your brands on it. You asked Andrew to help you find who was behind it."

He started to move away and Calvino shoved him against the fence in front of Renoir. Calvino pinned him with one hand, stared hard at him.

"You fuck. Running off to Denver." He felt Noah Gould quivering and let him go, stepping back, rubbing his shoulder.

Noah straightened his shirt, swallowed hard "It really isn't my problem anymore."

Calvino took a camera out of his pocket and snapped several shots of Noah with his two *yings* snagged at Renoir. "The thing with life, Noah. Just as one problem disappears a new one bites your ass."

Calvino crossed the street and watched Noah Gould climb into the back of the taxi with the two *yings*. Gould took the middle hump in the back, holding a container with the single piece of bruschetta. His smile had long vanished. What had replaced it? That thing the face does when surprise, disappointment, and shock converge in a single point of time.

Calvino stood on the sidewalk for a couple of minutes, then walked into a non-dead-artist bar because the booze was cheaper and the talk meaner. He ordered a double Mekong and Coke. He thought about how scared Noah Gould looked—not just a little frightened—but how muted and helpless his response was. He'd lived in the corporate world so long he had forgotten how to fight a real fight. It was easier and safer to flee and make a new life in Denver.

An hour after he came out, he went to his car. McPhail had gone. The inside of the car smelled of stale smoke. He rolled down the window, signaled, and drove home. As he drove, he thought about Weerawat's job offer. To become a *luk nong* of a powerful man, in Thailand, was a step up in rank. Calvino had been raised in New York City a different way. His mother had taught him that if you were self-employed, then working for someone else, no matter how influential, was not just a step down, it was climbing an altogether different kind of ladder.

Ratana had reminded him of something he should think about. That there was a difference between self-employed and unemployed and unemployable, and that he ought to seriously think about it. Let

Noah Gould take off for Denver. That wasn't going to stop Vincent Calvino getting what was owed. Weerawat wanted to hire him? Why not give him the impression that he was willing to go over to the other side? Most of the world lived by the rule that no man can stand long against a system and survive. But it wasn't Vincent Calvino's rule; it would never become a Calvino law.

Noah Gould must have understood that strong men in a weak legal system had an advantage. Andrew Danielson hadn't, and look what had happened to him. Ratana had earnestly asked him to think about Weerawat's offer with an open mind, free of prejudice, free of assumptions.

He'd done some serious thinking, though freeing himself of assumptions had been impossible. The frog in that coconut shell had some very sharp teeth. Somewhere inside that shell was the money he was owed. And he remembered what his grandfather, Vito, had taught him: never run, always face the threat, stand up to it, for better or worse. An honorable defeat is better than a coward's victory.

Calvino had turned his car around, found another parking place, and gone back to the bar with cheap drinks and laughing women.

TWENTY-SIX

CALVINO walked out of the bar with Noi. She had been working behind the counter and watched him drink three double Mekong and Cokes in rapid succession. Noi pegged him for a troubled, unhappy man in need of some loving. She held his hand as they walked to his car. He fumbled for his keys, dropping them in the street. He crouched down and in the reflected neon light tried to find them. He crawled around, reaching out with his right hand. He felt his trouser knee rip and his bare knee scrape against the pavement. Noi sat on her haunches, watching Calvino until she could take no more. She produced a small flashlight from her handbag and quickly followed the beam to where the keys lay.

"No good for you to drive," she said, giving him the keys. He didn't disagree. Leaning against his battered Honda, he tried to focus on Noi. But his left-eye and right-eye images refused to line up. She looked like two people. A tag team composed of identical twins. Calvino remembered that he had paid only one bar fine. He tried to focus on her face but the face split into two heads. He reminded himself this was an optical effect caused by drink. But now he wasn't sure.

One of them, in his vision-degraded state, had found his keys and persuaded him that driving wasn't the best career move. Calvino liked that. He leaned against the side of his car, rattling his car keys. He gave her a glancing kiss on the cheek. "I don't think I wanna drive," he said.

"That's good," she said. "Where do you live?"

He told her, shrugged, and started to walk. "It's close by." She ran after him, grabbed his arm, and hailed a taxi. On the short ride to Calvino's apartment, he sat with his head back, eyes closed. Noi woke him up as the taxi stopped in front of his apartment house. He paid for the taxi and climbed out as eight dogs—variously old, young, fat, skinny, mangy, and aggressive—ran full throttle toward the gate. The manager had let them out of her small dwelling, and they hit the drive barking and growling.

They knew his smell, and the barking gradually dwindled.

Noi froze with fear at the yapping dogs around her legs. She held on to Calvino as if her life were threatened.

"They bark but don't bite," he said. "Most of the time. If you kick them or growl at them, they might bite. So be careful what you say or do to the dogs."

Noi had heard more sober variations of that line before and had enough experience to know Bangkok dogs bite for no reason. Calvino took her hand and introduced her to each of the eight dogs, who had stopped barking and queued for attention and stroking.

"You see, the dogs love you. And he loves you. And she loves you. Stop being afraid."

"Okay, okay, they all love me. Can we go inside?"

Calvino's efforts weren't exactly calming or foreplay, but it was the best he could do.

Noi was still shivering from her fear of the dogs when she entered Calvino's apartment. He switched on the light. Unwashed dishes were piled in the sink, and newspapers, magazines, and junk mail spilled from the coffee table onto the floor. Along one window a row of plants, a series of shriveled black stalks, drooped and leaned in odd angles; neglect had doomed them. Whether they had been flowers or green plants or even plants at all would have stumped a botanist. The surface of wooden shelves and the curtains and sitting room furniture were covered in a layer of dust and dog hair. Blown through the open balcony from the *soi*, the dust and hair coated every surface, painting it an ashy brown sheen, the color of a desert floor.

Spider webs glistened in a triangular pattern over the bedroom door. He gave Noi his last fresh towel. She wrapped it around her waist, and fully clothed, disappeared into the bathroom. Moments later she screamed and ran out with just the towel around her. She'd surprised a rat that had been eating a piece of pizza in the bathtub. She never asked why there was pizza in the bathtub. Calvino went into the bathroom with a broom. The rat had already fled. Pizza crumbs along with tomato paste, cheese, pineapple, and ham were smeared in the bathtub. It was the pizza he had ordered the night after he had come back with the footage for Danielson. The remains in the bathtub were from his private celebration. The victory of getting the footage and the prospect of beginning a new, better life had been sweet and brief.

"*Noo tok thang kao san*," he said to her in Thai. The lucky mouse fell into the rice bin. Pizza or rice, whatever—what mattered was the luck to fall into a good life and that was a life without want.

That made her laugh for the first time since he had lost his keys.

"Are you a lucky mouse?" she asked, touching his cheek with her red polished fingernails.

It was what he wished to be. The lucky mouse who fell into a rice bin was the guy who married a rich woman. "I'd settle for being a lucky rat."

She had started warming up to Calvino. The Thai saying about lucky mice had made her feel connected, safe, as if he understood her in a certain way. She leaned forward with a longer, more passionate kiss. Noi crawled onto his unmade bed, pulled back the sheet, then took two pillows and pushed them against the wall. She leaned upright against the pillows, her legs crossed, still trembling from her encounter with the rat.

"Why your maid not clean good for you?"

"I don't have a maid."

"No maid?"

"And I cut my own hair." He demonstrated with two fingers as a pair of scissors, holding out a lock of hair.

None of this kind of information impressed Noi. She had just about decided he was normal when the money-on-empty gauge set off alarm bells in her head. Anyone cautious enough to carry a flashlight in her handbag knew the telltale signs of a customer who might not have money to pay her.

"Sorry," she started. "But I forget your name."

"Vincent," he said.

Her face darkened. She tried to say the name. "It's too hard."

"Call me Vinny."

That satisfied her. "Winee."

"One guy is a winner and the other guy is a Winee. That's me: Winee. That other guy."

He reached over and touched her arm but she shrank away. Calvino got out of bed and walked barefoot into the kitchen. He rinsed a glass he found under some plates in the sink. He poured himself a whiskey, rinsed another glass, and poured Noi a two-finger glass of whiskey.

Calvino came back into the bedroom with the two glasses, sat on the edge of the bed, and handed one to Noi. "The rat's gone. I checked."

"Turn out the light," she said, squinting from behind her hand.

Calvino got off the bed, switched it off. He couldn't see her on the bed in the total darkness. He opened the bedroom door, letting light from the kitchen spill through the crack. Noi had removed the towel and slid under the sheet, holding it around her neck. Calvino slipped out of his pants and shirt and climbed into bed next to Noi. He reached over and held her hand.

"Khun Winee has a good heart," she said. It sounded more like a question. But he pretended that she had meant it as a compliment.

Calvino grabbed her hand and placed it against his chest. He turned his head on the pillow, looking at her eyeball to eyeball in the dim light. "Not anymore," he said. "Just like you I've decided to put business first. How long did you say you worked at the bar?"

Without a blink she said, "One day."

One day that had cruised through three hundred and sixty-five nights, he thought.

He remembered slipping out of his underwear, and the next thing he remembered was having a splitting headache and looking at his clock. It was seven in the morning. A loud noise jarred through his sleeping mind. He opened an eye again. Light flooded through the window. The curtains had been pulled back to let in the morning sun. It was something Calvino would never do. He hated the sun in the morning. Noi stood fully clothed near the bed, looking down at him. Her handbag had dropped with a thud onto his dresser. She wanted his attention and short of a sledgehammer this was the best she could come up with.

With one eye squinted shut, he tried to read her face, to decipher what she was thinking and what she wanted.

He lifted himself on one elbow, yawned, looked at his watch, and shuddered. He fell back onto the bed, throwing the sheet over his head. Noi pulled the sheet back and sat on the edge of the bed. He opened his eyes. She stared at him, a flicker of a smile at the corner of her lips.

"Can I ask you a question?"

Noi nodded.

"Did we make love last night?"

It was wonderful, she said. "You make me happy too, too much."

Calvino couldn't remember a thing. "Good, uh?"

"You very good man."

That was coded language that meant she wanted money. Now, in her hand, before she left the room.

He leaned over and poked around inside the pocket of his pants until he found his wallet. He threw his trousers over a chair and missed. They fell in a crumpled heap, half on the bed, and half on the floor. Digging around inside his wallet, he counted his money without taking it out. He really thought he had had more than that. Noi sighed, reading all the signs of a customer who was short of cash.

"I go home. My mother is sick. I go take care of mother."

"Yeah, your mother's not too good? My mother, she's sick, too."

She thought that he was teasing her, making fun of her story, until he pulled out a photograph of a frail old lady with her white hair tightly curled, wearing a terry-cloth dressing gown. In the background was a black woman in a nurse uniform, all white teeth, smiling into the camera. His mother wasn't smiling. It was a reminder that her pain was because of him. That's why she had sent him the picture, and it was why he carried it. He handed it to Noi.

"Your mother?" Her face softened, rolling her head from side to side. "She looks so sad."

"When you're old and you realize your life is behind you, then, yeah, you feel sadness."

Noi didn't understand. Calvino figured he didn't have the vocabulary in Thai or English to explain.

He slipped his last fifteen hundred baht into her handbag. Money made a good substitute for understanding and explanations. If Noi was happy with the amount he had given her, she didn't show it. She lifted the handbag, pulling the strap over her shoulder. For a moment she hovered above him, as if she were going to give him a parting kiss. Whether or not that was what had been in her head, in the end she sat there at his side, rubbing her fingers along the leather strap. She looked at the photograph of Calvino's mother one more time, then rose and walked out of the bedroom. He heard the front door close behind her.

He had given Noi fifteen hundred reasons to leave. She knew the score and when she closed the front door, it was with a gentle touch that said thanks for the business.

TWENTY-SEVEN

A week after Calvino had climbed inside Weerawat's coconut shell, his first assignment came through. It had been a long wait, and at one point Calvino had felt Weerawat was avoiding him. He had wondered if Weerawat suspected that Colonel Pratt had wired him for the next time Weerawat showed his face. For days, Calvino had sat in his office, alternating between polishing his résumé for the WHO senior investigator job and pouring over Lovell's computer files of hundreds of documents, trying to make sense of the pattern of Weerawat's various offshore corporate offices. He had marveled at how Lovell could hold the intricate patterns and threads in his head, recall them at will, reveal any piece of the puzzle in a second. And he had waited for Weerawat's phone call.

When the call finally came, Calvino noted the name and address of the person Weerawat wanted checked out. It was a small matter, Weerawat had said. One of his real estate operations near Pattaya had a large amount of construction equipment and he suspected that one of the employees had been hiring out equipment off the books.

Employee theft and pilfering was the oldest corporate crime. Every security guide who ever worked for a company said the same thing: put an employee without supervision anywhere near cash or cash-like opportunity, and he or she will take the money and run. What made it impossible to stamp out was the employee attitude that what they were doing wasn't wrong; the company asset, which they had helped create, really belonged to them. Once they got their head around that moral dilemma, it was easy skiing down the happy mountain of plenty.

The telephone call had been brief and to the point, as if Weerawat had assumed the call was being recorded. Later that afternoon, a messenger had showed up at the office with thirty thousand baht in thousand baht notes. Ratana signed a receipt for the cash. Enclosed with the money was a typewritten, unsigned note: "Give him this money." Calvino flipped through the notes. They'd been marked with a blue ink stamp in one corner.

"I've got thirty thousand to deliver," said Calvino.

Colonel Pratt, at the other end of the telephone, listened. "Where?"

"Pattaya."

"He won't know that you're wired. Let him talk you through the plan. Once we have him on tape, then we've got enough to bring him in. Phone me if you have a problem," said Colonel Pratt. Sending along a police escort wasn't an option. Calvino had volunteered to go, but Pratt had thought twice about the wisdom of letting his friend walk into a situation that, at a distance, could get out of control.

"I've got a question, Pratt. Why wouldn't Weerawat just scare off Noah Gould? Or better yet, why not buy him off? Because that looks like what he did anyway. Why was it necessary to kill Danielson?"

Colonel Pratt cleared his throat. "Someone will replace Noah. They will get the idea that it is better to stay clear of Weerawat. He made a business decision."

"He worked out the numbers on a spreadsheet and Danielson's death made for a good bottom line," said Calvino.

"Weerawat's likely done a spreadsheet on you, Vincent. Be careful."

*

Eight kilometers outside Pattaya, Calvino found the small lane that eventually led to a large, open plain surrounded by rice fields. To the east of the rice fields was a large construction site. An oversized billboard advertised three-bedroom houses with swimming pools, showing a long-legged model on a deck chair in front of the pool. The name of the development was Harmony Village, and under the name a slogan ran in big, bold letters: "Come Retire and Live in Luxury."

He glanced at the map that Weerawat had emailed him. He laid it out on the passenger's seat. Harmony Village was the place marked on the map. He drove onto the construction site and parked next to a large earth-rolling machine. He got out of his car, leaned over the open door, and surveyed an open dirt area rimmed with earth moving equipment, tractors, trailers, cement mixers, and machinery for maintenance.

He locked up his car and walked toward the building. The open door was large enough for a tractor to enter. Calvino walked inside. Racks of electric tools lined one wall. The hot air smelled of oil and gasoline and grease. Another wall was pasted with large posters of Formula One cars and grinning drivers who looked like they had been gift-wrapped in their tight-fitting latex suits.

Several men worked on the engine of a tractor. Parts had been laid out in rows on cardboard. The hands of the men were black with oil and their grim faces were smeared with sweat and grease. One was on his back under the tractor, another handing him tools. No one had taken any notice of Calvino wandering around the building.

Calvino walked past the tractor to a workshop area with benches and more tools. He asked a man working on a muffler if he knew where he could find the foreman. The look of suspicion slipped into a look of fear.

"Khun Daeng expects me," Calvino said.

The worker whispered to a younger man, who led Calvino outside. They walked about a hundred meters. The man stopped and pointed to a Caterpillar D-4, an earth mover with tracks like a tank, heavy like a mechanical sumo wrestler. The D-4 was moving earth in the near distance beside a pond. That was the foreman, Calvino was told. His guide turned and, without another word, retraced his path to the workshop building.

Calvino crossed the dusty field, feeling the wind on his face. The man on the D-4 was in his late thirties, with dark-honey skin and pure black hair suggesting a hint of Khmer blood. He looked curious and watchful but, not noticing Calvino yet, he stayed in the cabin of the D-4, working the large blade. Blue Khmer tattoos had been inked on the back of his neck. The tattoos, like amulets, were believed to protect a person against bullets, knives, devils, or a *farang* dressed in a suit walking straight at him through an open field. In the sunlight, the tattoos streaked with sweat that looked like veins.

The foreman was using the D-4 to fill in a brackish pond. Calvino had been given his name: Daeng. That was a true Thai name. No Chinese or Indian blood mixed in his veins. Calvino had phoned ahead and asked if it was convenient to come out and talk about renting a D-4. Calvino told Daeng over the phone that he needed the D-4 for uprooting rocks, trees, and other obstacles so that the ground was a smooth, continuous surface. Calvino cupped his hands and called out Daeng's name. The roar of the tractor muffled his voice. Calvino moved in closer until Daeng caught sight of him out of the corner of his eye and killed the engine.

Daeng jumped down, adjusting his cap, and in a crablike walk crossed the space, stopping to kneel and pick up a large rock, which he threw into the pond. Daeng had a narrow face, eyes slanted as if expressing perpetual sorrow, and his hands strong and rough with calluses. He wore an old sweat-stained T-shirt, a pair of baggy green army pants, and plastic sandals. As he walked, he swung his lanky arms, double-jointed at the elbow. He twisted to find a cigarette. A layer of fine dust covered his face and neck and lips. Everything about Daeng translated as poverty, neglect, and struggle. Except for one thing: he had a cell phone clipped to the belt of his pants.

"Khun Daeng?"

Daeng *waied* him.

He wondered how someone like Cameron might read Daeng's expression. Weary, suspicious, fearful, or hungry for a bowl of rice noodles and chicken?

"I called you about renting the D-4. You rented one to my friend, Jim. Can you help me?"

Daeng lit a cigarette, lifted his head and blew out a lungful of smoke. His eyes looked Calvino over from top to bottom, sizing him up. Jim was a local contractor Daeng had rented equipment to in the past. But Calvino didn't look like a developer. He looked more like a businessman or a cop, the kind of man who got his hands dirty without getting them in real dirt.

"How many days do you want it?"

"Five days."

"Fifty thousand baht," Daeng said.

Calvino raised an eyebrow. "Expensive."

Daeng smiled, his teeth stained from tobacco, short yellow stubs worn down.

"Not expensive."

"You give me a discount? My friend, Jim, said you gave him a discount. He paid six thousand baht for one day. I pay cash."

Daeng played with his cigarette, rolling it between his finger and thumb. "Okay, okay. Same price as Jim. When do you want it?"

"Tomorrow."

Daeng wrinkled his nose. "Tomorrow, cannot. Friday, can."

"Sure?"

"Sure." Calvino counted out thirty thousand baht in marked thousand-baht notes. There wasn't much chance of getting a receipt. Calvino never thought to ask. He had the serial numbers from each of the notes. The blue ink stamp numbers on the right-hand corner of each thousand-baht note was a sufficient receipt.

"Where you take the D-4? You can't take far."

"Not far. I'll send my men to pick it up on Friday."

Daeng thought about this, counting the money, losing track, starting over, and recounting. Satisfied that he had the full amount, he stuffed the notes in the front pocket of his pants and fastened the button. He patted down his trouser pockets and smiled, lighting a cigarette before climbing back onto the D-4 and putting it into gear. A shaft of gray smoke shot from the exhaust as he carried on filling in the pond.

TWENTY-EIGHT

THE demonstrations around Bangkok wound down like an old clock. Crowds no longer gathered at Lumpini Park or Sanam Luang. After weeks of thousands of people turning out to protest, the whole machinery of protesting halted, stopped dead in its tracks. The newspapers called it a lull in a gathering storm. But storm wasn't quite the right metaphor. It was more like punch-drunk fighters after a slugfest. The bell had rung, and they'd staggered back to their corners, nursing their cuts and bruises, sucking water from a sponge. Needing a rest before the next round. They were exhausted after weeks of protesting to bring down the government. Their intense hatred of the government continued, a low burning hostility that with a small provocation would burst into open flames.

The demonstrations had given Ratana and Manee, Pratt's wife, a reason to meet. Such friendships had blossomed all over Bangkok; the demonstrations sealed people into pairs and communities. When the demonstrations had been called off, the relationships changed, going back to the pre-demonstration default. But the lull hadn't stopped Manee from phoning Ratana at work, asking her how she was getting on with her baby project. During one of those conversations, Ratana told her about the visits by Lovell and Weerawat. Both had been courting Calvino, and he had to make a choice.

"Could they have been courting you?"

Ratana smiled to herself. "I can always wish."

"Khun Lovell sounds *kai oon*," said Manee. A greenhorn translated as an inexperienced rooster. "He sounds like a much better match than Khun Weerawat, who has too many ladies."

After all, Ratana couldn't have them both. She told Manee how Calvino had come into the office one day and said he had made up his mind. He had decided to test Weerawat's offer by agreeing to a trial period. Ratana had thought this might anger Weerawat. Powerful men liked making conditions but hated to be on the receiving end of them. A *farang* asking for a trial period, a probationary period for the employer, wasn't something a Thai would ever agree to. It could be thought of as rude, insulting. It had worried her, but she had said nothing. She had put the call through to Weerawat herself just so she could hear his voice.

"I hope it is the right decision," she said.

"My husband says Vincent can take care of himself," said Manee.

"I encouraged him to take the offer. But now I am not sure."

She told Manee that though Calvino never said anything directly, he wasn't happy with the arrangement. But she felt some weight or burden had gone, and she wondered if she should feel guilty. Nothing had changed in the office routine. Calvino sat at his desk, agitated and brooding, waiting for Weerawat to phone. The decision to wire Calvino was a secret, as were the plans Colonel Pratt and Calvino had for Weerawat. They were confident Weerawat, who loved the sound of his own voice, would not disappoint them.

"He doesn't always show his feelings," Ratana added. Manee advised her not to worry too much. Vincent Calvino was quite capable of looking after himself, and if he'd decided to work for Weerawat, she could be certain that he had looked at the possibilities from every angle before making his decision.

Manee's words of comfort made Ratana feel a great deal better. In a perfect world, that feeling would have lasted a long time. The warmth of seeing a different future should have a shelf life longer than a bowl of mousse in the overhead Bangkok sun.

It lasted until three men in jean jackets, short hair, and leather straps with plastic police ID cards around their necks arrived at the office. They hadn't asked Ratana whether her boss was in. They walked into Calvino's office and found him working behind his desk. Two of the three were hard-looking men, slender, fit, in their early thirties, and unsmiling. Hard men with hard hands that looked like clubs with hairy knuckles. The third looked meaty around the middle. None of them looked like the kind of guy who spent his day directing traffic. Old enough to have seen and done things most people would not care to know about.

"Tell me about your business with Daeng. You saw him two days ago in Pattaya." His tone was unfriendly and hostile. He had square shoulders and rubbery features, with a mouth too small for the rest of his face.

"You're from Pattaya?"

They said nothing. These hard men fixed Calvino with their hard stares; they had no need to answer his question.

"Three cops from Pattaya. Isn't the protocol that you notify the police in Bangkok?"

Calvino thought, *Who the fuck are these men and why don't I throw them out of the office?* They had three guns and he had only one, and that was a losing equation.

"You haven't answered my question. What business did you have with Daeng in Pattaya?"

There was a long pause, a standoff silence, and the men were waiting to see how Calvino was going to play it. Was it going to be hard-ass *farang* or cooperate and bring in your supporting colonel if things start to get out of hand? "Why don't you show me your ID?"

"You read Thai?"

"I can read you," said Calvino.

Hard-ass, thought the Box Head. He took off his ID and handed it to Calvino, who looked at the plastic holder with photo—it was a Pattaya police identification badge—and then handed it back.

They still hadn't answered his questions, but that was beside the point. They were the boys, and it wasn't their job to answer questions, only to ask them. He wasn't wearing his wire. Pratt would be upset with him, but not as upset as he was with himself.

"Daeng, the foreman who rents earth-moving equipment?" asked Calvino, looking at the man with the rectangular head that looked like a suitcase and then at his partner, whose stomach looked like it had a permanent date with a hotel buffet. "That Daeng, I know. What about him?"

"He's dead." Box Head stared at Calvino as if reading his reaction to the news.

Calvino leaned his head against the back of his chair, rocked back, the bile rising in his throat, and drew in a long breath. This conversation wasn't headed in a direction that Calvino wanted to travel. His first reaction was to call Colonel Pratt, and his second thought was to phone Weerawat. They watched him too closely. There was no way he could get the wire from his desk without them seeing what he was doing. He guessed that these men knew about his connections. It hadn't stopped them coming to his office. They had some juice working not to be afraid of a Thai police colonel; not to mention that he worked for an influential figure with the power to have them snuffed out with a phone call.

"What's that got to do with me?"

"We checked his cell phone. You called Khun Daeng several times. The last time not more than thirty hours before he died."

Calvino was trying to figure out what was in it for the men in his office. Why had three men driven from Pattaya to tell him the foreman was dead? They arrived without an appointment, without anyone from the police force in Bangkok supporting them. This was not the usual way business was done. The cops, if they were cops, were out of their jurisdiction, trolling for information. The default explanation was usually apparent—they had come around because they wanted money.

Calvino decided to play it straight.

"Are you saying I had something to do with his death?"

"We are checking all leads," said the cop. He looked very pissed off, like a man staring at a closed sign in a gun-shop window.

"You didn't say how he died."

"He drowned in a pond," said the senior cop, who sat on the front of Calvino's desk. Another cop lowered himself into the chair opposite Calvino's desk.

"People drown all the time," said Calvino. "In bathtubs, *klongs*, ponds, the ocean, about anywhere there's water."

"He was hit in the head and then dumped in the pond. People don't drown like that all of the time." This man had a boxy head, a flat face with eyes sunk deep into it, flat nose, thin lips. Even when he smiled, he looked cruel.

"Was he robbed?"

"He had thirty thousand baht in his pocket. He wasn't robbed." The man sitting on his desk had the start of a potbelly, short hair, and enough Chinese blood to soften the features of his face.

"Who would want to kill him?" asked Calvino, looking at each of the three men.

"We thought you might have an idea about that," said the senior cop, a man with a perpetual frown, the corners of his lips curled down like an unmade bed, and with a high forehead and jug ears. Jug Ears had said very little so far, letting his men go the first couple of rounds to tire Calvino down.

Calvino looked away from the men and out of his office window. Customers were coming into the *soi* and disappearing into One Hand Clapping. "My idea is that it was probably personal or business."

None of the cops was amused. It was never a good idea for a *farang* to run the standard boilerplate evasion. It was one thing for the cops to tell this to reporters, it was another for the cops to hear it from a *farang* whose phone calls had predated the death of the victim.

"What did you talk about?" asked Jug Ears, who was now coming to dominate the conversation, his two junior officers hanging back, watching the show.

He took out a small notepad and started to write.

"I asked him to help me with some information about the theft of equipment."

Jug Ears looked up from the notepad.

"What'd he say?"

"Daeng said he didn't know anything about it."

"Did you believe him?" The cop with a boxy head and jug ears frowned as if to indicate he didn't believe Calvino.

"I gave him thirty thousand to find out the answer."

Jug Ears sneered, demonstrating the corners of his mouth could drop farther south than anyone could have expected.

"That's a lot of money," said the potbellied cop.

Calvino nodded. "A D-4 is a lot of equipment."

The cops looked at one another. The senior cop folded his notepad and put it in his pocket. They huddled in the corner of the office and whispered. The senior man broke from the group first, turning to Calvino. "We will check out your story. If any part of it is wrong, you can expect to have a problem," said Jug Ears. When a cop said you could expect a problem that was a code for ending up in a barrel dosed with gasoline and set on fire.

"You do that. Check it out," said Calvino, staring at the cops. They were determined, unsmiling men, the kind of men who moonlighted at knocking the designated target on the back of the head and dumping his body in a pond. Having finished their freelance work, they would get in their car and drive to Bangkok to interrogate the man set up to take the rap for the killing. They hadn't asked about money. That was a bad sign. The possibilities that lay beyond the usual extortion gave Calvino a feeling of dread. The men stood in his office, watching him. He suspected that matters had accelerated, and he was feeling the waterline rising over his head.

They flashed him one last long, communal stare, a mixture of contempt and hate. He could see it in their eyes, a purity of hatred that would allow them to kill him in a heartbeat. A moment later, they vanished. He heard their boots on the metal stair steps all the way down to the ground level. Sitting back in his chair, he closed his eyes. When he opened them, he saw Ratana sitting in the chair opposite him. She looked frightened and angry. "Phone Colonel Pratt," she said.

Weerawat had more than simple knowledge the cops would come to the office, thought Calvino. The spiders rattled around inside the coconut shell, spitting, darting from the dark places into the light, waiting to drag him into the web.

"I'll let Colonel Pratt know," said Calvino. "Don't worry about it. They're gone, and I doubt they'll come back."

"Those policemen shouldn't have come in the office like this."

"They delivered a message."

"Which was?"

"You think that you are protected. But we are standing with our boots on in your office. We have guns. How safe are you?"

Ratana left him alone. He sat at his desk in front of his computer. Noah Gould's photo with the two hookers stared back at him from the screen.

Noah had been caught red-handed, taking advantage of what time he had left before going to Denver. Maybe this was the only way out: you get on a plane and fly home. It seemed to be working for Noah. The cops barging into his office wasn't supposed to ever happen. It had never happened before. And now he was working for a powerful figure like Weerawat, it seemed impossible that it had happened.

He examined Noah's face on his screen. Clicking on the image, he zoomed in on Noah's eyes, blurry and shadowed, but enough fear showed, the unmistakable creases spiked by being caught off-guard. Had Weerawat sent the same three men around to visit Noah Gould, suggesting that it was a good time for him to ask for a transfer out of Thailand?

On Weerawat's first assignment, Calvino's mission had ended with a dead body stuffed with marked notes that he'd delivered. Daeng's cell phone showed Calvino's number as the last call he had received. He had to admire the care that had gone into the planning. Three Pattaya cops had made a point of letting him know that he was no one special. He was as open as any other *farang* mug on the street to taking a fall.

Calvino stuck his head around the corner. Ratana worked at her desk. "I want to talk with Weerawat," he said. He made certain the recorder was working on his phone.

She looked over her shoulder. "When?"

"On this side of now."

The downside of the patronage system was that more than one large fish hunted the same waters. Had Weerawat set him up with Daeng as a convenient way to get rid of two problems? Killing two birds with one finely thrown stone? Or had someone else used the opportunity to show Weerawat that his influence was finite? Nothing was ever as it appeared. One moment, a man sat in his office working in the twenty-first century, and an hour later, he walked onto a field and into the fourteenth century. The problem was that in addition to modern rules, Thailand had an unwritten set that had endured for seven hundred years. Figuring out which rules were in play—calculating where they stood in the arc of the centuries—slowed people down and made them anxious. It could make them come to a stand still. They had to be careful of the feudal overlord in a business suit who could have them drowned with a cell phone call. Calvino understood their confusion. He knew that a Thai business deal was always more than the paper and the numbers.

After Ratana finally got Weerawat on the phone, he denied everything.

"How you doing, Vinny? Everything okay?" Weerawat asked.

"Just peachy," said Calvino.

Calvino told him about the Pattaya cops showing up at his office, and Weerawat's joking voice went silent. His mood shifted to boss mode. He demanded Calvino give the names of the officers. But they hadn't given their names and he hadn't taken Jug Ear's name from the

ID. He couldn't assume the ID was real or the men were cops. Short haircuts and guns under their shirts was all the ID they required. In appearance they looked like cops. The conversation ended with Weerawat asking what kind of security chief wouldn't take down the names of all three police officers in such circumstances.

"You're right. I'm not too good at the job. I'll make it simple. I resign."

Weerawat exploded. "I'll tell you when you can resign."

"Any idea why Daeng ended up dead a day after I gave him the marked money?" There was silence at the other end of the line. "I'll give you a version of how it played out. When the cops pulled Daeng out of the pond, he still had the money on him. Not a single note missing. Who would know if they peeled off a couple of notes? You're next to a pond; no one's watching what you're doing. You peel off five, ten thousand baht and stick it in your pocket. Who's gonna know? But all of the cash was recovered. Don't you find that unusually noble?

"Then I tell myself, someone else must have known that I was meeting Daeng. I knew that I was going to see him. You knew because it was your assignment. How did this other guy or guys know? It wasn't from me. Okay, whoever this was, he or they saw us talking out by the pond, waited until I left, and then murdered Daeng and dumped his body in the pond." Calvino swung around in his chair, looked at Noah Gould's photo on his screen. He was starting to feel a brotherhood with this mug. "And you can't tell me why I'm in this awkward position. Who do you think I should ask?"

"I am the one who asks the questions," said Weerawat.

He was blowing out air like a whale surfacing after a deep dive. "You fire people who steal from you. Killing them isn't good business. You think that I had ordered Daeng's death? Is that what you are saying?"

Calvino thought of the celebrity, his face lined and strained. "That's exactly what I think. But I can't prove it."

Weerawat was smart; he talked as if he knew the conversation was being recorded.

The *mamasan* had cranked up the sound system downstairs. She'd loaded one of the jazz tapes, and Special EFX's song "Accounting" blasted through the two floors. The tenor sax made him think of Colonel Pratt, and how he liked to play the sax in his garden behind his house.

"Daeng was a little guy," said Calvino. "A small cog pulling a feudal wagon that ran over him. Better yet, a tadpole in a coconut shell."

"There is a Thai saying about slitting the throat of the chicken to scare the monkey."

Calvino smiled. The language was filled with monkeys, frogs, cobras, and elephants, an entire zoo to draw upon; he had already thought about the saying, and wished Weerawat had a little more imagination. "I know about the monkey and chicken story. What I can tell you is that I am not scared."

"That's disappointing," said Weerawat. He had lowered his voice, as if staring into a not too distant time.

"Life's disappointing. See you around sometime."

Weerawat had found a way to turn it all around. Calvino and Colonel Pratt's plan assumed that as head of security over Weerawat's empire, Calvino would have good access and a free hand to collect information on the ground. He had the perfect cover. Then the wheel had fallen off the wagon. Weerawat must've smelled something, a lingering hint of betrayal, wheels within wheels, agendas within agendas; a three-thousand-year-old Chinese tradition of watching an enemy's weakest point before attacking. More likely Weerawat found out that Lovell had been to Calvino's office. He had to assume Lovell had gone to Calvino for the same reason Danielson had gone to him: to cause him trouble. His people inside the department would have told him that Colonel Pratt was like a bulldog. When he found evidence of murder, he never stopped until he followed the evidence to the end.

Calvino put down the phone, sat back, looked out the window, and stretched his arms out, feeling the leather holster and handgun slide up his side. He had tried the obvious ploy, walking away as a preemptive strike; he had fired himself. Weerawat had seen through him. Walking wasn't an option. He either ran or faced the distinct possibility he'd soon be brushing up his Thai with Daeng and riding one of those big D-4s in the sky.

TWENTY-NINE

COLONEL Pratt sat at a back table watching a football match on the bar TV. When Calvino walked in, he looked over the room twice before he picked Pratt out. He had an ability to blend into the background. Calvino thought how good Pratt always was on a stakeout. He could make himself invisible. The times they worked together, Calvino watched as his friend went into one of those deep metaphysical states where he disappeared and stayed at the same time, saw everything, saw nothing, was part of the background, merged into the landscape.

They had arranged to meet at the English pub around the corner from Calvino's office. Calvino pulled the chair back and sat down.

"What's the score?"

"Liverpool's one goal ahead," said Colonel Pratt.

Calvino picked up the menu, his back to the TV. No matter how long he had lived in Thailand, the game would always remain soccer. He knew what everyone in the room was cheering a game that wasn't football. Try and tell them that. In a bar filled with Brits, it was safer for an American not give it a name. Football was a safe, neutral subject so long as it wasn't called soccer. Colonel Pratt wore his "I am concerned about your welfare" look. It gave Calvino a chill to see that policeman's skeptical, anxious face. He remembered that face from years before, in New York. Calvino had told him he would go to the wall for him when a Chinese triad gang had threatened to kill Pratt. They had come close to executing their plan. Calvino hadn't let that happen and, like his grandfather, had paid a price. Not a few years in prison, but the bar association had suspended his right to practice law. Sound of a rice bowl shattering, slivers as thin as spider webs.

That's what Colonel Pratt had told his wife when she asked about the hold this *farang* had over him. Calvino never brought the subject up with Pratt. Not once, though there were many chances to do so. But again, the point was *not once*. The colonel also understood that to act with such courage for a Thai meant he would follow you to the ends of the earth; he would die at that man's side if required. When Pratt tried over the years to tell Calvino that he was grateful for what he had done, Calvino shrugged it off. Changed the subject. Ever since Calvino had been fourteen years old and, at his grandfather's side, had seen Galileo Chini's *The Last Day of the Chinese Year in Bangkok, 1912*, he had understood that one day his destiny would take him there. Vito's father had sealed his fate, not Pratt. Siam had forever changed Galileo, Vito had said, and Calvino wanted to test himself against the tidal wave that pulled his great grandfather to Siam, moved him, frightened him, touched and repelled him, feelings that had caused Galileo enough regrets that he had a nervous breakdown in 1931. Calvino had gone to Thailand not because of Pratt but for more personal, family reasons, to search for something his great-grandfather had held in his hands, changing him forever.

Calvino was doing it again. This time Colonel Pratt wanted Weerawat. He knew that Calvino was making himself a nuisance to one of Weerawat's companies, and Weerawat had mentioned the problem to the right person, who passed along the solution: "Hire the guy, compromise him, get him on side. It's business." Vincent Calvino was climbing back into the eye of the storm without worrying about personal consequences to himself. The colonel wondered sometimes if Calvino had a death wish. Most people had such a wish but had the sense to step back in time. Calvino was dancing with Weerawat, and he loved keeping that half-step ahead of an asshole.

It was easy for Calvino. Weerawat had cost him his money, and Weerawat represented everything that Calvino despised. A life stuffed with flashy cars, models and actresses, and soaked in greed. It had been hard for the colonel not to say something when his wife, Manee, had said how disappointed she felt when Ratana told her that Calvino had signed on as Weerawat's security chief. He had gone over to the dark side. Colonel Pratt had said nothing other than, "Vincent knows how to take care of himself." The Vincent Calvino who stared down the Chinese triad gang hadn't vanished and never would.

"Should we order something to eat?" asked Pratt.

"Weerawat has found out."

"Found out what?"

"Enough for him to know I wasn't working for him."

"What did you tell him?"

"I told him that I resigned," he said, putting down the menu. "That I had to go up-country because my water buffalo got sick."

Colonel Pratt, a wan smile passing his lips, asked, "What did he say?" He tried not to let on how much he liked the way Calvino handled himself.

"He didn't exactly buy it."

"He was angry?"

"Spitting-viper fucked-up angry. He screamed into the phone that he would tell me when I could resign. I got it taped. And I said, 'Hey, man, my water buffalo. Don't you have any heart?'"

"There's something else, Vincent. The murder of a foreman in Pattaya."

Calvino rolled his eyes, slapped his forehead. "I was just gonna mention that."

"I had that feeling."

"But now I've lost face and . . ."

"No, you don't have to kill me. Only Thais do that, and only a small minority of us at that. So stop joking around, avoiding the subject, and tell me what happened at your office."

That made sense, thought Calvino. Ratana must have talked to Colonel Pratt's wife and a nanosecond later Colonel Pratt had the full story.

"I had three cops from Pattaya asking me about Weerawat's dead foreman. They said they were cops. They wore IDs but that doesn't mean anything. But they had the right haircut and they were packing guns. And I wasn't wearing the wire. They surprised me."

Colonel Pratt no longer watched the football match. "The evil that men do lives after them; the good is oft interred with their bones.'"

"None of them mentioned anything about Shakespeare," said

Calvino.

Colonel Pratt sipped an orange juice. The bar erupted into cheers as Liverpool scored.

Pratt took the commotion as an opportunity. He leaned over and said to Calvino, "If Weerawat does know, then he could be behind the killing."

"Weerawat knows, Pratt. And it could have been a leak from your end."

Colonel Pratt folded his hands on the table, looked up at the TV as Liverpool fans roared. The bar was full of shouts and applause as the scoring player ran around the field, chased by his teammates who embraced him.

"I don't know that and neither do you," Pratt said. "Weerawat's companies keep turning up in the Danielson investigation. Danielson worked for a law firm that acts as lawyers for Weerawat's family. And Danielson takes a case under the table that could ruin Weerawat. Danielson dies. Noah Gould is on the run to America. Weerawat wants to scare you away. It worked with Noah Gould."

Calvino shrugged. "I am not Noah Gould."

"Sometimes I wish you were." Colonel Pratt thought about what Shakespeare had said about evil: *Men's evil manners live in brass, their virtues we write in water.*

The waitress came and took their orders. Patrons filtered out after the game ended. "Weerawat is betting that I will cut and run."

"You told him that you quit. So he might think it worked. Like Noah Gould, you got shoved once and that was enough," said Colonel Pratt.

Calvino massaged his shoulder. The pain had jabbed him hard. Pratt was coming down hard on him. The benefit of the doubt was an old card he could no longer play.

"We wanted to play him, but Weerawat played us."

"Are you okay?"

"My shoulder is kicking up."

Colonel Pratt sat back as the food arrived. He watched as Calvino popped a painkiller, washed it down with beer, and rocked in his chair as if the motion would soothe away the hurt.

"Weerawat let you see what he wanted you to see. It's not your fault. I should have seen that coming." The colonel could not expect the *farang* to fully comprehend the ability of someone powerful like

Weerawat to play the shell game.

"If I'd been inside longer, I could have pinned the fake drug business to Danielson's law firm." Bangkok was a world of "could haves" and "almosts" when it came to making one more link to nail the big guy. The link was never made.

"Men like Weerawat have their own rulebook," said Colonel Pratt. "They have their own way of settling problems."

"There are lots of big guys," said Calvino. "They're big until their chair falls over."

"Everything in the Danielson murder case points to Weerawat. If we can find evidence to link him, he will fall hard."

Calvino let the colonel's judgment pass. The case was now the Danielson murder case. And Colonel Pratt was frustrated that Weerawat remained that one link beyond his grasp. He would wait until the colonel, in his own time and way, would slowly reveal the evidence to support a charge of murder.

"Is there such a thing as sufficient evidence to nail someone like Weerawat, Pratt?" The answer, Calvino knew, was only if someone benefited by taking Weerawat down.

Pratt unfolded his hands, examined his fingernails. Then he drank his orange juice. "I had a talk with Mrs. Danielson. And her lawyer."

"What did she say?"

"I asked her about her husband's allergies. And she said he had some. Dust, mites, feathers, cats. That kind of thing."

Calvino wondered where Colonel Pratt's investigation had been going. There had been lab reports and statements from members of the law firm, people at the Oxford and Cambridge dinner.

"And I asked her about insects," said Colonel Pratt. "Allergies to wasps or bees."

Calvino looked puzzled. "What's that got to do with Danielson's death?"

"Have you ever come across the word 'anaphylaxis'?" asked Colonel Pratt.

"Ana-*what*?"

"It's a severe allergic reaction to an insect sting. It's not always fatal. But it can be. If you're unlucky, it can bring on a heart attack."

Calvino sighed, glanced at the TV screen. The football game was over. Liverpool had won and a couple of drunks were pounding the bar with their fists and singing. "Danielson wasn't a lucky man," he said. "What'd his wife say? And, by the way, I've tried to talk to her."

"And?"

"She doesn't wanna talk. That can mean too many people and things are coming at her. Or she doesn't wanna talk, period."

"Vincent, the original medical report said that Danielson was stung by a wasp. But there wasn't a sting mark on his body. It made it easy to change the report and say the first report was wrong.

"We know that Danielson swallowed a couple of Zoloft. Maybe he had a bad reaction to the pills. Did you think of that? The first report could have got it wrong," said Calvino.

"There's no wasp venom in Zoloft." He had Googled Zoloft. The colonel had studied the chemicals that went inside the pill. He also knew that there was more than one way to deliver an ingredient.

"You think there was something funny about the pills?"

"It doesn't matter what I think. My friend found wasp venom in Danielson's blood."

Calvino scratched his head and held up his empty beer mug to catch the attention of a waitress. "That night in the restroom, Apisak offered two pills to Danielson. And Apisak works for Weerawat." He saw Colonel Pratt's eyes brighten, a smile cross his face. "The timing is important. I'd bet the farm that Danielson had just heard that his girlfriend Jazz was dead. He needed a little something to take the edge off. Lovell witnessed the whole scene."

"His presence is starting to look like it was an accident. Whoever wanted Danielson out of the way hadn't planned on Lovell being present to witness the pills." Colonel Pratt showed his hand for the murder charge.

Calvino's law: most murders fell into the category of either bad luck or bad blood. "Danielson's wife hasn't helped much."

Colonel Pratt finished his orange juice. "Talk to Mrs. Danielson, Vincent." An English couple in Liverpool shirts walked past their table, joking with each other. For them, their team had won. Nothing in their voices could have sounded more pure and innocent.

"You already did that. And she won't take my call. I've tried."

This was the ultimate card slammed hard on the table: "You

know her friends. Ask one of them to help you. They owe you, Vincent."

The friendship card, the connection to the heavy wiring card, the wild card that opened up the whole game. Calvino understood the game; he'd played before, and he was still playing his police colonel card every time he holstered his .38 police special and stood eyeball-to-eyeball with someone who wanted to scare him away.

It never came down to card counting; they were bonded by years of obligations and memories. For Calvino and Colonel Pratt, it wasn't a game. Because a game ended, and it had rules, winners and losers. The English fans began to clear out of the pub, finishing their drinks and calling for the bill. When Calvino examined the true tab that had been run up in this case so far, he found a dead massage girl named Jazz, a dead American lawyer, and a dead foreman in Pattaya. And Weerawat still hadn't cleared the bill.

Calvino had also been running up his own tab. He was still getting calls from the cops over Jazz's death in the massage parlor. Then there was the *mamasan*, who ambushed him on the stairs, demanding money, or cranked up her jazz CD collection full blast to remind him that he hadn't cleared what she said he owed her.

"You're looking for something from her," he said, meaning Millie Danielson. "Just come out and tell me."

"I want to know if she knew about her husband's girlfriend. You found Jazz. It's natural for you to ask her. The police have you down as the first person to enter the dead girl's room. He hired you, and he owed you money. Ask her to help you clear your name. Ask her for the money Danielson promised for the investigation."

She was going to write him a check sometime—in the late afternoon of her next life. This was an old Thai expression to let someone know they were in for a very long wait.

When a man knew someone for years, there was hint in the eyes that said something was bothering him. "What's in it for her?"

Colonel Pratt thought for a moment, rocked back in his chair, finished his orange juice. "Shakespeare wrote a play called *Antony and Cleopatra*, and there's a line in it that comes to mind when I think of Danielson: 'He hath given his empire up to a whore.'"

"And that's why she'll tell me to fuck off. The whore's dead. The wife got the empire. That's a grand slam home run. Out of the park. Talk to me?"

"If you convince her the home run wasn't a home run . . ."

How am I gonna do that? wondered Calvino. *The Risk of Infidelity Index* made *mem-farangs* see whores everywhere. Empires and wives were always closely interwoven. The Fab Four had hired Calvino to preserve the empire and their place in it.

"Her friends trusted you. You delivered. Millie Danielson will trust you. That's how it works with women," said Colonel Pratt.

That's how it worked with everyone: when you delivered the goods in a world where the goods normally went missing, suddenly you became a hero for just doing your job. Only Calvino didn't feel like any kind of hero.

"I'll see what I can do," said Calvino.

"Vincent, I want you to listen carefully."

"I am listening."

"Stay away from Weerawat."

Calvino grinned. "I have a program Lovell invented called The Lair. It lets me know where he is at all times."

"Where is he now?"

Calvino shrugged, gesturing with his hands. "Now, Weerawat could be anywhere. Maybe he's at one of those upscale joints on Soi 20. Maybe he's bareback with a girlfriend. Or he's playing cards and losing money."

"Some program."

"It's on my computer. You gotta punch in all of the variables to get a location read. Even then it can get it wrong," said Calvino, wiping his forehead with the back of his hand. He was sweating like a pig. "Just one request. You don't need a software program for this. Can you keep Weerawat away from me?"

"I'll see what I can do," said Colonel Pratt, smelling the smoky air. Nothing on Sukhumvit Road looked purely Thai anymore, not even the problems.

THIRTY

WHAT Colonel Pratt had asked for was one more small favor. *Nothing major*, he told himself. *It's a small thing.* Assuming that it was no small thing to interview the widow of a murder victim. Colonel Pratt had gone as far as he could with Millie Danielson. Calvino would make it casual and hope that with Millie's girlfriends whispering in her ear as to what a *mensch* he was, she wouldn't need no fucking lawyer, using his elbow to play a one-note scale on her rib cage, signaling her not to answer, interrupting her mid-answer. "What the widow means to say was that she doesn't know."

It would be just the two of them and the memory of Danielson, the person they had in common. Colonel Pratt told Calvino not to worry too much about the men who came to his office. Don't assume the men who came to his office were policemen; don't assume they were from Pattaya; in fact, don't assume anything. "But if they return," Colonel Pratt said, "phone me."

A wiry smile passed Calvino's face. "Yeah, I'll do that. Before you go to work, let me call my pal the colonel." The system had turned a blind eye to the grabbing and torturing of suspects. Torture was routine. Disappearances were common. It could happen to him; it could happen at any time. His friend was a Thai police colonel, but that didn't make him immune. It just made others more cautious before they acted.

They both understood the limitations. Placing a phone call was difficult when the boys were doing their thing, punching the button that sent an electrical charge through a suspect's balls. But Calvino appreciated the sentiment behind Colonel Pratt's offer.

As they walked across the restaurant, Colonel Pratt said, "That video you shot of the factory was interesting. The factory is owned by Weerawat's nominees."

"I know. Lovell had the lists of shareholders and directors."

He passed it along to the colonel. "I've been doing background checks on his nominees."

Colonel Pratt had found the usual nominees: drivers, maids, secretaries, lawyers, and friends. A domestic portrait emerged of the Weerawat clan and their helpers. "To take Weerawat down is to bring down a lot of other important people. That means finishing him won't be easy," said Calvino.

Colonel Pratt looked out at Sukhumvit Road, at the cars, taxis, and motorcycles. The hot night air was thick with humidity. It felt like rain. "I never said it was going to be easy. I didn't want you to get involved."

"I was already involved."

"Not to this level."

The Colonel meant the level where the fish tank explodes and all of the fish, alligators, frogs, and sharks swim straight for their meal. Calvino stood in their way.

"I haven't changed my mind."

"When you get the money from the Danielson case, stand aside, Vincent."

"And miss the chance to see Weerawat slide down his little mountain into a valley of slime? Not a chance." It had become personal. Sending goons to his office had made it such, and he had no doubt they had come on Weerawat's order.

A smiled crossed Colonel Pratt's face. "Watch yourself, Vincent."

"I can take care of myself." Instinctively his arm nudged his .38 under his jacket. Like an old friend, it was there, waiting for the right moment.

⋆

Outside the pub on Sukhumvit Road, the traffic was jammed in both directions. Calvino walked around the corner to the Villa Market to buy a bottle of Mekong whiskey and some bagels, lox, and cream cheese. Not New York quality bagels, but they were good enough when washed down with the Mekong. He picked up a yellow plastic basket. Stopping in the liquor section, he pulled a bottle of Mekong off the shelf, turning it over in his hand, reading the label. He felt a tap on his shoulder. Ruth Gould stood next to him, quietly studying his face.

"It is you," she said. "Vincent Calvino. Don't you remember me?"

As if he had so many clients that he would forget one who had agreed to pay him three thousand dollars cash. That was until husband Noah was transferred to Denver, Colorado, ensuring his entombment, a different kind of torture that was enduringly painful in its own way.

"Ruth, can you help me read the label on this bottle? Is this a good year?"

"It's a bottle of Mekong? It doesn't have a year, it has a bar code." Then she broke out laughing. "I almost believed you. That's very good."

"And I almost believed you. And your friends. You are very good. But I guess you had practice. What was it? Two, three private investigators worked on your cases before me. Yes, good, very good. All of you," he said, dumping the bottle of Mekong in his plastic basket.

"Look, Mr. Calvino. I know you're upset. You probably hate me and I wouldn't blame you. And that's what makes it all the more funny. About the Mekong and the vintage year." She started to laugh again. A couple of the clerks whispered, leaning over and nodding toward the laughing *mem-farang*. They gave the impression that they didn't see a lot of that happening, at least not in the wine and liquor section.

"What's so funny?"

My husband came home all messed up. He stormed into the bedroom, turned on the light, and just stood at the end of the bed trembling like some kind of madman. His lower lip did that quaver thing you see little kids do. Then he choked out the words that you and I had something going on. He said we were having an affair. Before I could say anything, Noah broke down, fell on his knees and buried his head in his hands at the end of the bed. It was weird. He'd come home drunk sometimes. But he'd never done anything like this. I was just hoping he wasn't going to wake up the kids with the way he was going on. I was about to say, Vincent Calvino, my lover, you've got to be joking. But he said, he not only understood why I'd done it but forgave me. He said that he had only got what he deserved. He told me how he'd been bar-fining girls out of the Dead Painters bars behind my back."

"Dead Artists bars," said Calvino.

"I got the dead part right," she said. "And Noah said that I had every right to do what I did going with you, and now that we were going back home, things would be different. We would get our normal lives back. I was hoping I'd get the chance to thank you." She opened her handbag and removed an envelope, and held it out for Calvino.

"What's this?"

"A thank you for saying whatever you said to my husband. For taking the initiative to bring him round to his senses. And I really hope that you don't hate me too much."

She walked away to the cash register. Calvino looked at the envelope. The sales clerks who'd been watching them now watched him. They were dying to know what was inside. He nodded in their direction, shrugged, and tore the end off the envelope with his teeth. He spit the slice of envelope on the floor. Then he blew into the envelope, closed his left eyes, and with his right eye squinting, looked inside. He looked up and winked at the sales clerks in their cute uniforms, short shirts, and heavy eye shadow, who had edged closer. One busied herself with a feather duster over a row of wine bottles. Calvino reached inside the envelope and extracted five one-hundred-dollar bills.

Ben Franklin stared out from the notes, the politician, inventor, diplomat, statesman, and whoremonger. He'd been stiffed out of another fifteen Bens owed to him. But he wasn't going to turn her down. He liked Ben. What wasn't there to like? The man had visited French, English, and American whorehouses. He could have invented The Risk of Infidelity Index. He was a man ahead of his time.

The two sales clerks grinned as Calvino showed them the money. He nodded at Ruth, who was standing in line at the cash register.

"Toy boy," he jabbed a finger into his chest. He put the Mekong back on the shelf, moved down the aisle past the two *yings*, pulled off a 1996 Bordeaux, and dropped it in his basket. One of Calvino's laws came to him: don't take any dry cleaning from a sumo wrestler, even if his mother begs. And don't take on an infidelity case from expat wives. He had broken the law and suffered. Humiliation and disgrace were close cousins, and he knew the whole miserable family. He wondered if they might have adopted him.

THIRTY-ONE

OUTSIDE Villa Market, Calvino passed a flower vendor wrapping a bunch of red roses and violet orchids for customers. He had seen the same vendor for years and remembered when she had been a young woman in white knee-high boots and a fresh smile. Middle age had overtaken her, robbing her of beauty and youth. It had also overtaken him. He'd been mugged by the years just like everyone else. He wondered if she thought the same thing when she saw him.

The tables in the large window of Starbucks overlooking Sukhumvit Road were fully occupied. People sat over their coffee talking, reading, or staring out the window. He took his time, walking slowly down Sukhumvit, counting four *reasons to stay* in Thailand.

One of the *yings* in a green tube top and jean mini-skirt came up to him. "You remember me?"

As a matter of fact, he did remember Mint. She had worked as a waitress in a hotel bar. "How you doing, Khun Mint?"

"I am *saabai dee*," she said, taking his hand. "You go shopping?"

He nodded as she eyed the shape of the wine bottle in the plastic bag.

"I go with you, okay?"

What he remembered about Mint was she never seemed to have a place to live. She stayed with a succession of friends but somehow things never worked out and she moved on. Mint was a floater, in between jobs, in between apartments, but the commercial possibilities her body offered allowed her to keep her head above water.

He reminded himself of another Calvino's law: never take a *reason to stay* back to your apartment unless she has her own place. Mint would have no reason to leave. That would be a problem.

"I've got an appointment. I can't."

A flash of a scowl crossed her face. "Okay, we go short time."

"Can't, baby. Next time." He left her just enough hope to scuttle away with a shred of dignity remaining.

Mint had almost taken the edge off feeling good about the unexpected payday and the expensive bottle of wine in his bag. He turned right onto Soi 33. Calvino recovered as he entered the *soi*, thinking that life was good. He was a middle-aged guy who just turned down a twenty-three-year-old girl who would have caused traffic jams in Manhattan. He had money in his pocket and a good bottle of wine, and he felt free and clean with Weerawat already fading from his memory.

⋆

As Calvino watched a middle-class Indian family go into Pan Pan restaurant, he turned into his *sub-soi*. He wasn't deep into the *sub-soi* when two things caught his attention.

The neon sign above the front of One Hand Clapping had been turned off. The area in front of the massage parlor was empty. Not a single *ying* or plastic chair to be seen. Not a single light was on inside. It appeared forlorn, abandoned, as if it had been not just closed but shut down.

Another thing caught Calvino's attention—Weerawat's Lexus, with the motor running, and parked beside the massage parlor. Calvino stood for a moment, eyes moving from the closed massage parlor to the Lexus. Red taillights flashed. The driver must have stepped on the brake. An interior light in the Lexus went on. The three men spotted him first.

Calvino felt his pulse kick into overdrive. His hand brushed against his .38 police service revolver. It gave him little comfort as he had a split second to choose either to turn back to Sukhumvit Road or make a run up the stairs to his office. They made contact. One Thai sat in the driver's seat, a second figure in the passenger's seat, and a third man sat in the back. He walked past the Lexus, increasing his pace. Calvino reached the bottom of the stairs when he heard the car doors slam. He was up the first flight of stairs when Weerawat called out, "Vincent, we need to have a talk."

Weerawat's work clothes were a slightly toned-down version of his nightclub outfit. He wore a white linen jacket, gray trousers and fashionable loafers without socks.

Calvino stopped on the stairs, holding his bag, staring at Weerawat. He was with two other Thai men. He recognized them as two of the "cops" who had come to his office earlier in the day. Box Head and Pot Belly. Jug Ears apparently was absent without leave.

"It's late, why don't we talk tomorrow?" This gambit might have worked with Mint, but Weerawat wanted something and wasn't going away.

"I want to talk now."

Calvino figured he didn't have a lot of choice. "Let's go to my office," he said, thinking that, on the way up the stairs, he would give Colonel Pratt a phone call.

Weerawat held out a key chain, rattled the keys, and shook his head.

"Let's go upstairs," said Weerawat. He pushed Calvino hard enough for him to pitch forward on the stairs. The force of the fall knocked his cell phone out of his hand. Box Head was on top of him, pinning him to the stairs. He reached inside Calvino's jacket and jerked the .38 police special from his shoulder holster. Then he picked up the cell phone and slipped it in his pocket. He had a screwy grin on his face, as if roughing up someone satisfied a deep personal need.

"My office is closed," said Calvino, looking at his own gun and the three men and calculating his chances of pushing Box Head into the others, giving him a head start to his office. What was he going to do when he reached the top and had to stop and unlock the door? They'd be on him. His chances were better keeping everything out in the open, public-like, where neighbors peeking out of their shophouse windows could watch the men on the staircase.

"Just keep moving."

Calvino clenched his jaw. "I know, 'and don't try anything stupid.'"

"Your mouth should stop moving."

Calvino lay sprawled out on the stairs as if performing the Bangkok version of the scissor kick. Only he wasn't in the water. Three against one did not make good odds. His own gun was now pointed at his chest, with Box Head's finger on the trigger. His phone rang in Box Head's hand. He handed the phone to Weerawat, who answered it. "Vincent's in a meeting. He will phone you back."

"Get up," said Pot Belly. His broken English came out more like "Gitup."

Calvino laughed when he shouldn't have smiled.

"You guys didn't find Daeng's killer?" said Calvino looking at Box Head and Pot Belly, who stood next to his mate half a shoulder shorter, and who had kicked Calvino in the calf. They had looked smaller when they had come to his office earlier. But he hadn't been on his back. Slowly he rose to his feet.

"Can you point the barrel away? The gun has a hair trigger."

Box Head kept the gun trained on Calvino.

"Vincent, we can clear this up." Weerawat nodded for Calvino to keep moving up the stairs. The two men had looked hard in his office; in the darkness, they looked like men who had little or nothing to say, and that was a worry.

I've got two sumo wrestlers with a handgun, thought Calvino. He wasn't going to be given the chance to say no.

With Pot Belly in front and Weerawat and Box Head behind him, Calvino continued up the next flight of stairs. They stood on the landing of the third floor, waiting while Weerawat unlocked the door of the vacant office.

Inside was a large, unused, and open office space. Hardwood floors and blinds over the windows. Calvino's office was one floor up; the massage parlor, one floor down. Where was the *mamasan* of One Hand Clapping? Where were all the *yings*?

Box Head and Pot Belly in their jean jackets and jeans, smelling of cigarettes and garlic, guarded the door. Calvino's .38 police special was no longer in Box Head's hand. That was at least some relief. Inside the empty space, Weerawat flipped a switch and a bank of overhead lights came to life.

Calvino stood in the middle of the empty room holding the yellow Villa plastic bags. It was a mystery that the wine bottle had survived the fall. He put that down as a sign of good luck.

"What do you want?" asked Calvino.

"You disappoint me," said Weerawat. "I asked something from you. But you don't listen. That makes me angry."

"You'll get over it." Making someone powerful angry was never a good thing. He knew that and he also realized that he had walked into one of those Thailand time warps. It wasn't clear which century's rules were in play.

Weerawat paced along the windows, turned, and walked back with his hands at his side, like he was thinking. He shook his head and sighed.

"You've become a major disappointment in so many ways."

"I can't report a lot of job satisfaction working for you."

Weerawat gave a long sigh and Box Head slammed a fist into Calvino's kidney. The punch was delivered with a sure expertise. Pot Belly moved in next and, using the full weight of his body, cross-checked Calvino against the wall. It knocked the wind out of him, and he collapsed on the floor. The bottle of wine, which had survived the assault on the stairs, was no more. Calvino dropped the plastic bag and the bottle of wine shattered with the sound of a gun shot.

The deep red liquid spilled into pools on the floor beside where Calvino sat on his knees and soaked through his pant legs.

"On your feet, now," said Weerawat.

Calvino held up his hand, one finger pointing up, asking for a slightly longer count. When he struggled to his feet, he looked down at the broken bottle and spit out blood. "That was a vintage bottle you just broke. Not just a bottle of bar-code plonk."

"There's nothing funny about this. But you don't get it, do you Vincent?"

"I liked it better when you called me Khun Vincent," said Calvino, sitting in a puddle of wine.

The two men, grabbing his arms, lifted Calvino to his feet, slamming him against the wall. "Do you think I could have my gun back?" Box Head slugged him. "I guess that means *no*."

Box Head and Pot Belly had even less of a sense of humor than their boss. Box Head's fist hit Calvino with a power punch to the gut. His eyes rolled back into his head, and he dropped back to the floor, vomiting the fish and chips from the pub and the two beers.

"Liverpool won tonight. I bet you guys didn't know that."

Weerawat nodded and Box Head slammed another punch into the side of Calvino's head. He looked up, the room and men spinning, trying to get his eyes to focus on Box Head and Pot Belly hovering above him, fists clenched. He was seeing four of them. He willed himself not to pass out. With his blurry vision, he kept them in his line of sight. Box Head must have been half a mind reader, as he kicked away the broken neck from the wine bottle. Calvino thought, *This counts as a double reason to leave.* He tried to hold onto the four good *reasons to stay* as one of the men kicks him in the ribs. He should have violated the law about not taking *yings* with no fixed address and gone to a short-time hotel with Mint. Calvino made a note to file: Be more flexible in applying the law.

"Do you still find everything funny, Mr. Vincent? Are you still laughing?"

The feudal serf showed a humble and passive personality to survive. Coming from New York, Calvino stumbled over humble and blasted through passive, and as he looked up at Box Head and Pot Belly, he realized the fourteenth century was a tough place for someone like him to live.

Calvino was surrounded by the mess on the floor—fish and chips and beer and bile, the sick smell of an up-country clinic midway through a long holiday. He sat in the middle of it, soaking up the liquid, the fumes, the disgust. The toes of Weerawat's expensive Italian shoes were a hairline fracture away.

Box Head clenched and unclenched his fists, waiting for Weerawat to signal another move. Calvino had had enough. Humble and passive was suddenly appealing.

"What can I do for you?"

Weerawat smiled. "That's what I want to hear." He paced in front of Calvino, who leaned against the wall as he sat on the floor, legs sprawled out in the broken glass, spilled wine, and vomit. "I want the original digital cassette you shot for Danielson. And any copies."

"I don't know from Wednesday what you're talking about," said Calvino.

Weerawat nodded at one of his men who then slapped Calvino across the face.

"Wake me up when Columbus discovers America. That's about 1492," said Calvino. He saw the dragon snaking down the street, climbing out of Galileo Chini's painting, the bells ringing, the sky going red, charging straight at him, and then for a moment the sky turned black.

Pot Belly moved in on Calvino's left side and hit him with a solid left. His ears were still ringing when he looked up at Weerawat.

"Do you have a learning problem?"

Calvino slowly opened his eyes, moved his jaw, and shook his head. Nothing was broken so far. Only a couple of people knew about the cassette. He turned over the shortlist in his mind. Once Pratt had taken it to the department, a lot of cops would have known about the cassette, and word would have spread.

"That case is over. Gone."

"Lovell said he gave you his case files. And he told us that you had the cassette of a factory producing medicine."

"You mean that fake shit you were making over on New Road?"

Box Head slapped him with the back of his hand. Blood splattered against the wall, and Calvino closed his eyes, his ears ringing.

What kind of ride had they taken the kid on? Or had he straightened Weerawat's shirt collar, adjusted Pot Belly's glasses, and smoothed out Box Head's sideburns? That seemed unlikely. Chances were they had beaten the shit out of him.

When he opened his eyes he saw Weerawat's face. "Lovell told us everything."

"Then he would have said that I don't have it," said Calvino.

Weerawat nodded and lit a cigarette. "We didn't get into details."

"I don't have the cassette," said Calvino.

Weerawat squatted down and stared straight at Calvino. Box Head lit a cigarette, and Pot Belly pushed up a panel in the blinds and looked out at the *soi*. The room spun around as Calvino tried to find his balance. "I can make you disappear. You have to understand that. No one will ever find you. They will believe that you ran away from a murder rap. That you slipped out of the country. You must believe what I am telling you."

Calvino shuddered, aching all over: his shoulder, gut, head, ears, and ribs. He tried to find a place that didn't hurt. People did disappear. A famous lawyer representing Muslims in the south had disappeared. And his face had been in the newspapers every day. If a celebrity lawyer could be made to disappear, then anyone could be bundled into the back of a car and taken out and shot, the body burnt, the ashes scattered.

"Where is the video?" An edge of panic entered Weerawat's voice, making it shrill and an octave too loud.

"It's with a friend."

"What's his name?"

"I don't want to get him involved," said Calvino, as the next punch struck above his left ear. The ringing sensation washed over him like a tsunami.

"Why did you give it to your friend?"

"He's a computer guy. Some of the footage is too dark. He's fixing it."

"His name?"

Box Head and Pot Belly, one on either side, stood ready to move in.

"Okay, okay. Wait. I've had enough. His name is Khun Prachai." He rattled off Colonel Pratt's private cell phone number. *If you are ever in trouble, use this number*, Colonel Pratt had said. The situation fit the colonel's definition of trouble.

Weerawat used Calvino's cell phone to dial the number. Colonel Pratt answered on the second ring. Weerawat gave the phone to Calvino and gestured for him to talk.

"Khun Prachai, sorry, *pee*, this is Khun Vincent and I need my cassette back. I want it back real bad. I have some people I don't want to disappoint. Could you bring it around to my office? . . . When? Now is a good time. It's a perfect time. . . . I know I sound funny. I fell down. But I'm okay."

After the call was finished, Box Head yanked the cell phone away from Calvino. Weerawat walked across the room, pushed back a slat in the blinds, and looked at the *soi*.

"Is he coming with the cassette?"

"He's on his way."

"He's a good friend?" asked Weerawat.

"My best friend."

For once Weerawat detected something approaching the truth coming from the mouth of the *farang*. "That's good, Vincent. In life, a man needs his friends."

Blood ran red between his teeth as Calvino smiled.

THIRTY-TWO

COLONEL Pratt arrived in Calvino's *soi* thirty minutes later. Pot Belly stepped out of the shadows. "Vincent is upstairs," he said. "I search you first."

As Pot Belly reached out to pat down Colonel Pratt, he took his eye away long enough for Pratt to catch him with a right hook in his oversized belly. He fell down on his knees, gasping like a carp in a water bucket. Four plainclothes police officers closed in, two of whom handcuffed Pot Belly and escorted him to a van parked outside the Pan Pan restaurant.

Pratt motioned for the remaining two police officers to stay at the bottom of the staircase. He saw that the lights in the second floor office were on. There should have been no lights in that vacant room. Box Head had opened the blinds and Colonel Pratt saw Calvino sitting on the floor. They were watching the approach. He saw that the man at the window had a handgun. Colonel Pratt held up the cassette so that Box Head could see. Weerawat moved into view, saw the cassette, and nodded, gesturing for Colonel Pratt to come up the stairs. Box Head stood at the open door. Colonel Pratt walked inside, with Box Head's handgun trained on his midsection.

"Hi, Khun Prachai," said Calvino.

"Vincent said you would bring the cassette. Please give it to me," said Weerawat.

Colonel Pratt carefully held out the cassette he had shown them from the stairs. He positioned himself by the window. He tilted his head to the right, then slowly to the left. Weerawat turned the cassette over in his hand, smiled, and slipped it into his white linen jacket.

"Now we can go home," said Weerawat.

Colonel Pratt's backup had seen the signal. Two plainclothes policemen charged through the open door, handguns drawn.

Weerawat clutched the cassette inside his jacket. "Give me the gun," said Colonel Pratt to Box Head. Weerawat nodded and Box Head handed Pratt his 9mm handgun. Calvino blinked away tears. It was finally over.

"You're under arrest," said Colonel Pratt. He had taken out a pair of handcuffs.

Weerawat grinned. "I've committed no crime. What we have is a misunderstanding."

"Think of it as an honest mistake," said Calvino. "He thought our employment agreement had a pistol-whipping clause. I thought it didn't. And so here we are." He walked through his own vomit to Box Head, smiled, and kicked him in the balls.

"Now give me back my gun, asshole."

Weerawat definitely didn't like the look of what Calvino did to Box Head.

"I'd like to phone General Theparak."

Colonel Pratt took away Weerawat's cell phone. "You can phone anyone after we book you."

"Do you know who I am?"

"If you've forgotten who you are, we will find out from your ID card."

"What are the charges?"

"Assault, illegal handgun, criminal trespassing, illegal confinement for a start."

"This man and the man downstairs are police officers," said Weerawat.

Calvino went through Box Head's jean jacket and pulled out brass knuckles, knives, and handguns. He was doubled up on the floor, hands cupped around his balls. Calvino knelt beside him, looking at the booty. "Shit, the guy's a walking armory."

Colonel Pratt squatted down, picking up one of the handguns.

"Is this yours?"

Calvino squinted at the .38 police special, his head spinning as

Pratt turned the handgun over and over as if it were hot. It made him dizzy as he tried to focus on the gun. Finally he raised his hand to say stop, it's okay, Pratt. "Give it to me." Colonel Pratt handed it to him and Calvino holstered the handgun.

"How do I look?" asked Calvino.

"Beat up." Colonel Pratt put the handcuffs on Box Head.

"That's how I usually look."

Another officer appeared and cuffed Weerawat.

"There's not that much difference." Colonel Pratt extended his hand. "Take my hand."

It was time to take the three men to the police station.

Weerawat and Box Head were taken downstairs to the van where Pot Belly was enjoying the secondhand smoke from the cop in the driver's seat and the faint smell of pizza from Pan Pan. Colonel Pratt knew exactly who Weerawat was; he also knew that the general who Weerawat wanted to phone worked the dark side, and had influence and power.

★

Colonel Pratt surveyed the wreckage. He picked up the broken wine bottle and read the label.

"You're going upscale, Vincent."

"I thought my luck had changed."

"Apparently it has."

Calvino's pant leg snagged a sharp object on the floor, ripped as he rose. Calvino sat down hard. He carefully ran his hand over the floor, avoiding the broken glass. He saw a straight line where the wine had been draining. "This is strange."

Colonel Pratt found a dry spot to kneel down. He found a latch recessed into the floor and he pulled on it, opening a trapdoor in the floor. Colonel Pratt and Calvino leaned forward, peering down into a room of One Hand Clapping.

"What do we have here?" asked Calvino.

They exchanged a look, and Calvino slowly lowered himself down to the room, finding his footing on a single bed. He climbed down from the bed and stood next to the window, staring out at Weerawat's Lexus. Colonel Pratt dropped down behind him.

Colonel Pratt continued to stand on the bed. He looked up at the trapdoor. No one in the room could see the outline of the door in the ceiling. The contractors had done a good job of hiding it.

Calvino had gone to the door. He ran his hand along the inside and across the hinges. The wood was still splintered. It was the same door he had forced open.

"What do you make of this?" asked Calvino.

The room was now familiar. It was the room where the girl had died. Like thousands of other identical rooms in the city except for a few details—broken door, secret door in the ceiling, and a dead *ying*, making for a hat trick of misery.

Colonel Pratt turned away from the window. "Time to go down to the station."

"Weerawat's got juice," said Calvino. He moved slowly, stopping every couple of steps, rotating his shoulder, his head, and feeling a sharp pain in his ribs. Something was busted.

"You did the right thing calling me."

From the tone of Colonel Pratt's voice, Calvino understood how close he had come to being swallowed up by the fourteenth century. He ached all over and parts of his body felt bent, broken, twisted in directions he didn't know possible. This was why Noah Gould had run scared. He had an idea of what Weerawat's men were capable of doing. Denver was suddenly a more inviting place than he had ever imagined.

THIRTY-THREE

AT the police station Weerawat and his two associates, Box Head and Pot Belly, had been given back their weapons and released. When they found out Calvino was also being released, Weerawat had asked the police to book Vincent Calvino for breaking and entering the empty third-floor office. For a moment, it looked like Weerawat was going to get his way. Colonel Pratt had personally gone to his superior in the department and explained that there was no evidence to charge Calvino.

"They say he killed a man in Pattaya," said his superior.

"There is no evidence."

The superior nodded. Box Head and Pot Belly turned out to be Pattaya policemen. The murder was outside Tonglor Police jurisdiction in any event.

"They say this Calvino assaulted the policemen after they found he'd broken into Khun Weerawat's office."

Colonel Pratt sat with his fingers pressed together, listening. "He says they forced him to go to the office and beat him up."

"It's a case of he said, and then he said. Only Khun Weerawat is not very happy with what he said. I suggest that we take the middle path," the superior had said. "We find a compromise."

No charges were filed against anyone and, after an hour, both sides were released. As Weerawat left the police station, he exchanged *wais* with the big shots. Calvino followed out of the station a few minutes later. Two officers gave him a stern warning to stay out of trouble. Colonel Pratt stood nearby, looking busy. No *wai*, nothing other than a strong suggestion that Calvino should watch himself.

He shouldn't be causing trouble for important people who would give the cops a major headache.

★

Calvino parked his Honda City in the visitor's lot of Lovell's apartment building, which was flanked by luxury condominium projects. Lovell lived in the heart of the well-off expat crowd, the ones with personal wealth or an employer who paid their rent. A water fountain gushed from the mouth of a lion as if the frozen animal had been condemned to a perpetual state of projectile vomiting.

Calvino wiped his own swollen face and touched his mouth, his lips dry and puffy from the beating.

The recessed lighting along the footpath illuminated a neatly trimmed hedge. The front of the building was a wall of blue glass. A security guard stopped Calvino at the entrance. He told the guard he was a friend of Lovell's, and the guard let him pass. A *farang* asking to see a *farang* was inevitably enough to get past security. The lobby was overstated opulence, gold relief on the dark wood paneling. Silver sculptures made from wire, steel, and bamboo towered at one end. *Someone's nephew had designed this under the influence of magic mushrooms*, thought Calvino. There was the top, and there was over the top. The lobby occupied a space a little farther out than over the top.

Calvino rode an elevator to the tenth floor. There were only two units per floor, and the guard told him to turn right and he'd find Lovell's apartment. He knocked on the door a couple of times before Lovell opened it, wearing baggy shorts and a Los Angeles Lakers T-shirt. He showed no surprise at seeing Calvino, or his bruised face, framed in the doorway. Nor was Calvino surprised to see the abrasions and scratches on right side of Lovell's face. It looked like he'd been in a wrestling match with a large cat and lost.

"You don't look so good," said Calvino.

"Try looking in a mirror yourself."

"Weerawat sends his regards. And Box Head and Pot Belly, they want you to know they miss you, too."

"It's not really all that funny, Mr. Calvino."

"You told them about the files from the law firm and the cassette."

Lovell looked up from a pile of perfectly folded shirts. "If you think I should be sorry, forget about it. They beat the shit out of me."

"That's always a reason to leave," he said.

"They knew about the air ticket Cameron gave me. That asshole had me beaten up."

Calvino smiled. "You finally figured Cameron out."

"You got that part right."

"Fortunately for you, Weerawat doesn't know about your perfect memory."

"Don't you think I know that?"

Lovell walked across the length of the sitting room, where two suitcases were open on the table and packed with shirts. Orange fabric walls, pink sofas and chairs, and a blue, puffy elephant framed on the wall. All that was missing from the room was a Hobbit family walking out from the kitchen, trailing meadow dust from their exceedingly hairy feet."

"You get slapped around and now you're going to run," said Calvino.

Lovell burst out laughing. "That's rich coming from you. Going to work for Weerawat. I can't believe you did that. You told me this incredible story about your grandfather stood his ground. Fought for honor. His courage doesn't seem to run in the family, detective."

"Where are you going?"

He looked over his shoulder, held up the airline ticket and waved it. "You see this ticket? It says LA. But does it matter, so long as it's out of this hellhole?"

Calvino leaned against the wall, watching him pack. "When you run away from a problem, it matters. Where you run isn't so important."

Lovell shook his head. He sat beside his case, leaning back on his hands. He looked up at Calvino.

"I took you for a fighter," said Calvino. "I thought you wanted to do the right thing and for the right reason. I thought you stayed because you wanted to find your boss's killer."

"I don't need to find Andrew's killer. He's found me."

"So, like Noah Gould, you're gonna run."

"Like Noah Gould, I plan to stay alive. It's not a bad game plan, detective. You might want to think about it as well."

Lovell renewed his packing. "How can you stay in a place like this? The corrupt and evil are never, ever punished. Weerawat's goons can beat me up, they can beat you up, and nothing happens. Why would you want to stay here?"

"People running away is why nothing ever changes."

"I am not running."

"I would've expected Noah Gould to say that, and then cut and run. But not you, Lovell."

"I don't have a job. I don't have a girlfriend. Come to think of it, I never had a girlfriend. She was my babysitter. I've been under twenty-four-hour watch since I arrived here. Now I can't think of a single thing that makes me want to stay. I want to live in a place where there is law. Where thugs don't beat me up. Where I can have a normal life. I don't expect you to understand what I'm saying. You've been here too long. It all seems positively normal for you. I don't want that ever happening to me. Now if you'll let me finish packing, I have a plane to catch."

Calvino walked across the sitting room and sat on one of the pink sofas.

"You wouldn't have something to drink?" he asked.

"In the kitchen, top right-hand cupboard. Help yourself."

Calvino disappeared into the kitchen, all white and chrome. It could have been the interior of a luxury ship he once saw in a magazine. He found the cupboard, removed a bottle of fifteen-year-old Johnnie Walker and poured himself a two finger shot. He found ice cubes in the fridge and dropped three into the glass, swirled them around and went back into the sitting room.

"The night of the Oxford and Cambridge dinner, do you remember who was at Danielson's table?"

Lovell looked up as he folded a necktie and laid it inside the suitcase.

"I've been over that with the police. It's in their report. If they keep reports. Or maybe they sell them to people whose names appear in the reports. I have no idea."

"When Danielson came into the restroom that night, did he say anything about being stung by a wasp or a bee?"

Lovell rose to his feet. "He didn't say anything about being stung."

"Some people have a severe allergic reaction to bee stings. It's called anaphylaxis. It can cause a heart attack. Did he have any allergies that you knew about?"

Lovell took a framed photograph of Siri that was on a side table between a rearing bronze horse and pencil-thin ballet dancer. He removed the photograph and packed the frame. Siri's photograph drifted like a leaf onto the floor. "An allergy can be inherited," said Lovell.

"I guess it can," said Calvino.

"He had a brother who died of something like that. The brother was older by three years. They'd been playing in a field and knocked over a hornets' nest. His brother ran but not fast enough. Six hornet stings were pulled out of his back and neck. He died a few hours later."

"Did Millie know about the brother's death?"

"It was hardly a family secret. Of course she knew."

"Do you think that Millie knew about the *ying* from One Hand Clapping?"

He left out the information that Millie and her girlfriends had been through several private eyes. It seemed impossible that even the most incompetent among them wouldn't have passed along information to Millie Danielson. She knew. Of course she knew all along about Jazz.

Lovell shrugged his shoulders. "How would I know what she knew or didn't know about her husband's family? Why don't you ask her?"

Calvino put down the glass of whiskey and walked over to the side table. He leaned down and picked up the photograph of Siri. She looked like a *reason to stay* in spades. "You live here alone?"

Lovell closed one of the suitcases and spun the combination lock. "She *used* to live here. But it already seems like a very long time ago."

Calvino glanced around the room. He'd already been in the kitchen and had a look round. The entire place was spotless, not just clean but ordered, organized, and rational.

"You've got a maid, right?" asked Calvino.

Lovell furrowed his eyebrows, knitting them together. "No, I don't have a maid. That's exploitation."

"You clean the place yourself?"

"That's normal. We are a different generation, sir."

"I don't have a maid. And I raise you one: I cut my own hair."

He looked down at the photograph, admiring Siri's smile.

"She left when? About a week ago?" asked Calvino. "Good-looking woman." In the back of his mind, he thought, *This kind of woman doesn't clean apartments. The fingernails broadcast the true story, and Siri's story is that she avoids physical labor. And she takes pride in keeping a distance from dusting, washing, and cooking. It isn't her style.*

"Yeah, a beauty queen," said Lovell.

"I never had a babysitter who looked like that."

Lovell sifted through a stack of underwear in the open suitcase, discarding some onto one of the pink chairs. "Lucky you. She works for Cameron. She's made that very clear."

"Danielson saw something different in you. Not just your memory. I saw that thing, or thought I did, the first time you came to my office." Calvino sipped his whiskey, holding up the glass to salute his host. "And you know what, that's why Danielson recruited you. He thought he saw a fundamental decency. Something he wanted to find in himself. I figure that's why he offered to help Noah Gould. He knew the risk involved. But he went ahead and took the risk. Weerawat or maybe his wife had him killed. Weerawat scared Noah Gould into leaving the country. You are about to run. I can't blame you. Most men don't have the guts to stay in the game. They fold and walk. They run. Men like Weerawat count on most men running away."

Calvino finished his drink and sucked on an ice cube, the cool making the inside of his mouth feel numb, and that felt good. He slowly opened his one eye that wasn't swollen shut. Lovell, an elbow away, refilled his glass with the expensive whiskey. Calvino lifted his glass to eye level. "But you know what, Danielson most likely made a mistake. He saw something that wasn't there."

Lovell's lip quivered, tears welled, and he turned and walked out of the sitting room, slamming the bedroom door behind him. Calvino let himself out. Walking past the lion with the endless ocean of water streaming from his mouth, he stood on Lang Suan, looking at the endless high-rise buildings filled with the rich who would do the same thing that Lovell intended to do. Run. That's what frogs did. They hopped away. Why should he have thought for a minute that Lovell was any different?

The coconut shell swarmed with scorpions, tails raised ready to strike, biding their time to score a fatal sting. The ethos of the neighborhood had always been to avoid the bite of a large spider and get back home alive. Escalate the shell game up a notch or two with scorpions, more punch, more venom, and bring in more capacity to deliver.

THIRTY-FOUR

CALVINO'S head throbbed—his face swollen, one eye half-closed, puffy, and black—as he slowly walked up the staircase. He stopped and looked at the spirit house in the distance. The memory of Ratana, the early morning sun on her face, offering flowers and incense sticks flashed through his consciousness, bouncing like an echo of an old song. She had wished upon a star—for a baby, for the end of the massage parlor, for new business, and for Calvino's mother in New York. If One Hand Clapping had really closed down, then she'd be inside dancing on her desk. Just getting one thing off a wish list was something, he thought. He slowly continued up the next two long flights, holding onto the hand railing, pulling himself one step at a time. In the morning, the pain of the hurt from the night before was much worse. When he reached his office, Ratana wasn't dancing on her desk or sitting behind her desk. She was standing at the door, waiting.

Her first words after looking him and up and down were, "I'm so sorry, Vinny," she said, fighting back tears.

"Sorry? I don't look that bad."

But it wasn't his physical appearance she was referring to as much as the state of his smashed up office. All of the drawers in his desk had been pulled out and thrown across the room. Papers and books and files covered the floor. The computer screen was smashed in and the hard disk from his computer had been removed. The motherboard had been stomped on and destroyed. Calvino walked around the clutter, the broken glass, the turned-over chairs. He squatted down and picked up an invoice for ten thousand dollars made out to Andrew Danielson. He crumpled it up and threw it at the wall. There were dozens of other printouts of the same invoice. The intruders had taken the trouble to print it many times and scatter the printouts across the office. His WHO application was also on the floor. He knelt down, picked it up, tore it in two pieces, and then tore those pieces again, throwing them across the room. He looked around the room. Galileo Chini's *The Last Day of the Chinese Year in Bangkok* was no longer hanging on the wall. The canvas had been slit dozens of times, leaving thin strips of bright red and yellow and orange. The dragon was gone. The slender figures of the Chinese in their pajamas and pigtails standing in the street of Bangkok in 1912 were no longer recognizable.

Maybe it had been the work of a single intruder—Jug Ears, for instance, who had received specific instructions. Destroy everything, including the oil painting. Jug Ears hadn't returned to Pattaya but stayed back, waiting for a chance to ransack Calvino's office. Calvino was certain Jug Ears had seen one of the Weerawat company reports on his computer screen.

Ratana stood with her arms folded in the doorway.

"They removed the hard drive from my computer," she said.

He looked over his shoulder. "They did a good job of it."

"I have a backup for my computer and yours, too, Vinny."

"Have you called the police?"

She shook her head. "Good," he said. "I want Pratt to see this first." Ratana had been smart enough to know that calling the police was not necessarily the first best move.

Manee had phoned and told her what had happened the night before. How Calvino had been beaten up bad but refused to go the hospital. How Weerawat had tried to have him arrested, and how Colonel Pratt had gone to a superior who found a compromise. She looked tired, as if she hadn't slept much the night before. "I want to tell you something."

She's resigning, thought Calvino.

"I've been confused lately. Between who is *khon dee* and who is *khon phan*. I made a mistake. I can't tell the good guy from the bad one. I don't blame anyone else. I should have seen what was so close to me. I took Khun Weerawat at face value. He is rich and powerful, so of course I thought he is good. I didn't ask how did he become rich. People at the demonstrations were asking this question. I am so blind I couldn't see the problem. I ask myself how I could have made such a bad mistake? I feel so stupid. I am so sorry, Vinny."

Calvino took a step forward over the clutter and, hugging her, said, "I thought I could fool Weerawat into thinking I would work for him. How's that for being stupid? That puts me at the top of the moron class."

She nodded, her chin quivering as she fought back tears.

"Let's get this office cleaned up," he said. "We have a business to run."

Ratana pulled him forward. "They want to scare you. That's why they wrecked the office."

Calvino saw his telephone under some papers. He lifted the papers with his shoe. The phone had been smashed. "They wanted my files. Now they know what Lovell gave me."

They had straightened up the worst of the mess when a middle-aged Thai man in a shirt, tie, and stethoscope around his neck came into the office. A round Chinese moon face without the craters. Calvino guessed he was in his early forties. The man tapped one wing of his glasses against the corner of his mouth, glancing at his watch.

"This is Dr. Somchai. I asked him to come examine you."

"Examine me? There's nothing wrong." He hated the idea of doctors, what they might find, what verdict they might make. Unless bone pierced the skin, then whatever was going on inside would eventually heal. Or not.

The doctor looked around at the damage but showed no reaction. "Take off your shirt." The approach was no-nonsense—forget the bedside manner.

By the time Calvino looked over his shoulder, Ratana had returned to the other side of the partition. He draped his shirt over his desk. "Now what?"

Examining the bruising and discoloration of the skin covering the ribs and running down his chest, the doctor frowned.

"Sit on your desk if you would."

"Sorry for the mess. I'm in between housekeepers," said Calvino.

"Don't talk," said the doctor. "Breathe in and hold your breath.

Hold it until I tell you to exhale."

Dr. Somchai placed his stethoscope against Calvino's chest, and then he moved it and listened again, until finally he leaned up. "Exhale. Your lungs have fluid."

"Yeah? Is that good?"

"No, that is generally bad."

"Lungs drain themselves, am I right?"

"Not to my knowledge," said the doctor.

The doctor pressed two fingers inward on one of Calvino's ribs. His eyes opened wide, and a sharp bark came from deep inside his throat. The doctor pushed again but this time more gently. "And here, does that . . ."

Calvino yelped as the doctor pressed another rib. "I believe it may be broken. You need a full set of X-rays. Your condition may be very serious."

"Can I put on my shirt?" His face twisted in pain as he reached for his shirt.

The doctor gestured with the stethoscope. "You have a hairline fracture on two ribs for certain. There may be another cracked rib. I can't be sure." He held Calvino's jaws between his palms and moved them up and down.

Calvino pulled away. "Is this also gonna hurt me more than you?"

The doctor packed away his stethoscope and sat on the desk next to Calvino.

"Don't tell Ratana anything," said Calvino. "Like lawyers, doctors have to keep their patients' secrets. Can you do that for me?"

The doctor blinked, lips parting slightly, a disapproving look in his eyes.

"No problem for me. But you should be in hospital."

"I should be dead."

Dr. Somchai didn't disagree with that assessment, at least not by much. *Unless he receives treatment, this private investigator might get himself dead*, thought the doctor.

As Calvino slipped into his shirt, he froze from the pain. He put down his arm, took a deep breath, and again tried putting on the shirt, this time successfully. He felt proud of that small accomplishment. "You wouldn't happen to have anything on you for pain?"

The doctor smiled for the first time, opening his black bag. He pulled out a syringe and a tiny bottle. He tore the wrapper off the needle and inserted it in the bottle, drawing the liquid into the syringe. "Slide down your trousers and turn around and face your desk."

Calvino rolled his eyes and did what the doctor asked. Dr. Somchai stuck the needle in Calvino's hip and slowly drained the syringe. "That should do it. You can pull up your trousers."

He grimaced, tightening his belt. "I could use some pain pills for later. That shot's gonna wear off in a couple of hours. I'd appreciate if you could help me out."

Dr. Somchai searched in his bag until he found pain pills.

"You have any allergy to any drugs?"

Calvino shook his head. "But I'm glad you asked. There's something I've wanted to ask you. What do you know about bee stings or wasp stings? Did you ever have a patient die from a reaction to a sting?"

"It's not the sting. It's reaction to the venom that kills people. It happens every year. We are strong in many ways but fragile, too. With all our DNA possibilities it doesn't take much for a misprint to make a sequence error. That little mistake is big enough to make a simple bee sting fatal."

He handed two packets of pills to Calvino.

"Thanks, Dr. Somchai. Can I ask you another question about bee stings?"

The doctor glanced at his watch and then nodded.

"Is it possible to get the bee venom other than in a sting?"

The doctor furrowed his brow. "Other than in a sting?" He looked confused by the question.

The effect of the drug had taken hold, making Calvino feel mellow and, for the first time since he'd been beaten up, pain-free. That take-it-for-granted no pain zone had returned. "It's like this. Someone has the reaction but didn't get stung by a bee. But the venom from the bee got into them another way. In a big enough dose to kill them."

The doctor looked at Calvino over his glasses.

"If the sting doesn't inject the venom, then what does?"

"I don't know. Maybe it's in the coffee."

"No. Coffee wouldn't work. It's too hot."

"Plain water, then."

"It would be diluted."

Calvino sat behind his desk. "There's got to be a way. Invention and murder are old friends. I'm certain if you put your mind to it, you could think of a way."

"If I had time to do so. But I don't, Mr. Calvino."

"How would you do it?"

The doctor tossed the needle and syringe into the wastebasket. "Do you know how people up-country kill dogs that bark too much or bite people? They poison them by putting arsenic in a piece of meat. They leave it along a path that they know the dog uses. When the dog finds the meat, eating or not eating it is up to the dog. The poisoner offers, but the dog chooses. It is the dog's karma to choose."

"I'll get the X-ray tomorrow, doc."

He held his bag. "That's really up to you, Khun Vincent."

"Where'd you learn to speak English so well?"

Dr. Somchai arched an eyebrow. "Our generation has no problem speaking English. Don't confuse us with the older generations like yourself."

That hurt as much as the two cracked ribs. "Which generation grabbed your namesake, Khun Somchai, the Muslim lawyer? The old geezers who think even educated Thais speak broken English or the younger generation who are fluent, hungry, and want what they want when they want it?"

Dr. Somchai looked away in silence. "No one knows."

"No one who knows will tell. That's different."

After Dr. Somchai left, Ratana came into his office and sat down.

"Dr. Somchai wouldn't tell me what was wrong," she said.

"He poked around. It wasn't anything that serious. I told him I'd get an X-ray tomorrow." He stepped around what remained of his computer, using his foot to lift up a large fragment of the motherboard. His office must have been entered after everyone had gone down to the police station. The timing was perfect. Weerawat had thought of everything, including splitting his team so Jug Ears could search and smash up his office. Ratana saw the grief on his face. He closed his eyes and bowed his head.

"He's got the hard disk with all of Lovell's files."

She started to cry. "It's all my fault. None of this would have happened if I hadn't pressured you to work for Weerawat."

"The good news is that the files are encrypted. It will take him a long time to break the code," said Calvino. Only his invoice folder and the one for the WHO application hadn't been encrypted. Whoever had broken into his office had printed out those files to send Calvino a message. But so far they had two hard drives and no easy way to get the information they wanted.

He reached over the desk with a handful of tissue. "Weerawat's got people on the payroll who will find a way to break open the encrypted files. We don't have a lot of time."

Blowing her nose, Ratana shook her head. She had been blinded by the Thai curse—the belief that money, status, and power automatically meant that Weerawat was "a good man." He had used his power to avoid charges and had come close to having Calvino charged with a number of crimes that would have tied him up for years. What troubled her about the miscalculation was that she had been physically attracted to Weerawat as he'd stood at her desk. The pull of his wealth, fame, and youthful appearance was irresistible. She would have done anything he asked. Now she felt a horrible weight of shame.

"It's not all bad news. One Hand Clapping is closed. I came back last night and the lights were off. I didn't see anyone today and the door was padlocked. Looks like they're finished. Your prayers have been answered."

"It's not so important now."

She already knew from Manee that the police had believed Weerawat's version of events. That Calvino had been caught inside the third floor and there had been a fight. It hadn't helped Calvino's position that he had admitted to the police that he had broken down the door inside the massage parlor and found a dead girl inside. And the *mamasan* had filed a complaint against him for damages. He'd refused to pay for the door he had ruined. It was all in a file.

A dead massage *ying* always presented a problem for the police. No one at the station cared why Calvino had broken the door. Only one thing stuck in their heads: he had torn the door off the hinges. He had put his shoulder into it. The police had heard that the *mamasan* had closed the massage parlor and left for Hua Hin, where she planned to open a beauty salon. Weerawat, Box Head, and Pot Belly had gone to look at the state of the massage premises. Weerawat had wanted to rent it but had to check the condition first. They'd been about to enter the massage parlor when according to Weerawat and his associates, Calvino had struck again. Colonel Pratt reported that a secret trapdoor had been discovered in that office. The police made more notes. Calvino sketched the trapdoor on a piece of paper. The police passed it around, each studying it closely before passing it along, until every officer had seen the drawing.

"So you've been in this room before," the cops had said.

"Never. I was on the floor when I found it."

"What were you doing on the floor?"

"I was being beaten up."

"But you had time to find this trapdoor?"

"My face found it." Calvino pointed to the side of his bruised face. "It found the trapdoor about the same time as it found his boot." He nodded toward Box Head.

"Before tonight, you didn't know about the secret door?"

"It's not my office. "Why don't you ask Weerawat how he has such an intimate knowledge of the building?"

None of the police believed the *farang*.

After his interrogation, Colonel Pratt escorted him out of the police station. To obtain Calvino's release without charges being filed, he had pulled a string the size of a rope suitable for anchoring an elephant to a tree. The whole time at the station, it had been Weerawat's word against Calvino's, and if the normal sequence of events had been allowed to play out, Calvino would been placed in a jail cell. And Weerawat would have shown his power. And the harmony of the universe would have been restored. But it hadn't worked out that way.

Weerawat had glared at Colonel Pratt and Calvino in the interrogation room. It was the look of a man saying it wasn't over between them. Be careful, be very careful. The interrogating police weren't too happy watching the *farang* walk out the door. No question about it, the police believed that Vincent Calvino was guilty of breaking and entering, and the police were not happy to see him walk.

The absence of any evidence of forced entry to the third floor had saved Calvino. A key had been used to gain access. Calvino's possessions didn't turn up a key to the office door. The police superintendent had told Colonel Pratt that they had a previous written statement that he'd broken the door inside the massage parlor. No matter that there was no evidence he—or anyone else—had forced entry to the second floor; he had been found by Weerawat and his two men (if their statement was to be believed) inside an empty office space. "What were you doing there?" the superintendent had asked Calvino.

"What was Weerawat doing there?" Calvino had responded.

"He owns the building. He heard someone upstairs. He went to inspect and found you."

It had been all downhill from the moment ownership of the building had become clear.

Weerawat's ownership of the building had come as a surprise to Calvino when he'd found it in the list of Weerawat's companies in Lovell's database. He'd been renting the office for years. The rent money had been deposited to a company's bank account. He'd had no idea about the owner of the building, other than it was a private Thai company with an address in Bang-Na.

The police were persuaded by Weerawat's coherent, rational story, backed up by two off-duty police officers, all of whom said that they had heard Calvino inside the third floor office space and that when they had gone to investigate, a fight had broken out. The virtue of Weerawat's story was its stripped-down simplicity. No complicated explanations or arguments. Building owner finds *farang* who already has admitted an earlier break-in one floor below, and the *farang* got hot-headed and resisted. The police officers had earlier interviewed him about the murder of a man in Pattaya. They'd returned to question him again only to find him on the third floor.

They were good. Their stories hung together so well that it was difficult to believe that wasn't what happened. Private investigators were good at getting locked doors open without force, though Calvino's personal record in the building suggested he lacked the skill to pick a lock. As Calvino listened to Weerawat explaining what had happened, he watched the show, observing that the police believed Weerawat's every word. Box Head and Pot Belly supported their boss with a nod or grunt right on cue as Weerawat spoke.

Calvino's law for police interrogation was: Keep the story simple, stupid. Explain too much as to why events happened in the way they did and before long it becomes a complex story and the cops get lost. Weerawat told a masterly story.

★

"Phone Millie Danielson. The number is in the file."

Ratana wiped her face, nodded, and returned to her desk to search among the chaos of papers for the telephone number. A moment later she came back. "I don't understand why you won't tell me what the doctor said," she said. "He looked unhappy."

"He said the office was in worse shape than me."

"I know he didn't say that."

Nodding, Calvino reached down and tried to get a dial tone from his office phone. After that failed, he used his cell phone to dial Millie Danielson's number. In the distance he heard a tenor sax playing. The mellow-as-honey sound of Andy Snitzer's "Only with You." The music was coming from below, over the sound system at One Hand Clapping. He stopped dialing and went downstairs, looking into the window of the massage parlor. He knocked hard on the door. After a few moments, Metta came to the door; looked out, and saw Calvino standing in front.

"Go away. Not open."

"Unlock the door, Metta."

He could hear the jazz playing and her playing for time. Finally she unlocked the door and Calvino stepped inside. She wore a fresh flower in her hair. Her lipstick, red and smooth, made her lips seem larger than he remembered. "Where's the *mamasan*?"

Metta held a small white rabbit curled up in a ball. She shrugged her shoulders. "She go away."

"When will she come back?" Calvino watched her nervously stroke the rabbit.

More shoulder shrugging. "Don't know. Maybe not come back. She scared."

"You're not scared?"

The rabbit gave her a feeling of comfort. She rocked it gently in her arms, keeping with the tempo of the music. "Jazz like this song very much. I want to play it one last time. I have a dream where she asked me to play this song. Her friend Andy liked this song, too. He asked her to play it many times. I never forget." Tears welled up in her eyes.

It was as simple as that. Metta came back to play one last song for a dead friend. Because she'd been asked to in a dream. Calvino brushed away her tears with his hand. She looked at his bruised face. "Someone hit you hard?"

"Yeah, they hit me hard."

She sucked air through her teeth. "Must hurt very much."

Calvino stuffed a thousand baht note in her hand. "Let me know if you hear anything from the *mamasan*. I'd like to talk to her."

She looked at the money and leaned forward and kissed Calvino on the cheek.

"When I see you first time, I think you a good man."

He touched his cheek where she had kissed him. "How did you open the door?"

Metta hesitated a moment, then pulled a key from her jean pocket. She held it out.

"Can I have it?"

Her eyes danced over his black and blue face. Eyes like her rabbit, curious, innocent, and afraid at the same time.

"I know what happened," Calvino said. "Jazz didn't kill herself. Don't worry about it. I'm going to find out who did it. Give me the key. It will help me find her killer."

She dropped the key into his outstretched hand.

"You help Jazz, I know you can."

Barefoot she stood in the door holding the rabbit, her head tilted to the side, whispering something in Thai to the small rabbit. Another kind of coconut shell; another rabbit pulled out of a hat.

THIRTY-FIVE

MCPHAIL sat in the Lonesome Hawk nursing a Jameson on the rocks, one arm around the waist of a waitress, the other flicking the ash from a cigarette. Calvino came through the door wearing sunglasses and a hat. The disguise didn't fool Old George for a moment. "What fucking milk wagon did you fall off, Calvino? You look like shit."

"I got rolled by a midget," said Calvino. "Small but powerful."

"That's my boy." Old George smiled.

Calvino slid into McPhail's booth. "What the fuck happened to you? It wasn't one of the Fab Four's husbands who did this?"

A waitress came out of the kitchen with two plates of tacos and beans and set them on the bar before a couple of regulars. One of them said, "I remember when the special was sixty baht."

The other said, "I remember when it was forty baht, soup and salad, too."

They were talking loud enough for Old George's benefit. He replied: "And I remember buying a building in Berlin in 1945 for two hundred cartons of cigarettes. What do you think that building is worth now? I could buy a cigarette company for the value of that building. The lesson is—are you morons ready for this?—fucking prices go up. What jungle school did you two go to for your education?"

Hunched over their plates, both of the men smiled, the tacos breaking in their fingers, spilling sauce, meat, lettuce, and cheese down their hands. One winked at George, his hands leaking juice. "So why raise the price of the special? You're already a rich Jew."

Calvino leaned his head against the back of the booth. His hands gripped his glass. "Don't do it," said McPhail.

The veins in Calvino's neck thickened, coming to the surface as he raised his head back and rose from the table. He walked over to the bar.

"That's enough," whispered Calvino, taking a taco from the customer's plate and pushing it hard against his face.

"Hubba, hubba," said Old George. "Go back and sit down, Calvino.

Calvino stood next to the customer, clenching and unclenching his fists. "I don't like what I heard."

"If you smash a taco into the face of everyone who says something you don't like, then I'm investing in taco futures in Mexico. Now go sit the fuck down."

George pointed at the customer, who peeled lettuce and sauce off his face. "Give him a Singha on my bill," he roared to a waitress. It was too late. He already had his wallet out and was stuffing cash into the chit cup. He walked out just as the beer arrived.

"Fuck you," said George as the customer passed him on his way out the door. Once the customer was gone, George turned to the DJ and screamed, "How many goddamn times are you going to play 'A Boy Named Sue'? Change the fucking music."

Calvino stroked his jaw, moving it slowly. One more punch would have split open the hairline fracture.

"Calvino ain't no Jewish name. What's your problem?" said one of the old customers across the bar.

"Hey, it ain't just the name that makes you a Jew," said Old George. "If your mother's Jewish, you're Jewish. It don't matter if your name is Vincent Calvino. His mother's Jewish." He left out that she lived in a rest home in New York and Calvino had been short of money to pay her bills.

Lovell came through the door. He looked around the dingy, dark bar. Everything looked worn out, broken down, used up. Calvino sat with McPhail in the booth, popping a pain pill and gulping down a Mekong and Coke. He pressed his cell phone against his ear, but when he saw Lovell walk in, he stopped talking. Lovell was dressed in a polo shirt, jeans, and tennis shoes, and the casual clothes made him look a lot younger. His face was puffy and bruised from the beating Weerawat and his men had inflicted.

"Are you two in the same boxing club?" asked McPhail.

"Same sparing partners," said Calvino.

The waitresses buzzed around Lovell, falling over each other to take his order. He ordered an iced coffee with no sugar.

"I thought you were in America," said Calvino.

"I thought you might be dead," replied Lovell, easing himself down on a bar stool opposite the booth.

"So far we're both wrong," said Calvino.

"Your secretary said I would find you here. She told me about the break-in. They ripped off your computer hard drives."

"They were encrypted. That gives us some lead time," said Calvino.

Lovell sipped his iced coffee, his eyes glancing at the walls decorated with branding irons, a Lonesome Hawk flag, an armadillo wood carving, assorted faded cowboy posters, montages of dusty photographs of regulars long dead. A huge stuffed water buffalo head occupied the paneled wall directly above Old George. Both the water buffalo and Old George tilted their heads toward the door, waiting for someone. Lovell lowered his glass, walked over to the booth and slid in next to Calvino. He reached over and, using the element of surprise, untied Calvino's tie and retied it. "Sorry, but it was making me nuts."

McPhail rolled his eyes. The waitress he held in a professional wrestler's arm lock slid her fingernails across the table and touched Lovell's hand. He jumped, nearly knocking over Calvino's drink. "You want a taco?" asked the waitress.

"It's not a trick question," said McPhail. "It's the special."

"I thought I saw someone wearing a taco on his way out," said Lovell.

"They're better eaten. But Calvino can help you turn one into an accessory."

Lovell reached into his polo shirt and pulled out a gold chain. McPhail's waitress swooned. Not only was Lovell handsome, he wore gold. This was a reason to stay for any *ying* working in a bar. Fastened to the chain was a thumb drive. Calvino recognized it immediately and smiled, nodding his head.

"I'm glad you decided to stick around," said Calvino. He glanced at McPhail. "Lovell was a Rhodes scholar."

"Fuck, that means he's really smart. You remember Arnold, the guy who used to work on the rigs and come around for thirty days? He said if you can't raise your IQ, then you move to one of those small African countries where the average IQ is around 70. Then you'd be a genius."

Old George pounded his table. "McPhail, you wouldn't be a genius on a desert island."

"Fuck you, George, you old Jew." McPhail leaned back. "It was a joke, Calvino." Calvino was too busy looking at the thumb drive to react to McPhail.

Lovell removed the thumb drive from his gold chain and folded it into Calvino's hand. "Ratana said she had a backup of the files I gave you. But just in case, here's another backup. Put it somewhere safe."

He paid for his iced coffee and got up to leave.

"Where are you going?" asked Calvino. Just then his cell phone rang. On the other line was Colonel Pratt. It was important—more than important, urgent.

"I'll phone you later," said Lovell.

He stood in front of the water buffalo head and stared for a full minute.

"Well?" asked Old George. "Haven't you ever seen a water buffalo before?"

"He looks at peace," said Lovell.

George cranked his head around and looked up at the water buffalo.

"Yeah, I guess he does."

THIRTY-SIX

CALVINO had never seen Chef Elmo in the restaurant at night. Every person had a place and time, and when one was shifted to another place and time, then something strange happened, as if that person had a new self. The man who ran the cooking class and the man he saw that night were different people. Night-time Chef Elmo circulated among the tables, laughing and joking with customers, making polite recommendations, listening to their stories, desires, and complaints with infinite patience and wisdom. He looked older, wiser at night.

Walking through the restaurant parking lot that evening, Calvino heard the gurgle from his lungs. His ribs hurt each time he breathed. He looked over the expensive cars parked outside Chef Elmo's tiny empire. The play of shadows and light made the lot seem strange in an exotic, other-worldly way. Out of another time. It was partly the light—the shafts of light diffused by the trees, a bouncing spotlight raking the moonless sky, and isolated rivulets of light along the verge between the driveway and the garden. In the center of the garden, an illuminated fountain shot jets of water through the trunk of an elephant rearing back on its hind legs.

In the daytime Calvino hadn't noticed the fountain, or if he had, the elephant hadn't fully registered. The grounds and buildings, all on one level, were originally a house in a compound. In the afternoon, the place was like a *ying* with no makeup, baggy shorts, and hair tied in a knot. Then one evening, inside a smoke-filled cabaret, the same woman comes onstage with all the right makeup, nails done, and tight-fitting dress and belts out a ballad that melts down the front row, rolling over them table by table, until her magic is everywhere.

He walked along the path. Around the compound was a three-meter stone fence. It was something he had seen hundreds of times in the green zone, especially along the back lanes. The magic wore off as fast as it possessed. The restaurant could have been in any neighborhood and in any big city. It was like Lovell's condo with the generic sculptures and painting, ornaments that speak of taste and grandeur, losing their identity.

The restaurant was out of his league. The price of a meal was a month's operating expenses, six months of lunches at the Lonesome Hawk. Eating the results of the Fab Four's cooking exercises didn't count as having dined at the restaurant. The women had cooked that meal. Chef Elmo had watched them. Guided them. He did the best he could. But the women weren't Italian. The food wasn't in their blood. The women thought they were cooking Italian, but they would also confuse a prayer rug with religion. Italians cooked Italian food. Everyone knew that.

Millie Danielson had suggested dinner at Chef Elmo's restaurant. He had agreed as it seemed his only chance at getting her side of the story, the side Colonel Pratt had sought but failed to get. She was waiting at a table when Calvino came through the door. The headwaiter gestured toward her before leading Calvino to the table. Millie Danielson looked at her watch and was about to say something when she saw his busted-up face.

"I know I'm late. I apologize." Calvino looked unsteady as he sat down.

An open bottle of French claret was on the table. About a third of the bottle was missing. From the breadcrumbs, he figured she was on her second basket of bread. She looked steamed. But then, she also looked a little drunk.

"The only reason I agreed to meet you was because you helped Ruth," she said.

"Ruth is a sweetheart. Noah's a sweetheart. Denver will be a better place once they arrive," said Calvino as a waiter smoothed a cloth napkin on his lap. "Could you bring some more bread?" he asked.

Millie Danielson refilled her glass and reached over and filled Calvino's glass. She didn't look like a grieving widow. A little drunk, irritated, and bored, but not any way near a state of deep mourning. Her dress with a scooped neckline screamed out, "I am available. Proceed to the front desk to fill out an application. *Stand in line, baby.*"

"And bring another bottle of whatever this is," he said to the waiter.

She drank without toasting Calvino, who held his glass out for a touching that wasn't meant to be. He smiled and drank half the glass. When he came up for air, she was staring at him.

"You are thirsty," she said. "Would you like some water?"

"I'll stick to the wine. But thanks for asking."

He knew the wine was expensive, and he didn't care. He wanted to show her he knew his own way to deal with pain. He took time to look her over. It was clear that she'd gone to a lot of trouble to make herself up, with a fresh hairdo, nails polished, the designer dress. Those fingernails tap-danced against the crystal glass the way a toastmaster does when he wants to get the attention of the audience. It worked every time. She had Calvino's attention.

"Noah—you know, Ruth's husband—isn't really so much bad as weak. That's the case with most men. They want to be good, to do good. Then a skirt goes by and they become weak. And the next thing, all the good goes out the window."

"A weakness that women use to their advantage," said Calvino.

"Men don't need much encouragement."

Calvino understood that these were the bitter words of a betrayed woman. Noah had been with the two *yings* in front of the Dead Artists bars, hearing a voice in his head: two good *reasons to stay*. Because he couldn't tune out the frequency, that made Ruth's husband weak; and if that were true, all men were weak. He smiled, drank the glass to the bottom and refilled it.

"Was your husband weak?"

It was better to get it out in the open. The waiter brought back another bottle of the same vintage, opened it, and refilled Millie's glass. He seemed to understand that neither of them had much interest in food and disappeared to another table.

Millie sipped her wine and didn't respond. "Have you ever met a *farang* husband," she asked, "who wasn't weak in the face of temptation? Or are you going to tell me that you're the exception, Mr. Calvino?"

"I am told that Bangkok's tough on a marriage," he said. Millie had read the *Index*. She knew the odds; she knew the upward trend. The bullish market for extramarital affairs was off the graph in Bangkok.

"What you mean is tough on a Western marriage. In this place, I don't find the women have sufficient means to keep their men inside the fence. I once had a border collie who learned how to open the gate latch. I couldn't ever un-teach him that trick. A man's like a dog who doesn't unlearn the trick that lets him on the other side of the fence."

"Did you know about the massage girl at One Hand Clapping?"

She nodded. "Jazz," she whispered. "Do you like musical names for women, Mr. Calvino?"

"I saw her body," said Calvino.

"Was it nice?"

"She was dead. Her wrists slit open, blood everywhere on the sheet, bed, and floor. Blood sprayed on the walls and curtains. It wasn't something you'd want to see. A lot of blood."

Millie shrugged off the image. If she had a picture of Jazz dead in the room, she showed no emotion. "I understand a lot of these girls decide to end their lives. Who can blame them?"

Calvino gave her a long silent look, broken by a hacking cough. He turned his head and spit blood into a napkin. The background noise from the other diners filled in the dead zone. *Not a hint of sympathy or compassion in her voice*, he thought. She was tough enough to play queen to Box Head's king on a chessboard.

"Sometimes they don't end it. Someone helps them along."

"What are you saying?"

"I'm talking about probabilities. The police say the probable cause of Jazz's death was suicide. Another probability is that she was murdered. She died only a few hours before your husband died. A coincidence? Maybe. Maybe not."

"And you think that my husband was murdered, too?"

"Yeah, I'm sure of it. Only I have a slight problem."

She raised an eyebrow. "What might that be?"

"I don't have any direct evidence."

"That puts your belief in the realm of faith, doesn't it? And exactly where do you think this faith is going to lead you?"

Calvino shrugged and ordered his dinner. He told the waiter that he wanted the special. The waiter asked him how he wanted it done. Calvino had no idea what the special was and so had no idea what to tell him. "Tell Chef Elmo it's for Calvino."

"Name-dropping," said Millie Danielson. The wine had taken effect. Her face flushed red and her mouth formed a pout as if she were throwing a kiss. But it wasn't a kiss. Her nails raked the side of the glass.

"How long did you know about Jazz?"

"You have blood caked along the side of your mouth," she said.

He used his napkin to wipe his mouth. "There, that's better," she said.

If Lovell had been at the table, he would have leaned over and wiped it for him. When he looked back at her, he was reminded that there were women a man would take a bullet for, and then there were women a man could easily put a bullet in.

"Thanks. Now tell me about Jazz."

"His current girlfriend?" She smirked. "For a few months. I usually find out about them after he finds one an apartment."

"How many times did this happen?"

Millie Danielson rolled her eyes, making a clicking noise with her tongue. "An eternal reoccurrence."

Calvino looked puzzled.

"Nietzsche, Mr. Calvino. Certainly even you have heard of him?"

"Beyond good and evil."

"Very good." Her faced brightened. "Nietzsche also said there is a morality of masters and a morality of slaves. He could have been Thai, don't you agree?"

"Nietzsche always reminds me that the masters don't always act morally."

"Ruth said that you were an intelligent man."

He leaned over the table. "Did you love your husband?"

Millie had expected this question. Her smile disappeared, her lips tightly pursed. "Yes, I did. I loved him very much." She said this with a mixture of disappointment and regret, rimmed with a thin layer of anger. Fumbling with her handbag, she took out a cigarette. "Do you mind?"

Wasn't it against the law to smoke in a restaurant? There were lots of laws that hit the wall of *mai pen rai* and bounced off. Calvino shook his head.

"I normally don't smoke."

That's why she carries a pack of cigarettes in her handbag, thought Calvino.

"But you and your husband grew apart," said Calvino.

She blew out a cloud of smoke. "Andrew passed HIV on to me."

Calvino reached over and helped himself to one of her cigarettes. They looked like a couple of White Russians plotting the overthrow of the Communists. "How long have you been positive?"

"Only a couple of months. You never think something like this can happen to you. And when it does, your world falls apart."

"Do you know how he got it?"

"Jazz. Or Jazz to the World, as I used to call her."

"Was he sure it was Jazz?"

She nodded. "I could sit around and feel sorry for myself. But why should I? With medication, HIV is something you live with."

"Some people have an allergy to the medicine." She didn't react immediately. "Did Andrew have any allergies?" asked Calvino.

She put out her cigarette. "He did."

She saw the look of surprise on his face. There was something touching about a grown man with a beaten-up face, looking sad for her and her dead husband.

"To the HIV medication?"

A long gray column of smoke curled out of her nostrils. "Andrew had a history of allergies. He said it had been his main inheritance from his parents. They suffered from allergies, too. His brother had been a kid when he died from a wasp sting. He had a bad reaction to some of the medicine he had to take. The doctors scratched their heads and finally worked out a combination that seemed effective. The irony is he didn't die of AIDS or an allergic reaction to medicine; he died of a heart attack. I really don't see how you can say that Andrew was murdered. I am certainly not aware of any evidence to support this."

Danielson had been HIV-positive, a gift passed on from a *ying*. He then passed it on to Millie. Also, he suffered from allergies. His brother had died from wasp venom. That wasn't something that happened every day. It was freaky enough to make Calvino refill his glass. And it got worse; even Danielson's medication for HIV had to be altered because of his allergies.

"Are you able to handle another?" he asked.

"As a man coughing up blood, you should take it easy."

"You're right. I should cut down. Starting tomorrow."

She saw that the second bottle was already half-empty. Calvino had picked away part of the label, peeling it back, as she had told him her husband's family medical history.

"Another bottle would be perfect." Her hand was back in her handbag. This time she pulled out a plastic box, opened the lid, and dumped the pills in her hand. Millie put them in her mouth, took a drink of water, tilted her head back, and swallowed.

"Who knew about your husband's condition?"

"I told Janet, who told Ruth, who told Debra. It didn't really matter. But it was a big wake-up call for them. That's why they asked your friend to bring you to class."

Calvino grinned. They had used McPhail. The Fab Four hadn't needed any convincing; they had gone on a search for a private eye to find out if their husbands were fishing in the same pond and might come up with the big one, like Millie's husband.

He thought about the other private detectives they'd recycled through their personal lives before he had come into the picture. None of that mattered anymore. Colonel Pratt had gone outside the normal channels to keep him out of jail. The night with Millie was for Pratt.

"Do you remember the name Weerawat? He's a business type."

"I've met him," she said.

A fat man at the next table erupted in laughter. It distracted Millie who returned to her cigarettes and wine. She'd pulled back one or two ticks on the emotional clock toward the cold, cautious side. Calvino's question had knocked her back, pushed her against the ropes just when she was starting to feel good and safe. The jolt of laughter from the next table gave her cover to withdraw from the conversation.

Calvino threw another punch as the waiter opened the bottle of wine. "Did he know about your husband's medical condition?"

The fat man's companion, a middle-aged Thai woman, spoke loudly into her cell phone. Calvino turned around, "Lady, we're trying to have a conversation."

Her reaction was hostile until she registered the condition of

Calvino's face. She lowered her voice and the fat man fed his face without looking up from his plate. Calvino turned back to Millie just as the waiter poured a mouthful in a clean wine glass. Calvino threw the wine back with no change of expression on his face. "Just like the first two bottles," he said. "I was asking you about Weerawat."

"And whether he knew about Andrew's allergy," she said. "I talked to Weerawat at one of those hi-so fashion shows. I can't remember where my husband had run off to, but I turned around and there he was. Weerawat. He introduced himself. I'd seen his photograph dozens of times in magazines, but I pretended not to know who he was. He told me that his company had a factory that produced a generic brand of the drugs for the government. He had an exclusive license. When I asked what kind of medicine, he said it was for people who had HIV. I think my face turned red. I wanted to die. But I smiled and tried to get hold of myself. I told him that I heard that some people had allergies to HIV drugs. I made a point of getting him to invite me for lunch. I saw there was some tension between Andrew and Weerawat, and later when I asked my husband about it, he said that Weerawat was a shady businessman."

"Did he mention Weerawat has a company that manufactures fake pills?"

Millie looked down at her plate. "He did."

Her honesty surprised Calvino. "When you went to lunch with Weerawat, did you talk about Andrew's allergies?"

She nodded. "Weerawat said that he had a niece who had all kinds of allergies. The more we talked, the more relaxed he seemed. At the end of lunch, I was pretty sure that I had brought him around."

"Did Jazz's name come up?"

A red blush streaked across her cheeks just as Calvino imagined it had happened at the fashion show. A combination of surprise, anguish, and guilt painted red tracks like a drunk's footsteps down the side of her neck. She sighed, shaking her head, biting her upper lip. "Her name came up."

"And what did Weerawat say when you told him?"

"I was half-drunk. It just slipped out. And he really didn't say anything. He had one of those Thai smiles that you could read anything into. Like some scam artist reading tarot cards."

"You mentioned the name of Jazz's massage parlor?"

"To tell you the truth, that's how it came up. Weerawat had told a lame joke, and when he saw I wasn't laughing, he asked why. I told him that I laughed at certain unusual images, like that Zen thing about the one hand clapping. And he said it was impossible for one hand to clap. I explained that it was the name of a massage parlor, and my husband had a fondness for one of the girls working there by the name of Jazz."

Over one lunch Weerawat had learned about Jazz and where she worked. Millie had also revealed Danielson's allergy history. All that information had translated into happiness for Weerawat, and he had responded with one of those generic smiles. He was putting together the pieces of a puzzle that had eluded him. Millie Danielson had given him the ultimate gift: power over the life of an enemy. If she had known the consequences of giving him this information, would she still have told him such personal details? Calvino didn't know this woman. But he had a feeling she had a good idea what it meant to say the things that she did over lunch.

"Why are you telling me this?" asked Calvino.

"I don't think you have any idea how powerful Weerawat is."

He had been thinking the same thing about her. Now he wondered if she had been shaving the handles off the truth, making a cup appear to be a bowl. "He could help a betrayed wife in a lot of ways," he said.

"Having my husband dead doesn't help me," she said.

"No life insurance?"

She laughed at the idea. He saw from the way her eyes looked down that she was avoiding an answer so that she didn't have to lie. The waiter came out with Calvino's special, ink-black truffles, and put the plate in front of him. They looked like three severed black testicles. The waiter then served Millie Danielson foie gras. Calvino looked up from the truffles and found Millie studying him as if he were a dead man walking.

"I didn't take you as a truffles man," she said.

"What kind of man did you take me for?"

"Someone who barrels straight ahead because he thinks he's right and so things will always turn out okay. You know what? That rarely happens in real life."

"Tell me what happens in your version of real life," said Calvino.

She lit another cigarette, blowing the smoke to one side from the corner of her mouth.

"You can fight him. But you won't be able to defeat Weerawat. Not with all the friends in the world. I'm telling you this because you made an effort to help my friends. I know they messed you around, changing their minds. But you still helped them. That's something in my book. And I can see someone beat you up." She put out the cigarette, making no effort to touch her food.

"It wasn't Ruth, Janet, or Debra."

She didn't smile.

"I wanted to return the favor and give you some advice."

"What would that be?"

She arched her eyebrow. "You're a smart man. Do I have to spell it out?" She could see from his expression that was exactly what it would take. "It'd be a smart move for you to head to the airport and go back to wherever you come from."

"I told you already. I'm from New York."

"Then go back. And I wouldn't leave it too long."

"You're telling me I don't have much time?"

The smile returned. "You catch on fast."

"Are you delivering a message?"

What he didn't tell her was that New York had changed in profound ways during the years he'd lived in Thailand, or maybe he had changed. All he knew was it didn't feel like the same New York he'd left. Or the same country. It was a strange, alien place on the map. Now he thought of New York as the place where his mother waited to die in a second-rate rest home.

"Going back isn't such a bad idea," she said. She stubbed out her cigarette and immediately lit another one. Her hands were shaking a little. Calvino leaned over and steadied them, letting the flame from the lighter touch the end of the cigarette. She inhaled deeply. The smoke calmed her.

"Then why are you staying? The local politics are turning nasty."

"When you're HIV positive, you stay where the medical care is cheap and servants look after the cleaning and shopping. You don't worry about politics turning nasty. They've always been nasty. Everywhere. All of the demonstrations for freedom and democracy, what does that mean to me? Not much."

THIRTY-SEVEN

CHEF Elmo wandered from the kitchen into the dining area. He wore a white chef's outfit and hat, making him seem pudgy, neutered, and all moon-faced with bloodshot eyes. He had a sheepish grin as he caught Calvino's attention. A politician's wave of the hand greeted Millie Danielson. Standing at their table, clicking his tongue, Chef Elmo examined the untouched food.

"You don't touch your food. It's no good?"

"We've been so busy talking, Chef, we haven't started." Millie lifted her hand for him to kiss.

After kissing the top of Millie's hand, he handed Calvino a note. "Please tell your clients that I am not a mailman."

A look passed between them. If Calvino had known Chef Elmo better, he would have seen all the signs of a man under stress, including nervousness and agitation. The persona of a celebrity chef rested on character tics. In Chef Elmo's case, happy diners assumed that a high degree of anxiety suited the role of a chef.

As Chef Elmo talked to Millie about his cooking class, Calvino scanned the note written in McPhail's handwriting. It read: "Follow Chef Elmo out through the kitchen. I'm waiting in the back. Keep smiling and pretend everything is okay." Calvino folded the note and stuffed it in his pocket. He lifted his glass of wine and toasted Chef Elmo. Millie raised her glass, too.

"To the chef," said Calvino. After taking a drink, he put the glass down. "There's a girlfriend problem. Excuse me for a moment. Chef Elmo and I need to talk."

She looked at Chef Elmo with a knowing smile. "It never ends, does it?"

He pulled his chair back and followed Chef Elmo through the doors to the kitchen. The chef didn't look over his shoulder. He crossed the kitchen quickly, passing the ovens and cutting counter, two industrial-sized fridges, and sinks, and entering a passage with large plastic garbage containers. Calvino caught a smudgy image of himself in the chrome fridge door. Not a pretty sight, he thought. He found McPhail squatted down between two of the containers, stroking a cat. He looked up at Chef Elmo and Calvino, one hand cuffing the cat's ear.

"You've got to get out of here," said McPhail.

"I'll tell Millie."

McPhail stood up, holding a machete, and the cat scrambled through between Chef Elmo's legs toward the kitchen.

"Not a good idea," said McPhail. He put a hand on Chef Elmo's shoulder. "Thanks Elmo. You did good."

"What's this about, McPhail?"

McPhail put an arm around Calvino. "You are in some real shit."

Chef Elmo pulled out a fist of keys and unlocked the back door, which opened onto a garden. He switched off the light above the outside door. Light from the neighborhood houses illuminated shadowy outlines of palm trees, banana trees, and yellow-striped bamboo taller than a two-meter stone wall at the end of the garden. No metal pointy pikes to impale intruders; no shards of broken bottles to slice their hands and knees. But getting to the wall was altogether another matter. Between the wall and the garden was a jungle of shrubs, bamboo, and trees. McPhail used his machete to clear a narrow passage through the bamboo.

Sweat rolled down McPhail's face. "Just a little bit more and we can get over the wall."

"McPhail, why are we going over the wall?"

He stopped hacking at the bamboo. Pointing at the restaurant with the machete, he said, "Because some assholes are waiting out front for you."

Calvino felt his heart thumping. The codeine had worn off and his ribs and head started pounding in a conga rhythm. "How many?"

"Two or three. And some cops."

"Over the wall it is," said Calvino. He thought of Box Head and Pot Belly waiting for round two. Coming out of the police station, they'd made it apparent a reunion would be shortly arranged.

With the smell of fresh-cut bamboo in the air, McPhail raised the machete and hacked at the bamboo, cutting out a small patch in the thick wedge of undergrowth. "Man, this is like a jungle. We have a few minutes before they find out you've done a runner."

"How would they know?"

He dropped the machete and put an arm around Calvino's shoulder.

"Good luck, buddy," McPhail said. "Pratt's waiting for you."

He cupped his hands together, forming a bridge. Calvino stepped into the hands and hiked himself up. One extreme burst of energy and he was on the top of the wall. He caught his breath and looked down.

"Thanks, McPhail."

On the other side of the wall, a pack of street dogs barked, and when they saw him looking down, they growled, jaws snapping. The dogs wanted him to take it personal. Calvino dropped to the ground. Reaching down, he pretended to pick up a rock, and wound up like a baseball pitcher. The threat was sufficient. The dogs fled, barking as they ran. Calvino looked around, trying to find some recognizable landmark. There was none. He had landed on the small *soi* to nowhere. Looking around, he failed to spot Colonel Pratt. The *soi* was secluded, quiet, the kind that rich people sought. He saw a car appear, a new metallic gray BMW pulled into a driveway. Once the BMW disappeared, there was no more traffic. It was the kind of *soi* used by those who lived on it. He could see to his left where the *soi* ended. On his right, a hundred meters in the distance, it formed a T-juncture with a larger *soi*. He hurried toward the T-juncture. A motorcycle passed. The driver hit the brakes, stopped, and looked over his shoulder at Calvino. The motorcycle driver parked his bike.

Colonel Pratt pulled off his helmet and waved Calvino over. Calvino broke in a run. He stopped at the curb and leaned over, holding his ribs. Then he slowly raised himself up. He'd never been so happy to see Pratt's face.

"McPhail said I might find you here," said Calvino. "I did a runner on a three-hundred dollar bill."

"The lady can afford it," said Pratt, holding out a spare helmet. "Put this on."

Colonel Pratt wore jeans, sandals, and an orange motorcycle taxi vest over the shirt. Calvino hadn't remembered a look of fear in Pratt's face. Not for many years, and then it had been the Chinese triad in New York that had caused him to look so afraid.

"You're gonna tell me something I don't want to hear."

Colonel Pratt's face became still, almost calm. "Lovell's dead."

A jolt of pain shot through his ribcage as a large shudder worked its way through his lungs and throat. He shook his head and looked away, and started to walk down the *soi*. Under his breath, Calvino muttered, "When?"

"Vincent, it's time to go. We'll talk about it later."

Calvino stopped, half-turned. "I wanna go home."

"You know that you can't go back. They'll be watching your office and apartment. You go underground."

One word. That is all it took for Calvino to fully understand the situation. "Underground" conveyed an immediate and powerful message that things had gone beyond what Colonel Pratt could control. Underground also translated into a feeling of numbness and futility. Old George told him that during the war he learned one important lesson of life. When you need an emergency exit, you've got no time to build one.

"You have to think smart, Calvino," Old George had said. "I'm surprised you've lasted as long as you have. The odds sooner or later will catch up with you, and then what?"

"What would you do?" Calvino had asked him.

Old George had looked to his left and right, and then leaned forward and whispered to Calvino. "I have a place. If you ever need it."

That time had come.

Calvino took the crash helmet and slowly pulled it over his swollen head. Pain shot down to the balls of his feet. He looked out through the narrow opening in the helmet. It was difficult breathing inside. He swung a leg over the back of the motorcycle. Colonel Pratt maneuvered the bike around; he drove to the back *soi* and turned left, taking a narrow footpath that came out to another *soi*. He sped through a latticework of small *sois* until he emerged near

Asoke.

The restaurant was far behind. Pratt pulled the bike into Asoke and merged into the flow of dozens of other motorcycles. He could pass for one of the hundreds of motorcycle taxi drivers carrying a *farang* passenger. It happened hundreds of times a minute, day after day. It took only a few minutes to reach the Sukhumvit entrance to Washington Square.

Inside the square, the parking lot near the old cinema with the name Mambo on the marquee was a zone of chaos. Machines and bodies jostled with each other, all sharp elbows knocking together in a confined space. Mambo shows, which had started at 8:30 that evening, had ended, unleashing hundreds of tourists from China, Hong Kong, and Taiwan. A swarm of the Mambo crowd surrounded Colonel Pratt's motorcycle. The crowd clogging the area were Mainland Chinese. Dressed in baggy, cheap clothes and sandals, their faces leathery from too much time in the sun. Hundreds of people rubbernecked each other, swarming as if someone had stuck a sword into a giant hive, all toothy grins, blocking all traffic. Colonel Pratt ran out of space to inch ahead in and ditched the motorcycle. He took off his helmet and climbed off the motorcycle. He was swept up in the crowd. Calvino struggled to keep sight of him as he fell one, then two, then three steps behind, unable to hold his own in the crowd.

Several group tour leaders walked down the steps from Mambo, shouting through megaphones. It took a few minutes for them to bring some order to the scene. The tourists followed their guides to huge buses, looking slightly disoriented, stunned to find themselves in the square at night, surrounded by a series of run-down shop houses. It could have been a mob scene in a movie about the Cultural Revolution. The Chinese smoked cigarettes as they waited their turn to board. A number of them wore wide-brimmed bamboo hats. Others had moon faces and their hair appeared to have been styled with a box cutter and a mirror. He knew from those heads he was in a sea with fish just like him. Two elderly bow-legged women climbed in that swinging side-to-side movement up the ladder to their bus. He saw their big round eyes staring at him out the bus window. He thought of his great-grandfather painting the ancestors of these people almost a hundred years ago. They didn't smile then; they didn't smile now. The Thais were always smiling.

That smile should mean something good, he thought. Even Box Head and Pot Belly had smiled as they beat the shit out of him. Calvino thought that they would have been smiling when they killed Lovell. He remembered those smiles from the pleasure of inflicting pain.

Calvino caught Pratt's eye as he emerged from the crowd. Pratt motioned for Calvino to follow him. They wound their way through the Chinese, who were in a good mood after the *katoey* show; they were laughing and joking and spitting their way as they walked to their buses. Calvino and Pratt were forced off the roadway as the buses started to move along the narrow lane. Once they had passed the entrance to the Lonesome Hawk, Colonel Pratt continued for another ten feet, stopped, looked in both directions, and then opened the door. Upstairs were four floors of hotel rooms. In the daytime, there were short-time rooms for rent. When they reached the third floor, Old George was at the top of the stairs, leaning on his cane. His ashen gray face, his humped-up shoulders, the thick glasses blurring his eyes—even at a distance these made him look like a composite of body parts stitched together from the bits alligator poachers had thrown back into the Florida swamps.

"You took your fucking time," said Old George.

"I had to climb over a fucking wall with two cracked ribs," said Calvino.

"There's always a wall to climb over. That's the meaning of life. Learning how to fucking climb and still be on time." Old George talked as he found the right key on his chain to open the door to one of the short-time rooms. He switched on the light, waited until Colonel Pratt and Calvino had gone inside, and then shut the door.

"You see, it's nothing much. But it is a place you can stay," said Old George. Pointing at the toilet at the far end, he added, "Don't flush toilet paper down the toilet, or everything backs up. That means plumbers. That means a problem. I know that it's not the Oriental Hotel. But no one will know that you're here." Old George looked at Calvino and then Colonel Pratt. "I'll see you get meals. Meanwhile, you two want to talk. I'll be staying across the hall tonight. It's too late for me to go back." He leaned on his cane and looked around the room.

This was the Bangkok underground.

After Old George had closed the door to the room and locked it,

Calvino sat on the sofa. "Tell me about Lovell."

"It's bad, Vincent." Colonel Pratt had photographs from the crime scene, and he handed them over. Calvino flipped through them quickly. He tried to register the images of Lovell's blood and brains spattered over the pink wallpaper and furniture of his condo. The generic sculptures and glass and chrome flecked with blood. Lovell lay slumped on his side, his head on the edge of the sofa as if he were looking into the camera. If they had beaten him, it didn't show that much on his face. Lovell might have been sleeping but for a ragged black hole in his forehead.

"When did it happen?"

"Someone heard gunshots and phoned the police. When the police arrived they questioned the security and neighbors. But no one saw anything. We never found out who called the police," said Colonel Pratt. "One of my friends was at the scene. He phoned me. He took pictures and sent them to me at home." He paused a long moment. The windowless, airless hideaway depressed him greatly. "Weerawat's people are looking for you, Vincent. So are the police."

"They think I killed Lovell? Are they nuts? I was having dinner."

Calvino sat on the edge of the bed and it sagged. He stared at his face in the mirror over the dresser. It had seen a thousand faces come and go in that room. His face was another monster mask of pain and regret.

"Lovell was killed before you showed up at the restaurant," said Colonel Pratt. "They will say you used dinner with Millie Danielson as an alibi. And that you killed Lovell because he wouldn't settle the money Danielson owed you. It's not what they think that matters. It's what they are told to think."

"They, they, they. Whoever *they* are, who cares what the fuck they say?"

"Vincent, it gets worse," said Pratt.

"How much worse?"

"The police found your .38 police special beside Lovell's sofa. The bullet that killed Lovell was fired from your gun."

"Box Head must have taken my fucking gun," said Calvino. "But you gave it back me at the police station."

"I gave you the .38 they handed me at the station. You would've noticed if it wasn't your gun," said Colonel Pratt. It had been a long time since Vincent Calvino had seen him break into a sweat. He wiped his brow. "You did check it, Vincent?"

"I'd been beaten up, Pratt. One eye swollen shut, the other half-open. What did you expect me to do, check the serial number?" Calvino unholstered his .38 police special. "I've got it right here."

"Check the serial number."

Calvino frowned, looking confused.

"The serial number on the gun at the scene is the same as the one registered in your name," said Colonel Pratt.

Calvino stared at the handgun in his hand as if it were an alien object. "They switched guns?"

Colonel Pratt nodded. "I know that. So does Weerawat. But it doesn't matter. He will say his men never saw your gun. He's got friends at the highest levels of this government. You can't touch him."

Calvino checked the barrel, running his forefinger to the end. "An untouchable who plants guns."

"Every gun has a different feel. You didn't feel the gun was different?" asked Colonel Pratt, taking the .38 police revolver from Calvino, turning it over, checking the serial number.

"All I could feel were a couple of cracked ribs, a bum shoulder acting up, and my face swelling up like a watermelon. Feel the gun? I didn't have any feelings left over. And who are they going to believe?" asked Calvino, looking at himself in the mirror over the vanity. The face he saw in the mirror looked like a dead man waiting to fall over. He understood the nature of belief and how like light it bent depending on the pull of gravity, and Weerawat was a huge gravity-pulling force.

Colonel Pratt nodded. "Do you understand, Vincent?"

"What about, Pratt?"

"Yesterday I received a transfer to an inactive post."

"You're not a cop anymore."

"I am a cop on ice."

"Freezing," said Calvino.

Weerawat has shown himself to be more than good. He's in a class of his own, thought Calvino. Weerawat had played him like the guys with their shell game on a cardboard box on Canal Street in New York. He'd let his guard down and failed to recognize the game Weerawat was playing. Hiring him as security chief was a brilliant way to set up Calvino for the murder of the foreman in Pattaya. Weerawat had that murder linked to Calvino. It gave him something important to fall back on no matter what. Weerawat had caught him wrong-footed, taking his gun, beating him up, switching guns, and using the one registered to Calvino to kill Lovell.

Weerawat had a bonus, too: Jazz's murder appeared on the surface consistent with Calvino's recent pattern of behavior. Weerawat had sketched out each of the murders for the police. Vincent Calvino was simply a very dangerous killer. As far as he was concerned, Calvino was protected by a police mafia source—Colonel Pratt. The same cop who had interfered, arrested Weerawat and his associates on their own premises, and had bailed him out even though he was implicated in two murders. Now he could say, "You see, by letting him go, you've let him kill again."

"What about Ratana?" he asked.

"Ratana's safe," said Colonel Pratt.

Calvino had been thinking about her and wondering how he was going to explain what had happened. "Of course she's safe," said Calvino.

"She's gone up-country with Manee. You don't need to know where they are. But they are safe." Colonel Pratt would have places up-country that no one would ever find. He thought of her face as she talked about making a mistake about Weerawat's character.

"Weerawat's appointment to a senior post will be in the newspapers tomorrow," said Colonel Pratt.

Calvino sighed, shaking his head. "Did you see this coming?"

"It's not over yet," said Colonel Pratt. "Something is coming down, Vincent. Things have gone too far."

"They say there'll never be another coup in Thailand. That those days are over."

"The government isn't led by a Prospero who can see the error of his ways," said Pratt. In recent days he'd been rereading *The Tempest*, one of his favorite Shakespearian plays.

"Prospero reformed by the end of the play," said Calvino, grinning. "You think guys like Weerawat are gonna reform? Next life in the late afternoon maybe."

Pratt started to say something else but thought better of it, looked away for a moment, and drew in a long breath. "All I can tell you is that Weerawat's photograph and the story of his appointment as a special senior adviser to the government will be all over the newspapers tomorrow."

Weerawat had taken a stand and sided with the government. His appointment would make others fear him. Rumors of the appointment had been circulating for some time, but such gossip was cheap. No one could be certain if it would ever happen. Colonel Pratt and his immediate superior had been among the first to find out the extent of Weerawat's reach. Both had been transferred to inactive posts. A warrant had been issued to arrest Vincent Calvino for the murder of Jazz and Daeng, the Pattaya foreman, and now John Lovell had been added to the list. They had witnesses who had seen Calvino with the dead man in Pattaya and had seen Calvino give him money. He'd busted open the door to Jazz's room. He'd been caught on the second floor and had used the trapdoor to drop down to the massage parlor room where the dead *ying* was found. And now they had Lovell's murder wrapped up with the presence of Calvino's handgun.

"Once I disappear into the gulag, that's it. I'll never come out," said Calvino.

"Stay out of sight for a while. Weerawat's afraid you can hurt him, so he's striking first."

Pratt pulled a bag of cheap phone cards out of his motorcycle taxi vest and handed them to Calvino. "Each card is a separate number. Use it once, then throw it away and use another. Just before you run out, phone me and I'll give you more cards. Don't use any number twice. When you phone, I'll give you a new number for your next call. That way they can't track our calls."

Colonel Pratt let himself out the door.

Calvino sat back on the bed looking around the room.

He turned on the television. All of the channels were in Thai. He caught a glimpse of Weerawat sitting on a padded chair, hands folded, smiling and looking into the camera. The interviewer asked him in Thai about his plans for the green zone, meaning the most desirable areas of Sukhumvit Road.

"It would be best to make certain the green zone has affordable housing for Thais," said Weerawat, smiling into the camera. "If foreigners want to live and work in the zone, they should first have a business visa. We have too many undesirable *farangs* in our country.

We should be more careful through tightened visa restrictions. Everyone thinks the *farangs* are rich. But it's not true. We have poor *farangs* causing everyone a headache. So my idea is to keep the green zone for Thais and business people."

He thought of Cameron reading the face on the TV.

Liar.

Calvino switched off the television. He had interrupted Lovell's packing with a nice speech about standing up for what was right. Lovell had listened and not gone to the airport. Now the police were hunting him for Lovell's murder.

Weerawat had been pulling the strings behind the police investigation. Along with his Uncle Suvit, Weerawat had worked hard to gain support and encouragement from the top officers. They had come a long way since Galileo Chini had painted their great-grandfathers with pigtails flying, streaking in front of the huge head of the dragon.

Everyone in the government and in the media was tripping over themselves to please him. They wanted to be on the right side of Weerawat because he looked like a winner, and people backed a winner.

Weerawat has to find me. He has to end it, Calvino thought. He lay back, shut his eyes, and fumbled in his pockets for a pain pill. He shook the bottle and dumped the contents into his palm. He had two left. Blinking, he threw both into the back of his throat and swallowed. *Just get me through the night,* he said to himself.

As Calvino drifted off, he saw Lovell's body on the sofa. He saw Weerawat looking out from the TV. Weerawat clenched his fists and jaws and stared straight into the camera, shouting about the need to cleanse the green zone of unwanted foreigners. If you don't have a business visa, then get out of the green zone. He saw the tour buses in Washington Square. The lines weren't Chinese tourists but *farangs*. They were in chains and heavily guarded. In the whispering, he heard them talking; he heard them weeping. They were being transported to another place. It was part of the program to weed out the undesirable foreigners, dissenters, perverts, unruly, and financially strapped. He saw a familiar face in the driver's seat. It was Old George, nursing a Singha beer and singing an old World War II song. He started the engine and drove into the night.

THIRTY-EIGHT

A ragged streak of light flashed across the room, followed by a rolling boom of thunder. Calvino woke up with a start. He sat up in bed drenched in sweat. He still had his shoes on. The lightning illuminated the room again. He'd been dreaming, and when he saw the outline of Old George leaning on his cane in the doorway, he wasn't certain that he was awake.

"You're screaming down the place."

"George? What time is it?"

"Three in the morning, and you woke me up. I've got other people staying here. You've got to be quiet."

"What do you want me to do?" asked Calvino. "I was dreaming."

Old George closed the door behind him and rested against the dresser. Calvino had rolled over on his side, his face pressed against the pillow. Slowly he rose up, holding the thumb drive that Lovell had given him with the backup files.

"What the fuck's wrong with you?"

"I was in a Thai court."

"What were you doing in court?"

Calvino shook his head. "It was a dream, George. The prosecutor is reading this long charge about how I've killed a Thai workman named Daeng and a massage *ying* named Jazz. After he finishes reading the charges he sits down. Everyone's staring at me. Two guards lead me in leg chains to the box. I'm barefoot, and I can feel the chains bite into my legs. I look around the courtroom but

I don't recognize anybody. The Thai judge looks down from the bench and says that before I testify I have to swear an oath. I ask him, 'What kind of oath?' And the judge is bored. He's just going through the motions. He says, 'You swear an oath on the Koran if you're Muslim. If you're Christian on the Bible, or if you're Buddhist, then on the Buddha's teachings.' The prosecutor and the others in the courtroom are waiting."

"What'd you say?" asked Old George.

"I said, 'I'm Jewish.' The judge isn't happy. I can tell from his face he's pissed off and just wants to get the hearing over. There's an executioner sitting at the prosecutor's table and he's sharpening a huge sword. The judge tells me, 'You must swear an oath as a Muslim, Christian, or Buddhist.' And I say, 'Even if it doesn't mean anything?' The judge is red-faced with anger. 'You don't believe in Jesus?' I shake my head. 'Or Mohammad?' I slowly shake my head, watching the sparks fly off that sword blade. 'Or the Lord Buddha?' 'Sorry,' I say. 'I don't. I don't believe in those religions.' The judge sits back in his chair, his face clouded with shock and frustration. 'Then swear in English,' he says. I blink a couple of times. 'Prisoner Calvino, did you hear what I asked of you? Swear whatever you want in English. Just swear. We need to get on with these proceedings.' I look at the prosecutor, the executioner, and then back at the judge. I shrug my shoulders, stand up in the box, cup my hands around my mouth, and shout, 'Fuck you!'"

"Then I woke up and you were standing in the door," said Calvino, toying with Lovell's thumb drive.

"If I were you, I'd be dreaming about a way out," said Old George. His eyes narrowed. "Are you interested in a container ship out of Klong Toey? It leaves the port the day after tomorrow for Hong Kong. You'd be safe there."

Calvino wiped his face and neck with a thin white towel and got off the bed. He paced across the room with the towel wrapped around his neck, holding the ends as he walked. "If they come here, it will be bad for you."

"Don't worry about me. Worry about you. Like in your dream, I say fuck them. I've been through a war. I am eighty-four years old. What can they do to me that nature hasn't already done?"

Calvino threw the towel down. "George, these are people who don't give a shit if you're old. These people would hurt you."

"Bring them on. I could use a little excitement in my life. Let me tell you something, young man. When you hit eighty your sex drive sputters and stalls out and packs it in altogether. Then you glide. You realize that you've spent most of your entire adult life fucking around in the big search. And what did you find after all that looking around? Screwing, sex, that's what. When you're young, you got to live with that. It's not easy. It's like taking a Jack Russell on speed for a walk twenty-four hours a day."

He raised his cane and pointed to a map of Florida on the wall. "In a week I am off to Florida. But you can stay here as long as you want." He looked around the room, caught sight of himself in the mirror and sighed. "It's been a number of years since I've been in this room. I ain't gonna tell you how many. So don't bother asking."

Ever since his fall the previous winter, George had moved slowly. No one saw him after lunch. He owned a twenty-year-old Toyota and parked it in front of the Lonesome Hawk. His driver, who was also the part-time DJ, hung around until it was time to drive Old George home. Then he helped him in and out of the car. That night, he had come alone in a taxi and got out slowly. He had stopped and leaned on his cane. He had untangled the key to the room for Calvino. The room had been George's private room. The one he used when the Jack Russell terrier in him had him fetching girls upstairs. It had been used for years. It was George's room. The room with all of his memories locked inside. A couple of times he had gone up to sit on the bed and remember. But with a cane it was hard going up the narrow old wooden stairs.

"You need to know what's involved, George. It's serious. The police think that I killed a man tonight."

"Did you?"

Calvino shook his head.

"That's good enough for me. Whenever they need a scapegoat, why is it they always point out the Jew?"

Calvino didn't have an answer. He poured himself a glass of water and drank it down. He'd never understood what it meant to be hunted. He knew that when the hunters marked a prey for extinction, if their intelligence and resources were good, they usually succeeded. He felt tired and scared. The hopelessness chilled him. Weerawat had put in motion the full force of the state. No one could ignore the power of such forces when turned on one man.

"You know the sad thing, George?"

"The world's a sad place."

"I walked straight into it. I had my eyes open, but I didn't see what was in front of me. You live here for years and years and think you've got it nailed. There's nothing you haven't seen or figured out. And then one day you wake up and you realize that you know nothing that matters. All that you think you know is less than a page in a thick book. Then they throw that book at you. It's still in the air. It's still coming at me. I'm trying to duck but I can't see any way out." He felt the presence of Weerawat's fence, the one that held him inside the square.

"I hate this rain," said Old George. "It makes my joints ache."

Calvino sat on the edge of the bed. "No more screaming, I promise."

Old George smiled. "If you were with a *ying*, that's understandable. But screaming in your dreams, that's bad karma. And it pisses off the other guests."

By the time Old George had disappeared down the hallway, Calvino had dressed and slipped on his shoulder holster. The answer had been in the dream. The Thais hated any public outburst. It set them on edge, made them crazy with anger, violent, and hateful. The more public the outburst, though, the fewer options they had to whack out the person standing on the public stage. As long as the limelight was shining, they stayed in the shadows, licking their wounds, waiting for the lights to go off.

He'd been a fool to think that he could hide out. Sooner or later Weerawat's men would find him, corner him, and finish what they had started. He used one of the SIM cards and phoned Pratt. He said he had figured out a way to put a very bright light on Weerawat.

"But you need something first."

"I'd like the security videotape from Lovell's building."

Colonel Pratt said, "I'll see what I can do."

"Any chance of getting my cassette from the Danielson case?" A long silence followed. "Then just the security video from Lovell's. It will have to do."

THIRTY-NINE

COLONEL Pratt parked his car in the street and walked thirty meters to Lovell's condominium. It was 8:00 a.m., and the traffic was jammed for a kilometer near a private school. Mothers behind the wheel of expensive cars stopped, deposited their children at the front gate before driving off. It reminded him of circling flight patterns at Don Muang as the planes crowded in, waiting their turn to land. He was glad that his children had already finished their schooling. They had turned out all right, he told himself. It seemed strange knowing that his career as a police officer with a future had effectively been ended. The superior officer who had given him the order had said, looking up from a folder, that his assisting Vincent Calvino had not been just unprofessional, some might think it amounted to aiding and assisting a fugitive from justice, and that if he continued down that path he should expect that a disciplinary action would be the next step. Threats within threats, like Russian dolls. He thought about his new superior's threat as he entered the condominium. His old superior had already entered the monkhood. That was always an acceptable end.

A uniformed guard stood at the front of the gatehouse. The guard saluted the driver of a Benz and pressed a button that lifted the cross arm above the driveway. The Benz drove through. In the back was a young boy on his way to school. Looking around the main courtyard, Colonel Pratt searched for the presence of police officers returning for another examination of the scene of Lovell's murder. Not a single officer was in sight. The absence of any police at the site of the murder surprised him. It was early morning, though, and they might have organized the team to return later in the morning or early afternoon.

Lovell's murder had happened the night before, and the investigation would have been only hours old. If he had been leading the investigation, his men would be covering the premises, questioning the guards, neighbors, handymen, or anyone else they found in the compound. Rather than crawling with investigators, the guest parking slots were empty except for a red BMW and a gray Camry. He showed the guard his police ID and asked where the security cameras were located. The guard looked at the ID, then Colonel Pratt, and handed back the ID. He pointed at a camera fastened to the roof of the guardhouse. There were also security cameras in the elevator and on each floor.

"I want to see the surveillance videotapes from 6:30 last night."

The guard shuffled his feet and looked away, smiling. "I cannot."

Pratt pulled a thousand baht note from his wallet. "I want a look. I am a police officer."

The guard stared at the money a couple of seconds before taking it, folding the note in two and stuffing it in the pocket of his uniform. He showed Colonel Pratt into the small office. The surveillance tapes were in a box on a table. The guard sorted through the tapes before handing one to the colonel. "From last night, starting at 18:00 hours and ending at 20:00 hours."

"I'll bring them back in a couple of hours," Colonel Pratt said, turning and heading toward the main entrance.

The guard, hands in his pockets, had not objected. He watched the colonel stroll down the driveway and out of the compound. He stopped and looked at the two cars parked in the guest zone. The BMW had Chiang Mai registration plates. Whoever owned the car was a long way from home, or else this was home, and he had his reasons to keep the car registered outside Bangkok. As he walked back to his car, Pratt was thinking that whoever had killed Lovell would have been captured on videotape. He felt a wave of disgust as he thought about the carelessness of the investigation. Not seizing the surveillance tapes was gross negligence. But there was a good side to it. If the police who had gone to the murder scene had been competent, the videotapes would have been gone.

Colonel Pratt drove back to his house and settled behind the computer in his study. He had a videocassette player hooked up to the computer. He shoved the surveillance tape into the player and hit the start button. A digital clock appeared at the right bottom of the screen: 18:06:37. The images moved slowly, with a built-in lag time. Hours could be put on a tape that otherwise would need replacing every ninety minutes.

Looking at the outside of Lovell's building was like watching time-lapse photography. The camera had been mounted on a platform that slowly arced a one hundred and eighty degree angle, including the entrance from the street, the walkway to the lobby, and the parking lot. Nothing much happened. Images moved across an empty entrance and lobby. A Thai woman in her thirties, dressed like an executive, carried a briefcase and used a security swipe card to open the entrance door. A car pulled into a visitor's spot. It was the BMW from Chiang Mai, and a young Thai in casual clothes got out, talking on his mobile phone. A security guard appeared in the frame, saluted the man and walked out of the frame. The BMW owner locked his car and walked to the entrance. Someone buzzed him in. At 18:48:42 a pizza delivery motorcycle and driver pulled into the frame. The security guard could be seen talking with the motorcycle driver, dressed in a pizza delivery outfit with a helmet, holding a large red thermo case. The security guard walked the pizza deliveryman to the main door and used his security card to let him inside.

At 18:52:19 the camera caught Vincent Calvino walking through the entrance and into the compound. The security guard saluted him, and they exchanged a few words. Colonel Pratt froze the picture and studied it carefully. He had no doubt that it was Vincent. He pressed the play button and at 19:06:44 the pizza deliveryman appeared, got on his motorcycle, and drove out to the street. A few minutes later, Vincent Calvino appeared in the frame again. The digital clock readout was 19:11:28. Calvino had been inside the condominium for less than twenty minutes. Enough time to shoot Lovell, get out, and drive to the restaurant for dinner with Millie Danielson.

For the next two hours, Colonel Pratt played and replayed the videotape.

The woman with the briefcase walked through the frame. She

disappeared into the lobby.

The BMW arrived and the owner talked into a mobile phone.

The pizza delivery guy dismounted his motorcycle with a red thermo case.

The security guard stretched out his arms and yawned in front of the entrance.

The security guard blew his whistle and waved a car out of the compound and into the street.

Vincent Calvino walked into the compound.

Colonel Pratt examined Calvino's appearance and exit, frame by frame. Calvino's .38 police special had been found at the murder scene. It was the gun registered in his name that had killed Lovell. And there was Calvino walking past the surveillance camera at the time the murder had happened.

The cars parked in the visitors' zone.

He stopped the videotape to look more closely at the cars in the visitors' zone. Calvino had just entered the gated compound at 18:52:19, the surveillance camera swept the surroundings, picking up not only Calvino but also the cars in the visitors' parking. The red BMW with the Chiang Mai registration plate wasn't parked in the third spot from the end. There was no red BMW anywhere in the parking zone. Colonel Pratt fast-forwarded the videotape to 19:13:12, a couple of minutes after Calvino had left the premises. The eye of the camera swept over the cars in the visitor parking. The red BMW and the gray Camry were parked in the lot. The cars had appeared and disappeared like rabbits in a magician's hat.

He used a safe cell phone number to phone Calvino.

"One hour," he said.

"What do you have?"

Pratt looked gray and tired as he caught a glimpse of himself in the mirror. He knew that he wouldn't have much time and that he would be followed.

"I'll show you in an hour."

"I've left the room. But not the area."

"Don't give me the location," said Colonel Pratt.

The chances were that the police had been posted to watch the Square. As soon as Calvino showed his face, someone would radio in his location.

"I'll meet you on the roof," said Colonel Pratt. "There's a ladder from the fourth floor to the roof. Look for a small shelter. Inside is a wooden bench."

"How do you know that?"

"I know."

"Pratt, bring your laptop. I need to borrow it."

★

Calvino found the shelter on the roof. He used another card to phone McPhail.

"I need more phone cards," said Calvino.

"No problem," said McPhail.

"You still logging into the Wi-Fi connection next door?"

McPhail laughed, "Free Internet. What's not to like? But isn't George putting you up?"

"Not anymore."

The shelter was over a row of shops on the park side of the square. It was a Plan B rooftop place that Pratt had scouted, a place to hole up in, in the event of an emergency, a location hidden from the street and with more than one exit. From this vantage point he could see traffic moving in and out of Sukhumvit Road. He had seen police coming into the square. More police than usual, and they were looking around, asking *farangs* and Thais questions.

★

Colonel Pratt heard sirens outside his house. His official, on-the-record mobile phone rang. His new boss was on the other end, ordering him to walk out of the house and give himself up. He packed a laptop and the videotape into a carrying bag. The senior cop at the other end of the conversation said they had information he'd taken the surveillance tape from a murder scene and that represented a serious breach in the investigation.

"The guard was shot."

Colonel Pratt felt a stinging sensation as if he'd been hit hard. "What?"

"The security guard you took the video from was shot dead."

The security guard would have been a loose end. One they had managed to weave into the story Weerawat was writing. Lovell had been killed by Calvino, and Pratt, his police colonel friend, trying to cover up, had shot the guard and taken the incriminating evidence on the security videotape. That closed the circle.

"Come out, now."

A direct, precise order issued from his superior.

Colonel Pratt had changed into his motorcycle taxi driver's shirt, pants, and orange vest. He peeked out the back door of his house. If he were surrounded, there was no evidence of police in the back. He hurriedly unlocked the padlock to the gate and slipped into a lane. He walked to a metal shed, unlocked another padlock, and rolled up the shutters. Unlatching the kickstand, he rolled out a Honda 200cc motorcycle. He shut the door on his way out and slipped the padlock back on. He rolled the motorcycle fifty meters before starting the engine and driving to the main street. A caravan of city buses roared past. Then a cement truck with the mixer churning barreled down the road. Pulling the helmet over his head, he eased into the traffic, overtaking the cement truck. He thought about who would have had the opportunity, the motive, and the expertise to have altered the surveillance videotape. Whoever had doctored the videotape had forgotten to match the two cars parked in the zone reserved for guests. They had been, in other words, clumsy, *muk ngai*—and had showed reckless disregard for getting something right. His boss had given him a direct order to go out the front door of his house. Now, with the laptop bag hung over his shoulder, he was on the run.

FORTY

THE entrance to Mambo was deserted except for three or four motorcycle taxi drivers who lounged on the front steps, sleeping or talking, or playing checkers with Chang beer caps. They were also the eyes and ears for authorities who wanted human intelligence on a *farang* coming in and out of the square. As an unofficial early warning system, they watched and reported.

When Colonel Pratt rode past the Mambo, the drivers eyed him, stretching out like cats, heads slightly lifted, curious who this driver was from outside the Square. He parked in the alleyway running between Mambo and Bourbon Street restaurant, avoiding the garbage. Rats scurried along the gutter, where steam rose out of the pipes. The alley smelled of urine and rotten vegetables.

Colonel Pratt glanced over his shoulder. No one had followed him. He cut across the back end of the square and kept walking until he reached the end of the row of buildings. Without missing a beat, he strolled behind the last building, edged down a narrow passage, and, looking up, found the fire escape from the night before. He pulled it down and climbed onto the first rung. As he climbed, he thought about his house, wondering if he might have seen it for the last time.

A few minutes later he was on the roof, walking bent over along the far edge, out of sight from those inside the square. Calvino waited on a small wooden bench under a shelter that overlooked the park and the Emporium. It was almost peaceful, he thought. The green of the "green zone" was a luxury, an indulgence, a freakish accident that had happened because somehow developers had fought among themselves to the point that a park was the only way to prevent bloodshed.

"You're becoming a regular in that taxi vest," said Calvino.

"Were you at Lovell's condo last night?" The colonel's mood, earnest and deliberate, suggested there was no room for small talk.

"I was nowhere near Lovell's condo."

"I have a surveillance videotape showing you going in and out of the condo at times that match the time of death. And the security guard." Colonel Pratt took a deep breath.

"What about the guard?"

"He was shot."

"When?"

"Not long after I paid him a visit."

Pratt opened his laptop and switched it on. After a moment, Colonel Pratt started the videotape from Lovell's condo building. Calvino said nothing as he watched the footage. He asked Colonel Pratt to play it back again. "Stop it there."

The camera froze on the pizza deliveryman.

"Can you do a close up?"

Colonel Pratt enlarged the image of the pizza deliveryman. His features looked grainy in the larger picture. The shape of Box Head's face would have been unmistakable. But he had a helmet on. It might have been him, or maybe not.

"Look at him. Don't you remember him?" In a blink, Calvino knew that it was Box Head.

Colonel Pratt looked closer, advanced the frame another couple of seconds.

Lovell's condo security camera had captured Weerawat's associate, one of the cops who had done most of the rib cracking on Calvino. His eyes peered from the helmet. Calvino had seen those eyes up close and personal. He'd never forget the wild pleasure in Box Head's eyes as Box Head was kicking him.

There had been a blue Khmer tattoo on Box Head's neck. Written in ancient Khmer, it was supposed to act like an amulet to protect him against misfortune, bullets, and knife blades. Instead it identified him.

"The tattoo," said Calvino. "I remember that tattoo."

Box Head, dressed in a pizza delivery outfit, carried a large thermo case to keep the pizza hot. He walked past the camera and nodded at the security guard. A few minutes later, he passed the camera again, returning from the building.

"Your gun was used to kill Lovell. You are on the surveillance videotape at the right time. The courts won't care about a tattoo or the fact the cars in the guest zone don't match."

"Is it possible you have the only copy?" asked Calvino.

"I don't know. Weerawat is doing whatever it takes."

"How did you get the tape?" Calvino stared at the Thai in the video who had kicked him in the ribs when he was down.

"From the condo security guard."

"Who is dead," said Calvino, looking away from the screen. "They figured you'd go for the surveillance tape."

Colonel Pratt looked at Calvino and then away. A couple of distant joggers in the park caught his attention. He hunched forward, frustrated and deflated.

"There's no way you could know it was a setup."

Colonel Pratt bit his lip. He shook his head. "I was the sloppy one, Vincent. These people don't leave loose ends."

Calvino leaned forward. Following Colonel Pratt's gaze, he saw the joggers in the distance running around the lake in the park. They seemed so free, so clueless about how easily anything might happen to them.

"Weerawat's smart," said Calvino. "He did an almost perfect job."

"The timing was crucial, Vincent. If you'd been somewhere else, before or after the setup, it wouldn't have worked."

"Millie Danielson," he said. She had sat across the table drinking expensive wine, doing a favor for Weerawat.

Colonel Pratt stared straight ahead. "I thought about her connection with Weerawat."

"She's smooth, Pratt. She worked Weerawat, but she was out of her league."

He thought about the container ship docked at the Port of Klong Toey and Old George's offer to get him on the ship. Colonel Pratt was right about one thing: getting the timing right was important.

How did Weerawat manage to have Box Head kill Lovell during the window of time when Calvino wouldn't have an alibi? Most questions come with a picture image answer. He saw Millie Danielson at the table, finishing the wine, waiting for him to return to the table. The widow who wouldn't talk to Colonel Pratt had agreed to have dinner with him. The dinner appointment would have pinned Calvino down to staying in the neighborhood and most likely at his office, working alone. Pot Belly would have been watching the building.

Pot Belly would have phoned Weerawat that Calvino was in his office, and Weerawat would have given the nod to Box Head. They were well organized. They didn't need to rely on guesswork or bets about Calvino's location. The rest of the building was empty. Calvino had stayed at the office alone working until dinner, going through the files, forming a picture in his head so as to know what questions to ask Millie.

Millie had planned the place and time with Weerawat's help.

"I phoned her friend Ruth," said Calvino. "The one Millie said had convinced her that she should see me. I found out that Millie's story about talking with Ruth was a lie. She hadn't talked to Millie for over a week."

They sat in silence watching the joggers, who looked like tiny stick figures circling the park. "How do we get out of this?" asked Calvino. "Old George can get me on a container ship to Hong Kong."

Colonel Pratt shook his head. "It's not a bad idea, Vincent."

"That's what I thought."

Pratt put a hand on Calvino's shoulder and quickly took it away. "We are driving in reverse. It's not a good time. Everyone's guarding their back."

"That doesn't sound like Shakespeare."

"What Shakespeare said was, 'Conscience does make cowards of us all.' And he wrote, 'The evil that men do lives after them. The good is oft interred with their bones,'" said Colonel Pratt.

"Sneaking out on a ship is cowardice," said Calvino. "I accused Lovell of being a coward for wanting to escape. He listened to me."

"Lovell made his choice, and you'll make yours."

Colonel Pratt had nowhere to run. His wife and kids were rooted in the city, and he had disobeyed the direct order of a superior officer. The wheels had been set in motion—more like tank tracks, rolling straight at him. But not like the iconic photograph of the man in Tiananmen Square staring down a column of tanks. It didn't work that way in Thailand. The driver of the lead tank would increase his speed and run over the man who dared to defy authority. That was the one act no one was permitted to do. Pratt rose to his feet.

"Where are you going?"

"I want to finish this. There are good people on the inside that I can go to. They will help."

"Pratt," he said.

Colonel Pratt turned and looked back at him.

"Thanks."

"Take care of yourself, Vincent."

As Colonel Pratt, the laptop strapped around his shoulder, wound his way along the roof and disappeared down the ladder and into the square, Calvino felt a chill of fear, sitting alone, looking at the sky. Galileo had written that the earth revolved around the sun and then he had faced the Inquisition. Galileo Chini painted a hellish vision of mankind revolving around sensuality. Calvino's world stopped and became silent. No dancing dragons, bells jingle-jangling, no gongs or drums. He had lost himself just as Chini had lost himself in his all-night sessions painting nudes. He had labored during the day over the frescoes in the palace. At night he'd escaped to mix his oil paints, watching the nude model reclined on the bed in a small, hot room, her body slick with sweat, as mosquitoes buzzed and dogs along the canals barked in the distance. Night after night, he had painted until his eyes blurred, canvas after canvas, wiping the sweat from his brow, cleaning a brush, working until just before dawn, then sleeping a few hours before slipping away to work again on the frescoes.

Chini had told Vito that Siam had a great mystical pull. He had been thirty-eight when he accepted the king's invitation to the kingdom. He had known no one in Siam. "After two years, I felt powerful forces quietly cementing me to Bangkok," he had told his son. "I knew that unless I escaped soon, I would never leave. I understood, then, that a young man who sets out for Siam never recovers from such an encounter. Siam imprisons him in the fine sensual luxury, the silky nights, the smell of orchids, the moonlight on the canals, the opium pipes calling to him, and the Siamese women who move without sound, ever watchful, ever caring, forever pleasing. My advice is to go to Siam before you are established, or if you never want to be established, or after you retire. Or if you are stuck, going nowhere, then flee like Corrado Feroci."

The weight of fame had sent Galileo Chini back to Florence, to meet Vito's mother, to father a child, to lose his nude model to Corrado Feroci, who, in turn, had abandoned her. She had sunk below the surface of the Arno River anchored with Galileo Chini's ceramics, her body swept away. Corrado Feroci, too, had gone to Siam to seek fame and fortune, but he had never returned. Vincent Calvino thought of himself as more like Corrado, who had never broken free from the pull of Siam. Galileo had stopped just short of that line and returned to Florence, but Corrado kept walking, crossed the line, and never looked back. Vincent Calvino felt the same line both men had reached was way behind him. He could never retrace his steps. Waiting for Weerawat's next move, Calvino's blood ran cold knowing there was no percentage in underestimating Weerawat's determination to set a whole new series of traps.

Becoming a plumber in New York had been a perfect revenge for the son of a famous Florentine artist.

Becoming a private eye in Bangkok had been a perfect revenge for the son of a famous New York-made man.

FORTY-ONE

THE lunch special came from the kitchen on old chipped plates. Puffy pastries with corn, carrots, string beans, and shrimp inside bloated shapes in the form of circles, blunt stupas, curled and warped. McPhail stared at one of the passing plates.

"UFOs," he said. Unidentified Fried Objects. The waitress set it down at the bar in front of a customer as two uniformed police came through the door. Old George sat, hands folded over his cane, head forward, watching from his usual place below the stuffed water buffalo head. One cop was seriously overweight, his uniform bunched up over his gut. Along with Fat Man was a second cop, who wore one of those quick draw holsters like a gunslinger from the old American west. Fast Draw had thick black hair and rough, hard hands. Fast Draw's hands looked as if they'd broken their fair share of bones.

"You see Vincent Calvino?" asked Fat Man.

"Never heard of him."

The cop didn't smile. "Why does everyone say you are his friend?"

"Why don't you ask them?"

He was an old man and they studied him, deciding what they could do or not do in a bar filled with *farangs* watching. The two cops split up and walked down opposite sides of the horseshoe-shaped bar. Customers stopped talking and stared into their plates. Fast Draw stopped beside a customer, tapping him on the shoulder with one of his rock-breaking hands. "You, do you know Khun Vincent?"

He was the *farang* whose face Calvino had pushed a taco into. He looked up from his UFOs, shaking his head. "Never heard of him."

Fast Draw glared at him, left eye twitching. He had moved close to the edge of the bar, squeezing between two stools. "I don't like *farangs* who come to my country and make a big problem. People who help such a *farang* are no good."

The *farang* never looked up from his plate, "I said I don't know the guy."

Then Fast Draw backed away from the bar. The two cops completed their circle around the bar and stopped in front of Old George. In the air-conditioning, Fat Man continued to sweat. The stains curved out from under his arms.

Fat Man held out his name card. "You see Khun Vincent, you phone me, okay?"

Old George looked at the name card and set it on the table, shoving it under a plate of UFOs. "What'd he do? Rob one of your politicians?"

Neither cop had any idea what the English word "politician" meant. They nodded, measuring up Old George, his cane, his bottle of beer, and the waitress combing out his ponytail. By the time they were opening the door, she was braiding it. "Not too goddamn tight. It gives me a headache if it's too tight," he barked. "And would someone change that fucking music? It reminds me of that fat cop and his sidekick."

"George, you are way fatter than that cop," said McPhail.

"Fuck you."

"They're watching you, George," said McPhail.

"Fuck them. Let them watch. They ain't gonna see nothing I don't want them to see."

One of the regulars from the bar shouted, "They'll be back."

"I am eighty-four years old. I am not worried about a couple of bent-out-of-shape cops."

"How do you know they're bent?" asked the customer at the bar.

"They are standing outside the bar. Aren't cops supposed to catch criminals? When is the last time you think those two caught anything more dangerous than a white envelope for their boss?"

★

It was day five since Calvino had gone underground, first in Old George's short-time room, then in an abandoned room, and finally in an empty room in McPhail's flophouse. McPhail had smuggled him in at three in the morning. Two days after the container ship had sailed for Hong Kong, Calvino was lying on the bed watching television when he heard a knock on the door to his room. Pratt's laptop with an open Wi-Fi connection was on a table. Lovell's thumb drive was connected to an external port. Calvino had been working on the computer for three long days. He had sent out five hundred and thirty-six e-mails.

He waited. He hadn't been expecting anyone. But whoever was on the other side wasn't going away. Knuckles rapped against the wooden door, stopped, rapped again. It was in sequences of three, with a pause, then three more. There was no peephole in the door. He got off the bed and paced across the room.

"Vinny, it's me. Open the door, please. I need to talk to you."

He'd know Ratana's voice anywhere. Unlocking the door, he opened it a crack, saw her standing in the hall, and then opened it quickly and pulled her inside.

"I told you not to come here. It's dangerous for you." He blinked a couple of times. Angry and happy at the same time to see her, Calvino had phoned her two days earlier to let her know that he was okay. Her mouth popped open as, for the first time, she saw McPhail's room. The ceiling had been strung with Christmas tree lights over a false ceiling fashioned from crinkled aluminum foil. Nude cutouts were pasted on the fridge door and sides. There were wooden statues of gnats from Burma, and dozens of erotic oil paintings hung on every inch of the walls.

He couldn't believe how happy it had made him to see her and he surprised himself by doing something: he hugged her, lifting her off the floor, as tears streamed down her cheeks. "I am so glad that you're all right."

"It's over," she said, patting him on the back. "Put me down, Vinny. You don't understand. Let me explain."

"You look great."

"You look terrible," she said, touching his face. "And this place, it gives me the creeps."

"McPhail's paradise."

Her feet touched the floor and he moved back, balancing against the edge of the vanity. He'd been watching the Thai news. There'd been nothing unusual. The best news was that she had showed up safe and sound at his door. She always talked in riddles. It was the Thai thing, keeping the possibilities open, a way out. His old anxiety returned as she walked around the room, looking at him with pity and sympathy as if he were someone in a hospital wearing a head-to-toe body cast. Maybe she'd come to say goodbye? He could hardly blame her. With her boss under suspicion of murder, it would have taken a miracle for her not to bolt.

"I understand," he said. "You've come to say goodbye."

She shook her head. "No, I'm not going anywhere."

He pointed at her. "Why are you here?"

"Sit down and listen."

He moved from the vanity and sat on a chair. Ratana looked around the sparse room. On the wall a lion played a flute while a naked woman danced. There was a dresser with a mirror, a chair, a bathroom, and a window with opaque glass like in a public restroom. Newspapers and clothes were scattered on the floor. On the dresser was a half-empty bottle of Mekong, whiskey glasses, and an ice bucket with three inches of water in the bottom. And Pratt's laptop.

"I thought you'd gone up-country with Manee."

"I came back."

"I've got work to do. You should go. It's not safe for you to be here." He thought it had to be Pratt and the surveillance videotape. Pratt would have told Manee and she would have phoned Ratana. "The security videotape had been doctored. Someone spliced in footage from the night I went to see Lovell. They edited it into video footage from the night Lovell was murdered."

"It's not about the tape. It's about Lovell's files."

He sighed, bowed his head, running his fingers through his hair. "I feel responsible for what happened to him. He was on his way home. I went to his condo and convinced him not to leave. I threw all the big ideas at him, about honor, dignity, integrity and doing the right thing. Look where it got him. Fucking dead."

Ratana cautiously moved to his side and squeezed his hand.

"Listen to me. You've done it, Vinny."

"Done what?"

"The world that matters knows about Weerawat. John knew Khun Weerawat was dangerous. But he didn't know how to deal with him. But John told me 'the detective' would find a way."

Calvino had no illusions that the police would close down Weerawat's piracy businesses. Weerawat's influence was too great. He was a lord above the law. Calvino had worked it out. On Lovell's thumb drive were all of the files, confidential memos, charts, emails, corporate structures, and interlocking directors and shareholders, names, dates, places. He had organized it in cross-indexed files, giving it the beauty and grace of the double helix shape of DNA. It was the code for the lifeblood of Weerawat's empire.

Calvino had uploaded all the files to a Yahoo account and, to be on the safe side, uploaded them again to a Gmail account. Working next to the nude cutouts on McPhail's fridge, Calvino had surfed the web for in-house lawyers who worked for the major drug companies, auto companies, and film production houses. It had been a long time since Calvino had done this kind of research, going through all of the State Bar Association directories, industry groups, and congressional staff records for versight committees. He had found a website for Cameron's old law firm in New York and addresses for all the partners. Another website for the Ethics Committee for the New York State Bar Association had yielded more names and emails.

Calvino had even remembered some classmates from law school and looked them up. They'd gone on to better things in corporations and major firms. They had become judges and politicians; they'd made real careers. He'd had no idea how well plugged into the system they had become. He added their names, then others he could find for people at government agencies and local embassies.

When Calvino had his list, he began sending out his e-mail. He told his story, the real story that shined a bright spotlight of truth on Weerawat. He provided links to the files, showing evidence of Weerawat's factories turning out fake products and shipping them throughout Asia and Europe, tracing his business enterprises to the Isle of Man, the British Virgin Islands, and Hong Kong. The revenues were enormous, making Weerawat powerful enough to rise above the law. No one dared to challenge him. But the evidence Calvino sent could make a criminal case, and the people he was writing were also powerful people. *Let them do the work, pull the levers, exercise influence,* Calvino had thought. Within twenty-four hours, telephones would be ringing all over the world. They would shout down the roof. No one would be able to shut them upCalvino had all the files from his office, and he'd made notes, drawn maps, and added names of people. He had sent them the evidence a lawyer would need to make a criminal case. The new way of getting the message out was direct mail to the people involved. These were powerful people. *Let them do the work, pull the levers of power, exercise influence*, Calvino had thought. They were connected to the right journalists, congressmen, and big shots at every level of government in the phone book. These companies made huge donations to political parties. They would shout down the roof in a single, loud voice. No one would be able to shut them up.

Ratana opened a copy of *The Nation* on the bed. On the front page was a photograph of Weerawat. One of his smiling stock photographs that revealed nothing. The story under the photo was short and to the point. Weerawat had left Thailand for an undisclosed country to undergo medical treatment. The story said that he would remain outside Thailand for some time, and that he had informed the government it wasn't possible to take up the advisory position he'd been offered.

Ratana flipped to page four, and there was a story about an ex-cop who had confessed to being the hit man behind several murders, including those of a workman in Pattaya, a massage girl in Sukhumvit Road, and a *farang* named John Lovell. There was a photo of Box Head. He looked like he'd been beaten up. Calvino wondered how many hours the police had worked on him to get the confession. And whether Weerawat's family had made an arrangement to pay cash to Box Head's family as part of the deal. The newspaper report speculated that the ex-cop had been acting on behalf of a mastermind. But there was no mention of Weerawat's name.

Calvino looked up from the newspaper.

"The police aren't looking for me?"

"Not any longer."

"Pratt has seen this?"

She nodded. "He wanted me to be the one to tell you."

The colonel must have things under control, Calvino figured, or he wouldn't have sent her. He would have come himself. It made Calvino smile to think how relieved Pratt must have felt once the story had broken. But in what direction would the story go? The government had a way of containing and disposing of bad news.

It had all been a misunderstanding, a lack of communication, an honest mistake, thought Calvino. That was what the system always belched up from its gaseous intestine when it suffered indigestion. It was the fall-back position used by the authorities to meet allegations that were embarrassing. When the deceits and deception fell apart, it was never, "We're sorry." It was always, "No one is responsible. It just happened and now it has not happened."

"Colonel Pratt asked me to give you this," Ratana said, taking a 9mm Beretta out of her handbag.

"What else did he say?"

"He said it might take some time to get your .38 police special back from the department."

"Did he say anything else?" Calvino took the Beretta in his hand.

"He said it was a throw-down. Whatever that means. And it would be wise to stay off the streets after ten o'clock tonight."

Guns, like women, had a history. Bodies they'd been with, bodies they'd left behind.

"Don't worry about returning it." She reached into her handbag and handed him a padded envelope. "And he said you should have this." Colonel Pratt hadn't said what was in the envelope, and Ratana hadn't asked.

Calvino looked at the envelope. Written on the front in large handwriting were the words: "'The game is up.' William Shakespeare, *Cymbeline,* Act 3, Scene 3." Calvino nodded and stuffed the envelope in his jacket pocket.

He felt the weight of the gun in his hands. The first touch was soft and passionate. *A throw-down gun was like a throw-down woman; they come with the past wiped clean.* The Beretta had a good weight. *The throw-down had belonged to other people, but no one knew her prior owners, what they had wanted from her, what they had done to her, or why they'd thrown her away*. He checked the clip. It was full. *Women and guns—when they became a throw-down no one could ever trace them, check their story, ask the compromising questions based on an understanding of what had gone on before. There was never a before, only an after.* Calvino holstered the weapon.

"Tell Pratt, if you see him before I do, thanks from Vinny."

After Ratana closed the door on her way out, he opened the envelope. He removed the silencer and screwed it onto the barrel of the Beretta. A perfect fit. He checked the ammunition; Pratt had loaded the magazine with subsonic rounds. Just short of the speed of sound, the bullets would travel at three hundred and forty meters per second, more than enough velocity to kill. With the silencer, the subsonic rounds provided absolute silencing.

Calvino sat down in front of the laptop, setting the Beretta beside the keyboard, and opened one of Lovell's subfolders with the name tag The Lair, Lovell's software program. When Weerawat was afraid, Calvino wondered, where did he hide? The newspaper hadn't said where Weerawat had run because the writer didn't know. Lovell's Lair game asked a few questions then showed one likely location: on the New Road, near the Chao Phraya River. Calvino had been there before, videotaping the fake drug factory.

Calvino waited until dark, packed the Beretta in his holster and the silencer in his jacket, and took the Skytrain to Saphan Thaksin station, getting out in a crowd of tourists, students, and office workers. He walked down the Skytrain stairs, taking the exit to New Road. Climbing through a hole in a fence, he followed the pavement through a playground. At one end a group of Thais, shirts tied to their waists, sweat rolling down their faces, played the French game of *boules*. It was one of those ancient games once played by Roman soldiers for amusement in between battles. He watched them for a couple of minutes, the thrower eyeing the balls on the ground, shifting his weight to the balls of his feet, checking the distance, and then making an underhanded throw. He made a direct hit on one of the stationary balls, knocking it out of the circle. *The game is up*, thought Calvino, as he moved on toward the street.

Lovell had had a list of Weerawat's secret, private places. Calvino knew the way to this one; he'd been there before. He walked at a good pace, keeping his head down. Making himself a figure no one would notice, hurrying along the road.

When he reached the *soi*, the drizzle had turned into rain. He opened a shopping bag and removed a black rain slicker, putting his head through the hole; the slicker fell around his shoulders and arms. He pulled the hood tight over his head. A couple of steps into the *soi*, he noticed something had changed since his stakeout. CCTV cameras covered the street, picking up anyone walking or driving through the checkpoint. A couple of uniformed security guards sat at a table, two legs of it positioned in the street. They were watching a drama on TV.

Calvino turned around and walked back to the main street. A quarter of an hour later he reached the next *soi* with access to the river. He entered and walked toward the end, finding the passage used by fishmongers to drive their pickup trucks to the wharf. He'd gone through the back door to his destination. On the wharf side there were no guards, just glistening wet surfaces, neon light washing the gray cement, rats scuttling in the gutters, and stacks of crates waiting for the fishing boats to dock. The stench of dead fish and fresh entrails and blood fogged the air. At the far end, men and women in hip boots sorted fish from pickups, raking them into large plastic containers. They were far away and hadn't seen him at the other end of the wharf. Staying in the shadows, Calvino came out onto the street, keeping close to the buildings, his black rain slicker merging into the darkness. A couple of schoolgirls in their white blouses and blue skirts biked past, laughing. They hadn't noticed him in the dark. He felt sweat running down his back under the rain slicker; these things weren't made for the tropics.

Turning the corner, he saw the factory entrance halfway down the road. Before there had been trucks going in and out, and workmen working to load the trucks. Now nothing on the street moved, except for a skinny feral cat darting across the road and disappearing between cracks in the fence running along the wharf side. The piracy operation had been shut down. The other buildings looked empty; no lights, no movement. A wind blew rain from the river. The heavy air smelled no longer of fish but of tar and oil. In the far distance, a long-tail boat headed upriver. Spirals of white steam rose from an opening in the gutter, rolling over the street and beaten down by the rain. The street was dark except for some lights in a window where the blinds were closed. A horn from the river wailed a long blast followed by two short wails, leaving the *soi* in silence. Calvino worked his way down the empty *soi*, stopping a few feet away from a large, open building of two stories, made of stone and wood. Inside the front was a shrine decorated with small lights.

He freed his arms through the side slits in the slicker, removed the silencer from his jacket, and screwed it onto the barrel of the Beretta. He edged forward, swinging around the side of the building. He thought of tossing a small stone against the window. That only worked in the movies. He waited for what seemed like an eternity. Then Jug Ears opened the door. His knees bent, he rose with two large suitcases. He stared straight into Calvino's eyes. It took a second for him to register what was in front of him. Man in black. Seen the face before. *Farang* named Calvino, and I once broke his ribs. He started to lower the suitcases, his right hand moving down for the handgun in the shoulder holster.

The suitcases had touched the floor when Calvino shot him. The round from Calvino's Beretta caught Jug Ears an inch above his right eye. Neither the gun nor Jug Ears made a sound. Fragments of bone and pieces of brain sprayed against Calvino's rain slicker, and Jug Ears collapsed, dead before he hit the ground.

He pushed the body inside and away from the entrance. Then stepping over it, blood dripping off the surface of his slicker, he crouched down in the entrance. You shoot someone up close and personal, and there is sure to be a blowback of blood. Lots of blood had been distributed in a fine spray.

Upstairs there was movement. Pot Belly shouted over the booming sound of drums and gongs, "*Mee arai rue plao wa?*"

From above, Calvino heard the volume of music cranked up, the sound leaking through an open door. The recorded sound of drums, cymbals, and gongs echoed from the top of the staircase.

Calvino moved to the side of the staircase and waited. Pot Belly cursed and started down the stairs. Pot Belly and Jug Ears had been moving suitcases to the ground floor. They must have been close to leaving. Calvino could see Pot Belly's shadow on the wall above him, with the silhouette of a gun in Pot Belly's hand. Halfway down, he stopped. Calvino could hear his breathing, the way a man's breath catches in his throat when he's afraid. He called out Jug Ear's name again. Calvino waited until Pot Belly cleared the last step, and then he came out of the shadows and shot him at close range. A 9mm round ripped through Pot Belly's throat; the second round entered the front and exited the back of his skull. Blood sprayed in an arc over the railing and against the wall, showering the floor. Pot Belly slumped to the floor, his gun skittling across the marble floor. The silencer couldn't silence a handgun hitting the floor, but the soundtrack of the dragon dance muffled the noise.

Calvino stepped over the body and walked up the stairs, sidestepping the pools of blood. The second floor was dark and empty. Calvino continued up the next set of stairs to the third floor. At the end of the corridor light shone from the door left ajar. The Beretta in his right hand, Calvino pushed the door open with his left. Moving low and fast, he entered the room, his back to the wall, pointing the gun at Weerawat, whose back was turned to him. To one side were two dozen large suitcases stacked on four trolley carts. Weerawat had plans to leave, and he wasn't traveling light.

Inside the room the sound of drums and gongs ricocheted off the walls. Weerawat, dressed in a black jogging suit, knelt on a cushion in front of the shrine, incense sticks clutched between the fingers of his hands. It was a large Chinese shrine, the kind used to worship ancestors. Above the shrine was a series of old grainy photographs of elderly Chinese faces. The wall was covered with oil reproductions of Galileo Chini's paintings. The most prominent was a life-size canvas of *The Last Day of the Chinese Year in Bangkok.* Around the room were dozens of framed nudes he recognized as the work of Chini. These were original oil paintings. Calvino moved close enough to watch Weerawat's lips moving, chanting. He could see the soles of Weerawat's feet in the reflected red light.

Pointing his Beretta at the back of Weerawat's head, he leaned over and switched off the music. Weerawat froze, his head slowly pivoting around. He showed no surprise, his face tranquil, serene even, as if he were coming out of a trance. Calvino stood in the door, his black slicker dripping water and blood in small pools at his feet. Weerawat's eyes moved from the puddles to the area behind the door. "They're downstairs," said Calvino. "The music got too loud for them."

An imperial curl of Weerawat's lip suggested he had uncoiled from his fugue-like state. "Your great-grandfather was a great painter," Weerawat said. "One day I should tell you the whole story of how our great-grandfathers were once friends."

"You had Lovell killed."

Weerawat's head slowly rotated upward to a painting above the altar.

"Notice the figure in the foreground of *The Last Day of the Chinese Year in Bangkok*? He was my ancestor. He knew the painter.

More than simply knew him. My great-grandfather supplied opium to Galileo Chini. Galileo had become an opium addict. That often happened in the old days. *Farangs* would start with one opium pipe, and that led to another, and soon there were many pipes to fill and smoke. Galileo and my great-grandfather found shared interests. It was more than opium. My great-grandfather found the women Galileo used as models. He arranged for Galileo to paint some of the most beautiful, desirable women in Bangkok during that time. Some might call them prostitutes. But I think that is unkind. Look closely at the paintings. Inspired, wouldn't you say? Opium dreams in oil. Each painting is an original. Not one has ever left this room. My great-grandfather accepted them from your great-grandfather as payment for services rendered. As you see, our two families go back a very long way. If our great-grandfathers could do business, become friends, why can't we try to do the same?"

"That first day in my office, you saw Galileo's painting on my wall. You said nothing. You looked upset. Why?" said Calvino, carefully watching Weerawat's hands as he carefully placed the incense sticks in a jar of pure white sand.

"It was a reproduction."

"I know it was a copy."

"The painter had painted the Chinese letters for treachery and betrayal on the dragon's head. Cleverly painted them as part of the eyes and mouth just above my great-grandfather's head. It hurt my dignity to see this. This insult to his memory and honor caused me to react. You're a foreigner and don't understand the meaning of the dignity of a Chinese family."

"Did Lovell insult your family dignity? Is that why you had him killed?"

No fear, no emotion showed on his face as he continued to hold the incense. "Sympathy, Mr. Calvino, is a good thing. You should look it up in the dictionary."

Calvino kept the Beretta trained on him. "I have looked it up. 'Sympathy' is one of those words that falls between 'shit' and 'syphilis.'" He pulled back the hood from the slicker. Calvino's face was soaked with sweat, his hair wet and matted. His eyes were bloodshot, wild with anger and pain.

Weerawat thought this was a difficult man to placate, and even more difficult to kill.

"You see the painting on the left?" He waited until Calvino looked up at the painting of the nude woman and continued. "When a man paints a woman with such feeling, you know that she has touched him, won his heart. She was seventeen and Chinese."

She sat facing outward, her legs hooked behind, leaning on her hands, fingers closed, the slender arms and shoulders inviting. No pubic hair showing. Knees pointed outward. Eyes closed, hair brushed away from her face, lips full but unexpressive, as if she had been lost in a dream. No woman naturally sat in that posture. Every detail of the model's body had been carefully positioned. It was the kind of painting that drew the eye, focused attention.

A large sunburst of a smile pulled Weerawat's lips back. From the corner of Calvino's eye, he saw Weerawat's right hand slide under the cushion. His hand lingered until Calvino looked up at the paintings, and then when it came out, it was difficult to see the small black metal object. Weerawat's hand held a subcompact 9mm GLOCK, black like his jogging suit. He half turned on the cushion, bringing the GLOCK into firing position. As he turned, his foot knocked the side of the shrine. Calvino looked back and rolled over on his side. Weerawat's eyes were wild, his lips parted. One shot fired wide. Calvino positioned himself as a second shot missed him by an inch and squeezed off two rounds from the Beretta. Both rounds hit Weerawat's chest just above the heart. The impact of the rounds knocked Weerawat back. Calvino's third shot punched through Weerawat's skull two inches above the hairline.

Weerawat slumped forward. The first shot had slammed him against the shrine. The Christmas tree lights scattered in a light show across the floor. Calvino kicked the GLOCK out of Weerawat's hand. He knelt down and examined the weapon, small enough to cup in the hand; it held a ten-round clip. Model 26 was like a painted catwalk beauty whose attitude shined in capital letters.

He reached under his rain slicker, pulled out a cell phone loaded with one of the one-time-use cards, and phoned Colonel Pratt. "Bring a van. There's a ton of luggage." Colonel Pratt said nothing. The conversation had ended.

When Colonel Pratt's investigative team arrived, they would examine the gun, take down the model number, and after work buy a lottery ticket ending in 26. Calvino smiled, thinking about the superstitious nature of most people, and reminded himself, to be on the safe side, to buy a lottery ticket. He squatted beside the body, the Beretta still in his right hand, and looked at the paintings, one at a time.

Shots had split the air but were silent, unheard. Calvino inhaled the smell of cordite, took it deep inside his lungs. He was his father's son more than Galileo Chini's great-grandson. But blood was blood and never to be denied. The sound of the two rounds fired from the GLOCK would have been heard outside. He glanced at his watch. It wouldn't be long before the police arrived.

Calvino remembered the first time he'd gone to Florence. He had been only fourteen years old when he stood next to Vito gazing upon Galileo Chini's masterpiece at the Pitti Palace. What would Vito have made of this room? What would he have felt about Weerawat's stories, the opium, the prostitutes procured for art?

Calvino had no answers. He drew a long breath, looked up at the nude oil paintings—had they been received by Weerawat's great-grandfather as payments for opium? What kind of man had Galileo Chini been? Once, after a long discussion about Calvino's family, Pratt had quoted Shakespeare, *Two Gentlemen of Verona*, "The private wound is the deepest." Calvino unscrewed the silencer from the barrel and dropped it into his jacket pocket. The shots had attracted no attention and no lights had come on in surrounding buildings. Calvino stood in the door and looked one last time at the Siamese nudes painted all those years ago by Galileo Chini. He had found his reason to stay, and he had found his reason to go.

He thought of his great-grandmother with the tiles of those images in her coat pockets as she fell into the Arno River. It had all happened a very long time ago; it had all happened a moment ago.

Calvino broke open one of the suitcases, and files, agreements, and deeds spilled onto the floor. He reached down and picked up one of the documents. It concerned a low-cost government housing project. Most of the documents were in Thai. He flipped through them until he found one written in English. It was for the sale of seventy-three *rai* of land to a government agency. Another department bought thousands of units. The sums were staggering—billions of Thai baht payable to a private company. Calvino shoved the documents back into the suitcase.

In the luggage were the thousands and thousands of documents that had been stored in Lovell's brain. Calvino looked around the room one last time and then walked down the stairs and to the back of the shop house. He opened a window and climbed through, into a courtyard, and then walked down an alleyway, hearing the long and short wails of a horn from the river. He listened for the wailing of police cars. There was none. It seemed strangely quiet as he worked his way back through an empty warehouse and emerged on the wharf. Boats had docked. Some of the men sat smoking cigarettes, eyeing him as he passed. He guessed that one of the boats had been waiting for Weerawat. It would wait only so long and then leave.

He didn't have to wait long at the end of the pier. A freelance long-tail boat docked. He squatted down as the Thai boatman asked him where he was going. "Klong Saen Saep, Italian Thai Tower," he said. The boatman wanted three hundred baht but accepted the two hundred baht counteroffer.

Calvino climbed into the boat and worked his way to the front. The engine coughed a large gray cloud of smoke as the boatman pulled away from the pier. The public boats had stopped running a couple of hours before. Once the long-tail boat turned into the canal, the only light was from the houses and shops along the canal bank. Calvino glanced around. A heavy spray of black water made it difficult to see the boatman. He had spread his rain slicker over the side of the boat. He eased the Beretta out of his holster and slipped it over the side of the boat; another hundred yards along the *klong* and he slipped the silencer over the side. The noise of the engine, the spray of water, and the darkness were the cover needed to dispose of the weapon. In the old days there had been floating brothels on the *klong*. Now there was little traffic at night; the sound of a TV coming from a house was muffled by the roar of the long-tail engine.

The boat engine cut out and the boatman glided the long-tail to a pier under a bridge. Bracing himself as the boat rocked, Calvino climbed from the front to the middle, where he stepped onto the pier. He paid the boatman and walked, hands in his pockets, the rain streaking his face, until he reached the top of the bridge.

The traffic was light. A taxi, then a motorcycle, a couple of cars, and then what he had rarely seen in Bangkok: an empty street. He looked toward Petchaburi Road on his left and wiped the rain from his face. Blinking hard, he looked again at a huge, gray high-rise office, a mountain of sharp angles carved out of steel and glass. Neon office lights on the upper floors wrapped a horizontal grid around the building, forming a mouth, and two stories above on either side, offices were lit, making the slits for eyes. Calvino stopped on the street and stared at the building. Sculpted from light and shadow was the face of a monster, repellent, threatening, overpowering. It was the only face on the street that wasn't human.

The game is up, as Colonel Pratt had said. By the time he was back on Sukhumvit Road, he saw the first soldiers in camouflage combat uniforms, carrying M16s. The TV and radio played martial music. The coup d'état that they said could never happen again was in progress. He checked his watch; it was past 10:45 p.m. Weerawat was dead; the government was gone; the world had changed. Several soldiers stood at the entrance to his *soi* as Calvino turned and walked past them.

Back in his apartment, he turned on the TV. All the stations played patriotic music. He stripped off his clothes, threw his shirt and trousers in the bathtub, and filled the tub with water, leaving them to soak. He went into the bedroom, lay down on the bed, and slept. And in his dreams he saw a young woman, her coat pockets weighed down with tiles with painted images of Siamese nudes, standing on the bridge above the Arno River. He watched as Livia's arms rose from her sides and she looked at the sky. Livia jumped, holding her head high, arms stretched out, suspended for a moment like an angel, the rim of the sun starting to crack the dawn sky, before disappearing into the fast-moving current below.

★

The telephone woke him up. What he remembered wasn't the dream but that he had killed three men the night before. Anyone who says they felt nothing, or had some intellectual insight the next morning hasn't ever killed anyone—felt and remembered the shark teeth bite of anger, the sting-ray's tail of hatred, or the bile of bitterness backing up in the throat.

"Man, where were you last night?" McPhail was on the line. "The army's taking over."

"I missed it."

"There were tanks on Sukhumvit Road."

Calvino put down the phone. He smiled, thinking how Old George had called him stupid for not boarding the container to

Hong Kong. Weerawat should have been on that container, or on one of the boats docked at the wharf. His dozens of pieces of luggage were ready. He only had to say his final goodbye at the family altar. He was going to run. Lovell had stayed when he could have run. He gave Lovell that; he wasn't a runner.

The office was empty when he arrived. He hadn't expected to find Ratana there, with soldiers in the street. But not long after he'd entered, Ratana came in and sat across from his desk.

"You should have stayed home," he said.

"I'm glad the army did it," she said. "And I'm glad that you are okay. I was worried."

Instead of Lovell, it would have been him going up the chimney in smoke. In a fairer world, it should have been him, a wisp of gray smoke disappearing into the Bangkok sky. But the world was neither fair nor just, nor rational, nor predictable. Some were made gods; others died because they defied the gods.

"There's something I need to tell you," he said.

She unwrapped the yellow scarf from around her neck and dried her eyes.

"When I went to his condo that night, he was packing. I said he should stay. He's dead because he believed in what I said. And I don't even know if I believe that."

"John knew exactly what he was doing, Vinny. He stayed because of me."

"What do you mean because of you?"

"We had started to see each other."

Calvino cocked his head to the side. "You were seeing him?"

"Believe it or not, I have a life."

"You and Lovell?" He tried to imagine them in bed together.

"I had a test. I'm going to have a baby." It was the way she said it. Her voice breaking, like a song, a melody filled with sadness. "Why did he have to be so idealistic? Why couldn't he see the trouble he was in?"

Ratana's eyes searched his face as if he held the answer. He wouldn't have made that mistake. He hadn't made that mistake; her boss knew when to go underground.

She choked back a loud sob. "I had this feeling that something terrible would happen. I told him to please leave. But he refused. He wouldn't listen. When I heard he'd been shot, I didn't cry. I was too numb. I had already gone through his death a hundred times in my mind."

She'd given Lowell the ultimate reason to stay.

Ratana left him alone. Soon after, Colonel Pratt phoned. "Weerawat's left the country. He wasn't the only one to flee."

Calvino assumed the conversation was being monitored. "I slept through the coup."

At the other end, Colonel Pratt cleared his throat. "You've not been well lately. Catch up on your rest. See a doctor."

"I'll do that, colonel."

"'He that dies pays all debts,'" said Colonel Pratt.

He thought of Pratt looking at the phone, smiling. The debt had been squared.

As Calvino crossed Soi 22 to Washington Square, he thought about the way Pratt had chosen his reply. Outside in the square the sun beat down from overhead. A few scattered, puffy clouds hadn't stopped the searing heat. Old George's Toyota was just pulling out. The driver stopped the car as Old George rolled down the window. "Where in the fuck do you think you're going?"

"It's Liberation Day, George."

"I just had the cops in asking about you yesterday."

"Thanks for what you've done."

"You're fucking crazy. Get on the tanker to Singapore, Calvino. Get out of this place while you can. You know these things never end. There's only a pause, and then it starts all over. You don't wanna be part of that. Or do you?" Old George smacked his lips as he started to roll up his window.

"There's been a coup, George. It's a new day," said Calvino.

"New day, bullshit. You don't know what comes next. Go ahead and ask your Shakespeare-quoting buddy. He'll tell you there is never a new day. Just the same play with new actors."

Calvino watched as the ancient Toyota turned right at the corner of the square and disappeared.

FORTY-TWO

COLONEL Pratt sat in Calvino's office, stirring sugar into a cup of coffee. One sugar; then he added milk and stirred again slowly. Calvino stretched back in his chair, hands behind his head. There had been a number of shots fired during the coup d'état. Those fired by Calvino and the two missed shots fired by Weerawat. It had taken Colonel Pratt and three colleagues two hours to remove the bodies and the luggage, and another two hours to clean up, file reports, and arrange for the disposal of Weerawat's body. They had been waiting for Calvino's call, a couple of minutes away from the scene.

"But he had already confessed according to the papers."

Colonel Pratt paused. "His lawyers claimed the confession was under duress."

From the photograph in the papers showing Box Head's bruised face that would not have been a difficult point to press before a court. " So Box Head wanted to retract his confession. He figured he had nothing to lose with Weerawat gone."

"I had photos of his dead friends," said Colonel Pratt.

Calvino listened as Colonel Pratt talked about the next round of Box Head's interrogation. "I put the photos on the table. He looked down at the dead men. A couple of minutes later he admitted that it was him in the surveillance videotape dressed as a pizza deliveryman, and that he had gone to Lovell's condo and shot him point-blank. It was the close-up of that frame with his Khmer tattoo on the neck that broke him." He left out the details about the beating Box Head had received.

"Wasn't that tattoo supposed to protect him?" said Calvino. "It doesn't look like an amulet is always your best friend. Except when it is." He thought of the amulet Weerawat had clutched.

"Tomorrow he's scheduled to reenact the crime." Colonel Pratt blew on his coffee before taking a sip. "We told him if he confesses, then no death penalty. He'll get a discount. He had a visitor from Weerawat's family. After that meeting, he started chirping and nobody could shut him up. They told him Weerawat had fled the country and that two of his associates were dead. An hour later he confessed to killing a workman named Daeng in Pattaya. He'd hit him on the head and dumped his body in a pond. He also killed Jazz. We had two teams hammering him for the name of the mastermind. We all knew who that was. But he wouldn't say Weerawat's name. He'd already earned his discount from death to life. And he had his deal with Weerawat's family. He shut up. I thought I saw something in his eyes. Maybe fear. Or hesitation. Loyalty or respect, I don't know. Whatever it was I saw, it wasn't enough to pull him in the direction we wanted. There will be other days. He will tell us what we already know." An absolute certainty in Colonel Pratt's tone indicated Box Head hadn't sung his final song yet.

"What will members of the old government do if they think Weerawat's alive?"

Colonel Pratt scratched the back of his neck—prickly heat. "A lot of people are on the run. But Weerawat is different. He gave us an opportunity. And all the evidence we need. If he's dead, then the others involved know they have certain options open to them. But if Weerawat's missing, he could be dead, or he could be alive and in hiding. That makes it more complex; they can't be so certain that if they choose one path, it will be a mistake. We can squeeze them by letting them know we are negotiating a deal with Weerawat. That will get them to turn on each other."

"From what I saw in the one suitcase, there are going to be a lot of questions involving some important people. Will they get away?" asked Calvino.

Colonel Pratt rocked back in his chair. "There's too much evidence."

Calvino smiled, "But is it sufficient?" They both knew that documents disappeared, and documents could be rewritten, altered, or faked. Witness testimony and family name might trump the most damning document.

Pratt flexed his jaw and shrugged his shoulders. "Maybe they'll find a crawl space to come out the other end untouched, or maybe not. Keeping Weerawat's fate open-ended is enough of an edge to keep them off guard."

Backdoor construction deals, fraudulent land transfers, airport procurement scams, and offshore companies with Weerawat's family at the hub of the wheel. There would be committees; there would be investigations, reports, recommendations; and there would be compromises.

"What about you?" asked Calvino.

"My transfer to the inactive post was cancelled." A hint of a smile passed the colonel's lips. "It's a rite of passage, Vincent."

As far as Calvino was concerned, there were two rites of passage that made a man understand the nature of the world—the first time someone shot at him, and the first time he had to find the money for a payroll.

"What are they calling what they did to you? A typographical error?"

"There are ways to smooth over problems which you wouldn't understand. But we need to avoid conflict. Harmony has to be restored. If it takes a coup to make that happen, then it must be done. With Weerawat and the government out of the way, no one will have any memory of him in the department. No one was ever his friend or went to dinner with him or was seen in a society page photo with him. Or did business with him. He's a non-person. His power vanished the night of the coup. In a couple of weeks no one will remember him or talk about him. His disappearance will be old news."

"I sent hundreds of emails to lawyers in big drug and film production companies. And auto companies. Weerawat ripped off airbags and brakes, too."

"The factories are already closed down. When we move, we move fast. That is what the *farangs* wanted. We did it. They don't want publicity. They want the piracy operation shut. We got what they wanted."

"Journalists might start asking questions."

"The only questions they will ask will be about the coup. Weerawat is already history. The new government will know nothing. No one from the old government will say anything. No one will say anything."

The question is always, what do you bring to the party? It was rarely asked but always assumed. What Calvino was asked to bring was his silence. It was to be his gift to the god of social harmony and face. If he could bring that prize to the party, he could stay.

"What about Danielson?" asked Calvino.

Colonel Pratt shrugged. "Heart attack."

"Yes and no." He called for Ratana to bring in a file.

She came into his office and put the file on Calvino's desk. "Explain to Colonel Pratt what Lovell told you happened at the Oxford-Cambridge dinner."

Ratana explained what Lovell had told her. "He had been in the restroom retying his bow tie when Apisak came in. A few minutes later, Khun Andrew came in. His face was grayish white, and sweat was dripping down his neck. He pretended at first that everything was okay. But one look at him indicated he wasn't telling the truth. He said he'd just received some very bad news. He was shaking and sweating.

"Khun Andrew was in the midst of a full-blown panic attack. Apisak saw it first. He asked Khun Andrew point-blank if he was having an anxiety attack. He avoided the word 'panic.' Apisak said he saw the signs—he had the same problem—and pulled out a bottle of prescription medication. Apisak dumped one red pill into his hand, threw it into the back of his mouth, and swallowed. He offered pills to Lovell, who declined, and then to Khun Andrew. By this time he was having trouble breathing normally. He took the pill and swallowed it."

Colonel Pratt had the original autopsy report which had surfaced after the coup. That report mentioned an unusual description of the ingredients, which included a large amount of synthesized wasp venom. Danielson had an allergy. The pill Apisak gave him was the cause of his death.

"John didn't know what had happened."

Colonel Pratt sat impassively, listening, his fingers touching. After Ratana finished, she looked straight at the colonel. "John would have told you. I am sure of it."

"Danielson was cremated. Lovell is dead. But there is no evidence to directly link Weerawat or Apisak."

"That means nothing can be done," she said softly.

"It is messy. It isn't fair or right. But Weerawat's world has collapsed. But those who think he may be alive can see that his uncle can't help him, and Cameron's firm has pulled back from him. The new government has announced they will seek Weerawat's extradition. The official line is that he's on the run. As for Apisak, he will find that others who matter won't forget. It will take time, but he will do something that will incriminate himself and I'll be waiting."

"Sooner or later, they will find out Weerawat was killed the night of the coup," said Calvino.

"That won't happen."

There was no catch of doubt registering in Colonel Pratt's voice. Whatever came down with the corruption cases, Weerawat's body would never be found. Calvino had no doubt about Pratt's ability to cover the crime scene and dispose of Weerawat's body. How or where, he didn't ask; he didn't want to know.

The office telephone rang. Ratana went back to her desk and answered it. He thought, *This is the first day of my life.* He could have fled to Hong Kong, or to Singapore. But he was back in the saddle in Bangkok, settling in, thinking about the weekend. Pratt was back on the job, and as soon as his superior officer left the monkhood, he would also be reinstated. Their transfers to inactive posts had been explained as a miscommunication, a mix-up, according to the official version. Everyone was allowed to save face.

Ratana put the call through to Calvino, who leaned back at his desk. He raised the receiver to his ear. It was Ruth. "I thought you and Noah were in Denver."

"The transfer is off. Noah's taken a job at a bank in Bangkok."

He would recognize Ruth's voice from the bottom of a fish barrel.

"You're staying?" he asked, giving Colonel Pratt a wink.

"Of course, I'm staying. I'd like to hire you again."

"I think that I can fit you in, but I'll need a retainer."

"That's not a problem, Mr. Calvino."

"All of it up front."

She understood completely. A couple of grand had been only a small down payment to finance a long-term matrimonial war. Her husband had gone back to the front line and Calvino would be paid to follow him. By staying in Bangkok, Noah Gould had decided to play for keeps, light the matches, squat in the dirt, throw them one at a time into a bowl of gasoline. Weerawat was out of the picture. He was no longer afraid.

Before lunch, Ratana placed a letter on Calvino's desk. Most mail was either junk mail or invoices. This was an actual letter with a return address at the New York office of the WHO. He ripped open the envelope and read the letter. "We would like to inform you that you are on our shortlist for the position of senior investigator. Please contact me for arrangements for an interview in New York."

He had torn up the application form. Ratana must have sent in a replacement. She would have done anything for him. He lowered the letter, thinking how she had devoted her life to looking after him with an unshakable loyalty. He felt her waiting on the other side to say something about the letter.

"I'm not the guy the WHO wants," he said, balling up the letter.

After a moment of silence, "I am sorry, Vinny." Her voice carried no hint of sadness.

He couldn't see her face. Was she smiling? "Time to get back to work. It's nothing to be sorry about."

She looked around the corner. "You're not upset I sent in the application?"

"You did the right thing."

Now she was smiling.

FORTY-THREE

LUNCHTIME at the Lonesome Hawk started around 10:30 a.m., when the first real drinkers drifted in and ordered beer or cheap bar whiskey. The waitresses sat in the corner booth next to the window, putting on their makeup. These customers were more thirsty than hungry. The need for food wasn't so much gnawing at them as the need to get down the first shots, fast and red hot. The waitresses, with expiration dates long past, held no interest for them. One customer leaned over the bar as the bartender turned around, saying, "Honey, what was the name of that guy who bought you your teeth?"

"Khun Dan," she said.

He returned to his conversation, "The guy's name was Dan. And he had a good heart. Well Dan said last night during the coup d'état he saw dancers from Nana Plaza giving flowers to the soldiers. Everyone was smiling and all happy like one big family."

Feeling good after that first beer, they looked around and saw others feeling good, getting into that early drinking space. The bar was transformed into a pocket of the past, a place of mutual understanding, shared experiences, and alcohol-fueled history, a narrow ledge where men could pretend they had some control. A place where they knew who they were, and what it meant to be drinking beer mid-morning.

Old George waved his arms like a madman and screamed across the bar at his driver-cum-DJ to change the fucking music from "I Left My Heart in San Francisco," which had been played six times. "I hate fucking Tony Bennett. Can't you change that music? Or do

I have to do it myself?" He tapped his cane on the floor.

Calvino came through the door.

"Look who we got here. Vincent Calvino. You got yourself out of the hot seat. Now where are you looking to jump? The frying pan? Don't get too cocky. Once they find out they can fuck with you, they may go away, but they always come back."

"Thanks, George." Calvino gave him a hug and kissed him on the forehead.

"Get off me, you! They're gonna say Jews are fucking queers."

"Vinny slept through the coup," said McPhail.

Calvino rotated his head to one side, then the other. "I was tired."

From the bar, one of the regulars raised a bottle of Singha. "It's no joke. You can get hurt bad with all those tanks."

"You disappoint me, man," said McPhail. "I thought you'd be in the middle of it. Running down Sukhumvit Road, jumping on a tank."

"I was out like a light. Didn't hear a thing," said Calvino.

McPhail was in a booth nursing a Jameson and watching the TV that was mounted on a small platform on the wall. The BBC news ran a feature about the transplant of a still-beating heart into a man's chest.

"Hey, Vinny. Have you seen this? The guy gets a live heart put in his chest. It's like removing an old engine and slapping in a new one. I asked this little one what she thought."

McPhail squeezed the waitress who sat next to him. "She's upset. And I asked her, 'Hey, baby, why are you upset?' And she says, 'His heart not stop.' Man, and I'm thinking that the Thai definition of death is the heart stops. If the heart is still beating, they must have killed the guy to harvest the heart. There is no Thai phrase for brain death—heart still beating but brain gone to the other side."

Calvino ordered a Mekong and Coke and the special. Meatloaf. He hated meatloaf almost as much as Old George hated six rounds of Tony Bennett singing "I Left My Heart in San Francisco."

"No gravy," he said.

"I hope this new government won't appoint someone like Weerawat. He was downright scary with all that talk about a quota on the number of *farangs* in the green zone."

"Next it'll be the Yellow Star of David," shouted Old George from his perch.

"Nothing ever really changes," said one of the customers at the bar. "They only want our money. They don't want us."

"The generals are talking to the people up-country," said someone at the bar. "Trying to calm them down."

"Send them money. Cash will calm them down," said McPhail. "Send money. Those are the first English words they learn."

A couple of months before the coup one of the papers had run a feature on the green zone and the various popular theories for the name. First, green was (thanks to the American dollar) the universal color for money. Second, the area between Soi 4 and Soi 55 had more parks and trees. And third, all around the world in dangerous places, the green zone was the place of safety for the rich, an enclave where the terrible acts of violence were less likely to occur.

With the soldiers at the intersections and tanks in the streets, the feature appeared dated, out of place, from another time and place. No one could be certain what policies or personalities would survive, and that gave a large measure of hope the green zone idea would fade away.

"Those boys got themselves stuck, and everyone expected them to charge ahead or retreat. What I didn't expect or see coming was the army taking over. You can't predict an ambush from the flanks. Isn't that right, George?"

"You got that right. How do you think we took Berlin?"

"The Russian army took Berlin, George. That's a fact," someone shouted from the bar.

"What the fuck do you know? Were you in Berlin in 1945? Fuck the Russians."

Calvino slid out of the booth and went to the bar. He leaned over and whispered to the bartender, gesturing at a customer. He asked her to send the man a drink on his bill. She nodded. He watched as the bartender opened a bottle of Singha and set it in front of the customer. He looked up, surprised. The bartender whispered, and pointed at Calvino. It was the same guy whose face he'd smashed a taco into. The same customer who told the cops he'd never heard of Calvino. The customer raised the beer and mouthed "Thank you."

Back in his seat, he looked at the meatloaf on his placemat.

"What was that about? Buying that lizard a drink." said

McPhail.

"Colonel Pratt asked me if I had any enemies. And I said private investigators are in the business of making enemies, dealing with enemies, standing up to enemies; but their enemies rarely kill them. And he said this was Thailand and different rules applied. Enemies never forget or forgive. They hunt each other down to the grave."

Calvino had taken the colonel's advice to heart. A sweet smell of apple pie came from the kitchen. The cook swung open the doors and brought the steaming pie to the booth. A waitress took away the meatloaf. The cook wore oven gloves and a toothless grin as she set the pie plate down. Standing next to the booth, she couldn't stop grinning. Her dream was that Dan would return one day and buy her a set of teeth.

"What's this about?" asked Calvino.

She winked. "It's for your secretary. Please give to her." The bamboo telegraph had been working overtime.

There were enemies in Thailand, and there were friends. When he made the calculation, it came out that the number of friends always won. The upside number of friends was a good *reason to stay*.

"You're the man," said McPhail.

"You got that wrong, McPhail. It was Lovell who was *the* man."

Lovell, the kid, who had a thing about bow ties, the one who called him detective. The father of Ratana's kid. He was the man.

He was the man, a fish out of water who had gone upstream to mate and die.

But he had left his mark. He'd drawn a line in the sand. The kind of line that good men drew, the kind of line that good men knew which side to take a stand on. He had done that. Vito had done that. How many men could look at the sky one last time and say that? Not many, thought Calvino. Not many at all.

ACKNOWLEDGMENTS

Vincent Calvino fans often asked me the question: why aren't the novels available in the United States and England? I would answer that the publishing of international crime fiction is a relatively recent development. It certainly wasn't established when *Spirit House*, the first in the series was published in 1992. By the time this novel, the ninth starring Vincent Calvino, was published in 2007, perception, taste, and interest has shifted. Readers are far more adventurous in the fiction they read these days.

The series was born in Thailand, where my original publishers are based. Though books in the series have been translated into Chinese, French, Italian, Hebrew, Norwegian, Thai, and Spanish, Vincent Calvino's journey to New York has been a long one and many people share the credit.

Barney Rosset and his partner Astrid have been supportive for more than a dozen years, seeking ways to bring Calvino home. Barney's pool game improved considerably on his trips to Bangkok.

Galen Williams, founder of *Poets & Writers,* was an early fan of the series and provided a constant source of support and assistance over the years.

When Marc Allen wrote in late 2006 that he loved the Calvino books and wondered why they weren't available in the States, I wrote back, "Vincent Calvino also believes this is a mystery." Along with his colleague Munro Magruder, they started a personal campaign to find an American publisher. About the same time my friend John Paulos, a best-selling author in his own right, suggested that I send several of the novels to his agent, Rafe Sagalyn. Rafe read the books as did his coagent Bridget Wagner, and they offered to represent me. They had a passion for the Calvino books. Less than two weeks later, Bridget Wagner, who has a magic touch, e-mailed to say Morgan Entrekin shared their passion. It seemed a matter of good karma.

Since the time I lived in New York from 1984 to 1988, I had followed his career. From the beginning of 2007, Morgan had heard from Munro Magruder, who had kindly passed along one of the Calvino novels, saying, "You've got to read this." When Morgan spoke with Atlantic Books in London, his English partner, Ravi Mirchandani also said he'd been a long time fan of the series. And then, about the time Morgan was thinking about making an offer for the Calvino series, he had lunch with an old friend, who happened to be an old Asia hand. He said he was about to offer for a private eye series set in Asia, and his friend replied, "Would that be the Vincent Calvino series from Thailand?" Lastly, Morgan discovered that Grove Press founder Barney Rosset and I were longtime friends. The decision to publish the Calvino series took on an inevitability.

At Grove Press, I had the privilege to work with Jamison Stoltz. All writers should be so fortunate to have an editor like Jamison who has the eye of a sniper and the heart of an artist.

Vincent Calvino owes a large debt to a number of people.

John Stevens was responsible for my initial trip to New York. I stayed at his place in 1984 for two weeks and managed, through his contacts, to sign on as a civilian observer with the NYPD. It was on patrol with NYPD I saw a different New York and met a number of people who inspired the character of Vincent Calvino.

Ronald Lieberman who in 1990 suggested on a beach in Phuket that I should consider the idea of a private eye series set in Asia.

Oxford University professor David Vaver, who kept me informed on the many intellectual property issues, which most authors sooner or later must confront.

Author Joe Glazner, who read and provided useful insight on an earlier draft of this book.

Norman Smith, who knows more about Southeast Asia, weapons, special ops, and who has provided advice, counsel, and support since the beginning of the series. Norm has been my foremost advance reader, taking time to go through early drafts, and finding errors and omissions. J. C. Cummings, who served with distinction in the U.S. Air Force, like Norm, has on more than one occasion, saved me from making an error about weapons, trucks, and machinery.

Bernard Trink, George Fetherling, Kevin Burton Smith, Mark Schreiber, Richard Ravensdale, Chris Johnson, Fabio Novel, Paul Owen, Dr. Ian Corness, and Paul Wilson, who over the years have written articles and reviews about the Calvino series, spreading the word about Vincent Calvino both in and outside of Thailand. Their efforts brought the series to the attention of readers who otherwise would have never heard about the Bangkok private eye.

My wife, Dr. Busakorn Suriyasarn, carried out the role of adviser, critic, and soul mate. From Thai proverbs to current Thai slang, she was a constant source of inspiration. I can't image how an author without such a wife could find the resources to bring the very best out of his writing.

Ratchawithi Rd.
Yothi Rd.
Sri Ayutthaya Rd.
Royal Turf Club
Rama 5 Rd.
Sawankhalok Rd.
Rama 6 Rd.
Luk Luang Rd.
Krung Kasem Rd.
Prachathippatai Rd.
Ratchdamnern Nok Rd.
Sri Ayutthaya Rd.
Petchburi Rd.
Phayathai Rd.
Bamrung Muang Rd.
Rama 1 Rd.
Krung Kasem Rd.
Charu Muang Rd.
CEN
Charoen Krung Rd.
Banthat Thong Rd.
PATHUMWAN
CHINATOWN
Horse Racin
Phayathai Rd.
Henri Dunant Rd.
Chao Phraya River
Charoen Krung Rd.
Rama 4 Rd.
BANGRAK
Maha Nakhon Rd.
Si Phraya Rd.
Somdet Chao Phraya Rd.
Thaniya
Patpong 2
Patpong 1
Surawong Rd.
Lat Ya Rd.
Mahesak Rd.
Charoenrat Rd.
FINANCIAL DISTRICT
Charoen Nakhon Rd.
Silom Rd.
Surasak Rd.
Sathorn Nua Rd.
Sathorn Tai Rd.
Krung Thonburi Rd.
Somdej Phrajao Taksin Bridge
Somdej Phrajao Taksin Bridge
Narathiwat Rd.
Chong Nonsi Rd.
CENTRAL PIER
Saphan Taksin